W9-BFV-503

SOUL TAKEN

Titles by Patricia Briggs

The Mercy Thompson Series

MOON CALLED	NIGHT BROKEN
BLOOD BOUND	FIRE TOUCHED
IRON KISSED	SILENCE FALLEN
BONE CROSSED	STORM CURSED
SILVER BORNE	SMOKE BITTEN
RIVER MARKED	SOUL TAKEN
FROST BURNED	

The Alpha and Omega Series

ON THE PROWL
(with Eileen Wilks, Karen Chance, and Sunny)

CRY WOLF

HUNTING GROUND

FAIR GAME

DEAD HEAT

BURN BRIGHT

WILD SIGN

MASQUES

WOLFSBANE

STEAL THE DRAGON

WHEN DEMONS WALK

THE HOB'S BARGAIN

DRAGON BONES

DRAGON BLOOD

RAVEN'S SHADOW

RAVEN'S STRIKE

Graphic Novels

ALPHA AND OMEGA: CRY WOLF: VOLUME ONE

ALPHA AND OMEGA: CRY WOLF: VOLUME TWO

Anthologies

SHIFTER'S WOLF
(*Masques* and *Wolfsbane* in one volume)

SHIFTING SHADOWS

SOUL TAKEN

PATRICIA BRIGGS

ACE
NEW YORK

ACE
Published by Berkley
An imprint of Penguin Random House LLC
penguinrandomhouse.com

Library of Congress Cataloging-in-Publication Data

Names: Briggs, Patricia, author.
Title: Soul taken / Patricia Briggs.
Description: New York: Ace, [2022] | Series: Mercy Thompson
Identifiers: LCCN 2022014338 (print) | LCCN 2022014339 (ebook) |
ISBN 9780440001614 (hardcover) | ISBN 9780440001638 (ebook)
Subjects: LCGFT: Fantasy fiction. | Paranormal fiction. | Novels.
Classification: LCC PS3602.R53165 S68 2022 (print) |
LCC PS3602.R53165 (ebook) | DDC 813/.6—dc23/eng/20220401
LC record available at https://lccn.loc.gov/2022014338
LC ebook record available at https://lccn.loc.gov/2022014339

Printed in the United States of America
1st Printing

For Ann Peters, my Trusty Assistant, aka Sparky,
who makes everything in my life work better.

SOUL TAKEN

PRELUDE

~~~

HE STOOD IN MERCY'S BEDROOM, IN THE HEART OF THE
home of his enemy.

He frowned a little. No, she wasn't his enemy anymore. His
ally, then. She had asked for his aid—something even his Mistress
seldom did, untrustworthy servant that he was.

He had helped Mercy—maybe—and then she had, she had . . .
done something to him. He wasn't sure what to call that, either,
because it had felt as though she had saved him until the effects
wore off and he understood that she might have destroyed him
instead. Hope was the most deadly of emotions.

He didn't think she was his enemy. But certainly not his friend.

He held the silk fabric of his treasure carefully. It was very old
now, though not as old as he was, and he seldom got it out of its
protective box for fear of damaging it. He brought it to his nose
and pretended that he could still smell the rich jasmine perfume
she had worn to cover the scents that healthy human bodies used

to carry in a time before daily—or even weekly—baths. He missed those scents; everything smelled weak and pallid to him now.

This frail cloth, a gift to the person he had once been, was his touchstone, a reminder that once he had been whole. Once there had been joy. He was taking a chance leaving this here, this last scrap of his soul. Mercy was unpredictable, and she brought chaos in her wake.

He brought the embroidered silk belt closer to his body at the thought of releasing it into chaos. But only for a moment. Because Mercy, unlike himself, did not harm the innocent. She would keep this bright and pretty thing safe, he thought with sudden relief at the truth of that, understanding, at last, the impulse that had moved him to bring the belt here.

He lay down upon Mercy's bed, put his head on her mate's pillow, and held the loops of the silk girdle against his cheek. He closed his eyes.

He was not a Christian, had never been that he could remember. But the ironic words of the child's prayer came to him.

> *Now I lay me down to sleep,*
> *I pray the Lord my soul to keep,*
> *And if I die before I wake,*
> *I pray the Lord my soul to take.*

He laughed silently as tears rose in his eyes. His mouth moved without sound against the old silk belt, mouthing the words "*Ardeo. Ardeo. Ardeo.*"

I burn.

1

~~~

"MERCY."

Adam peered down at me. His feral, golden eyes held my gaze. Only a few bits of darkness lingered in the bright depths, like bitter chocolate melting in butter. Icy rain dripped from his forehead onto my face, causing me to blink.

The gold was worrisome, I thought muzzily, wiping my cheek with a clumsy hand. I should pay attention to the dangerous gold in his eyes.

"Pretty," I said.

Someone stifled a laugh, but it wasn't Adam. His frown deepened.

I had just been . . . well, I couldn't remember exactly, but it had definitely not been lying on the wet ground, icy rain—or possibly very wet snow—sluicing down on my face as I stared up into Adam's wild eyes. I reached up with a hand that didn't want to obey and closed my fist on the collar of his shirt.

Though my brain still wasn't tracking quite right, it didn't take much thought to make a connection between the splendid headache that seemed to be centered around my temple and my position on the ground. Something must have hit me hard. I figured I'd be—cold water dripped on my cheek—right as rain in just a minute, but judging by Adam's expression, it might not be soon enough to prevent an explosion.

That could be bad. Worse than if Adam merely lost out to his wolf. His usual wolf. The flash memory of the twisted version of a David Cronenberg–inspired movie werewolf worrying at my throat with huge, already bloodstained teeth served to wake me more effectively than the cold water splashing my face from the skies above us had.

I sucked in a breath with a sudden surge of adrenaline that seemed to extinguish the last few dark bits of humanity in Adam's eyes even as it left me thinking more clearly. Neither he nor I knew if the vicious monster the witch Elizaveta had cursed him to become when she died was gone or merely biding its time.

Adam had warned the pack about the possibility that he could turn into something more dangerous, a monster that he couldn't always control. But in true werewolf fashion, they seemed to look upon it as a new superpower Adam had achieved rather than the terrifying threat it was. They hadn't witnessed it firsthand.

After the full moon had come and only Adam's usual wolf form had answered that call, Adam had been relieved. His temper, already easily roused, had continued to be on an even-shorter-than-usual fuse, but I thought that could be attributed to the unusual strain of the past few months. And yet . . .

I examined my mate's face for a hint of the monster and saw . . . Adam. He carried the experiences of this past year, and despite the werewolf-bestowed youth, his eyes looked older. There was a tightness to his features due to the bite of Elizaveta's curse and the various horrors of the past few months. He still had the confident air that was so much a part of him, but now it looked as though it was riding a war-weary soldier.

I tugged a little harder on the collar of his shirt.

He blinked and a ring of darkness solidified around the outside of his irises. Reassured, I tugged hard enough to choke him, ignoring the soreness this spawned in the newly healed muscle of my right arm where an assassin had shot me shortly before Adam's monster had eaten her.

I couldn't have pulled Adam down to me if he hadn't wanted to come. He was a werewolf and I wasn't. I could have levered myself to him, but I didn't have to make the effort. He bent down and brushed my lips lightly, with a wry tilt of one eyebrow that told me he knew what I was up to but he was willing to play my game.

He sat all the way down on the ground, ignoring the slushy mud, and hauled me into his lap. It was like sitting on a furnace. My whole body softened into him, into his warmth and the rich smell of home. For a half second there was another scent, a more rank scent—or maybe that was just my imagination, because when I inhaled again, I smelled only Adam.

I leaned my head into his shoulder, which was as hard as stone. That wasn't just because he was tense with anger; he was just in that kind of shape. What little softness there had been was worn away, leaving only muscle and bone behind. There was no give to him, but if I'd wanted soft, I would have had to look for someone who wasn't the Alpha of a werewolf pack. Someone who wasn't Adam.

When my temple touched his collarbone, I hissed, and he went rigid. I'd almost forgotten. This had all begun when something had hit me in the temple and dropped me.

"Was it Bonarata?" I asked. That didn't seem right. The Lord of Night, vampire ruler of all he could survey, was in Italy. But we'd killed all the witches, hadn't we? Even Elizaveta was dead. And the fae-ish smoke dragon was gone to wherever fae-ish smoke dragons go.

There were a few more smothered laughs. If there were enemies around, there wouldn't have been people laughing—and Adam wouldn't have sat down on the ground.

Someone said, in a whisper that was not quite quiet enough, "Dang, she's going to have another black eye." Honey, I thought. She usually had better sense.

Adam tightened his arms and growled, a sound that no completely human throat could have made. He was very and continually unhappy about the damage I took as his mate—a position more usually filled by a human, who would have been kept out of events whenever possible, or a werewolf, who could hold her own. I wasn't either of those things; I was a coyote shapeshifter, a member of the pack in my own right, with all the privileges and the duties that entailed. I didn't let them—or Adam—coddle me. It wouldn't have been good for any of us, no matter how hard it was on him.

"Hey, boss," said Warren's casual voice, the one he used when he thought he wasn't talking to a rational being.

I glanced over to see that the tall, lanky cowboy had taken a deliberately relaxed stance about ten feet away. It would have been more convincing if his eyes hadn't been showing a hint of gold. A couple of yards behind him, the pack hovered in a mud-spattered, silent aggregate.

Adam looked, too.

Under the impact of Adam's attention, the pack backed away. Warren turned his head so he wasn't even looking in our direction.

But his voice was still calm and steady as he continued, "You sure you should be moving her around? Mary Jo should maybe see if she has a concussion."

Mary Jo was a firefighter, and she had EMT training.

Again, Adam didn't answer, and the tension grew. Which was exactly the opposite effect our outing to the pumpkin patch was supposed to engender.

OUR PACK, THE COLUMBIA BASIN PACK, WAS UNAFFILI-ated with any other werewolves, the only one on the North or South American continent that did not belong to Bran Cornick, the Marrok. His goal was the survival of the werewolves, and he was ruthless in that pursuit—which was why we'd ended up on our own.

A wise pack, bereft of the Marrok's protection, needed to keep its collective head down if it wanted to survive. Unfortunately, that wasn't an option for us.

It wouldn't be vanity to say there wasn't another pack as well-known as ours anywhere, at least in the eyes of the mundane world. Adam, our Alpha, my mate, was recognizable on any street corner in the US. That had begun as an accident of his contacts in the military, his willingness to talk to news agencies, and the good looks that had been the bane of his life long before he'd become a werewolf.

But it was *my* fault that the whole pack suffered along with him.

A few years ago, the worst thing most of the people (and other sentient beings) living in the Tri-Cities of Washington State had to worry about on an epic scale was the possibility of one of the Hanford nuclear waste tanks—filled with the caustic sludge by-products of the early, experimental years of nuclear science—leaking its goop into the Columbia River. Or possibly exploding.

There were nearly two hundred of the aging tanks, some holding as much as a million gallons. Each tank contained a unique mix of very bad radioactive soup, and worse, due to the secretive nature of nuclear weapons development, no one really knew exactly what was in any of them.

There really were scarier things than monsters.

Anyway.

The Tri-Cities, in addition to being right next to a Superfund cleanup site, were about an hour's drive from the Ronald Wilson Reagan Fae Reservation, which the fae had turned into their own seat of power in their (mostly) cold war with the US government.

Because it suited them and because I claimed the Tri-Cities to be under our pack's protection (it was a stupid heat-of-the-moment thing), the fae let it be known that they acknowledged and respected the Columbia Basin Pack's right to protect our territory and the people, mundane and supernatural alike, who lived within it. We had signed a bargain with them that we would do that—and, more significantly, they would not harm anyone under our protection.

We hadn't had a choice, and neither, I am pretty sure, had they. But bargains with the fae, even when both parties entered into the agreement with the best of intentions, tended to end badly, which was why the Marrok had cut us loose.

No one wanted a war between the fae and the werewolves. If our pack stood alone, whatever happened between us and the fae—or the vampires, other werewolf packs, ancient gods, or demons—*werewolfkind* would not be forced into that conflict. Our pack's demise would not start a war between the supernatural world and the human, so long as we stood alone.

Or so everyone hoped.

The bargain with the fae made the Tri-Cities a neutral zone where humans could rub shoulder to shoulder with the magical world because they were protected. We had suddenly become a point of interest in national, international, and supernatural politics—and there were consequences.

Weaker supernatural beings flocked to a place of (perceived) safety, causing, among other things, a housing shortage. Hotels were booked solid and the Airbnb market went through the roof, because there was now a "safe" place to go see fae mingling with regular folks.

More quietly, predators came here, too, creatures who did not think they had to worry about a mere pack of werewolves interfering in their plundering of the rich hunting ground the Tri-Cities had become. We'd killed two of those predators in the past week alone.

Our pack was fierce. Adam was awe-inspiringly awesome. We had support from the fae—though admittedly that was nearly as dangerous as it was useful. The local vampire seethe helped us for their own reasons. Our pack, all twenty-six of us, bore the brunt of protecting our territory, and because we were not affiliated with the Marrok, we weren't going to get any more wolves very easily.

Adam had responded to the situation by turning us into a finely tuned fighting unit. Some of that meant training in fighting techniques. Some of it meant becoming a more tightly knit pack.

Which was why Adam had rented a giant pumpkin patch and corn maze on a Tuesday night in October so that our pack could play together.

Who knew that a pumpkin patch could be dangerous?

OCTOBER IS A FUNNY MONTH IN EASTERN WASHING-ton. Some days are eighty degrees and sunny, some days are thirty degrees and pouring rain or sleet. Our playdate had turned out to be the latter, with the addition of forty-mile-an-hour wind gusts.

Warm in Adam's arms despite being wet through, I tipped my chin so I could see the ground and note the growing mush of mud and icy slush. The owners of the pumpkin patch had really made bank on us because only the most desperate parents would have paid money to come out here in this weather.

Over Adam's shoulder, the flapping of paper drew my eye to the billboard near the exit of the corn maze. On one half of the board, sodden paper hung limply or flapped from pushpins and staples, revealing a rough plywood surface that needed a new coat of paint.

On the other half, plexiglass covered a movie poster showing a shadowy figure with a sickle and the title *The Harvester* in old-style horror lettering. A white sheet of laminated paper taped to the plexiglass announced special showings of the movie beginning this Saturday, with an opening event that included a guest appearance by the Pasco-born screenwriter.

As I watched, the combination of wind and rain tugged the

announcement free. It fluttered to the ground and landed upon something small and suspiciously orange, about the size of a soft-ball. I wiggled to get a better look.

Oh, dear Lord, I thought, staring at the orange perpetrator of my once and future doom with dismay. *I am never going to live this down.*

As far as I could see, all the pack members who weren't actively hunting in the maze had spread out across the maze exit to avoid getting too close to Adam. They saw where I looked, and several of them flinched or ducked their heads.

"Tell me," I said, in a voice that was *not* whiny, or at least not very whiny, "that I didn't just get hit in the head by a pumpkin."

"You *might* not have gotten hit in the head by a pumpkin," said Honey, with added sweetness in her voice. She knew what kind of trouble I was in. "It was orange, but also small and hard, so we're pretty sure it's actually some kind of ornamental gourd rather than a variety of pumpkin. We were discussing the matter right before—"

"We were playing baseball, waiting for the last group to make it through the maze," said Carlos, one of the other wolves, apologetically. "If we'd been using softballs, we wouldn't have hit anywhere near you, but these things aren't round. No predicting where it might go."

"Makes it more interesting," said Mary Jo soberly, with a wicked glint in her eye.

Mary Jo was nearly as muddy as I was, her short blondish hair plastered tightly to her head. She was the smallest in the group of werewolves. Not many of them could have taken her in a fight, though—as she'd proven.

She held a three-foot-long piece of two-by-four in her hand.

Presumably it was a makeshift bat. I wondered if that bat had been the one that sent the pumpkin . . . the *gourd* bulleting my way. If so, I was pretty sure it wouldn't have been on purpose. She and I weren't buddies, but she didn't hate my guts anymore.

I was pretty sure.

"Most of the gourds just smoosh when we hit them," said George, tough and confident. He'd been a police officer a couple of different times in a couple of different places. He was currently working at the Pasco Police Department and had been with them for as long as the pack had been in the Tri-Cities. He was one of the wolves who had traveled with Adam when he'd moved his pack from New Mexico.

George had just a hint of apologetic laughter in his voice as he bent to pick up the assault projectile and give it a little toss, for all the world as though it were actually a baseball. "But the hard ones are almost as good as the real thing."

I sighed and patted Adam. I'd been hit in the head with a gourd, knocked out, and dumped in a mud puddle. As a boost for my ego, it was pretty awful. As a boost for the pack's team spirit, it might be the best thing that could have happened, as long as Adam didn't decide to defend me.

A dollop of mud slid out of my hair and over my cheekbone. The story of how I'd been taken out by accident was going to be told and retold until it was a pack legend. At least it hadn't been a proper pumpkin.

I bet it is going to be a pumpkin in retellings, I thought dismally. Stories like to grow as they are passed around, becoming more exciting and less likely. I could see it now, some distant future in which a pack sat around a campfire and told stories about the stupid coyote shapeshifter who thought she was a werewolf until someone bashed her head in with a pumpkin. Or something like that, anyway.

I might have writhed in humiliation for a few more minutes, but Adam's thigh muscles flexing under mine reminded me that he, at least, was not amused by the Pumpkin Incident. The minute I got up, Adam was going to go after the baseball team, and the whole point of this production would be lost. But if I didn't get up soon, he was going to think I was really hurt, and that wouldn't make things better, either.

But he was really warm. And, I have to admit, I'm a little perverse. Adam is flat-out gorgeous. It's not my favorite thing about him—and it was one of the reasons I'd held off dating him for such a long time. He is absolutely out of my league. That doesn't mean I don't enjoy his looks. What woman wouldn't? But when he is angry . . . yum. Just yum.

He was very angry right now. It was distracting.

I pushed my face against his neck, tipping my lips until they touched his ear, and breathed, "You and I have a hot shower in our future. Could be fun."

I could feel him go still. I realized, even if I hadn't meant it, I'd done the best thing I could possibly have done to change his focus.

Another soft laugh from the peanut gallery reminded me that we had an audience. We were sitting in slush—or at least Adam was—and I wanted a hot shower. I intended to do something about both of those.

To that end, I sat up, and in a loud and (this time) deliberately whiny voice, I asked, "Did you guys have to knock me into the mud?"

"If you choose to stand next to the biggest puddle in the whole ten-acre playground, you don't get to complain when nature takes its course," said Warren mildly, though his wary eyes brushed past me and hesitated on Adam before he looked away again. "We didn't do it on purpose"—all of them had been careful not to name the actual culprit; Mary Jo wasn't the only one with a makeshift bat—"but if you're going to provide us with that much temptation—"

The team of wolves inside the corn maze had been making a lot of noise for a while. Sometimes it sounded like it was coming from just over the wall of corn and sometimes from farther away—as was consistent with wolves playing tag in a maze. Everyone was looking at Adam and me, and Adam was looking at me—so I was the only one who saw Zack burst out of the exit.

He was running at top speed, his raised fist displaying a multitude of damp ribbons that proved he'd found the waypoints scattered throughout the maze. His face was turned to look behind him and held a sort of gleeful terror that told me Sherwood (our designated maze monster) was in hot pursuit.

I didn't even have time to open my mouth to warn anyone.

Zack's shoulder hit George at full speed, knocking the much bigger man into the mass of the gathered people. Zack himself tumbled all the way over George's falling body and into Mary Jo, who dropped more from the unexpectedness of the impact than its force.

Just before Mary Jo hit the ground, a giant wolf leaped over the top of the cornstalks—which was a feat that not all the wolves in our pack would have managed, because the wall of the maze was not only nearly ten feet tall but at least that wide—and this wolf did it missing one rear leg. From my vantage point on Adam's lap, I could see the instant in which Sherwood (the three-legged wolf) took in the whole scene.

I had no doubt that he could have landed safely. But with an expression of satisfaction in his eyes, he chose to belly flop in the deepest part of the puddle I'd already fallen into. I felt just the lightest touch of magic, then everyone, including Adam and me, was doused with icy mudwater.

Zack crawled off the top of the pile of people, wiped his face with his forearm, then showed Adam and me the fistful of ribbons, now even wetter than before. "I brought out all fifteen ribbons. My whole team gets steak dinner at Uncle Mike's, right?"

The rest of Zack's team, Joel in the lead, emerged from the maze at a much steadier pace. They looked, if anything, even more drenched than the rest of us—but they were laughing like lunatics. Zack's team was the last through and the only one to make it out with all the ribbons.

Sherwood stood up and shook, splattering them (and Adam and me) with more water, his expression smug.

Adam had curled around me to protect me from the worst of it, so I could feel the exact moment at which he relaxed and laughed.

ADAM TOOK ME HOME WHILE THE PACK CLEANED UP.

"Privilege of rank" was all Adam said when I protested that we should help in the cleanup. But I knew that the reason we were leaving was because he was still worried about me.

I was fine. I'd had concussions before, and this was not one. But I wasn't going to argue with Adam—I just rolled my eyes at Mary Jo behind his back.

She stuck her tongue out at me and crossed her eyes. We had been getting along better recently. Some of that had to do with the utterly charming deputy she was dating—so she wasn't lusting after Adam. I thought about it for a second and decided that maybe all of it had to do with her new boyfriend. I liked that she was happy.

Adam caught her expression—she hadn't been trying to hide it from him—and turned to look at me. But he was too late; I had my eyes front and center and my face innocent.

"I heard your eyeballs roll," he told me, which was a phrase he used on his daughter, who had been the empress of eye rolls when she was thirteen.

I laughed.

"We'll see you all in an hour at Uncle Mike's," Adam told them.

"We've got this, boss," said Warren.

I GOT WAYLAID TELLING ADAM'S DAUGHTER, JESSE, about my bruise and all the mud, so Adam had the shower running before I got up to our room. I started stripping out of my muddy clothes as soon as I closed the bedroom door. By the time I walked into the bathroom, I was already naked—and Adam had turned off the water and was reaching for a towel.

"Nope," I told him, swiping the towel out of his hands and dropping it on the floor.

He narrowed his eyes at me—or at least I think he did. I wasn't looking at his face.

"You're hurt," he said.

"Pish-posh," I scoffed—an expression I'd stolen from Ben. Most of his British words were NSFW, but I liked "pish-posh." "It's a bruise. It'll go away. And you promised me sex in the shower."

"I think that was you promising me," he told me.

"You, me, who cares?" I grabbed his hand and dragged him back to the shower. "Nudge."

It was a big shower, plenty big enough for two.

"No fair deploying the WMDs," he pretended to grump. "Nudge" was our code word, never to be resisted but also not for overuse. But I could tell he approved of my plans no matter what he said.

"When you are dealing with a big bad wolf, you have to deploy all the weapons you have," I explained, turning on the water.

I did not wince when the water stung my cheekbone. He saw it anyway, putting one hand up to protect my face.

"I did not expect joy," he told me, kissing the sensitive skin just behind my ear.

"What?" I asked, distracted.

He pulled back and met my eyes, his own dark chocolate, the pupils wide with passion. "You bring me joy," he said clearly. "I never expected this. I don't deserve it—but I am claiming you for my own."

"Well, yes," I told him. "I thought we'd established that when I claimed you for my mate and then my husband. I get you. You get me. No take-backs."

He laughed. Kissed me.

I buried my face against him and just breathed in. He brought me joy, too. But he also brought with him this steady certainty that I had someone in my corner.

When I was a teenager, my home had been torn away with the deaths of my foster parents. My foster mother had died trying to become a werewolf. Unwilling to live without his mate, my foster father, Bryan, killed himself, leaving me alone at fourteen. I spent the next two years living on my own on the outskirts of the Marrok's pack, under its aegis if not its certain protection. When I was sixteen, I lost even that.

I'd learned to stand on my own two feet by then, though. I'd lived a mostly solitary life for years and thought I was content. Then Adam showed up and turned my world upside down.

I wrapped my arms around him, taking in his solid presence, this man of duty and solid strength, this man who loved me when he could have had anyone. There were no words for how much I loved him. At least no words that I knew. But I did know how to show him.

That was *joyous* fun for both of us.

When he carried me out of the shower a limp, thoroughly loved mess, he whispered, with a growl in his voice, "No take-backs."

UNCLE MIKE'S WAS A PUB RUN BY FAE FOR THE SUPER-natural denizens of the Tri-Cities. From the outside, it looked like a somewhat-seedy dive located in what had been an old warehouse in an industrial area of Pasco, not a place where anyone would expect to find a pub.

There were quite a few bars and pubs in the Tri-Cities where the tourists could meet some of the fae—carefully selected to make good impressions. There was even one pub that was currently the setting of a low-budget reality TV show about tourist and fae interactions. Uncle Mike had opened his pub for the tourist trade briefly, but the need for us to have our own place, where we could be ourselves, was too great. Petitioned by his usual customers—and a few of the more unusual ones—Uncle Mike had closed his doors to the general public once more.

By the time Adam and I arrived, most of the pack was already in the private room that we'd reserved even though we'd left them the mess at the corn maze to clean up.

They greeted our lateness with unrestrained hilarity—since some of them had overheard my earlier proposition to Adam of a shower with benefits. Their humor was tempered by an under-current of cheer that bubbled through the pack. Knowing that Adam and I had a strong bond made the wolves feel safer. Some-times the pack's keen interest in my . . . no, let's be honest, in *Adam's* sex life made me uncomfortable.

But I understood. Werewolves have one place of safety, and the Alpha is the center of it. Adam's strength and stability were the core around which our pack thrived. Adam had had a rough few months, and anything that made him happy was good for the pack. Our lovemaking was not and could not always be private when it was so important to the pack's survival.

The night was filled with moment-by-moment retellings of the fun and disasters of the evening, with Sherwood the star of the show. He had not given anyone easy victories, making Zack's triumph especially sweet. We'd missed it, but apparently Zack's team had hoisted him over their heads in the parking lot and carried him into Uncle Mike's in triumph.

Our lone submissive wolf often shied away from attention, but Zack looked relaxed and happy tonight. I noticed various pack members walking by his table so they could high-five him, pat him on the shoulder, or even just casually ruffle his hair. Like happy Alpha wolves, submissives made the pack safer, too. Zack's quiet contentment spread over the room like a blanket in winter. With the exception of Warren, I noticed, with faint worry.

Warren was usually as imperturbable as any dominant were-wolf I'd ever known. But he was visibly more tense than he'd been at the corn maze. I wasn't the only one who'd noticed. A little space had opened around him where he sat in his usual place, right next to Zack.

Zack lived with Warren and his human mate, Kyle. I mean lived with like a roommate, not like a *roommate*. It had started out as a temporary arrangement, but none of them were making any effort to change matters. It made me feel better that our most vulnerable pack member (besides me) was living under Warren's protection.

Like Warren, and despite a lovely interlude-with-shower, I was more than usually out of sorts. After we'd dressed, Adam had told me the real reason he'd decided on an after-the-corn-maze party. I had not been happy to learn he'd been keeping a few things from me.

I nursed my limeade and kept my seat while Adam wandered around the room, doing his part to keep the cheery atmosphere going. Which was smart of him, because I might love him, but right this moment I was pretty unhappy, and by holding back information, Adam had made himself a convenient target of my ire.

Like Warren, I'd been gaining a few surreptitious glances. But it was Zack's fellow victorious teammate, Joel, who breached the leave-me-alone I was projecting as hard as I could.

Joel pulled out Adam's chair and sat in it. He examined my face without speaking. He was the one who'd decided to join me; he could start the conversation.

After a few minutes, he said, "You're angry about something."

"Very," I lied.

I wouldn't have tried to lie to one of the werewolves. But Joel was the other pack member who wasn't a werewolf (besides me). His senses were a little different, and he was new at the whole supernatural business.

I'd known Joel (pronounced the Spanish way, though he didn't get upset when people said it wrong) on a casual basis longer than I'd known anyone in this room, though he was nearly the newest member of the pack. My day job was as a VW mechanic, and he'd been fixing up old wrecks since long before I'd run the shop.

He'd found himself, by an accident of ancestry, the target of an ancient god, and the incident had left him possessed by or in possession of the spirit of a tibicena—a volcano canid ("dog" wasn't quite the right word for it). For months he'd been unable to regain his human shape for long enough to resume a normal life. Luckily for everyone, he had been able to keep the sizzling tibicena at bay most of the time, leaving him wearing the body of a black-brindled presa Canario, a beast nearly as intimidating as most werewolves.

He'd been doing better lately, though. Last week, he and his wife had moved from pack headquarters (Adam's and my house) back into their newly renovated home—taking with them our rescued-from-Underhill boy, Aiden, to keep everyone safe. Aiden was gifted with fire, and he could help if Joel lost control.

"You are not angry," said Joel, frowning at me like I was a recalcitrant engine mount—a puzzle to be solved. "That was a lie."

So much for it being easier to lie to Joel than to one of the werewolves.

"I am a little angry," I said.

He examined me closely. "All right," he said slowly. "That wasn't a lie. Who are you angry with?"

I didn't answer because there wasn't a truthful answer that didn't sound like I was thirteen. Only adolescents can say things like "fate" or "the world" and not feel like cringing afterward. By the time a person was my age, they should know that life isn't fair and quit pretending that it ought to be. If I wanted to be truthful, I'd lost my anger at Adam, to which I'd been clinging, after about ten minutes of watching him tend our pack.

He would always try to carry the weight of the world on his shoulders alone. If I didn't like it, I shouldn't have picked him as my mate.

Joel and I had been speaking very quietly and there was a lot of noise in the room—music, laughter, chattering. But now he turned his face so that no one could see it.

"I know who hit you," he said.

It took me a second to realize he thought I was upset about the Pumpkin Incident, because I'd all but forgotten about it. "It's not that," I said. "And unless you judge that the hit was deliberate—in which case we are dealing with an entirely different matter—don't tell me." I thought about it and said, "Actually even if you think it was deliberate, keep it to yourself. I'll figure out who it is eventually, and they will pay." And that would be better than if Adam found out someone had deliberately hurt me.

Joel grinned and there was a spark of red in his eye. "I've been enlightened about your perfect revenges. Jesse told Aiden, who told me that there was a spectacular incident involving a chocolate Easter bunny. You've been hiding your light under a barrel."

I mistrusted that spark in his eye; the tibicena could be malicious. We were in a mostly wooden building, and Aiden wasn't here to draw out the fire. I had no doubt that Uncle Mike could control a normal fire, but I'd prefer not to have to find out if he could handle the tibicena.

"We don't talk about the Easter Bunny Incident," I told him earnestly. "And it was Easter bunnies. It's not my fault that laxatives come in chocolate flavor."

Truthfully, I was a little on the fence about the Easter Bunny Incident. The result had been perfect and satisfying. But my adult self figured if the bunnies had laid out the werewolves, they could have actually killed someone, especially if one of my victims had decided to pass a chocolate bunny on to some mortal child.

As an adult, I preferred to be more measured and prudent, at least sufficiently prudent not to kill anyone I didn't mean to. But the Easter Bunny Incident had persuaded the whole of the Marrok's pack to quit messing with me. Everyone except Leah, the Marrok's mate.

Joel laughed, as I'd intended him to, and the red spark in his eye receded.

Awesome, I thought. One disaster at a time was always a good thing.

"I would have loved to have been a fly on the wall," he said. Before he could say anything more, someone called out his name. He gave me a rueful smile and headed in that direction.

That was also good. Because he hadn't asked me what was bothering me if it wasn't getting hit by a pumpkin. I didn't want to tell him that I was scared. Evidently he hadn't smelled it on me, either—which was why I was concentrating on my anger, juvenile though it was. Hopefully that would fool sharper senses than Joel's.

I wasn't alone long. Ben, fair hair and blue eyes lending a

deceptively harmless air to his face, was the next to approach me. He pulled up a third chair to my two-chair table, to avoid taking Adam's. Ben had been a wolf long enough not to encroach on Adam's territory, even if it was just a chair.

Ben had, at one time, been the most dangerous of Adam's wolves. Not because he was the most powerful but because he was the most likely to lose control and kill someone. He'd been sent to the Columbia Basin Pack to get him out of trouble in the UK, and anything requiring that much distance indicated that whatever he'd done, it hadn't been good. Not bad enough, in someone's judgment, for him to have been eliminated, but not far off. He'd been getting better over the past couple of years, both more stable and more happy.

Even so, like Adam, he'd had a rough few months. He'd stayed awhile with us, recovering from being possessed by a smoke dragon, moving back to his home only a couple of weeks ago. He seemed to be okay, but he'd lost about fifteen pounds he didn't need to lose, and he wasn't gaining it back.

"Observe me gutted," he said. His aristocratic English accent had been softening, and I hadn't realized just how much until it returned in force. "It was I."

"Who was you?" I asked.

"I hit you with the pumpkin."

I met his eye. We stared at each other for all of twenty seconds before we broke. His lip twitched once. Then twice. And that was it. I laughed until my stomach hurt and tears welled.

"It wasn't that funny," he said, but he was laughing, too. He didn't look at all dangerous.

"With a pumpkin," I managed in a fair attempt at his accent because that made it more absurd somehow.

I needed a good laugh, and the hangdog expression on his face combined with the confession of pumpkin mayhem was priceless.

Honey, walking by with a pair of beers, shook her head. "Confessing, was he?" she asked me.

She must have gone home—or somewhere—to shower and change, too, because she was groomed back into her usual elegant self, complete with trousers and silk shirt. She was one of those women who knew how to wear makeup so that it drew your attention to her features and not to the makeup.

I nodded. "He hit me with a pumpkin," I said, assuming a wide-eyed expression of astonishment to accompany my version of Ben's English accent.

Ben was facedown on the table by this point, and he slapped it once. "With a pumpkin," he agreed in a choked voice.

Honey grinned at the pair of us—the expression making her perfect face more human. "If I didn't know better," she said, "I'd ask what you've been drinking." She looked at me. "Did you hear that Human Resources asked Ben to change how he answers his phone?"

"No?" I said in a tell-me-more tone.

"They informed me that 'What the fuck's your problem?' was inappropriate," Ben said without lifting his head.

"I heard it took two weeks before they asked him to go ahead and resume his old phrase," Honey said.

"All of the new ways he answered his phone were even worse," said Carlos from a nearby table.

"It only took them six days," Ben said smugly.

Ben was dragged off by a pair of pack mates not long after that and I was left alone.

Adam sat back down in his chair, replacing my empty glass with another limeade.

"Ben fessed up," I told him. "There was no secret plot to make you a widower via flying itty-bitty pumpkin. It was an accident."

"I saw the two of you over here laughing like loons," he said.

"He hit me with a pumpkin," I told him, in my bad British accent. "He was gutted."

Adam laughed.

2

GEORGE WAS THE FIRST TO LEAVE.

"I just got called in early tonight," he told Adam, raising his voice to be heard over the music, as they exchanged hand grips. "Something went down at one of the grocery stores."

Adam tensed. "Violence?"

George shrugged. "They are keeping it quiet for now—or they just don't know yet."

"Stay safe," I said.

"You should talk," George said, his eyes going to my bruised face. "I've taken bodies to the morgue who have been hit just there. Weak place in the skull."

"Me, too," said Adam, though his voice didn't tighten. I realized that he must have been thinking that when he saw me fall at the corn maze. Sometimes knowledge only makes things worse.

"Not dead yet," I reminded them. "I am hardheaded, I guess.

When it's my time, I'll go, and it will probably be something stupid. But if heaven is kind, it won't be a pumpkin that takes me out."

"Fair enough," acknowledged George with a faint smile. He touched his finger to his forehead in a final salute and headed for the exit.

"Let's go talk to Zack," Adam said.

Step one of the final planned task of the night. My stomach clenched, but at the same time, I felt an odd sort of relief. Waiting around sucked eggs.

"You don't need me for this part," I told him.

He gave me a half smile. "I like having you around."

I left my fresh glass by the empty one and followed him to Zack's table.

"I need you to stay for a bit after everyone else goes," Adam murmured to him. "I can give you a ride home when we're done."

Next to Zack, Warren grunted, lifted up his hips, and pulled out a Subaru key fob that still had the dealer's tag attached. "I'll catch a ride home with someone. Zack, you take my car."

"*You* have a new car?" I asked. Ever since I'd known him, Warren had driven a battered old epoxy-and-blue-and-rust truck.

"Present from Kyle," Zack said, taking the fob from Warren without an argument.

I was momentarily distracted from my worry. Warren didn't take presents that big from Kyle.

Warren and Kyle had lived for a long time in the World War II–era duplex Warren used to rent instead of Kyle's upscale house because Warren was opposed to depending upon anyone else. Even after they had made Kyle's house their home, Warren had clung to his apartment for a while. Accepting a gift as expensive as a new car was as big an admission of trust as anything I'd ever seen from him.

Kyle had bought a very nice wedding ring for Warren, too. I'd picked it out with him a few months ago. He'd come with me to get my lamb necklace fixed at the jewelers and seen the perfect ring.

Kyle had told me that it was too soon. Warren had been alone a very long time and he had trouble trusting anyone. Kyle was a smart man; no doubt he was right. But he'd bought the ring anyway in happy anticipation.

"That's a new thing for you," I said. "And I don't mean the car."

"My truck is too noticeable," said Warren, his mouth tight with something that might have been embarrassment. It also might not have been.

I frowned at him.

"Kyle has me trailing people around," Warren said too quickly. Warren was a private detective who did work for Kyle's law firm. "He decided I needed something that blended in with all the other cars."

It sounded like Kyle might have made that decision over Warren's objections, though that was a little unlike him. That might explain the extra tension that Warren was wearing tonight.

"I'd have gone Honda or Toyota for blending," I said, leaving that evidential sore spot for Kyle and Warren to work out. "But Subaru makes a good car, too."

No one asked me about Volkswagen. I was bitter about the new Volkswagens ever since the turbo-diesel incident.

"I'd buy Mercy a new car to replace the one she used to squish her enemy against a dumpster," Adam said, "but she'd have my hide."

"I'm a mechanic," I told him with mock coolness. "I have to drive an old car. It's the rules."

He smiled at me, and my breath caught in my chest at the warmth in his eyes. "Okay," he said. "As long as it's the rules."

ABOUT TWENTY MINUTES LATER, THE PACK BEGAN drifting out singly or in small groups. Adam stood by the door, touching each one as they left. Sometimes he'd hug them, sometimes it was a brush of his fingers on their cheeks or a pat on the shoulder. A good pack leader knew what his wolves needed.

I retreated to our table, sipping my third glass of icy limeade. I should be with Adam, but I wouldn't be able to hide my tension. It was important to let the pack be happy tonight. A few of them looked at me, and I rubbed my cheek in answer. My headache was real enough, even if it wasn't my problem.

Adam said something to Darryl, his second-in-command, that made the big man laugh. Auriele, Darryl's mate, reached up and smacked Darryl on the top of his head, but she was laughing, too. Darryl hadn't competed because he and Adam had set up the stations around the maze, but Auriele had. Her team had made it out in time but hadn't found two of the ribbons.

Sherwood got up to leave. He limped a little on his way to the exit, proving that he'd given his all to the games in the maze. Usually, he was so graceful that most people wouldn't notice that he had a prosthetic leg.

Rather than interrupt Adam's conversation, Sherwood started past. Adam, without taking his attention off the other two wolves, caught Sherwood's arm, holding him where he was. Sherwood stiffened, drawing back—and Adam didn't let him go.

Nor, despite the quick, almost worried glance Darryl gave Sherwood, did Adam allow their good-byes to be hurried. When they left, Auriele was frowning.

Adam said something to Sherwood, and Five Finger Death Punch's "A Little Bit Off" belting through the overhead speakers made sure no one else heard what it was. The big man stared at Adam with unfriendly eyes for a moment, then took a deep breath. He made a deliberate effort to relax his posture, gave Adam a quick nod, and turned back to stride toward me.

Showtime, I thought, taking a deep breath. I needed to be calm.

Sherwood's limp was not in evidence as he prowled toward me. I did not think that was a good sign. Wolves don't show weakness before their enemies. Not that anyone who knew him would think that having only one leg made Sherwood vulnerable in the slightest.

I'd never heard of a werewolf missing a limb before. Werewolves either die from injuries, or they heal them. If a leg gets severed, it should regrow.

In the case of a human who was crippled or missing a limb prior to becoming a werewolf, there are ways to fix that. Those ways are horrible and involve reinjuring the damaged but healed body part. I'd heard that those methods had been tried unsuccessfully on Sherwood.

Sherwood had been found in the laboratory of a collection of black witches who had been taken down by werewolves a few years ago. No one knew how long he'd been there or what had been done to him, but I'd been confined in such a place for a bit, and I still had nightmares.

His rescuers had brought Sherwood to Bran, who had forced him to shift back to his human form. Maybe because he'd spent too long as a wolf, maybe because the witches had done something to him, Sherwood had no memory of who or what he had been.

Bran had known Sherwood's identity, but for his own Bran-reasons hadn't seen fit to tell Sherwood, or anyone else. Instead, Bran had thrown up his hands, given the three-legged wolf (or one-legged man) a name, and sent Sherwood Post to us.

I'd first thought the move had been for Sherwood's sake. Bran had told me that Sherwood had complained about the horrible Montana winters and asked for assignment to a pack that lived in a warmer climate. Most places have better climates than Aspen Creek, Montana.

After the last few months, months during which Sherwood had proven to have some useful and unusual skills, I was beginning to think Bran might have had other reasons for sending Sherwood to us.

Had Bran known what was going to happen here? Had he known our pack would become the center of fae political maneuvering before we did? Because Sherwood came to us not long before I'd made our territorial claim on the national news. How had Bran known? And if so, why hadn't he warned us that he'd be forced to leave us (*leave me*, some childish part of me murmured) out in the cold without the protection of the Marrok and the whole of the wolves under his aegis?

If I thought too much about Bran's planning capacity, I usually ended up with a headache. I didn't need more of a headache, but I couldn't keep myself from wondering.

Had Bran, knowing that we would need every advantage we could muster, given us Sherwood Post as a secret weapon? Sherwood wasn't just any werewolf. He was witchborn. Maybe. Or at least he could manipulate magic with skill. His power didn't smell corrupted, nor did it smell exactly like witchcraft. And he had a lot of magic for someone who wasn't tainted by black magic.

I didn't know quite what he was. But I did know he was *someone,* a Power whose name would be known. Someone a few of the really old wolves would probably know on sight. We had only a couple of those—Honey and Zack. Age is one of those things that you just don't ask, but you get a feel for it after a while. I knew that Honey didn't know who Sherwood was, but I was not so sure about Zack. Zack could keep secrets.

Bran might have given us Sherwood as a weapon, but Adam thought it was about to explode in our faces.

Sherwood slid out the chair Adam had been using and sat in it. There was a significance to that, just as Ben's not sitting in it earlier had been significant. This left Sherwood facing me, his expression as grim as I felt.

Now is the winter of our discontent, I thought. I'd taken a Shakespeare course in college that had been taught by the drama department instead of the English department. Mostly that meant we'd had to memorize a lot of the famous speeches. They bubbled up now and then. I didn't think that Sherwood would bring glorious summer, no matter how much all concerned might wish it.

I liked Sherwood and had done so ever since the day we'd talked on the top of a very tall crane and ended up fighting back-to-back. Nothing tonight was his fault, any more than it was Adam's. Sometimes—quite a lot of the time—being a werewolf just sucked.

I decided the best way to calm down was to have a conversation, something to distract us both. Not that Sherwood was a good conversationalist at the best of times. But there was one sure way to get his attention.

I asked, "How is Pirate?"

Some of the stress left Sherwood's posture at the mention of his cat. But not all. If Adam was right, and Adam was always right about this kind of thing, Sherwood knew that we were in trouble, too.

"Pirate extends his greetings," Sherwood said solemnly, "and expressed his regrets that his evil roommate would not bring him tonight. He bids me tell you that he will endeavor to teach said roommate the error of his ways—probably by coughing up a hair ball on the bed."

He caught my surprised look, and color flushed up his cheeks. He adjusted his chair, and it gave a warning creak—he was a big man.

It was true, Sherwood did usually bring Pirate anywhere he could, and cats did tend to exert their dominance over their homes. If he could speak, Pirate might very well have given the message Sherwood related.

But this was *Sherwood*. I had expected a simple "Fine." Maybe, if he was feeling unusually garrulous, he might even have said something like "Angry at being excluded." The longer and funny story was not like the Sherwood I knew.

The silence between Sherwood and me grew awkward. More awkward. I had a million questions rising to my tongue, and I couldn't ask any of them until Adam joined us.

"Oh, look," I said gratefully, because awkward silences tended to make me babble, "here's one of Uncle Mike's minions. Do you want something to drink while we wait?"

A server had come into the room via the kitchen door, glanced around to the few remaining guests, then started toward our table, now the only one still occupied.

Before Sherwood could answer me, I met the eyes of the wolf who quite possibly would kill my mate tonight, and babbled another question off the top of my head—one that I blamed on my earlier internal sound bite from *Richard III*.

"*Are* you Shakespeare?"

Sherwood went still. Almost carefully, he turned his head toward the approaching waiter. I was pretty sure that it was to hide his expression from me.

Because there was only one reason for me to ask him that.

Adam had told me, in the aftermath of our shower this evening, that the pack bonds had informed him Sherwood's memory was back. Sherwood's reaction told me that he was right. Adam had no idea why it had happened, but that wasn't the important thing just now. We had in our pack a wolf who was suddenly very, very dominant.

I'd been told that Adam was the fourth most dominant wolf in the New World. It went Bran, his two sons, then Adam. But Adam thought the new, improved version of Sherwood was more dominant than Adam was. That was a problem, especially under our current circumstances.

"Four glasses and a pitcher of water," I told the waiter before he could ask us anything. "And when there are only four of us left here, could you close the door and give us privacy until we leave?"

"Right you are," he said, with a nod and a touch of his finger to his forehead and a bare glance at Sherwood. This waiter was a new one to me and he looked human. He didn't smell like it, though.

"I wonder why Uncle Mike gets along with the goblins better than most of the fae do?" I mused when the waiter had gone, giving Sherwood the opportunity to ignore my last question.

I didn't really think he had been Shakespeare. But the pack had a betting pool about who Sherwood had been. When he'd found out about it, he'd bet that he was—or rather *had been*—

William Shakespeare. I was pretty sure that had been a joke. Iambic pentameter was not something anyone would expect from Sherwood, who seldom spoke five syllables when one syllable would do.

"Don't know," Sherwood told me shortly.

I took my cue from him and quit talking. He leaned back in the chair, head canted to watch Adam talk to the last few lingering pack members.

Adam looked relaxed, the smile on his face genuine. Adam had been in a lot of battles. Unlike me, he tended not to fret about them in advance, not if it was "only" his life on the line. Next to Adam, Zack leaned casually against a wall as if he had tried to find a place where he might not be noticed. But no wolf would overlook a submissive. I saw him smile and nod at something one of the exiting wolves said.

"Do you think Zack is necessary to keep my temper under control?" asked Sherwood, his voice a rumble that carried right over the music.

The last few wolves were gathered around Adam, and I watched as they all turned to look at us. I doubt they'd been able to understand what Sherwood had said, but they probably hadn't missed the ugly tone in his voice.

I saw some alarmed faces. Zack glanced over and away. Adam didn't react in any way I could see. Honey frowned and started toward us, but Adam said something quietly enough that I couldn't catch it. She aimed her frown at Sherwood.

Adam raised a brow at me, then hustled Honey and the last of the now obviously worried wolves out, following them through the door. Presumably he would reassure them—or tell them the truth. He'd do what he thought best. Zack glanced at Sherwood and me, hesitated, then trailed after Adam.

"Is Adam worried I'm unstable?" Sherwood persisted.

How to redirect an angry werewolf. I was experienced at this, having grown up in the Marrok's pack of too-unstable-to-inflict-on-anyone-else werewolves. I just had to pick my weapon. Make him madder? Or make him think? One was certainly easier than the other, but I picked option two because it was less likely to end in disaster.

"You didn't answer my question," I said evenly. "Why do you think I should answer yours?"

I smiled my thanks to the waiter, who'd brought a clear pitcher foggy with the condensation clinging to its cold sides and set it down in front of me. The waiter smiled back, displaying sharp yellow teeth as he cleared away my empty limeade glasses. He stayed as far away from Sherwood as he could.

"It is not like you to play games," Sherwood said, after the waiter had left us via the door leading directly to the kitchen.

"Adam asked that I not start any serious discussion until we were alone," I answered, pouring myself some water. And in case he didn't know which question I was talking about, I continued, "I shouldn't have asked about Shakespeare, but I couldn't help myself. That betting pool has taken on a life of its own."

He looked at me a moment. Then he heaved a sigh and said, "No, I'm not Shakespeare."

"No," I replied to his previous question. "We don't think you need Zack to keep your temper under control."

"Then why do you need him?" he asked.

"Because having a submissive wolf in the room makes conversations between two dominant wolves easier," said my mate, striding through the doorway with Zack trailing behind him.

Adam offered the empty chair Ben had used to Zack in a way

that reminded me, as Adam's manners sometimes did, that he was a product of another time. There was something protective and gallant in the old-fashioned action. It didn't have the air of a man pulling a chair out for a lady, but it wasn't far off.

Once Zack was seated beside Sherwood, Adam brought another chair over to sit beside me. He was close enough that his leg pressed against mine. In no way, shape, or form did his touch make me safer, but I felt like it did.

A movement by the exit door caught my attention as Uncle Mike looked in.

Uncle Mike gave Adam a somewhat ironic salute and slanted an unreadable look at Sherwood—or maybe Zack, it was hard to tell. To me he gave his usual wide grin, his "I'm just a friendly innkeeper, darlin'" smile that I found significantly less reassuring than I had before I knew him well. My ongoing wariness seemed to amuse him, though, so I'd learned to not let it show.

Uncle Mike touched a controller I'd assumed were lights, but instead the music stopped. He stepped back into the corridor and made a gesture, meeting my eyes meaningfully before he moved out of sight behind the closing door. There was a funny sort of pop as the door shut, something that my ears didn't quite hear but I knew was magic.

Sherwood's eyebrow climbed.

"I asked Uncle Mike for a bit of privacy," Adam said, and I realized that I hadn't needed to say anything to our waiter. No one would disturb us—and no one would overhear us, either.

I wondered if that magically enhanced privacy was the reason for Uncle Mike's look. Maybe. Probably.

But Uncle Mike was old. And I was pretty sure that he knew

who Sherwood was—or had been. That look . . . had he glanced at Sherwood first and then me? I couldn't remember.

"What do you want to do?" Sherwood asked bluntly, drawing my gaze back from the closed door.

He looked a little . . . more *real* than I was used to. I blinked and the impression faded, leaving me not quite sure what I'd seen.

Probably it was my subconscious acknowledging that he was *more* than he had been, I decided. Possibly the impression had been aided a little by the intensity that the two dominant were-wolves at this table couldn't help but generate. I wasn't Adam, to read the fine points in our pack bonds, but I could feel the magic warn that trouble was imminent if something didn't give.

I hadn't heard the invitation, but Adam had told me he would ask Sherwood to our table, as a guest. For the majority of were-wolves it wouldn't have had any effect. They aren't fae, who ob-serve guesting laws by necessity. But Adam was sure that Sherwood was old, maybe old enough that guesting laws would mean some-thing. Conditioning wasn't magic, but it tended to linger.

The little table, designed for two, made a fragile barrier be-tween Adam and Sherwood. I wondered if I should shove the table over a foot—Zack and I didn't need a barrier between us.

Instead of directly answering Sherwood's question, Adam poured himself a glass of water. He was being careful to keep his gaze away from Sherwood's face, except for brief, sweeping glances. Sherwood, I noticed, was doing the same.

Adam took a drink and, with the formal politeness of a dow-ager duchess in a Jane Austen movie, said, "I don't know what they do to this, but it might be the best water I've ever tasted."

We all knew that it was an invitation to Sherwood to accept

the hospitality of the table. What he did in response would set the tone of the negotiations.

Sherwood looked at Adam a moment, not quite long enough to initiate active conflict. Then he looked away, sighed audibly, and relaxed his shoulders a degree or two.

With a quirk of his lips and a touch of showmanship, he filled his own glass. As if it were fine wine in a crystal goblet instead of battered barware, he brought the drink to his nose and inhaled. He sipped it, working his mouth as if rolling it on his tongue.

The room's dim lights caught his hazel eyes. I couldn't recall if I had noticed what color his eyes were before. Which was a little odd, now that I thought about it.

"Nothing magical," Sherwood said, a not-so-subtle reminder that he was adept with some sort of magic.

He took a second drink. "Not magical *anymore*, I should have said. They've purified it somehow."

He put the glass down deliberately, as if putting an end to the theater. Adam glanced at Zack and me, then nodded his head toward the pitcher.

Zack and I each filled our glasses and drank. The water could have been out of a sewer and I wouldn't have noticed, not just then. I swallowed quickly and set the glass down. Zack took his time. No one spoke until he put his glass down, too.

"Just about two weeks ago, something happened to you," Adam said in the same conversational tone that he'd used to talk about the water. "I felt it in the pack bonds as you came back into your power. As if a firework sparkler turned into a fusion bomb. Quite extraordinary."

Even now when I sought Sherwood through the pack bonds,

he felt the same as he always had. Adam thought Sherwood was doing something that kept me and all the pack unaware of his true power. Either Sherwood had not bothered to hide what he'd become from Adam—or he couldn't hide himself from the Alpha of his pack. I thought it was the latter.

"Something died," Sherwood said. He gave a brief, unhappy smile. "You could ask Charles about that if you'd like to. I heard that he was in the right place when it died, but I haven't talked to him about it."

"Something?" I asked.

He shrugged. "Something. Someone. An old foe. By its death, it released me."

It wasn't the time for stories now. I'd call Anna and see if she knew anything.

"You remember yourself," Adam murmured.

"Yes," agreed Sherwood, in an equally quiet voice.

"I gave you time to come to me," Adam said. "But you didn't. For the sake of the pack, I could not let it lie any longer."

Danger scented the air, a sharp, almost storm-front quality that was as much possibility as odor. I couldn't tell if it was my nose warning me or the pack bonds.

"I understand," Sherwood said. "My identity is a problem."

"I don't care who you are," Adam said heavily, "or were."

"He's not Shakespeare," I said cheerfully into the heavy threat gathering. "He told me so."

Briefly a smile lightened my mate's face. "There will be several of the pack disappointed."

"Six," I said. "Including Sherwood. They might have won two hundred and four dollars and eighty-three cents, split between them."

"Life is about disappointment," murmured Zack. "Who keeps putting pennies in? What do you do if they win?"

I had a plan for that, but Sherwood interrupted me before I got the first word out.

"You don't care who I am?" asked Sherwood, sounding . . . not distrustful exactly. If Adam had lied, we'd all have heard it.

"I don't have any money in the betting pool," Adam said mildly. "And I'm curious. But who you were doesn't matter for the pack's welfare."

"*Darned* curious," I said confidentially, bumping Adam's shoulder very lightly with mine.

I had been raised by werewolves. I knew how to manage them. The key to keeping two dominant wolves from killing each other was to keep things from getting confrontational. Zack and I were both working to lighten the atmosphere, our voices reminding Adam and Sherwood that this was not a duel and not a fight. Not yet.

To that end I continued, "Maybe even expletive-deleted curious. Starts with an 'f' and isn't 'firetruck.' But he won't say so in front of me."

That Adam wouldn't swear in front of me had become, fairly recently, a matter of some hilarity in the pack. A few of them were trying to get him to swear on purpose. That's how I learned that Adam apparently swore a great deal—rivaling our pack execration champion, Ben—when there weren't any females in the room. When I'd confronted him, he'd blamed his time in the military.

Adam didn't look at me, but I caught the edge of his dimple peeking out, as if he'd thought I'd been funny. Proof that he wasn't as annoyed with the pack antics as he pretended—and also that his nerves were titanium.

This could go so wrong, and there were very few ways it could go right. Which disaster came to pass depended on Sherwood, and I didn't know who this Sherwood was.

He wasn't paying attention to me, so it was safe to examine him. I stared at him as if my eyes could take his surface and read the depths. Sherwood's eyes really were hazel—almost green. I couldn't believe I hadn't noticed them before.

There was a black tattoo on the side of his neck, a tattoo that was so old it was hard to discern anything about it other than that it had probably not been done with a modern technique. That made sense because werewolves are hard to tattoo, but if they have ink work done before they are Changed, it stays with them.

I hadn't realized he had a tattoo at all.

Sherwood had been in our pack about five months and I had never seen the tattoo on his neck that was the size of my hand? It wasn't even something a high-necked collar could have covered completely—the edge of the tattoo touched his jaw. The button-down shirt he was wearing obviously didn't hide anything. I tried to remember how Sherwood usually dressed—but I just didn't pay much attention to what people whose names weren't Adam wore.

I thought of Uncle Mike's meaningful look. Had he done something to Sherwood? Or had he seen something about Sherwood that had changed?

I looked at Zack. Did he look real?

Yes. But it didn't feel any different than usual. Did that mean that Sherwood usually didn't look real?

While I puzzled over Sherwood, the conversation had lingered a bit on swearing, with Zack leading the conversation. No one laughed, but the tension had died down a bit when Adam returned to the original topic.

"Curiosity aside, I don't care who you are or were," he said.

Adam hadn't been slouching—too many years in the army. But now he straightened further and leaned forward, careful not to cross the edge of the table, which was still serving as a small and only partial barrier between the two dominant wolves. "What I do need to know is what you now mean to the survival of my pack."

"Because I am more dominant than you are," Sherwood said, his voice a low rumble. He held up a hand, and when he spoke again, most of the aggression was out of his voice. "Sorry. That has not been established. Let us say that I am too dominant to fit in the space I have occupied in the pack."

Zack drew in a shivery breath as he finally figured out that this meeting was about something a lot more serious than Sherwood regaining his memory.

Zack hadn't been briefed by Adam like I had, and Sherwood only felt different in the pack bonds to the Alpha. Having a werewolf in the pack who was, even possibly, more dominant than our Alpha was both unexpected and possibly disastrous. Sherwood, without taking his attention from Adam, put a reassuring hand on Zack's shoulder.

Adam took a moment before he spoke.

"The pack's situation is precarious," Adam said. He glanced at Sherwood and then away. It was a look that human males don't do much—good werewolf manners, one Alpha to another—equal to equal.

Sherwood nodded slowly, giving Adam the same look-and-away deliberately, completing the acknowledgment of equality that Adam had begun. A step back from the assertion of superiority that both wolves could accept better than mere words. A lot of communication between werewolves was nonverbal. That was why this conversation was happening in person instead of over the phone.

"Everything hangs by a thread the fae have managed to spin here," Adam told Sherwood. "Not just our pack's fate or the fate of the peoples—wolves, fae, human, and other—who live here in our territory. It may be the thread that leads the entire world away from the probability of annihilation of whole categories of sentient peoples. We, all of us, stand upon a precipice. If our pack can continue the illusion that this, our home, is a safe place for all, the Gray Lords might manage to negotiate a peace that holds."

Sherwood's lips twisted, but it wasn't a smile, not really. "I hadn't thought you were that much of an optimist. How many witches have you met that you think peace is possible with them? Vampires? The fae barely look up from assassinating each other."

He didn't sound like Sherwood, I thought, but what he said still sounded familiar, like listening to a few lines from an old movie I couldn't quite place.

"I know you understand what I mean," Adam said impatiently, his voice a little hoarse with the wolf, though his eyes were still dark. "Isolated violence is different from genocide. A battle is different from a war."

Sherwood tipped his head in admission. "Yes. But you know and I know that even if the Gray Lords manage to work out some kind of peace—it will not last. The humans are just beginning to remember what their ancestors understood. And they are afraid. In this case, knowledge will not make them less afraid."

I'd grown up listening to variants on the theme. Sherwood

sounded, I thought, like someone who had been watching world events for a very long time, like Bran.

"You think like an immortal," Adam said, echoing my thoughts. "Of course, peace doesn't last any more than war does. We"—he waved a hand around in a swirling gesture as if indicating every thinking being on the planet—"tire of peace, eventually. But I know war. And every day I can hold it off is valuable to me, and to its victims."

"Fighting becomes a habit," I offered, more to break up the intensity that had developed between Adam and Sherwood again than because I really had something to add. "But so can peace, if you give it time."

But Adam nodded at me as if my point had been important.

"Peace kills fewer people," he said. "And if we get a peace that lasts for a century or a decade, it is worth fighting for."

Sherwood raised an eyebrow at Adam. I frowned at him. There was something about that expression.

Adam nodded. "Fighting for peace—I know how stupid it sounds. I fought in that war, and it didn't seem to help anyone at all."

He sighed, took another drink. When Adam spoke again, his words had weight, though he spoke quietly. "I am responsible for my pack. For the lives of those living in my territory. For those I love. That responsibility gives me a *duty* to strive for peace."

Sherwood scowled at the corner of the room. "You didn't bring me here to discuss the possible outcome of the Gray Lords' politicking."

"I think that might be the heart of the matter," Adam said, soft-voiced. "The Gray Lords' politicking leaves us operating on the edge of what we can do, with failure not an option if our pack is to survive."

He allowed Sherwood to think about that for a minute. The other wolf shrugged, managing to convey sympathy rather than indifference.

"Because our pack is standing between those who live in our territory and those who would harm them, held there by honor and by a bargain with the fae, my actions are limited," Adam said. "And I think that yours are, too."

"I don't want this to happen," Sherwood said. "But avoidance has obviously gotten me nowhere." He waved a hand to indicate the discussion we were having. "You are a good Alpha, but I am not going to die tonight."

A pack could not have two Alpha wolves. One of them would have to submit to the other, or die.

"There are the usual choices," said Adam.

None of them would work, I thought bleakly. Adam had already been through them with me.

When Adam didn't continue, Sherwood turned one palm up in invitation. Despite the tension of the situation, I found my attention drawn inexplicably to him again.

Sherwood took up space, physically as well as metaphysically. The only one in our pack bigger than Sherwood was Darryl. Unlike Darryl, Sherwood wasn't handsome, but there was something about the structure of his face that inspired trust. It was, I suddenly realized, the face of someone people would follow off a cliff, a Rasputin, maybe.

Or a Bran.

A cold chill traveled down my spine as my subconscious stirred.

"You can leave," Adam said neutrally, and his words brought my attention back to the matter at hand with a jerk.

Here we go. I offered up a prayer, and helpless to stop myself, I put a hand on Adam's thigh. Hopefully, he wouldn't find it distracting, but I needed to touch him.

"Is that what you want me to do?" Sherwood asked, but not as if he were seriously considering it. There was a subtle challenge in his tone that made the room harder to breathe in.

To someone who had not understood what Adam had spent the last quarter of an hour saying, Sherwood's leaving would be an easy solution.

Adam met his gaze and held it this time. The possibility of violence sharpened, the smell of it like ozone in the air before a lightning strike.

"No," Adam said into that waiting maelstrom. "You were a gift from the Marrok to my pack. I don't throw away gifts."

Sherwood gave a sudden, fierce smile that changed the waiting violence, gave it pause, as he said, "A gift from Bran Cornick and you didn't run? Maybe I was intended as punishment."

I hadn't ever seen quite that expression on Sherwood's face, but I'd seen it somewhere.

It was gone in a moment, but his hazel eyes were still crinkled at the corners as he continued softly, "Or maybe this whole situation was intended to be punishment for me instead."

Adam gave him a wry smile in return. "I am absolutely sure that all three could be true at once. This is Bran Cornick at work. He is good at that kind of planning." After a second, he added, "Or taking credit for planning when the whole situation is a total accident."

Sherwood gave a crack of laughter and quaffed the water in

his glass with the flair of a pirate downing a mug of ale, complete with slamming the empty glass on the table. He did not break either glass or table, though it was a near thing.

"If Bran planned this," I said grimly, "I'm going to make sure he regrets it."

Sherwood gave me a sardonic look. "This is beyond raw eggs and peanut-buttered seats."

"Yes," I agreed. "It is."

"You know I can't let you leave," Adam said. "We are just barely managing our part of the balance the fae have constructed here. If the pack fails, the whole house of cards falls down and this chance of peace will be gone. The pack cannot afford for you to leave."

"*Let.*" Sherwood showed his teeth.

It was Adam's turn to shrug. "Leaving is a choice you might have. If you wanted to leave, I would fight to keep you—for the good of our pack." His eyes flashed yellow. "The wolf requires it of me because you might be the key to the pack's survival. I—my wolf would fight to the death to keep you."

The words rang in the air, and Adam let them hang for a moment. The pause wasn't on purpose. He was fighting his wolf to form words. Adam's control was very good, but the wolf he carried—even not considering Elizaveta's parting gift—was uncommonly wild.

I squeezed his leg. He put his hand on mine. When I turned my palm up, he gripped my hand so tightly it verged on pain.

Sherwood spoke, soft-voiced, into the silence. "For those very same reasons, I could not leave."

Adam nodded. I knew that he had not really expected Sherwood to be able to leave. If he had been able to leave his pack when it was in trouble, he would not be the level of dominant that could challenge Adam.

"If my wolf could be persuaded that the best thing for the pack was for *me* to leave . . ." Adam's voice was deeper, even though his eyes were almost entirely human.

"I couldn't do that," Sherwood admitted.

Adam nodded. "We need every wolf. If you need me to stay— and you do—you will have to defeat me in combat or my wolf won't accept you as Alpha. And because you need me to stay, your wolf won't let me leave, either."

"And you couldn't go any more than I could," Sherwood said wryly.

Maybe, Adam had said to me as we drove to Uncle Mike's, *Sherwood will see something I don't. Maybe he'll see a way through this. Maybe he can bring something to the table that will change the situation.*

Adam had said that Sherwood felt to him as though he was a Power on par with some of the more ancient wolves in Bran's pack. Maybe with Bran himself.

I hoped so. I hoped that Sherwood was the greatest, most powerful warrior the werewolves had ever had. Because maybe, maybe if he was better than Adam by more than a little, Sherwood could beat Adam without killing him.

Adam was a very, very good fighter, and he did not think that he could beat the Sherwood Post he now shared a pack bond with. For the first time ever, I wished that I didn't trust his judgment.

"If you want the pack," Adam said, "tell me. It won't change how hard I fight . . . but it might change some of my choices when we battle."

Zack leaned across the table to put a hand on my arm, though I was pretty sure I hadn't made a sound.

What had happened to my tidy life where the most dangerous thing I did was tinker with old cars?

Adam's hand, still clasped tightly with mine, reminded me that I knew exactly what had happened to my contented, safe life. I inhaled his rich scent and thought, *Worth it. Worth every bruise, every moment of terror, to be Adam Hauptman's mate. Even if it ends tonight.*

Adam was worth everything.

"What if—" Zack's voice was almost breathless. He stopped speaking as if he were trying to put something difficult into words.

When I looked at him, he didn't appear worried or sad or anything else I would have thought appropriate. Instead, there was something approaching awe in his face. Zack's hand was still on my arm, but the rest of his body was twisted around so he could look Sherwood in the face.

"What if?" I asked when it didn't appear he was going to finish.

To my surprise, Zack gave me a brilliant smile. He let go of my arm and sat back in his chair. "What if everything just remained the same?"

All three of us stared at him.

Around the question of who is Alpha, there is no room for wishes or wants. Any doubt about the ability or suitability of their Alpha makes the whole pack more dangerous—not to their enemies but to themselves and to their allies.

Warren is more dominant than Darryl, my rebel self observed. *And because Warren wishes it, Darryl is still our second.* But I knew that the situation wasn't remotely the same. Darryl wasn't an Alpha, and neither was Warren.

"You know it doesn't work that way," said Adam. He might have been answering my thoughts, but he was talking to Zack. Because the other wolf was a submissive and as fragile as any were-wolf I'd ever known, Adam's voice was gentle.

In response, Zack turned to stare at Sherwood.

Submissive wolves don't generally do things like that.

I looked at Sherwood to make sure he wasn't going to take offense. And all the little niggling things my subconscious had noticed finally came together and I saw what Zack had seen.

Sherwood was giving Zack a fond-but-exasperated look. It was a look I'd seen directed at me, but not by Sherwood.

"You're a Cornick," I said in shock. "I'd recognize that exas-perated expression anywhere. Samuel uses it when I beat him at chess."

3

~~~

I KNEW . . . I *KNEW*. BUT I WAITED FOR SHERWOOD'S RE-
sponse in case I was wrong.

Beside me, Adam quit breathing for a moment, his body tightening like a bowstring. Once I'd pointed it out, he saw it, too.

Bran Cornick, the Marrok, looked like a grad student most of
the time, though he was the most powerful werewolf in North
America and possibly the world. His firstborn son, Samuel, shared
his hair color, but was about eight inches taller and fifty pounds
heavier. Bran's younger son, Charles, took after his Native American mother more than his father's side of the family.

It was only when the Cornicks were together that it was apparent
they were closely related. Their alikeness was subtle, the way they
moved, the expressions on their faces—but it was unmistakable.
Sherwood looked more like them than they looked like each other.

There were no other Cornicks that I knew of. Bran's parents
were dead. Charles and Samuel were his only surviving children.

Samuel had no surviving children. I didn't know about Charles, but he was half-Salish, and Sherwood showed no signs of having Native heritage. Besides, though Charles was a couple of centuries old, Adam had told me that he thought Sherwood was one of the really old wolves.

"*You* beat Samuel at chess?" asked Sherwood. I noticed that he didn't comment about being a Cornick.

"Sometimes," I answered. Twice was sometimes.

"A Cornick," said Adam. Only someone who knew him very well would have heard the relief in his voice.

"Does this help?" I asked him. I thought it did, but I wasn't sure why.

"If he is a Cornick, it might," Adam answered.

Sherwood half lidded his eyes. That was a Charles-like expression if I'd ever seen one. "If I am?"

"Well, there are going to be a lot of disappointed people in the betting pool," I said, to buy Adam a little time to think. "But Ben will be happy."

I didn't understand why I felt relieved that Sherwood was a Cornick rather than any of the scary monsters in the betting book—assuming that being related to Bran meant that Sherwood *wasn't* Merlin, King Lycaon, or the Beast of Gévaudan (someone had written "He's dead, idiots" beside the Beast of Gévaudan in block letters). The problem of Sherwood's dominance did not just go away because we knew he was related to the Marrok. I knew that it didn't. But reality apparently didn't affect how I felt about it.

Adam looked at me. "Ben said that Sherwood is a Cornick?"

"Ben said 'Bran's flunky,'" I said.

"I am no one's flunky," Sherwood growled, sounding so much like Bran that I couldn't imagine how I hadn't seen it before now.

I paused. How *had* I missed that resemblance until now?

We'd fought side by side, Sherwood and I. We had bonded sitting way too high up in the air on a freaking huge crane designed to build nuclear power plants in Japan, overlooking the Columbia River in a way I hoped never to see again. And I hadn't noticed he had a tattoo on his neck? Hadn't noticed that his eyes were the same hazel as Bran's? Put like that, the answer was obvious.

Magic.

If I were going to send an amnesiac wolf out into the world, and that wolf was old and powerful enough to have amassed the kinds of enemies that such a one would accumulate, it would be better if everyone didn't immediately know who he was.

Pack magic is hunter's magic, very good at stealthy things like camouflage and muting sounds. I wouldn't have thought that pack magic could have hidden Sherwood's actual appearance from other werewolves, but Bran was Bran. I was happy to believe that he could figure out a way to use pack magic to hide Sherwood in plain sight. Something that made people not really see him. Something that made him look less *real.*

Bran had given Sherwood a disguise to protect him from his enemies when he could not protect himself. Magic that had melted away today in Uncle Mike's, in the halls of a Green Man. I remembered that odd look I'd gotten from Uncle Mike as he gave us privacy, and wondered if it had been on purpose or by accident.

Moreover, thinking about how no one had hinted anything about Sherwood, I was pretty sure that his disguise was not something Bran had done just for Sherwood's move to our pack. I could see a few old wolves holding their tongue about Sherwood's real name. But no one who looked at him and also knew Bran could fail to understand what they were looking at. Bran must have disguised Sherwood almost as soon as Sherwood regained his human shape. I couldn't think of any other way for Bran to keep all the wolves quiet.

"Not a flunky," agreed Zack, interrupting my racing thoughts. He still had a rapt look on his face, like an acolyte meeting a saint—or maybe a teenager meeting a rock star. "His right hand. His problem solver." His voice sank to a whisper as his lips curled into a smile. "I have heard stories."

"You think you know who I am," Sherwood said.

Zack started to nod but paused and shook his head slowly. "No. Maybe. Maybe not. But I know who you have been. And I heard a story from a wolf who was there, in Northumberland. The strangest thing in the whole business, she said, was that *you* didn't have any trouble following the lead of an Alpha a lot less dominant than Adam for a couple of years."

I glanced at Adam, who shook his head. He didn't know what Zack was talking about, either. But unlike Adam and me, Zack had reason for his belief that Sherwood's identity meant we had a path forward without blood being spilled. If Sherwood had managed to be part of a pack without killing the less dominant Alpha, then he could do it again.

Sherwood said with a growl in his voice, "Northumberland was six hundred years ago. At your age, you should know better than to believe stories."

Zack, who still cringed when the other wolves growled too close to him, gave Sherwood a serene smile. "Stories have power. My friend is—" Here his voice hesitated, and the smile faded. "She *was* not one to exaggerate."

"A Cornick," said Adam. "I think we can manage things differently if you are a Cornick."

Sherwood glanced at the three of us and shook his head in what looked to me something very like dismay.

"Bran Cornick abandoned you," he said. "And even if he had not, I am not he. And you have such—" He searched for a word.

"Faith," I supplied.

"Hope," Zack offered.

"I'm not going to say 'charity,'" said Adam with amusement. "But yes."

Sherwood shook his head and raised his arms up in a hopeless gesture. "Being a Cornick is not magical. Trust me, it does not solve any problems."

"No," I agreed. "But it solves *this* kind of problem. There never was a Cornick who couldn't turn a bad situation to his advantage." And that was true. They were all, even Samuel, ruthless and focused. "And killing Adam is not to your advantage."

Silence fell for a moment.

"Point to you," Sherwood said. He looked at Adam. "Though I don't know why you are so convinced I'd be able to kill you if I tried. Bran did not think so, or he wouldn't have sent me here."

"I know what you are," Adam said.

"And I know wha—" Sherwood stopped speaking midword. His pupils suddenly enlarged to engulf his irises to the point where his eyes were black with only a thin ring of wolf yellow.

"Magic," he rasped, surging to his feet so fast that his chair fell on its side.

Adam was a half second behind him. I don't know when Zack got to his feet, only that all four of us stood for a long minute, alerted by Sherwood's reaction. But no one made any further move. I couldn't smell any magic besides Uncle Mike's, but I trusted Sherwood's abilities over mine.

Nothing happened.

With my senses expanded for battle, the steady tick of the old-fashioned clock on the wall was annoyingly loud. Zack let out his breath, but no one else relaxed.

Adam, staring intently across the room, said, "By the fire-place."

I looked, but it didn't appear any different to me than it always had.

The old stone fireplace took up most of the far wall of the room, maybe twenty feet from where we sat. The gray stone was blackened around the hearth, with soot streaks reaching all the way to the ceiling. It had the appearance of something ancient, something that had been heating this room for centuries, though I knew that the building that housed Uncle Mike's had been built in the early 1950s.

I inhaled to ask Adam what he'd seen and caught a familiar scent.

"Sulfur," said Zack.

"Brimstone," I said. The difference between sulfur and brimstone was not chemical but magical.

Brimstone meant witches. I was, as usual, armed with the cutlass the pack had given me. But I had no intention of getting that close to a witch if I could help it. I pulled my carry gun. I held the 1911 in a two-handed grip, keeping it pointed at the floor until I had a better target. It took an effort to keep my hands steady, and I found it uncomfortably hard to breathe.

I wasn't ready to face witches again.

I didn't have nightmares every day anymore, but there were still nights when I had to drive to the burnt-out remains of Eliza-veta's home to see where the witches had died before I could go back to sleep. Last Friday there had been a *For Sale* sign next to the driveway. I wondered if I had a moral obligation to tell some-one just how many dead bodies—some of them human—were buried there. I was sure that no one would ever find the ones Zee had buried, but I had the feeling that the witches wouldn't have done quite so thorough a job of it.

Adam had his gun drawn, too. I hadn't been paying attention to see when he'd drawn it. Zack had a knife as long as his fore-arm. The only one who wasn't obviously holding a weapon was Sherwood, but a werewolf is never really unarmed. At that point I finally noticed what Adam had seen, a slight stirring over the blackened remains of the last fire someone had lit.

"I see smoke," Zack said, "but nothing is burning."

We could have rushed over, but Adam was staying put. We all waited beside him, almost like we were a team and Adam was our Alpha. I could feel the pack bonds rise and settle around us in preparation for battle. Sherwood felt to me as he always felt. The bonds thought Adam was the Alpha, too.

Black smoke began to trickle out of the firebox mouth, then flowed out and down, as if it were a little heavier than the air around it. The cloud of smoke ebbed and writhed in reaction to something—at first I thought it was just the invisible air currents in the room. But gradually it gathered in a rough circle on the battered floor in front of the hearth, a purposeful shape. As more smoke entered the room, the circling darkness grew higher and more dense, forming a rough cylindrical shape that stretched up until it was as tall as the big mantelpiece that topped the fireplace.

Then she stepped out of the smoke.

She was clothed from head to foot in black, like the charcoal color of the smoke. There was some magic about that, too, because my first impression was that she was wearing a Victorian era widow's dress complete with lace veil and feathered hat. But when I blinked, the clothes were made of smoke that wrapped around her like black velvet. The big ostrich feather drifted off into nothingness around the edges.

The brimstone blunted the effectiveness of my nose, and the smoke blurred the edges of her body. I could not tell who or what she was until she reached up with hands covered in black tatted lace—or lacelike smoke—and pulled the veil up to reveal Marsilia, Mistress of our local vampire seethe.

There was something different about her. Her eyes were closed, and the golden glory of her hair was veiled. Against the blackness, her flawless features could have been made of porcelain rather than flesh. Arched brows so pale that they were almost invisible teamed with the high cheekbones to frame her closed eyes.

She usually darkened her brows and her lashes, I thought, though makeup was generally the last thing I noticed about anyone. But the effect of all that paleness was startling, and not at all the impression she usually made. I caught a glimpse of something just below her jaw—a dark mark. A wound, maybe. But before I could be certain, the smoke drifted up her neck again. Something about the too-white face and the encircling darkness reminded me of a porcelain death mask.

She looked vulnerable.

Marsilia didn't do vulnerable. And this dramatic entrance was unlike her, too. She could do drama, but this was drama without a point. We all knew her, knew that she was scary—so why the smoke and brimstone?

I tried to tamp down my adrenaline as I coughed to clear my throat. There was no need to overreact.

Marsilia was our ally. She was not a witch. Though she was scary, and she disliked me, she did not feature in my current nightmares. And still, staring at that pale, perfect face, I did not put my gun away. This was not like her, and that worried me.

Marsilia was an old vampire, and old vampires, like most old supernatural creatures, picked up talents and bits of magic throughout their lives. Marsilia could teleport. I hadn't known that she could do this smoke-thingy, and I didn't know why she'd bothered. Surely if she were trying to be scary, teleporting directly in was as scary as anything else she could have done.

Maybe she'd figured out who Sherwood was, too, and this show was for him. She was old; maybe she'd known all along who he was and had been waiting for us to figure it out.

She stood with her eyes closed for as much as three seconds. No one spoke because Adam did not. I'd have thought that seeing Marsilia would have lessened his tension—Marsilia and he liked each other—but it didn't seem to.

Without opening her eyes, she pulled the veil back down to hide her face again. Only with her face behind the black smokey lace did she turn her head fully toward us. I saw the glint of something that might have been her eyes, though it was more red than brown.

"Where is my Wulfe?" she asked.

For a second I thought she was speaking about one of our pack—none of whom belonged to her. Then I realized she was talking about her second. W-U-L-F-E, not W-O-L-F.

Wulfe was a very old vampire, older than Marsilia. He was witchborn and a wizard, which meant that he wielded two entirely unrelated forms of magic in addition to whatever magical power just being an old vampire brought him. He was also bug-nuts. The combination of power and unpredictability made him the single scariest vampire I'd ever met—and I'd met Iacopo Bonarata, who ruled Europe.

Lately Wulfe had been stalking me.

"How should we know? He belongs to you," I said, my voice sounding weirdly normal amid all the theater. "I haven't seen him since last Thursday."

He'd been standing just on the other side of the glass when I looked up while I was doing dishes, startling me into dropping a Pyrex baking dish on the edge of the sink. He'd been gone when I looked back up from the disaster of sharp glass in dirty dishwater. That was the last time I'd *seen* him.

Two days later he left a gift for me on Adam's and my bed, a very long, green silk belt embroidered with phoenixes from one end to the other. Between every seven birds was the word "*Ardeo.*"

It was old. Very old.

Google translated the Latin as "I burn." It was, apparently, meant to be taken in an erotic way and not as an offer to turn oneself into a pile of ashes. I didn't think it was magical—it didn't have the feel that the fae artifacts had. But Wulfe had left it on my bed, so I figured all bets were off.

Presently it was stored in our weapons safe until I figured out what to do about it.

More worrying than having custody of such a thing was how it got onto our bed. Adam had been unable to determine how Wulfe had entered the house unnoticed.

While it was true that vampires (among a few other supernatural creatures, according to their nature) could not enter a home without invitation, Wulfe had been brought inside when unconscious while everyone involved had been too exhausted and battered to make better choices.

Even so, our house was filled with werewolves. A vampire shouldn't have been able to traipse around unnoticed. Especially since Adam's pillow had been pulled out from under the covers and noticeably—probably deliberately noticeably—dented, as if Wulfe had lain beside the belt for a while.

It had been the second time Wulfe had made it up to our bedroom without anyone seeing him. The first time he'd just left a note covered with heart stickers, the kind kindergartners put on Valentine's Day cards.

That's when I'd asked Joel and his wife to move out and take Aiden—our fire-touched rescue boy—with them in case Joel wasn't able to control his tibicena.

"Because of Wulfe?" Joel had asked.

"Because I don't like the way Wulfe treats Aiden like a threat," I told him bluntly. I hadn't told him I was just as afraid for Joel, because that wouldn't have been useful.

Joel had packed up his wife and Aiden and moved out. That reduced the people living in our home to Adam, me, and Adam's daughter, Jesse. I was pretty sure Wulfe viewed Jesse as a noncombatant in our current weird stalker dance, leaving only Adam and me as targets.

But I wasn't going to tell Marsilia all of that. Primarily because if Wulfe could waltz in and out of our home, I wasn't going to advertise it to the enemy. Ally. Frenemy.

"You have seen him," she said to me. "All know that Wulfe hunts the Columbia Basin Pack Alpha's mate."

Her words were formal, almost stylized. This was the Mistress of the seethe speaking, and it sounded like a threat to me. I just wasn't sure what kind of threat.

Marsilia's attention lingered on me a moment, but I wasn't going to say anything until we knew more about what was going on. This time I was sure that it was a red glint I saw behind the black smokey lace. I'd seen vampires with eyes that glowed like that—they'd been very hungry. It made me glad she was all the way on the other side of the room.

I wondered if she was wearing the veil to hide her eyes or to protect us from her gaze. I was (mostly) immune to vampire magics, but Adam and Zack were not. I didn't know about Sherwood. Marsilia had captured Samuel with her gaze once, so I didn't assume Sherwood was safe.

Marsilia took a step closer to us, the smoke following her like a black wedding train. "There has been peace between us," she said.

"Yes," Adam agreed, his stance changing a little, Alpha werewolf speaking to the Mistress of the seethe.

"We have come together to keep this territory safe from other predators," she said.

"Yes," Adam agreed.

Supernatural beings in confrontational, or semi-confrontational, interactions tended to restate the obvious. I thought it was to make everything absolutely clear so that if death resulted, it would not be by misunderstanding.

"All know my Wulfe has been oft at your door of late," she said. The archaic wording was unusual. Marsilia, like my friend Stefan (who was also an old Italian vampire), had mostly kept her Italian accent, but otherwise she spoke colloquial American English.

"He's been stalking me, yes," I agreed dryly.

"And now he is gone," she said. "Others say that he is dead and your pack at fault. Adam Hauptman, if you would keep our alliance, you will find my Wulfe, prove he is not dead." She might have invoked Adam's name, but the hairs on the back of my neck were certain that she was still looking at me, no matter how much that veil hid.

"Wulfe's a vampire," said Sherwood, speaking for the first time. "He's already dead."

Sherwood distracted her from me. She looked at him, tipping her head sideways in a motion more wolf than vampire. I wasn't sure how to read that. Maybe without the subtle disguise Bran had given Sherwood, she, too, recognized him.

But it was a brief pause. She looked squarely at Adam, and he tensed under her regard, even though her veil was now almost opaque.

I gripped Adam's wrist, leaving my gun in my left hand. I could shoot left-handed, though not as well as with my right or in a proper two-handed grip. Sometimes I could extend my limited immunity to vampire magic to someone by touching them. And keeping Adam free of Marsilia's influence was more important than whether or not I could hit the side of a barn.

Adam growled, a low rumbling in his chest. He twisted his hand until it closed over mine, so we stood hand in hand.

Marsilia didn't seem to notice.

"If you do not find Wulfe, all will know what happened to him," she said, sounding suddenly tired. Her next words were rushed, a little more like her usual self, though the word choice was still off. "All will know that you prey upon your allies. Upon those who count upon your support. There will be war between your pack and the vampires."

She disappeared, smoke and all, with the suddenness that I was more used to from her. Almost in the same breath, Uncle Mike opened the door, taking three quick steps into the room with the attitude of a sheepdog scenting wolves. I thought I caught a glimpse of a blade in his right hand, but his body blocked my line of sight. When he turned to us, there was no sword in sight except for the cutlass hanging from my belt.

"My apologies, Adam," Uncle Mike said. "I'd not have thought any enemy could have trespassed my wards here in the heart of my home."

"Marsilia isn't our enemy," said Adam in a thoughtful voice, holstering his gun. "Not yet, anyway."

WHEN WE EXITED THE BUILDING, I HEARD UNCLE MIKE turn the lock. The big new sign had been turned off, along with the rest of the building's exterior lights. There was a staff lot on the other side of the building, so our vehicles were the only ones left in the main parking lot. I checked my phone—and yes, it was that late.

We didn't discuss Marsilia's visit. We were on Uncle Mike's ground; whatever we said would probably be overheard. Adam hadn't told Uncle Mike much about Marsilia's visit—just that she had brought us a message. If that message turned out to have larger implications, Adam would share it with Uncle Mike.

Uncle Mike hadn't pushed the issue.

Sherwood was parked near the entrance. The parking lot had been mostly full when Adam and I had arrived, so we were parked near the back of the lot, the black SUV blending in with the shadows where the parking lot lights didn't extend. A maroon Subaru Outback was parked near us, presumably Warren's new car.

We were almost to the SUV when Sherwood, who'd stopped by his car, said, "Adam."

We—Adam, Zack, and I—turned to look at him.

Sherwood stood with one big hand on the top of his car and the other on the open door. He was not looking at us, his gaze turned back toward Uncle Mike's.

"I know who and what I was," he said heavily. "But there are a lot of holes in my memory. Zack is correct that for the better part of two years, six hundred years ago in Northumberland, I ran as second in a pack with an Alpha who was not as strong as Warren is. But I do not remember why it was necessary or how I did it."

A train rolled by on tracks that were less than a half mile away.

"It can be done," Adam said. "Are you willing to try?"

"It can be done," Sherwood agreed. He gave Adam a half smile. "I don't want to fight you for the pack. I am not convinced I would win—but I think that we would damage each other and our fight would damage the pack. I will see what I can do. But in the meantime, you should help me keep clear of Darryl and Warren—because the pack sense is that I am the fourth male in the pack."

He had been steadily rising in the ranks, without violence, since he'd joined us. As an old wolf, he should be tradition-bound, but he still chose to add "male" into his statement—a recognition that our females held rank, too. And furthermore, that their ranking was complicated, caught as it was between tradition and reality.

"Yes," Adam acknowledged.

"That will only last until Darryl, Warren, and I are in the same room for an extended period of time. Changing the organization of the pack without purpose is not a good idea."

Adam and Sherwood exchanged a brief, rueful glance.

The stability of the pack was the key to werewolf survival. A stable pack helped the individual pack members stay in control of their wolves. Unstable packs resulted in wolf and human casualties. Human casualties scared people. Frightened people came hunting with pitchforks, guns—and in our modern era, more lethal weapons. Weapons that could kill even werewolves.

Our pack needed to be more stable than most to survive the pressures we were putting on it. Which is why Sherwood had to stay away from Darryl and Warren—to avert running into a situation when the confusion about where he belonged in the pack might force a fight.

"You don't need to avoid me?" Adam asked.

Sherwood considered it. Then he shook his head. "You know," he said. "Our talk tonight seems to have made a difference." He glanced at me with a frown. "Or something did, anyway." He made a fist and touched his own chest. "The beast is willing to bide its time. I think that we can work together safely. For now."

He got into his car and the rest of us watched him drive away.

Only when his taillights were a block down the road did Zack take out the Subaru fob and unlock Warren's new car with a beep.

Adam caught the driver side door before Zack could close it. "Is there anything I should know about Sherwood that you know?"

Zack said, "Most people think that wolf in Northumberland was Samuel, you know? But Samuel's a white wolf and the wolf in my friend's stories was gray."

Adam nodded as though Zack had answered his question.

"What happened?" I asked. "I don't know the story."

"Sorcerer," Zack said. "Man made a deal with a demon, but this one stayed in control longer than most—and he paid attention to what victims he took. People who didn't draw notice—whores, the sick, the very poor. Was active for a long time, a little over a century, as my friend figured it."

"A century?" I asked. "Was the sorcerer a werewolf?"

He shook his head. "Hid himself in a monastery. Made him difficult to find. Especially as he fed the demon sparingly." Zack raised an eyebrow in irony. "Power of the spirit over flesh was something those monks practiced, apparently. He wasn't anyone important. He wasn't after power or wealth. He just didn't want to die. And the demon kept him from doing so."

Zack smiled wryly. "He'd have been better off a werewolf. Any human who could control a demon for a century would have made a good werewolf."

"No one hunted him," Adam said, "because he wasn't causing trouble."

Zack nodded. "Not for a while. Eventually his kills started getting more public. And they looked like animal kills."

"Framing the pack," I suggested.

"Or possibly losing control," Adam said.

Zack tipped his head toward Adam. "That's what they thought."

Zack looked at me. "We don't get sorcerers much anymore. There aren't a lot of people who believe in demons."

"We had a run-in with one a couple years before you got here," Adam told him. "A vampire."

Zack's eyes grew wide. "Nasty."

Adam nodded. "We handled it, as it happens. But the Marrok showed up in case we needed him."

"They didn't have something like the Marrok in those days," said Zack, then he smiled. "Well, I suppose they must have done, given that Sherwood came to help. They just didn't know it, eh? My friend told me she thought Sherwood was just some wolf, joined their pack and lay low for a while. Called himself Jack Hedley, which was a common surname around those parts. But when the pack started actively hunting the sorcerer, he took point. He's the one who figured out that the sorcerer was living in the monastery. He organized night patrols that ran the area around the monastery. After a few months, the patrol came upon a kill."

In a faraway voice, which held enough horror that I was fairly sure that, though he hadn't been present for this one, he'd seen something similar enough to picture the scene quite clearly, he said, "Some little boy, maybe two years old. They later found he'd been abandoned at the monastery for care."

There was a short pause as Zack collected his thoughts.

"Their Alpha had been leading the night's patrol when they heard the cries. He was fast and he had a little boy about that age. He outstripped the pack and got there before the others. If the monk had been purely human, he'd have died with a werewolf's fangs lodged in his neck."

"But he rode a demon," Adam said.

Zack nodded, but said, "The demon was doing the riding by the time the rest of the pack got there, she said. Just finished boiling the skin off their Alpha and in the process of burning him from the inside out. He was still screaming while most of his body was already ashes. My friend, she was an old wolf when I knew her, and she told me it was the most horrible thing she'd ever seen."

By now it was obvious that Zack was avoiding giving a name to the friend who'd told him the story. There were a lot of reasons for things like that, and good werewolf manners meant not asking.

"There they were." Zack's voice was a bit dreamy. "This pack of werewolves surrounding a little old man in the robes of a monk, and they were too scared to move. And then Jack Hedley stepped out of the shadows. He hadn't even been on patrol that night. She never did find out how he knew where to be. He wasn't even in wolf form, but he called a challenge to the sorcerer.

"She thought he was a dead wolf, no joke. But she was near enough the edge of the pack to try working her way around through the shadows, hoping to get behind that old monk, see? She had a burning need to kill him for what he'd done, though she figured to lose her own life in the process. But she had to get close to him to do it.

"The sorcerer sent green lightning out of his hands to strike old Jack down. It hit him right enough—and caused no damage. Jack took everything the demon-ridden monk had to throw and just stood there. When the demon stopped, Jack smiled at him and turned into a beast."

71

Zack looked at Adam and nodded, as if in answer to a question. "I haven't seen the beast you carry, but if the description you gave is accurate, it's not the same thing at all. This was a wolf—twice the size of a normal werewolf. Only this Jack, he changed like Mercy changes, between one eyeblink and the next."

He took a breath and closed his eyes, and when he spoke, it was obvious that he was reciting someone else's words. "A storm rose from the ground, tearing up rocks and hunks of earth, flinging them into the air. We wolves, we flattened ourselves in fear and wonder as the Great Beast fought the demon, not with teeth and claw but with magic meeting magic. The air crackled with it, and lightning rained down as though the end were nigh. Four of us died—three were lightning struck and the other was just dead with no sign of what killed him. And when it was over, the demon having been driven from his host, Jack stepped from the Great Beast as if he were throwing off a winter coat and snapped the monk's neck."

Zack shrugged. When he continued, the words were in his own voice. "That's the end of it. Jack left. Another Alpha took over. The monk was dead. Another monk found his body with the poor child, and the monastery decided God and his angels had struck the man down for his wickedness while wearing the cross. One of the wolves in her pack swore he'd seen Jack before, called him Cornick. My friend knew Bran—and Samuel, too, for that matter. She thought that other wolf was right, but she never managed to find out just who he was."

"The Great Beast of Northumberland is in the betting book," I said. I hadn't been able to get anyone to tell me the story of the Great Beast, even though three people had bet on it. None of those had been Zack.

"Maybe Sherwood should go through the betting book," Zack suggested.

I grinned at him. "That should be interesting."

Zack made to shut his door again.

"One more thing," Adam asked.

Zack waited.

"Is there something I should know about Warren?"

Zack hesitated, then shook his head. "Nothing that's my place to speak of. Not right now."

"There is something?" I said anxiously.

Zack smiled at me. "He's smart. If he needs help, he'll ask for it."

ADAM WAS QUIET ON THE WAY HOME. I DIDN'T SAY much, either. It was late, I had a pumpkin-induced headache, and Zack had just given us a lot to think about. But the biggest take-home of the night was the message Marsilia had given us. I wished I was sure what that message really was.

Adam was probably doing the same thing without the head-ache. I treated myself to a pause in my deliberations so that I could enjoy the play of the dashboard lights on my mate's face. Werewolves don't age, but I still thought he looked older than he had a few months ago.

The witches had inflicted some deep internal wounds. The poison had been drawn, but there were still scabs and scars that remained, exacerbating his already infamous temper. He worried about the monster Elizaveta had cursed him with. His cheek-bones were sharper, and there were hollows under his eyes.

He caught my look and grinned suddenly. "Like what you see?" he asked.

Adam had anti-vanity. He knew he was gorgeous, and though he was happy to use it as a weapon, it didn't much affect him otherwise. I suspected it embarrassed him.

Not wanting to tell him that I'd been assessing rather than admiring (primarily assessing, anyway), I pressed my face against his shoulder. I closed my eyes and inhaled, feeling my headache abate just a little.

"I love you," I told him. "I know we have a lot on our plate again, but I'd like to take this moment to tell you that I'm glad you and Sherwood don't have to fight."

"Maybe," he cautioned.

"You'll figure it out," I said confidently. I was a little surprised that I was able to be so confident. I suspected it was because we had another disaster on our hands for me to worry about.

What had Marsilia meant with that performance? It wasn't out of character for her, just out of character for her with us. She knew that it wouldn't impress us the way it would impress someone who didn't know her. So what had it accomplished that a normal meeting would not have?

She had left us no openings to question her, and I had a lot of questions. How did she know Wulfe was gone? Where was the last place she'd seen him? What was she hiding with her veil and the brimstone? Why had she needed to hide her eyes?

The brimstone was particularly interesting because it meant we couldn't smell anything but the brimstone: not emotions, not whether she was telling the truth, and not any incriminating scents like blood, either. It was possible that the brimstone could have been part of the magic she'd used to create the smoke effects and not an attempt to mask scents. Possibly she'd used it for both reasons.

I didn't think she had used the brimstone to lie. I couldn't use my sense of smell to tell me that, but my instincts were that she was telling the absolute truth. So far as it went.

"Did she not want us to believe her?" I asked when Adam turned onto our road. "I mean, I think she was telling the truth—it had that feel. But the brimstone, the smoke, the veil are all the kinds of things the vampires use to confuse the issue."

"I think," Adam said slowly, "that Wulfe is missing, and she needs us to find him. I am sure that the theatrics were partially to clue us in that there are other things at play, possibly things she can't tell us."

"Like maybe someone is going to question her?" I asked.

"Or has forbidden her to tell us," he agreed.

"Bonarata?" I asked, and didn't like the quiver in my voice at all. Bonarata, Marsilia's maker, was the only one I could think of who could possibly make Marsilia do his bidding.

Adam reached out and gripped my hand.

"Last I heard he was still in Italy," he said. "But my information is a couple of weeks old. I'll check again. I think that you are looking at the right scale. Someone powerful enough to get Marsilia's tail in a twist, and possibly to capture or manipulate Wulfe."

I shivered.

"It's not time to panic yet," he told me. "Marsilia thinks we can make a difference. She's not stupid, and she understands power games. We'll start with Wulfe and work our way to Marsilia's real problem. It is possible that there are just things she didn't want to tell us. Marsilia is not beyond being manipulative for her own ends."

"Keep an open mind?" I said.

He smiled at me. "Usually works better at this stage of the game."

4

WE PULLED IN TO FIND LIGHTS ON AT HOME. I'D BEEN looking forward to going directly to bed, though it had been unlikely Jesse would have gone to bed before she found out what happened tonight.

Adam parked in our usual spot, looked at the cars, and said, "Looks like Jesse has friends over."

One of the cars belonged to Jesse's best friend, Izzy, and the other was Tad's. Looking at Tad's car, I sighed theatrically.

Adam raised an eyebrow.

"I miss Tad," I told him mournfully. "Zee scared away the last assistant I hired before he'd worked a full shift."

Four weeks, three people who no longer wanted to work for me. I really regretted the first two.

The last one I was pretty sure I'd have had to fire in a few days anyway, because he didn't know how to fix things without directions. People like that don't make good mechanics. They can work at a new shop, where all they have to do is replace the part that a computer tells them needs to be replaced.

But working on old cars is generally a matter of understanding why cars run and what can interfere with that. Fixing them can be quirky. I have used bread tabs and dental floss when the new parts don't fit a forty-year-old car the way they would have fit the car when it was new.

"If Zee is going to scare all of your help away, you should make *him* hire the next one," Adam told me, not for the first time.

Tad, my former assistant and Zee's son, had taken a new job.

"I have to take it," Tad had assured me earnestly when he'd turned in his notice, which was handwritten on the back of a shop receipt. "They were very persuasive—and it comes with a free education. If I don't take it, I might have a partial college education forever and be stuck in a job like this."

Tad had once had a full-ride scholarship to an Ivy League university back East. He'd left it unfinished and never told me why. More interestingly, he'd never told Zee why, either.

I thought that Tad hadn't talked to me because he was worried I might tell his dad, which was sound reasoning. I didn't think he was worried about what I'd do. But if I ever found out who had sent our Tad home with his optimistically sunny view of the world ripped away as if it had never been there . . . maybe he was worried about what I'd do, too. I might not be a powerful fae like his father, but I was pretty good at revenge.

When he'd left me the first time, finding a good assistant to man the phones, do the billing, and help out in the shop hadn't been too difficult. But then Zee had only been coming in now and then when I got behind or he got bored. Since matters had heated up around the Tri-Cities, Zee came every day.

"To keep an eye on things," he'd told me.

To keep a watch out for Tad and me, I understood. He wasn't unhappy that Tad had taken a new job, under the circumstances, but he was old and cranky and had very little patience. It took more than a few weeks to see through the crusty interior to the (very small and well-hidden) kindness beneath. I hoped I could find someone before I woke up one day to discover *I* was the new assistant.

I glanced at Jesse's car as we walked by it, and I took stock of it reflexively. It still needed a new paint job, but we'd sprayed the exposed metal with an undercoat that would stop the rust even if it gave the old car a somewhat leprous appearance. There were no new dings, no key marks, no spray paint.

As the daughter of the local Alpha, Jesse had watched her world get smaller and smaller as our enemies had grown more numerous and more powerful. She was human and a target for anyone who wanted to attack our pack.

Jesse had altered her plans to go to school in Seattle on her own, knowing that we could no longer spare the manpower to give her the protection she'd need living in a different city. There was a pack in Seattle, but since we had been separated from the Marrok's care, they could not help us. Jesse had also turned down her best friend's offer to co-rent an apartment next to the local Washington State University campus because she was afraid that our pack trouble would affect Izzy, too.

It wasn't just supernatural attacks she had to deal with. Adam was a celebrity, local and otherwise. And everyone in the Tri-Cities knew him and his family (Jesse and me) by sight.

The first week of classes, a group of students organized by the anti-supernatural organization Bright Future had begun following her around with protest signs everywhere she went. While they were doing that, someone vandalized her car with a can of spray paint. Parking lot cameras caught an unhelpful image of a hooded figure in jeans and tennis shoes.

Jesse told us about the car because she hadn't been able to get the paint off before she had to come home. But Izzy, who had been witness to some of the rest of the harassment, called Tad and told him about all of it.

Tad showed up while I was still trying to get the spray paint off. I know a few ways to get paint off, but it's tricky to do that without removing the car paint, too. Tad was better at it than I was, but when we'd finished, a new paint job was inevitable. I'd called and made arrangements, but my painter does show cars and was a couple of months out.

The next morning, Tad was waiting next to Jesse's car when she came out to drive to school. The ensuing argument got pretty heated. I was in the living room, but my hearing is very good. I didn't start out deliberately eavesdropping, but I didn't try to tune it out, either. Adam came in about halfway through the argument, just about when things got interesting.

That's how we learned that the car had been the tip of the iceberg. The only reason Adam stayed in the house was that when Jesse drove to school, Tad was in the passenger seat.

I don't know, don't *want* to know, what Tad did, but Izzy told me that the people with signs only made a brief appearance that morning, and did not reappear again after Tad spoke to them. When the three of them walked to Jesse's car at the end of the day, it was in the same condition it had been in when they parked it.

That night, the pack made a formal offer of employment to

Tad. It took some string-pulling to get Tad enrolled late, but we managed. Adam said that the school's reluctance to bend the rules of entry had only been pro forma. Tad's grades were high enough that he qualified—and the school hadn't known what to do with the protesters. They were more than happy to let us propose a solution that suited everyone; it just took a couple of days to manage that within the established rules.

Tad had cheerfully accepted Jesse's somewhat scattered approach to her first semester at college. I was pretty sure she'd added the women's studies Comparative Sexuality class to see how far she could push him. Tad rolled with whatever she threw at him. After dealing with Zee his whole life, Jesse was easy.

I didn't know what would happen once she picked a major, but maybe matters would quiet down so it would be enough for Tad to be on the same campus rather than needing to be on the same class schedule. For now, at least, Tad and Jesse were fine.

"It's a Tuesday," I said to Adam. "Isn't it a little late for them to still be up?"

"Wednesday morning now," said Adam. "Did Jesse say anything to you about having plans?"

"No."

We'd warned her about the Sherwood problem before heading to Uncle Mike's. If she'd had plans, it was entirely understandable that she'd forgotten to tell us about them. Adam opened the front door, and laughter and the scent of fresh-buttered popcorn rolled out of the kitchen. They didn't seem to notice our entrance.

Adam winked at me and then announced, "Parental curfew," in a drill sergeant's voice that could have awakened the dead.

There was the sound of a chair scraping the floor, then Jesse bolted out of the kitchen and threw herself at her dad. She had, for the time being, eschewed her usual bright-colored hair dye. Her newly natural honey-brown hair, which was making its first appearance since she was about thirteen, made her look uncomfortably like a real grown-up. She didn't look less adult in her frantic relief.

Adam hugged her hard. "All is well," he told her, which was true as far as it went. But Jesse was used to that; her dad had been the pack Alpha since the day she was born.

"The thing that we thought might end up with Adam dead looks like it will work out okay," I told her dryly as her feet hit the ground again. "We have another situation to replace it that might end up with Adam dead. Or me dead. Or maybe the whole pack. But at least we solved one deadly situation before we picked up another one."

"Business as usual," said Tad, who'd exited the kitchen with a little less speed than Jesse.

He was only tall when compared to his dad, but he had a sort of lanky grace that made him look taller. His ears stuck out, and his nose was flattened as if he'd spent time in a boxing ring. He was still attractive, but it was an effect of expression rather than bone structure. Of course, his appearance was a matter of choice rather than genetics. He was half-fae and half-human, but powerful enough that he could adopt a glamour like the full-blooded fae in order to hide his other-than-human appearance.

Izzy, full name Isabella Norman, tagged along behind Tad. She was slender and doll-sized, with curly brown hair—and was a lot tougher than she looked. She and Jesse had been casual friends for a long time. When Jesse started taking heat from other high school students as her father's position as the werewolf pack

Alpha became better known, Izzy had jumped into the breach. For that alone I would have liked her, but she was also a genuinely good person.

She wrapped a hand under Tad's arm and leaned around him so she could see us better. "Hey, Mr. H, Ms. H, glad you're both still alive. Mom wants to know if you want more of the orange essential oil—it's on special this month."

"I'll take two," I said. I'd been experimenting with using it in my baking. Sometimes it worked, sometimes it was awful.

"Don't you have school?" Adam asked, addressing all three of them.

"Not until eleven tomorrow," Jesse said. "And we are working on an assignment, anyway."

"*The Harvester*," said Izzy in a tone suitably sepulchral. Then she grinned and said, "You know, the new horror movie? The one written by that Danson guy who graduated from Pasco High? Apparently he went to school with our English Lit teacher, from kindergarten through college. We were given the assignment of watching it and reporting on it."

"The screenwriter claims that it's based on a local urban myth," said Tad with a grin. His hand covered Izzy's where she touched his arm.

Aha, I thought. They're dating. No wonder she'd called Tad when Jesse had been in trouble.

"The problem, ladies and gentlemen," announced Jesse in a voice meant to mimic their instructor's, "is that there is no urban myth of that sort around here. Have fun picking it apart."

"I don't think he likes his old schoolmate much," murmured Tad with laughing eyes. "Jealousy is a terrible thing."

"I get the impression that it's not jealousy," said Jesse. "It feels more personal than that. Like maybe Danson stole Dr. Holbearth's girlfriend." She paused. "Or they dated and had a bad breakup."

"*The Harvester* had a pre-opening midnight showing tonight," said Izzy. "We thought we'd get a running start on our assignment. And also miss out on the crowds." She shook her head. "One out of two isn't bad. That theater was packed."

Tad's eyes caught mine meaningfully, then traveled to Jesse. He and Izzy had taken Jesse out to distract her from her worries over her father, I interpreted. I gave him a little nod of thanks.

"It was *so* bad," Jesse said. "I mean even worse than the usual B-horror-movie bad. The villain, for no discernible motive I could figure out, dressed up like a scarecrow, took a scythe down from an old barn in the back of the farm he'd just bought, and started killing people in ways designed to be as bloody and disgusting as possible."

"It was a sickle," said Tad in the patient tone of someone who has said that before.

"And it was supposed to be possessed," Izzy said. "The old woman, the first victim, she said as much. 'That old scythe is hainted.'"

"'Hainted'?" I said. "The movie is supposed to take place here, right? Isn't a 'haint' a Southern term for a ghost? Like Georgia Southern. Southeastern Washington is still in the Pacific Northwest."

"Oh, *that's* what she said," Jesse exclaimed. "I couldn't tell what she was talking about. Well, if they knew the stupid thing was haunted, why did they leave it hanging around in a barn? Why didn't they just burn down the barn with the scythe in it?"

"They did eventually," Tad pointed out. "If the barn burned

in the beginning of the movie, they wouldn't have had a possessed guy armed with the *sickle* slicing people in half all over the place."

"He beheaded a couple of them," said Izzy. "Is it still slicing them in half when it's more like removing ten percent or so?"

"All I know is that I'll never get that hundred and eight minutes of my life back," Jesse said. "Are you really sure it was a sickle? Everyone in the movie called it a scythe."

"'Sickle' doesn't sound as cool as 'scythe,'" Izzy said, frowning at Tad.

"When the son of an iron-kissed fae who is the most famous smith in all of mythology tells you what a tool is called, you should believe him over someone reading a part," Adam advised. He wasn't smiling, but his dimple was making an appearance.

"A scythe is what Death wields," I told them. "Long-handled. Like a pike or that weird thing Adam's alter ego Captain Larson uses in ISTDPB4." ISTDPB4 (Instant Spoils: The Dread Pirate's Booty Four) was an interactive computer game that the whole pack played together on a regular basis. "A sickle has a handle that fits your hand—like a sword someone bent in a circle."

"What's an iron-kissed fae?" asked Izzy. "And Zee is famous?"

"Infamous," I corrected.

Zee's history wasn't a secret, precisely. Though I didn't go out of my way to talk about it. But Izzy was all but family, and if she was dating Tad, she should know what she was getting into.

"Thanks," Tad told Adam and me dryly before addressing Izzy. "My father is one of a small group of fae who can handle iron and steel. Dad made a few famous weapons back in the day under one name or the other." He flapped his free hand airily and went on in a casual tone, "Killed a few famous kings, a saint . . ." He cleared his throat and said, "A god or two, maybe. That kind of thing. Stories get exaggerated with time. Most of the fae who are older than a couple of centuries have stories told about them."

"He made jewels out of the eyes of the sons of a king who enslaved him," Jesse said tightly, her tone substantially different from Tad's breezy delivery.

I knew that story—it wasn't about Zee. I didn't *think* it was about Zee. It was about Wayland Smith, a somewhat mysterious character who appeared in various medieval chronicles. I'd done a paper on him once, in college.

Jesse didn't read a lot of old Germanic legends, so where had she gotten it?

"And goblets of their skulls," she continued. "And he served that king and his wife wine out of those jeweled goblets. Beguiling them so they drank from the skulls of their sons."

The tightness of her voice told me that she'd come upon that story very recently.

"Who told you that?" I asked before Tad could.

"Tilly," said Jesse, sending a cold chill down my spine. "She doesn't like Zee or Tad."

That she didn't.

Tilly was the name Underhill had given herself when she took on the form of a child so she could play with her human toys. Aiden had been one of those until he escaped.

Tilly might look like a feral eight-year-old girl (or any other age she picked that day), but she was the personification of a land of faerie that had destroyed the courts of the fae and driven them out of her borders, locking her doors against them. The fae claimed that it had been the increasing use of iron that had closed the doors to Underhill in the old country. But I noted that the fae had been locked out, not locked in.

When Aiden had come to live with us, Tilly had installed a door to Underhill on a wall she built on the property line between this house and my old house. And apparently, she'd been telling Jesse stories.

"When did she tell you that?" Adam asked, his voice very calm and quiet.

"Since Aiden left, she's started showing up when I go outside alone," Jesse said, answering Adam's real question. "I asked Aiden. He told me that there wasn't much she could do given the rules she is constrained by. He advised me not to let you know she was bothering me, because then she'd know she was bothering me. She'd look on it as encouragement. And maybe you'd try to renegotiate the rules. He thinks that she's as bound up by rules as she is willing to be. Any negotiations are likely to backfire. I thought I should listen to him when he talks about Underhill."

Adam grunted unhappily. Jesse was right. Aiden was probably right. But I expected that Adam would go have a chat with Tilly the next time she showed up anyway. Hopefully it wouldn't happen until he'd had a chance to cool off.

"She told you that story was about Zee?" I asked.

Jesse nodded.

"Your dad," Izzy asked Tad, "can make jewels out of someone's eyes? And goblets out of children's skulls? And he *drank* out of them?" She'd let go of Tad's arm and taken a step back while I wasn't paying attention to her.

Maybe if it had happened in the past century, I might have had a different attitude about the story. But that tale was from the *Poetic Edda*, written a thousand years ago, more or less. It felt like a cautionary tale, not something that happened to real people. I couldn't see Zee, my old friend, doing something so horrible.

Okay, I could, actually. Because he'd done something similar fairly recently.

"When people live a very long time, they have room to change," I said, carefully not saying that Zee had changed.

Tad gave me a look that said, *Thanks, but please don't try to help.*

"I *warned* you that my father was not just a grumpy old man," he told Izzy. "I told you he'd done some very terrible things."

She gave him a look that would have done credit to a kicked puppy.

I wanted to tell her that even if Zee had been terrible once, he didn't do things like that anymore. But it would have been a lie. I was pretty sure that parts of the bodies of the Gray Lords who'd held Zee and Tad captive in the fae reservation were still turning up in unexpected places. The fae, even the powerful ones, had started to have a certain tone in their voice when they referred to Zee.

There hadn't been, as far as I'd heard, any jewels that were formerly eyeballs, though. I hoped that Tilly had been wrong—mistaken, not lying—that *that* story had been about Wayland, who *wasn't* also the same person as the Dark Smith of Drontheim, who had become my Zee.

But I had to admit, if only to myself, that it was altogether too plausible, given the stories I knew about the Dark Smith. One of the Gray Lords had told me that Zee had made Excalibur. There were stories that attributed Excalibur's making to Wayland.

"But he's so nice," said Izzy.

We all stared at her. Zee was my mentor, my friend, and I loved him. But "nice" wasn't an adjective I'd have used to describe the grumpy old smith. He could be kind, yes, but "nice" implied something less . . . dangerous.

Izzy's back stiffened at the incredulous look Tad gave her, and when she spoke, her voice was defensive. "Last week I had a flat and called Jesse to tell her I'd be late. She said since I was only a mile or so from the garage, she'd see if someone could come help me. Ten minutes later your dad showed up with a new tire. He changed my flat, told me I needed new brakes. He followed me to Mercy's garage, where he fixed the problem, then gave the whole car a once-over. He wouldn't let me pay him." She glanced at me. "Though I suppose I should have been paying you."

I shook my head. "Up to Zee. I don't argue with his decisions."

She continued, "He gave me a free soda—told me I needed fattening up."

Like the witch in Hansel and Gretel, I did not say. I wondered what the old smith had been doing. I would have expected Zee to fix a flat for one of Jesse's friends. The rest of it made me uneasy. It was out of character for Zee—or maybe I was just freaking out about the story of the jeweled-eyed skull cups.

Izzy glanced at Tad and then away. She looked at Jesse and evidently found that easier. Tad's face told me that he wasn't happy about Izzy's story, either, but it wasn't worry or concern I saw there; it was banked rage.

Tad wasn't someone who overreacted. And I didn't think he was freaked-out about the story of the skull cups. Or maybe he was. The skull cups were not the only thing that Wayland Smith had done in that story.

"He asked me if we were dating," Izzy told Jesse. "I told him yes. And he smiled at me like he was happy about it."

She drew in a breath, as if bracing herself, and then looked at Tad. But he'd already replaced his previous expression with one of calm interest.

There was a snap in Izzy's voice when she said, "And now you tell me that he made jewels out of children's eyes."

"That was me," said Jesse, but Izzy wasn't listening to her.

"There are a lot of things I could say," Tad told Izzy. "Most of them add up to he is a force of nature. When one of those is trapped, horrible things can happen."

She crossed her arms over her body as if she were a little cold, and her voice was softer. "Can I think about this for a while? I know I said I knew what I was getting into. But maybe I should have read more fairy tales."

He smiled at her, but his eyes were shuttered. "I told you there might be a few times like this." He looked at Adam and me, glanced at Jesse, and then put a light hand under Izzy's elbow.

"Let's go talk outside and let these people get to bed."

She took a deep breath, put her hand over his—in exactly the reverse gesture that they'd assumed upon entering the room.

"Okay," she said. As they left through the front door, she turned and said, "Night, Jesse. Good night, Mr. H. Ms. H, I'll give my mother your order. And"—she paused on the other side of the doorway—"I'm glad you made it out alive again."

Tad pulled the door shut behind them.

"Me, too," Jesse said. "I'm glad you made it out alive again, too."

Adam gave her a one-armed hug, making her stagger a little because he was paying attention to the door—or rather the people who had just walked through it. She might not live here, but Izzy was a staple in the Hauptman household. Adam was protective.

"I know," Jesse said guiltily. "I shouldn't have dropped the stupid jewel story on her tonight. I guess my head was still caught up in that horror movie and the worry that my dad was going to be dead when I got home." She paused. "And I've been thinking about that skull story since Tilly told it to me this weekend."

"I imagine," I said carefully, "that Tilly could tell a story so that it would linger until it could be released to cause as much harm as she could manage."

They both looked sharply at me.

I shrugged. "Or maybe she just enjoyed sharing something horrible with you. But I wouldn't bet on it."

"Magic?" Jesse asked.

"Don't ask me," I said. "Maybe just the power of storytelling. It's nearly Samhain, isn't it? When the fae are more powerful?"

Adam frowned at me.

I gave him a grim smile. "Oh, Tilly has been talking to me, too. Interesting that she's been leaving you alone."

"Do we have a problem?" he asked.

"With a door to Underhill in our backyard? How could that possibly cause us any problems?" I gave him a look.

He laughed. Sometimes laughing is all that you can do.

We heard two car engines start and drive away.

"I hope it works out," Jesse said. "Tad is exactly what she needs to give her a little confidence. And he could do with a little coddling and someone to fight dragons for."

Adam squeezed Jesse more carefully this time. "Better they find out now," he told her.

"Still," Jesse said, "I wish I'd kept my mouth shut."

"Izzy's tougher than she looks," I said confidently. "She'll be okay."

"I hope so." Jesse turned her attention back to Adam. "And you are *really* okay?"

"He's *really* okay," I said. "And the only reason I'm not saying that, like Izzy, *Adam* is tougher than he looks is because—"

"He looks pretty tough," Jesse agreed, finishing the old joke. She stepped away from her dad again. "So the situation worked itself out?"

"Sherwood didn't want to kill Adam," I said. "I told you that would save the day." I had not been as sure of it as I'd tried to sound.

"Good." Then she frowned. "Did you find out who he is? Was he Rasputin?"

"There are photos of Rasputin," I told her. "And Rasputin doesn't look like Sherwood at all." Except a little around the eyes. "We still don't know who Sherwood is. Was."

"You didn't find out?" Jesse asked. "Really? Weren't you curious at all?"

"He's related to Bran," Adam told her. "Closely. Brother, son, father, uncle—something really close."

She blinked at him. "To the Marrok? There's a werewolf related to the Marrok that's not Charles or Samuel? I haven't heard of any. Have you?"

For some reason, both of them looked at me.

"No?" I said.

"You were raised in the Marrok's pack," Jesse insisted. "Surely someone said something?"

"Not that I recall," I said. "I'll call Samuel and bug him."

"Why not ask Sherwood?" Adam said.

"Did he sound like someone who was going to spill the beans

to you?" I queried. "He talks more, but he doesn't say more. He hasn't changed that much." I found that reassuring. "We'll get it out of him one story at a time." I thought a moment. "Though I might make him go through the betting book and say yes or no, because apparently the Great Beast of Northumberland is a yes. Still, Samuel is an easier nut to crack."

"And we haven't heard from him in a while," Jesse added.

Jesse had had a bit of a crush on Samuel when she was younger, and the effects lingered. But instead of pursuing the subject of Samuel or Sherwood, she asked, "So what is the new situation that might end in death and destruction?"

"Marsilia gave us a puzzle," I told her. "We aren't sure exactly what it means. Nothing horrible tonight." I paused. "Probably."

Adam leaned over and kissed Jesse on the forehead. "Bed," he said firmly, for all the world as if she were still a child.

She smiled at us both. "I'm asleep standing," she confessed. "Night, you two."

I waited until she was upstairs in the bathroom brushing her teeth before taking out my phone.

"I'm calling Stefan," I said quietly. "I got the impression that we might want to get on finding Wulfe or following Marsilia's clues as soon as possible."

"Good time to call," Adam said neutrally.

It was two in the morning, but Stefan was a vampire. He wasn't one of Marsilia's vampires anymore—but they had ties that went back all the way to the Italian Renaissance, when they had both been human. He'd also been keeping an eye on Wulfe once the other vampire had decided to start stalking me.

Stefan would know what was going on. I was a little surprised he hadn't contacted me about Wulfe's disappearance before Marsilia had.

Stefan's cell phone clicked immediately to voice mail. I didn't leave a message.

"Maybe he's talking to someone," Adam said.

"I'll try the house," I said. I didn't like that he hadn't answered.

The house phone was picked up after four rings.

"Hello?"

I knew most of Stefan's people—neither he nor I called them sheep (unless Stefan was feeling particularly bitter). To Stefan they were more than a collection of easy meals and prospective fledglings, and whatever else vampires did with their toys. To Stefan, they were family.

When Marsilia had killed some of his people, as a way of making a show for the spies of Bonarata, Stefan had never forgiven her for it. And he had loved Marsilia—not in a romantic way, I didn't think, but love nonetheless.

The voice at the other end of the line was husky and hesitant, making it unfamiliar. It might have been Rachel, who was Stefan's usual spokesperson with the mundane world. Rachel was the one who typically answered the phone if Stefan wasn't there. It didn't *sound* like Rachel, but it could have been. If she'd had a bad cold.

"This is Mercy," I said, and was treated to a dial tone humming in my ear. I quit trying to pretend there wasn't something wrong.

I looked at Adam.

"I'll call Tad back," Adam said. "As soon as he gets here,

we're headed over to Stefan's." He frowned at me. "And you take some more aspirin. No sense being exhausted and in pain."

I DIDN'T TAKE ASPIRIN, OF COURSE; IT WAS IBUPROFEN. Adam was of a generation that used "aspirin" to refer to any painkiller. The NSAID knocked the edge off my headache, but I suspected I'd need sleep to really deal with it. Too bad it was growing doubtful that sleep was in my near future.

Stefan's house was in Kennewick proper, about a twenty-minute drive from our home. I called Zee—he was used to me calling in the middle of the night.

"Still working," I said, trying not to think about skull cups. "Can you open tomorrow?"

"Yes," he said, and hung up.

Adam called his security company and told them he'd be gone for a week, though available in an emergency. I thought about that for a minute and called Zee back.

"Can you handle the shop this week?" I asked, expecting the same yes and click of a disconnect.

"It is bad, then," said Zee instead.

"Probably," I told him. "Signs point to all hell is about to break loose."

Zee snorted. "Situation normal, you mean," he said, echoing his son's earlier observation. "Ah, well. At least I can count upon not being bored in the near future." He disconnected.

I was pretty sure that meant he was good to run the shop for the week.

"Zee is right. This is becoming a habit." Adam frowned.

95

"Maybe we should make arrangements for the new normal. Would you object to moving Sherwood into your old house? Without Joel and Aiden, it isn't safe to leave Jesse home alone, and it's not fair to expect Tad to play bodyguard more than he already does."

My house, a single-wide manufactured home that had replaced the one that burned to the ground, shared a back fence (now partially a wall, thanks to Tilly) with Adam's house, even though they were more than a football field apart because they both were on acreage. My house had sat empty since Gabriel, my previous assistant, had left for college.

The house next to it was empty, too, having been the scene of a pair of brutal murders, though as of last Friday, there was a hopeful *For Sale* sign on it. I wondered if it was still haunted.

My house was. Which was one of the reasons it was empty. The other one was that though the door to Underhill on our back fence allowed Tilly access to our house, it was also on the back fence of *my* house. I wasn't willing to rent the place to someone who couldn't protect themselves from Tilly, and that somewhat restricted the pool of renters.

"If Sherwood is willing," I said. Sherwood could probably protect himself better than we could protect ourselves. "He's just renting the place he's living in, right?"

"Your house would be an upgrade," Adam said. "But living that close might push us to the fight that we just narrowly avoided. I'll ask and trust his judgment."

"It's a little like finding out King Arthur has been a member of the pack in disguise," I said.

"He's not King Arthur," Adam said with a growl in his voice.

"Probably not," I agreed in a hushed voice. Maybe a better person would have stopped when faced with that growl instead of being inspired to push their luck a little further. "But it's exciting. Maybe he knew King Arthur. Or Robin Hood." I sighed happily. "All of the history he has packed in his head."

"I am not jealous," Adam informed me. "I know when I'm being teased."

I laughed and turned to rest my forehead against his shoulder. "Do you suppose he will give me an autograph?"

"I'll autograph you," Adam murmured.

"Only if I get to autograph you, too," I purred happily. Flirting didn't have to make much sense. "Werewolves are hard to tattoo, so I'll use Jesse's glitter pens. Do you want hot pink or baby blue?"

He laughed because he thought I was joking. He was probably right, though I might have done it if Jesse's mom, Adam's ex-wife, hadn't finally moved back to Eugene. Though I doubted that she'd have paid attention even if I'd scrawled *Mine* in glow-in-the-dark lettering across Adam's forehead, there had been days it would have made *me* feel better.

"What's wrong?" Adam asked.

I lifted my head. "Nothing, why?"

"You quit laughing."

"I love you," I told him.

"I love you, too," he answered. "Why did that make you quit laughing?"

"We were talking about jealousy," I said. "And marking territory. You're probably lucky Christy finally moved when she did, or you might have ended up with my name written across your face in Sharpie."

He grabbed my hand. "Your name is written across my heart," he said, because he could say things like that and have them sound serious. When I tried, I sounded like someone trying out for a Hallmark movie.

I kissed his shoulder. "You just don't want to wake up with Sharpie on your face."

"It would look unprofessional," he agreed.

5

~~~~~

STEFAN'S HOUSE WAS NEARLY AS BIG AS ADAM'S AND mine, and for much the same reason—it might need to shelter a lot of people at any given time. Unlike ours, it sprawled out instead of up, and was set in a neighborhood of upscale houses built around half a century ago.

The outside lights were on, and several of the windows were dimly lit, as if reflecting lights deeper in the house. Only the basement windows were absolutely dark, but I knew they were painted black. Stefan told his neighbors that he had a movie theater downstairs.

Adam pulled his brand-spanking-new SUV into Stefan's driveway. It looked exactly like the last two SUVs, which had suffered tragic deaths this year. Adam told me that in his worst year, suffered *before* he and I got together, he'd lost six vehicles—but they had been a lot cheaper. I asked him if they'd all been black, and he'd laughed. But he hadn't denied it.

Adam parked next to Stefan's Mystery Machine, not that anyone else would know what it was. The old VW bus's paint job was shrouded in a protective cover.

"I thought you had gotten it ready for him to drive again," Adam said.

"I did." I tried to keep the worry out of my voice. "After the smoke dragon took him for a ride, he told me that he didn't suit the bus just now." But I took the cover as a good sign. *Not now but someday*, it said.

"The cover's a good sign," said Adam. "Stefan is planning on driving it again someday."

Our mating bond did things like that sometimes, when Adam wasn't keeping a close eye on it. I'd gotten used to having my thoughts come out of his mouth—or possibly his thoughts run through my head before he spoke. I didn't like it. But when our bond had been suspended a few months ago, I'd learned that I preferred chafing under its inconveniences to silence.

I'd gotten used to sharing part of my inner self with Adam. It didn't leave me in a blind panic anymore. Mostly.

"I was just thinking that," I said.

He grimaced. "Sorry."

He understood. I took a breath, leaned against him, and kissed the side of his jaw.

"It was a good thought," I said. "I haven't had a chance to really talk to him since the smoke dragon."

Stefan had bowed out of the last few bad-movie nights. We held them at Warren's and kept them down to eight or ten people—up from the days of our four-person maximum, but still more manageable than if the whole pack showed up. I should have approached Stefan after the first one he missed, but the vampire and I had a *complicated* relationship.

He was one of my oldest friends; I'd met him very soon after I'd moved here. He'd protected me from Marsilia for years before I'd known I needed protecting. He'd bound me to him at my request, to save me from another vampire. It had worked—and that was not the only time that bond had saved me.

But a vampire's bond is not like the bonds of the pack or the mating bond I shared with Adam. A vampire's bond is one between master and slave. Stefan had never used it that way, but he could. It scared me.

Adam ran a thumb across my cheek—the one without the scar because the scar could be sensitive. He didn't say anything, because he knew all about Stefan and me, about my misgivings. I knew that he struggled with it sometimes himself. There was nothing useful to say, but his touch helped a lot.

We walked side by side in companionable silence to the front porch. I glanced up at the dimly lit windows and realized why there had been an itch on the back of my neck since we'd driven up. Stefan, like Adam, had been a soldier, albeit in a much different kind of army in a much different century. He would never have let his people present themselves as a target. Those windows should have been curtained.

Adam, who had gotten ahead of me while I looked at windows, lifted his hand to knock just as a strange scent drifted through the air. I took two quick steps and caught Adam's arm before it landed on the door.

He stopped midmotion, raising an eyebrow at me.

Stefan's house was more soundproof than most, but it was

unlikely the occupants hadn't heard us drive up—or seen our headlights. We weren't going to take anyone by surprise.

Still, instead of speaking, I tapped my nose and mouthed, *Fae.* No sense advertising what we knew to anyone listening.

Adam inhaled through his nose and shook his head. He couldn't smell it.

That told both of us I was probably smelling magic rather than body scent. Usually I could tell one from the other, but this scent was very faint, almost as if someone had taken some pains to hide it.

I have a quirky immunity to magic. It works best for vampire magic for sure, and for everything else it is hit-and-miss. Tad and I had spent an afternoon experimenting with it after we'd faced down some witches. He thought I'd been remiss not figuring out what kinds of magic worked on me. After he'd pointed it out, I'd had to agree.

It hadn't been a productive afternoon. In the first place, Tad only worked fae magic. I didn't want to involve the vampires, and the only witches I knew were now dead. It turned out that my immunity to magic, when dealing with fae magic, really did appear to be random. The same spell thrown at me the same way affected me sometimes but not always. We asked Zee to help, but he refused, saying, "Chaos is not predictable. To imagine anything else would be dangerous."

But some immunity was better than none.

I glanced into the dimly lit windows and saw no one moving about inside. Those vulnerable windows, added to Stefan's unanswered phone, fairly shouted that neither Stefan nor his people were in charge of the house. Someone inside that house used fae magic.

I wondered if this situation was tied up in Marsilia's mysterious message and Wulfe's apparent disappearance, or if it was some entirely new problem. A coincidence.

I don't believe in coincidences much. I knew the thought was Adam's, but I agreed.

I tried to send back a question: *Do you think Marsilia sent us into a trap?*

She would know that the first person I'd contact if I were looking for Wulfe would be Stefan.

"I'm beginning to think that all of our vampires are in trouble," murmured Adam into my ear, so softly that a werewolf standing five feet away would not have heard him.

He stepped in front of me, pushing me behind him as he started to knock on the door again. Obviously, he intended to go in first.

In a physical fight, Adam was the tank and I . . . well, I was a predator, too. In our four-footed forms, Adam's wolf was more than eight times my coyote in weight. I was a hair quicker, but his werewolf was considerably better armed.

In human form, which for me was the better shape for fighting, I had years of martial arts training backed by a recently hard-earned black belt. I carried a gun and a cutlass. But even there, Adam was a better fighter. He'd spent most of his life in battles—first as an army ranger and an LRRP (long-range reconnaissance patrol, essentially a scout) in Vietnam. After the war, he'd been Alpha of a werewolf pack and served in that role for almost half a century.

But in a fight where magic was a strong possibility, even an unpredictable immunity to magic made me less vulnerable. It made sense that I should go first.

I caught his arm. Continuing our probably useless attempt to be stealthy, I wiggled my fingers to indicate magic, tapped my chest twice, and then held up one finger by itself.

Adam's lips tightened and a streak of white appeared on his cheek when he clenched his jaw. Given that reaction, it surprised me when he nodded. He made a downward gesture with the flat of his hand, indicating a space about knee height.

That made sense, too. I was a more difficult target in my coyote form, more unexpected and quicker than when I walked on two feet. I hadn't managed to prove it to myself one way or the other, but I thought that my immunity might work better when I was wearing my coyote self, too.

I glanced over my shoulder at the road that ran by Stefan's house. It was a fairly busy one, but at this time of the very early morning, when the darkness ruled, there was no one around. I stripped quickly out of my clothes and changed as I dropped my underwear on the ground. Unlike the werewolves, my shifting was both painless and virtually instantaneous.

I felt one claw catch in fabric that tore and hoped it was my underwear. I'd been wearing a new shirt my youngest sister had sent me for her birthday. I usually gave her something on my birthday, too. I don't remember when it started or why, but it was a tradition now. This shirt was a T-shirt that said *When the Zombie Apocalypse Comes, Remember That I Am Faster Than You* in glow-in-the-dark lettering.

I shook myself to get rid of the last of the changing tingles and pressed my shoulder against Adam's leg to tell him I was ready.

He fished my carry gun out of the pile of clothing, checked it, and tucked it into his waistband. He hesitated a moment, then simply drew my cutlass from its sheath, holding the blade against

his body where it would not be seen by any passing motorist—
though the road was still quiet.

I made a noise. The cross guard was silver.

"It's not a cross guard," murmured Adam almost inaudibly.
"It's a guard with a knuckle bow. Only the knuckle bow is silver.
I'll be careful."

I paused. It wasn't the correction. I knew the cutlass didn't
have a cross guard. A cross guard formed a cross shape with the
blade. I'd made that mistake with Auriele once and been treated
to a five-minute lecture that ensured I *always* called it a cross
guard out of sheer perversity. We were getting along better these
days, but now it was a habit.

I had not remembered, if anyone told me, that only the knuckle
bow was actually silver. That was a good thing to know.

But I hadn't called it a cross guard out loud. I couldn't talk in
my coyote form. He'd read my mind again.

It didn't matter that I'd just tried to do that with him a few
minutes ago. My breath hitched as if something were tightening
around my throat. What if he could read my mind all the time?

"Not usually," Adam told me softly, his attention still on the
door and what lay beyond. Evidently our plans should be silent,
but he didn't think it made sense to worry about a stealthy approach. "But a few times tonight. You must be a little tired, or it
might be the knock on the head. I do not lie to you, Mercy. We
can talk later if you need to."

He didn't lie to me, that was true. Most werewolves quit bothering with lies because any other werewolf and quite a few of the
other supernatural creatures can hear a lie. I could. Adam didn't
lie even about very painful things. The reminder that he would

tell me what he knew allowed me to allow our bonds, pack and mating, to lie lightly upon me again. As soon as I quit struggling, I could breathe.

With me standing in front of him, Adam had to lean forward to knock on the door, three sharp knocks. When nothing happened, he rang the doorbell three times, too. Having given anyone inside a chance to welcome us, he landed a swift kick on the door, splintering the frame as if it were a movie prop.

The door swung open to an apparently empty house.

I could smell old blood, various cleaners, and personal scents that made up Stefan's usual household smells. The fae scent that didn't belong was present, but no stronger than it had been outside.

I padded cautiously over the cool flagstone of the entryway to crouch in the darker shadows beside the old upright piano that occupied the small space between the entryway and the living room. This allowed me to get an unobstructed view of the living room—which was apparently unoccupied. When nothing stirred, Adam stepped into the room, bringing my cutlass to guard position.

It had initially surprised me that he had chosen the blade over a gun, his or mine. But guns were loud and would attract neighbors. Whatever we were facing in Stefan's home would not be made better by adding a bunch of human cannon fodder into the mix.

The cutlass in the hands of a werewolf who knew what he was doing would be quiet and nearly as deadly as a gun. Possibly, depending on what kind of fae we faced, more deadly. I hadn't seen him fight with my blade, though I'd seen him fight with other swords and swordlike things. The cutlass was unlikely to give him any trouble.

I'd had time to think about the fae magic I'd been smelling. Fae had very distinctive odors, depending upon the magic they used. Some of them smelled earthy or like water. Others smelled of fire or woodlands. I used to think there were only earth, air, fire, and water, until I encountered more fae. Some of the Gray Lords smelled like hunting cats or lightning. Some of them just smelled like themselves.

This fae smelled . . . like nothing I'd ever scented before. Not so much a different scent, but *less* of a scent. It had to be magic if Adam couldn't smell it. But it didn't smell right even for that. I had no idea what we were facing.

Adam shut the front door behind us. Any close examination would reveal the damage to the latch, but people driving along the nearby road shouldn't notice it—not the way they'd notice a door hanging open with light spilling out onto the porch steps.

I'd been inside Stefan's house a couple of times before, enough to know the general layout. The entry and living room could have belonged to a 1920s craftsman, contrasting starkly with the soul-less exterior that had been built to match the other houses in the area. The flagstone entry gave way to dark oak floors covered with scattered Persian rugs, Shaker-style couches, and chairs built with more dark wood and woven earth-tone fabrics.

The living room opened to a larger, more airy space that was the dining room and kitchen. The look here was modern and sleek, with lots of shiny chrome softened by earthy tiles. The two parts of the house should not have blended as well as they did, not without walls to soften the change. But the overall effect was, *usually* was, homey. But that wasn't how Stefan's home felt now.

The atmosphere reminded me of childhood expeditions to the

haunted mansion at a traveling carnival, nerve-tingling but also sordid. I could not tell exactly what was causing it: the fae whose magic I could still sense, or the ghost who sat watching me from the big couch that took up the long wall of the living room.

I'd met Daniel before he became a ghost. Now the fledgling vampire sat on the middle section of the Shaker couch, absolutely motionless, as vampires often did. He sat near a big Tiffany floor lamp that was the source of the light reflected in the outside windows. That he did not cast a shadow in the light was the only real sign he was a ghost.

That's not to say that he wasn't creepy. His eyes were on me, white and pupilless, as they had been the only time I'd seen him alive. Or as alive as vampires got, anyway. He was, as he had been then, half-starved and frail, his hair only a stubble on the pale globe of his shaved scalp. Tears dripped slowly down his emotionless face.

Daniel was not a ghost I would have been comfortable living with—but Stefan didn't know Daniel was still in his house. Or if Stefan did, it wasn't because I'd told him about it.

I tried to ignore Daniel because too much attention from me strengthens ghosts. He was not what we were hunting here, and Stefan would not thank me for making his dead roommate more powerful.

Adam stopped in the center of the living room. He turned very slowly, taking his time peering into the shadowed hallway that led to the bedrooms, then at the open basement door. He didn't see Daniel, but I hadn't expected him to.

Adam moved without a sound, but not because he needed to. The splintering of the front door had been loud enough to alert anyone in the house who hadn't heard our car drive up of our presence. It was an involuntary reflex he reverted to whenever there was danger about. I thought that he might have learned to do that before he'd ever become a werewolf, when he'd hunted and been hunted in Southeast Asia.

I felt like we were being hunted now. My impression that this was a trap had settled into an instinctive certainty. I just couldn't tell if Adam and I were its intended prey—or if it had been set for Stefan.

I was going to feel really stupid if I was overreacting and Stefan and his people were at the seethe, or out on a team-building exercise. I made a mental note to ask Stefan if he did team-building exercises, then thought about what kind of team-building exercises a vampire might do and decided it might be better not to ask.

I told myself that the fact that Daniel was the only ghost I could see was good news—since I could not hear anyone in this house, which should have at least eight normal humans and a couple of fledgling vampires in it at this time of night. If they had been violently killed recently, there would be more than one ghost here. I put my nose to the floor and tried to pick up any hint of the thing we were hunting.

I made a full circle of the living room, a quick-time perimeter slink, with my nose on the floor, finishing back at Adam's side. There were no sounds or scents to direct our hunt, so I paused to see where he wanted to go next.

I didn't much want to move on to the bedrooms, where tighter spaces would make fighting anything nasty more difficult. As for the basement . . . spending some time in the basement of a black witch might have left me with just a bit of basement-itis, because I didn't want to go through that dark doorway.

Adam took two steps forward so he could get a better look at the kitchen and dining area. I would have started heading into the kitchen, but Daniel's whitewashed eyes caught mine. He wasn't, had not been, one of the ghosts who interacted with the real world, so it caught me by surprise when he looked from me up to the vaulted ceiling.

I followed his gaze. I yipped a warning, but it was too late. Something pale the approximate size and shape of a VW Beetle dropped from the ceiling on top of Adam, flattening him on the floor with a boom that rattled the house.

I leaped upon its broad and smooth back, hoping to find a place I could get some teeth into, something that might get it off Adam. I'd expected to land on something soft, but the surface was as hard and cold as an ice-skating rink. My nails landed with a click, and I had to scrabble to stay on top of it as it moved under me because I could find no purchase.

The creature was near white with a greenish cast in the warm light of the floor lamp. It looked as much like a spider as it did like anything else I'd ever seen. Its body was divided into two rounded segments, one—the one I'd hopped onto—much larger than the other, and it had six long legs with two joints in each. If someone who had never seen a spider tried to make one based on a kindergartner's description, it might have looked like this creature. Especially if the kindergartner was afraid of spiders—and couldn't count to eight.

Fine "hairs" covered the hard shell of the body in patches, and they had more in common with cactus spines than with anything as friendly as actual hair. They dug into the tough bottoms of my feet like fiberglass fibers. The connection between body and head was hard, too, covered with plates like armor, and gave me no place to worry at with my teeth.

The legs were covered in longer slivery needles that lay down against the surface. I'd learned how to kill porcupines without getting a muzzle full of quills. If I bit at just the right angle, maybe I could avoid being stuck.

I had to try something because Adam was beneath it.

It shuddered, shivering like a maraca, complete with sound effects. I felt my feet slipping, so I flung myself back off the creature in the hope that once I was on the floor, I could get traction to pull off a leg strike.

The smaller round section, which turned out to be its head, spun as it tracked my motion. It was an uncanny movement—as if it were connected to the body like a trailer ball instead of bone or sinew. It reminded me of the way an owl's head moves, but creepier. I got a brief glimpse of its open mouth—no teeth or tongue but dangling bits that wriggled—and it spat at me, a cupful of clear liquid that it obviously thought of as a weapon.

I accepted its judgment and sprang out of range as if the spit were acid. It landed on the wood and the edge of a Persian carpet and dissipated in a fog. I decided to continue to treat the spider spit as if it was dangerous.

In the back of my head, I kept track of how long Adam had been down beneath the creature. Seconds were hours in a fight, and I had counted three already.

Fortunately, Adam on the ground was the farthest thing from Adam helpless. While I was trying for a good angle of attack for one of the legs, Adam surged to his feet under the weight of his attacker and flung it into the piano with thunderous effect.

Stefan's piano had survived when someone heaved me into it a while back.

Either Adam threw harder or I didn't weigh as much as the Volkswagen-sized monstrosity. The piano collapsed in a shower of splinters, ringing soundboard, and broken wires that lashed the creature hard enough to leave a few small cracks in its shell.

The spider-thing righted itself with a stomach-turning flutter of spindly legs. Then it skittered—if something that large could be said to skitter—back toward Adam.

Looking only a little the worse for wear, he waited for it with a calm face and my cutlass at the ready. It leaned back and balanced on four legs, striking at Adam with the two closest to him.

Adam avoided the first limb with a subtle twist of the weapon and a slight movement of his body. He caught the leg with a glancing blow as it swept past him. He didn't hit it hard, but the blade sang out as if the leg were metal.

My cutlass wasn't the thick-bladed version made famous in cartoons and bad pirate movies, though it was stout enough. Its blade was slightly curved, and short enough so that it could be used in close quarters—like on a pirate ship. Zack told me they'd picked it because the length suited my arm, and also because it was a prize for winning the pirate computer game the whole pack was obsessed with.

Adam's first strike had been to test the way the blade felt against the leg, and he'd gotten some feel. The spider-thing's second leg was only a hair's breadth behind, and on that one Adam tried to take out the joint. Again, he didn't hit it full force—as he would have with something that was ordinary flesh and blood. Instead, he caught it a glancing blow, the way he would have dealt with another, equally strong blade.

He thought that whatever formed the outer layer of the leg was as strong as or stronger than steel or he'd have hit it differently. Again, the blade sang out as it rebounded a bit off the leg.

There were going to be no easy victories here—and I was afraid that I was as useless as sunscreen in Seattle. I was fast enough, I thought, to avoid its attacks. But if that cutlass in Adam's hands wasn't doing much damage—neither could I.

I did take a good look at the creature's underside in hopes of finding some weak point, but it was, as far as I could tell, made of the same stuff as the rest of it.

Adam took a third strike at the joint between leg and body. The creature could put its body anywhere from flat on the ground to about six feet in the air, and at that point the joint was level with Adam's shoulder. It didn't make that clanging sound, but I couldn't see that it did any damage at all—visually, anyway. The spider-thing jerked back with a hissing noise of about the same volume as dropping water into hot grease. So he must have done something.

He'd struck the leg with a steel blade, and it had flinched. But it hadn't reacted like most fae would have when hit with cold iron. The steel hadn't left scorch marks or burned it. If the iron in the blade gave Adam any kind of advantage against this fae, it wasn't much. There were fae who could tolerate iron and its more civilized child, steel—Zee was one of those.

I was in the middle of puzzling out the fae-thing's weaknesses when I realized that I couldn't smell the spider-thing at all—it wasn't the source of the fae magic I could still scent.

The creature had so little scent, in fact, that I wondered if it was using magic to disguise that. I'd never heard of any of the fae doing that before, but it didn't mean that they couldn't. This six-legged spider-thingy just might be a case in point. With no scent to go by, there was no reason for me to be so certain that this creature was fae. But I was sure.

If it wasn't the fae I'd scented, somewhere in the house was another fae creature working magic. I put that thought in the back of my mind because I wasn't going to leave Adam fighting alone, even if I hadn't been much help to this point.

As I watched Adam's graceful, deadly dance, I had time to consider larger implications. It was fae. It attacked us, unprovoked, in the house of our ally.

If we'd encountered it in, say, a barn, as a not-random example, I wouldn't have been that worried about it. Any single fae might attack us—but the fae community would take care of it if we weren't able to. However, this was in Stefan's house. Stefan, who was the bridge between the vampires and the werewolves. Could this creature's presence in Stefan's house be part of whatever Marsilia had tried to warn us about?

Was one of the Gray Lords holding our vampires prisoner? It might account for Marsilia's oddly dramatic method of giving us a quest as well as her indirect communications.

One of the spider's legs sliced down through the muscle of Adam's calf, and I hissed in a breath as blood poured out. Adam didn't react to it other than to pull power from the pack bonds to increase the speed of his healing. I decided to worry about whether or not we could kill Shelob (with apologies to Tolkien) before looking at the possibilities of even bigger disasters.

Adam grimaced briefly, and I smelled scorched flesh. His grip must have touched the knuckle bow. He backed farther into the living room, giving himself more space. Of course, that gave the spider-thing more room, too.

Instead of closing with Adam, the spider-creature rocked its body back even farther, like a rearing horse—except the bottom end of its body stayed on the ground. The sharp ends of the creature's legs were leaving gouges on Stefan's floor. It placed a leg on either side and raised the other four, twisting its odd head around until it could see Adam. The long hairs on the legs lifted away from the shafts of its legs, sparkling a little with warm golden light as they reflected the illumination from the amber glass of Stefan's Tiffany lamp.

I flattened myself against the wall and moved very slowly around the edge of the room. If I could get behind it while Adam kept it busy, maybe I could do something.

I didn't know what, as my fangs were apparently utterly useless against it, but *something*. I thought about the thin cracks the breaking strings of the piano had left in its back. Unfortunately, I couldn't lift a piano and throw it.

I felt Adam's awareness of me even though he didn't look my way. He stepped forward to attack. I wasn't sure if it was because it was the right thing to do or because he didn't want that spider-thing noticing me when the wall I was skirting got too close to the creature.

The fight looked like a demonic fencing match, with the speed of both participants and the added weird grace of the thing's long legs. The oddest element was that the body of the creature was largely stationary. Raised up as it was, I could see the underbelly more easily. I still could not see any spot that looked soft. The only difference was that it was even more heavily furred with the nasty slivery hairs. The precise strikes of its legs made me think that it had fought someone armed with a sword before.

As it had with me, it flung spit at Adam.

In the short period of time that I'd been examining the thing's underbelly, Adam had acquired a long red strip along his cheek. I couldn't tell if he'd been smacked by a leg or splattered with some of the spittle. His leg had quit bleeding, but he was favoring it ever so slightly.

Adam shifted his grip on the cutlass and punched with the knuckle guard instead of using the blade. He targeted one of the exoskeleton breaks from the creature's impact with the piano, and his blow left a starburst pattern of hairline cracks about eight inches across. But I smelled burning flesh again.

He jumped away and I could see that the knuckle guard had buckled around his hand. He pried at the metal to free himself as the silver burned his skin wherever it touched. As soon as he'd pulled the knuckle guard away from his sword hand, he dodged under a flashing leg and hit the creature in the same spot, this time with the point of the blade.

There was a great cracking sound, like glass shattering. For an instant I thought he'd broken the thing's shell, but then I realized the sound had come from the wrong direction.

Beside the damaged piano, on top of the broken plate-glass window he'd evidently jumped through, the king of the goblins stood. Why he chose to jump through the window instead of kicking open the damaged door, I couldn't say.

He wore no shoes but was apparently unconcerned by the glittering shards of glass under his feet. He wore only a black loincloth; his body, like Adam's, was refined to only muscle and sinew, though on him it looked stringy, almost as if his muscles worked differently than ours. His extra-jointed four-fingered hands flexed on the pair of short swords he carried as he stepped off the broken window, shaking his shoulders to shed stray bits of glass. If I'd done something like that wearing nothing but a loincloth, I'd have been dripping blood. His skin was tougher than mine.

He spared a yellow-green glance for me, his lips quirking upward. I don't know if I amused him somehow or if it was just the anticipation of violence. Larry the goblin king was fond of violence.

Adam had kept the fae creature too busy to pay much heed to the sound of the window bursting—and the goblin made no more noise than Adam had as Larry's first cautious steps turned into a sprint. He leapt atop the spider much as I had, though more to one side, deliberately unbalancing it. The creature fell forward and had to use one of the legs it was attacking Adam with to catch itself.

The tip of the leg had dug into the wood, putting the leg under tension. When the goblin knocked it down, the leg twisted further. Adam's cutlass, sweeping upward to hit in a previously damaged joint, snapped the leg in half.

The shorn bit of leg flew at me, and I dodged right into the open doorway of the basement stairwell as the sound of the creature crashing into various furnishings echoed throughout the house.

My paws skidded on the smooth wood of the step, and my speed pushed me right over the edge. But my four-footed form is more agile than my human one, and I caught myself on the third step before I rolled all the way down. I hoped Stefan wouldn't get too upset by the deep scratch I'd put in the beautiful figured wood of the step.

The spider-thing's leg had followed me through the doorway and rolled over the edge of the top step behind me. As I gained my footing, it rolled through the empty space between the steps of the open stairway and fell to crash on some hard surface below. I couldn't see the floor, because the basement was *dark*.

I dug my claws into the wood of the step again, with the intention of flinging myself back up into the fray wherever I might do some good. Then I realized what I was smelling and stopped.

The elusive fae scent I'd been tracking wafted up from the depths of the basement in thick waves of chill that raised the hairs all over my body with the expectant buzz of power. It felt as if, by coming through the doorway, I'd stepped past some barrier that had been restraining both the scent of the fae and the feel of its magic.

And as I paused, I realized that I could not see my feet. As if the basement were a pool of darkness and I was standing knee-deep in it.

This was more Larry's territory than mine, and I tried to be sensible about admitting when something was over my head. I'd have gone and fetched him except for two things. The first was that the battle royal was still going on upstairs. The second was the feel of the magic.

After spending that time hidden in the witch Elizaveta's basement, I'd gotten a sense for spell-casting magic. There's a warp and weft to it, just like a good winter sweater. The magic filling Stefan's basement was in the process of being gathered, spun, and woven into something big.

Spell casting of this complexity was the sort of thing that did not allow the caster to pay much attention to anything until the spell was done. If the fae lost focus, the spell would fail, probably in a spectacular way. But if I had to pick between a spell deliberately launched at us by an enemy and a chaotic magic bomb of some unknown effect, I would take the unknown any day.

Maybe that was because I wasn't a spell caster.

To stop the spell, though, someone was going to have to trot down the stairs, into the blackness. That someone was going to have to be me.

Ears pricked, I started down the stairs at a rapid pace. I didn't need eyesight much because stairways are regular in shape. I could have made less noise, but the feel of my nails digging in was reassuring. And I did not think that silence would save me.

Stefan's basement staircase was an elegant affair, open underneath the railing and underneath the stairs. In horror movies, this kind of staircase always meant that someone could reach underneath a step and grab unwary feet. I was not sure there were more wary paws in the universe just now than mine.

As I descended into darkness, I concentrated on what my ears told me. But the battle above was loud, full of crashes, breaking glass, and an odd crunch or two. I thought I heard Adam grunt in pain. Below me was silence. If someone was breathing down there, they were doing it quietly.

About eight steps down, one of my raw feet—the punctures made by the hairs on Shelob's back meant that it hurt to walk—came down upon a thin film of ice. I inhaled and the air felt as if it were fresh off a glacier. It could have been a side effect of whatever spell was being formed. Or it could be the start of a directed attack. If I was wrong about what the spell caster could do while wrangling all the magic, then I was in trouble. I'd spotlighted myself at the top of the stairs, and those same stairs made it clear what my path had to be.

Deciding I'd had enough of being a target, I jumped over the railing, dropped about a foot, and landed on something that felt like it might be a bookcase. My landing was awkward because I'd

expected it to be a lot longer drop, and because there were orna-
ments and pots and other things under my feet. I knocked a fair
bit of stuff onto the floor, which sounded as though it might be
about a six-foot drop.

Stefan's basement was very deep. I bet if I checked the original
plans, this house didn't come with a basement like this. I moved
and something cylindrical that felt uncannily familiar rolled under
my feet and followed the rest of the mess down to the floor. Maybe
it was a cane or something else that felt like the walking stick. I
was distracted from that by a high, whistling cry that hurt my
ears, followed by a thundering crash from above, as if a body the
size of a VW had fallen into something.

Beside me, at about the right place for the bottom of the stairway, I heard a sharp snapping sound that reminded me of the
cracking of an ice floe on a Montana river in spring. The sound
echoed throughout the house with an impact that hit my bones
with a physical blow. Then the bookcase I stood on fell over, with
me on top of it.

I scrambled over a mess of books and other things on the floor
and bumped around until I found something to hide beneath and
quit moving. My shelter might have been a low table or a high
bench.

"Mercy?" Adam called out from above.

When I looked up toward where the doorway should be, I saw
nothing. I'd known the light from above couldn't illuminate the
basement. I hadn't realized that meant I couldn't see the light
from upstairs.

"Mercy?" Adam called a second time.

I didn't want to answer him. My movement to my current lo-
cation had been camouflaged by what I had to assume was the

sound of the destruction of the stairway. If whatever called the darkness was also blinded by it, I didn't want to make a sound and reveal my hiding place.

Too close to me, no more than ten feet away, something screamed, the sound starting in a register that I'd bet a normal human couldn't hear—above the note a dog whistle makes—and then rattling down the octaves until my skin tried to crawl off my body.

Toward the end of the scream, I felt a very quiet click—and the basement was flooded with light. Adam and the goblin king, both battered and bleeding, stood where the top of the stairs should have been. I was right: I was in a large room, a library, roughly the size of the living room and kitchen above, but there was a hallway that led off to other rooms.

The stairs—or what I presumed to have been the stairs—looked like a pile of overgrown matchsticks that had been left under a sprinkler during a heavy frost. Or like the Fortress of Solitude from the old *Superman* movie with Christopher Reeve. All of that I took in peripherally, because first, I looked where the scream had come from.

A sturdy Stickley library chair had been pulled directly in front of the stair landing, which was still mostly intact, if white with frost. Crouched in it was a . . . well, a woman, I suppose. She was the same drowned-body color of the spider above, but her flesh looked too-soft rather than armor-hard, like the skin of a balloon that has been inflated too long.

She was thinner than a living human could have been, with pale gray hair that hung around her in long braids with small black beads woven into them. Her hands were abnormally long-fingered and black tipped—and she had six fingers on each hand.

Her eyes were solid black. I couldn't tell what she was looking at—me, Adam and the goblin king, or Daniel, who was sitting on the ground directly between her and me. Maybe none of us or all.

In front of her, attached to the newel posts of the broken staircase as well as the wall behind her and the arms and legs of her chair, was a web woven in ice. Her lips twisted in an ugly smile as she reached out one finger to touch her web.

I could feel the magic form into something coherent as her finger neared the thread of her weaving. Out of time to plan or consider my actions, I simply bolted right through Daniel. I leaped into the middle of the web, and her finger touched me instead of it.

THE SNOW COVERED THE TOPS OF MY KNEES AS THE bitter cold slid down my lungs and tried to freeze my nostrils together. The tips of my ears and my fingers burned with the cold.

It was too bad I had somehow shed my coyote self. The fur would have done me a lot of good. As it was, my snow-covered feet and calves were significantly warmer than the rest of my naked body.

I stood in a vast empty field of snow. It was tilted just a little, like high mountain meadows sometimes are. On three sides, at a distance that was too far for me to see clearly, were great dark fir trees. I didn't want to turn around to see the fourth direction.

I did, of course.

My bare toes touched the edge of a precipice over a deep hole as black as the snow I stood in was white.

"Be careful," said Daniel, and I turned to see that he was standing beside me, leaning forward over the empty space.

He stretched out an arm toward the darkness, then turned to me and said, *"Hic sunt dracones."*

Latin, I thought, not Italian. It took me a second and then I realized why the words were familiar.

I said it out loud. "Here there be dragons."

He nodded. *"Hic sunt leones."*

"Here there be . . . lions?" I said.

He nodded again. He spread his arms out, as if he were a great bird preparing for flight. His fingertips brushed my shoulder.

I took a slow step back. And then another.

"Hic sunt—" Arms still outstretched, as if he was planning on jumping, Daniel gave me a sad smile, then turned from me to face the chasm of darkness. In Stefan's voice, he said, "—wolves."

"Stefan?" I whispered, but my fear of the empty black was too much. I wanted to move toward him, but I took a third step away instead, forgetting that, in places like this, geography doesn't follow the rules.

This time there was nothing beneath my feet, and the blackness reached out and touched me.

Hello, Coyote's daughter, the void said.

6

"BREATHE, DAMN YOU," GROWLED MY MATE.

I sucked in a breath, because Adam told me to. But the rest of me was still falling, consumed by the darkness. It took another moment for me to understand that I was lying on the tile floor of Stefan's basement library with the fading taste of empty blackness in my mouth.

I tried to stand up. But when I had stood on that icy snowbank, I'd been in human form, so that's the body I expected to be in. My four feet all seemed at sixes and sevens, and I scrambled in something approaching panic until Adam helped me up.

I stood shaking, my breath rising in a mist around me, though the earlier frost that had covered the basement was just dampness and a few small puddles now.

Adam was sitting beside me, next to a broken chair. He brushed a hand over his forehead and closed his eyes, his other hand firmly threaded through the hair on the ruff of my neck. I could see the pulse pound in his neck as he breathed out. I wanted to tease him about swearing at me, to distract us both from the last few panicky moments, but I was wearing my coyote self, so I whined at him instead. His fingers tightened on me.

His breath didn't make a fog. Mine quit after my third breath expelled the last of the air I'd inhaled wherever I'd been. If I'd been anywhere at all.

I glanced at the ruined library for clues to how much time had passed. Daniel was still seated where he'd been, staring off into space. I wondered if he was flying through the darkness with his arms open wide—or if I'd just been knocked unconscious and dreamed the whole thing.

Light footsteps and a sense of motion called my attention to Larry padding out of a dark hallway, a bronze short sword in each hand. The left one dripped a thick black liquid that was the wrong color for blood, though that's what it smelled like to me.

Larry looked first at me and then at Adam. The blades of his swords caught fire for a moment. When the flames died, the bronze looked freshly burnished and a fine ash drifted to the floor.

"Did you kill her?" Adam asked. I presumed he meant the spell weaver whose web I'd broken.

"Yes. She was mostly dead anyway. I just gave her the coup de grâce." The goblin king frowned at me. "No one told me Mercy is a spell breaker." His voice was mild, but there was something dangerous in his face.

"No one told *her* that, either," Adam said, his voice rough with the wolf riding him. "Possibly because she's not one. I cannot give you all of our secrets, Goblin King. But let me say that

Mercy is Coyote's daughter, and that means the magic of the dead has difficulty with her most of the time. Magic in general is weird around her."

Adam opened his eyes, finally, and I saw they were gold. Adam and his wolf had been vying for control an awful lot over the past twelve hours or so. I didn't think that was a good thing.

Courteously, Larry averted his gaze, though he'd continued to approach until he was a few feet away. He judged it nicely, I thought. An inch closer and Adam would have risen to his feet. Given the color of his eyes, just that much motion could have been enough to shake another werewolf's control.

"That was not vampiric magic," Larry said.

"Sometimes . . ." Adam stopped, and his hand tightened on me. There was a long pause before he continued, "*Sometimes* other kinds of magic don't work on her. But her resistance to fae magic is very, *very* hit-and-miss."

Larry sat on his heels so that he was eye level with both of us, though he still avoided Adam's gaze.

"Her gamble paid off this time, then," he said. "That spell would have leveled this house and killed us all." He met my eyes and said, "Of course, breaking it the way you did might have leveled the city."

He looked around and took a deep breath, half closing his eyes. "Or not. Reckless and lucky. I like that in an ally." His lips quirked up. "But not in a mate, eh?" He wasn't looking at Adam, but that was who the last sentence addressed.

"She puts up with a lot from me, too," said Adam, his voice sounding almost normal. He loosened his grip on my ruff, his touch becoming a caress. "Did you clear the basement, or do we need to do that still?"

Larry said, "I killed the web weaver, and she was the only one alive down here. Or in the rest of the house. My watcher told me that a white rental van was here at sunset, and Stefan's people left in it."

"All of them?"

Larry shrugged. "The two fledgling vampires, my watcher was certain. None of the rest of Stefan's people are a threat, so she did not note them particularly. We should check upstairs, but there is no one down here. No one came to see what all the noise was about."

I had mostly recovered from my trip to the freaky cold place while they talked. I thought that we should go before whoever had planted the spider-fae people decided we needed more fun. I sneezed to get Adam's attention and then looked up at the first-floor doorway.

"Right," he said. "No sense hanging around here."

He stood up, sweeping me into his arms as he did so.

"Ready?" he asked.

It was a warning rather than a question no matter how he said it. With no further ado, he tossed me up and through the doorway at the top of the no-longer-in-one-piece stairway.

I cleared the doorway and flew forward another three feet before my paws touched the ground. I almost skittered into the viscous body of the first spider-thing, which looked as if it was halfway to turning into a gooey puddle, but I caught myself with an additional insult to the once-polished wooden floor.

I looked around at the remains of Stefan's house. If there was an unbroken stick of furniture in the living room, it was buried somewhere under all the rest. There were holes in the walls, and the window Larry had jumped through was not the only one that was going to need repair.

A noise behind me made me turn to see Adam finish pulling himself over the threshold. As soon as he rolled clear, Larry leapt through as well, landing lightly on his feet. Goblins were agile creatures.

I changed back to human so I could speak. The added weight made my feet hurt more, but it was bearable.

"Do you know who these fae were? Is this an attack aimed at Stefan? Or is it an attempt to bring down our treaty with the fae?" I asked Larry.

"We need to talk," he said. "But somewhere else, please. Your house?"

"We need to go to the seethe now," I told him.

Stefan was alive. I'd know if he were dead. But vampires were as territorial in their own way as the werewolves. He would not have willingly allowed fae to take over his home. Something had happened to him—just as something had obviously happened to Marsilia. And maybe it was the same thing that had happened to Wulfe. But if that were true, why hadn't Marsilia just sent us after Stefan? In any case, the seethe was the obvious place to go next, and it was roughly four in the morning so someone would be up.

Adam didn't argue. He just handed me my clothes. It *had* been my panties I'd caught with a claw; the shirt was okay. I pulled on my jeans and stuffed the torn cloth in my pocket. Then put on my bra, various weapons harnesses, shirt, socks, and shoes. Adam handed over my gun.

"This isn't going to be fixable," he said, showing me the cutlass. It was bent. The tip was broken off. Blackened holes pockmarked the blade as if someone had sprayed it with acid.

I glanced at the dead fae, less substantial now than it had been a few minutes ago. "It did its job," I said. "But I think I'll get another one. Maybe this time without the silver cross guard."

"It isn't a cross guard," said Adam. He snorted afterward because I had said the words with him.

Larry said quietly, "We do need to talk tonight. There are things you should know."

Adam said, "You can come with us. Or I could call you while we drive there or while we are driving home afterward."

Larry frowned, looked at the floor, then at the puddle of dead spider-thing. "Don't go to the seethe."

"What do you know?" I asked.

"At your house?" Larry suggested, pointedly walking to the front door as he spoke. He was still barefoot, and he still didn't pay any attention to the glass crunching under his feet.

My own feet, punctured by the spines on the fae's back, were oddly numb. That should have been a good thing, because they'd hurt like the dickens when I'd first regained my human shape. But I lived in the land of cheatgrass, where the arrowhead-like seed-pods could burrow into paws and fester out months later. I hadn't had it happen, but my cat had. I needed to remember to look at them—or have someone else look at them.

I'd wait until tomorrow, I thought, shivering a little as the autumn air blew in through the broken window. I looked at Adam—who was watching me.

I shrugged and followed Larry out of the house. Adam shut the door. It looked as though a good wind would make it pop open again, but if someone wanted to get into the house, there was a gaping hole where the window used to be.

All three of us walked to the SUV.

"You have reason to warn us away from the seethe?" Adam asked.

"Not warning you away," Larry disagreed. "But I have some things you need to know. I'm not willing to talk where I can be overheard. Not on the phone."

Adam looked at me.

I needed to find Stefan. Horrible, horrible things could be done to people who are as tough as vampires were. I recalled his voice, "*Hic sunt* wolves." The edge of fear in it made me think that finding him was urgent.

I rubbed my forehead and realized that my hand was a little sore, too. Had I really heard Stefan? It didn't matter. We still needed to find him.

I looked back at Stefan's house with the broken door and broken front window.

"Larry?" I asked. "Why didn't you just come through the door?"

"The window was easy," he said. "And people expect you to come through doors. I don't much like doing things people expect me to do. That trait contributes to my long life."

I thought of Marsilia in her black smoke gown, and of Stefan's house being emptied and invaded. All the questions and none of the answers. Perhaps I should make a decision that would contribute to my chance of living a long life.

"Maybe invading the seethe should be done in daylight hours," I said. "And probably we should bring some backup."

Adam raised an eyebrow. "Invasion? My intention was to knock on the door. Just like we did here." He looked at Stefan's broken front door and made a thoughtful noise. "There is a very good chance it might end up the same way this one did."

"Let's not do that now," I suggested.

Adam said, "All right. We'll go to our house." Adam looked at Larry. "Would you like a ride?"

There was no sign of another car.

"I have one," Larry said, giving a whistle.

Out of the shadows on the far side of the shrouded Mystery Machine trotted a largish pony wearing neither bridle nor saddle, her hooves clopping on the driveway cement. She was one of those odd, found-only-in-ponies colors. Her body was seal brown, and her thick mane and tail were a light, almost silvery gray.

As Larry swung aboard her, she gave me a wicked look, pinning her ears and crinkling her nose. Larry soothed her in a language that was not Welsh (which I'd grown up hearing people speak) but related somehow. Cornish, maybe. I'd heard him use it before. Someday I'd ask him what it was.

He should have looked ridiculous on such a small animal—his legs dangled almost to her knees—but they suited each other. She sidled and he followed her movement with the grace of a born horseman. Bran's son Charles rode like that.

"I will meet you at your house," he said—and they were off at a brisk canter.

Horses make noise when they run, the impact of their weight hitting the ground and the strike of the hoof. They make more noise when they run on hard surfaces like roads and sidewalks. Larry and his pony made no noise at all.

LARRY WAS SITTING ON OUR FRONT STEPS WHEN WE drove in. He had taken the time to change into more usual clothing—boots, jeans, and T-shirt. Behind him, Tad leaned against the door, as if he were blocking Larry's way in. Their body language made me think that they weren't friendly.

"Magic ponies travel fast," Adam observed to me, though I was pretty sure his attention was on the tableau on our porch.

"I wouldn't have gotten on that pony if you paid me," I said, hopping down to the ground and shutting my door as quietly as I could. We were a ways from the neighbors, but sound travels in the night. I didn't want to wake anyone up.

Keeping the neighbors happy when your house is often filled with a pack of werewolves is both vital and difficult. Not many people are crazy about werewolves running around. Pack magic can sometimes help keep the noise down, but we weren't fae, who could manage illusions to hide the damage when we were attacked.

I baked cookies and took them to the neighbors whenever anything happened that might worry them, but two of the eight houses on our road were for sale. And last time I brought cookies, the nice lady who lived in the big gray house did not come to the door even though I could hear that she was home. It was probably a good thing that we didn't live in a normal city neighborhood like Stefan did.

"Larry, glad you made it," Adam said, soft-voiced for the same reason I hadn't slammed my car door. "Tad, thanks for helping out."

Larry nodded without getting to his feet. Tad straightened and took a couple of steps forward, his eyebrows climbing up at the sight of Adam's battle-torn and mucked-up clothing. Tad glanced at me, but my torn clothing was tucked in a pocket where he couldn't see it. I imagined that the bruise on my face was fully formed by now, but I'd had that the last time he'd seen me.

I answered the question on his face with a shake of my head. We hadn't found Stefan yet.

"Don't get me wrong, overtime is awesome," Tad said, not inquiring further in front of Larry. "But I was thinking it might be easier if I rent your little house, Mercy. Or at least the house that is standing where your old trailer house was before it burned."

"Adam and I were just discussing approaching Sherwood to move into it," I said slowly, because having Tad move in might be better than Sherwood. I glanced at Adam.

"We haven't talked to him," Adam said. "And having you there might be a better idea. We can include rent as part of your salary."

"There are a couple of downsides you should be aware of," I said.

"Underhill's gate." Tad tipped his head toward the back of our house. "She won't bother me. I'm small potatoes by her measures. She both dislikes and is wary of my dad. One or the other might intrigue her, but both together keep me safe until after she decides what to do about avenging herself on the rest of the fae. Dad thinks so, too."

Larry laughed, his wide grin showing sharp teeth. "Is that what she is doing? Well, someone is going to have a fun old time when that happens."

Tad gave him a long look, then his shoulders relaxed a little. I don't know what had gone on between them before we arrived, but it must not have been anything too bad.

"I think they are still surprised that she dislikes them," said Tad in a sour tone that reminded me forcibly of his father.

"More fool they," Larry said. "I'm looking forward to the fall-out."

Tad grinned at Larry. To me he said, "I can move in Saturday."

If Wulfe continued his stalking of me, though that seemed to be in question, would Tad be safe from him? Probably, I realized with a hint of relief, for the same reasons he was *probably* safe from Underhill. And if not? Tad could handle himself, possibly even better than Sherwood.

Most of the time, the half-blooded children of fae and mortal were much less powerful than their fae parent. But once in a while, the cross produced someone with unexpected and powerful magic. I would have been very hesitant to say that Tad was more powerful than his father, but only because I had no idea of the extent of the power of either of them.

There were, however, more problems with my house.

"Underhill was only the first thing. The house is also haunted by my murdered neighbor," I told him.

"The Cathers?" Tad asked, his lips curving down. He'd known my neighbors, too. "Which one is lingering?"

"Anna," I told him. "It's not been very long—she still might fade. I don't know how much you'll see and hear, but she's there every time I go in. She scared the pants off the HVAC lady last week."

I had mistakenly assumed I was the only one who could see my neighbor's ghost because that was the way it usually worked. I'd let the technician in and left her to do her work. I hadn't gotten ten feet outside the house before she'd come tearing out as white as a sheet. I wasn't going to let anyone else go in there without a fair warning.

Tad shrugged. "Anna and I traded casserole recipes. I'd guess we'll still get along. I'm used to ghosts. Dad's place is haunted, too."

I winced. It was. It had been not much of a haunting until I accidentally paid too much attention to their ghost. Apparently, it was now knocking stuff off shelves and hiding small but important things like car keys.

"He can always decide to move out if it's too much," Adam told me.

"Okay," I agreed.

"Settled," said Tad. "See you Saturday, if not before then." He waved at the three of us and headed for his car.

"Larry, what happened between you two before we got here?" I asked. It wasn't idle curiosity. I needed to know if my various allies couldn't be trusted to be alone together.

Larry shrugged. "I think he was guarding your house from me. I could have eased his mind, perhaps."

I heard an equine snort, though the pony was not anywhere I could see. Larry grinned over his shoulder; evidently he knew where she was.

The grin was gone but a smile lingered in his eyes when he turned back to us. "Your lad seemed to be taking his job very seriously. I might have pushed him a bit to see how he handled it. You left the Iron Kissed's son here as protection for your daughter, yes? Good idea."

"Thank you," said Adam dryly.

"Especially since my people say you sent the Fire Touched and the demon dog away," Larry said. It wasn't quite a question.

"Yes," Adam agreed.

Larry gave him an exasperated look. "I am plying you for information, my friend. A single-word confirmation of something I already know is not useful."

"Yes," said Adam, amusement in his tone.

The goblin heaved an exaggerated sigh. "Did you send them away for your safety or theirs?"

"Maybe they moved because their house remodeling is finished, so they can move back in," I suggested. The fae lie with questions all the time—I didn't expect Larry to believe me.

Larry smiled at me. "And took the Fire Touched with them to help the tibicena stay under control," Larry agreed. "But their house has been finished for a month or more at this point. Why now?"

"You know about Wulfe stalking Mercy," Adam said. It was not a question. The goblins "observed" people of interest. It was part of what made them valuable allies. "We worried that Joel and his wife might become collateral damage," he told Larry. "And we sent Aiden with him to make sure the tibicena stays controlled."

"Speaking of Wulfe," I said, "do you know where he is?"

Larry heaved himself to his feet with pretended effort. "This discussion needs to move inside."

Alarmed that he might have noticed someone watching, I took in a deep breath of the night air and gave the darkness around us a careful look. Beside me, Adam did the same thing.

Larry's mount—who smelled only incidentally like any equine I'd ever gotten a whiff of—was still around somewhere nearby. But I couldn't detect anyone else.

"No intruders," Larry said, observing this. "But there are creatures who can hear very well living nearby." Like Tad, he tipped his head to indicate the back of the house. "Very, very well."

It was a warning.

"Inside the house is better?" I asked.

"It's warded by your magic-wielding wolf," he said. "Nothing can listen in." And if there was something a little rueful in his tone, we all ignored it.

I knew that Sherwood had warded the house. Larry had just made me realize that I didn't understand exactly what that meant. Wulfe hadn't had trouble getting in despite Sherwood's wards. But Wulfe was a law unto himself.

I glanced at Adam, who was holding the door open in invitation. He didn't seem perturbed by Larry's remark; likely he had already known what Sherwood's magic was doing.

After a quick glance up the stairs to where Jesse was sleeping, Adam took us down to the basement so we wouldn't wake her up. The main room of our basement was set up for the pack to relax or play in. Furniture tended to get moved around—and battered.

Someone had pulled two couches to face each other. One of them was brand-new. The other would need replacing soon, and someone should probably have cleaned the hair off it. Adam took a seat on the battered one. Larry sat across from him.

I got a folding chair from a small stack leaning against the wall, popped it open, and set it next to the couch Adam was on. I sat on it backward.

"If I sit with you in that comfy couch," I told Adam's raised eyebrow, "I'm going to fall asleep. I have now officially been awake for twenty-four hours and change."

Adam frowned at me in concern—though I knew that he'd gotten up at the same time I had. But he wasn't going to send me up to bed, or grumble at me in front of Larry, any more than I would do to him. He turned his attention to Larry.

"Why are we here instead of the seethe?" Adam asked.

Larry gave him an intense look. "The goblins have alliances. We have always had alliances. We do not have allies."

I got what he was saying before Adam did, I think. Allies. Friends. People who actually cared about each other. That was quite an offer from the goblin king. In the long history of the fae, only parts of which I was familiar with, the goblins had been thoroughly indoctrinated in the idea that they stood alone.

Adam sat back and considered that. "Why us?"

Larry pursed his lips. "Complicated question. Werewolf packs take care of their own. Only if a situation might impact the pack's safety—or the safety of a wolf in the pack—do they step into the business of others."

He smiled at me with teeth in full display, but when he spoke, his voice was a whisper. "Coyote's daughter changed your pack, Adam Hauptman. She changed you. The Columbia Basin Pack is suddenly full of heroes who take on anyone to protect the innocent, the helpless, even enemies." He paused. "Even goblins. 'Might for right,' in fact."

"*Camelot*," I said involuntarily, recognizing the quote. When Adam shot me a glance, I said, "'Might for right' is a quote from the musical."

"Well, you aren't King Arthur," said Larry dryly. "Of course, neither was he. But that's the point, really. What you are doing might change the way we all live together."

He smiled at me again. "My youngest goblins love playing heroes with your wolves. Even some of the old ones have gotten into the game."

Adam said, "Like you did at Stefan's house. If I'd asked for help, it would have been one thing. Riding to the rescue unbidden is another altogether."

"Indeed," he agreed. "I would like my people and yours to be friends."

Friends share important information.

"We were at Stefan's today as the result of a chain of events," I told him. And then I described Marsilia's dramatic performance and her telling us we needed to find Wulfe and how that led us to Stefan's house.

Larry said, "I was at Stefan's because one of my goblins called to tell me you were there."

"That was quick," I said, because there had been maybe ten minutes between when we'd parked the car and when Larry had shown up.

He shrugged. "I was nearby. I had a feeling." He paused, considering his options. Possibly organizing his thoughts. Or maybe just to make sure he had our attention. With Larry, it could be any of those.

"Should we call Beauclaire?" I asked.

Larry shrugged. "As you wish, though I wouldn't ask for help from him myself."

Which hadn't been what I'd meant.

"This feels more organized than a couple of upstart fae attacking Stefan. If there is a group of fae attacking the vampires, trying to break the treaty, Beauclaire should know about it," said Adam, to clarify what I'd meant.

"Not fae," Larry said with a shrug.

"Oh yes they were." I tapped my nose.

"Half-bloods?" suggested Adam, watching Larry intently.

Larry put a finger in the air to indicate Adam had the correct answer. "The Gray Lords would not consider them one of their own. Those creatures do not have the power to break any treaty."

Larry said "the Gray Lords" with a hint of distaste. Like Schrödinger's cat, the goblins were both fae and not-fae at the same time. I'd found if I kept to that assumption, I seldom offended anyone.

"Half-bloods," Adam repeated, leaning forward. "In service of whom?"

"Themselves?" I suggested. Tad, who was half-fae, did not belong to any group of half-bloods, but he'd told me that he'd been approached a few times.

Medea, my cat, emerged from the shadows to hop onto Larry's lap. It was probably because we were so tired that all three of us stopped speaking to watch her. She turned around two times and then settled down and started to purr.

"My people eat yours," Larry informed the cat.

Medea kneaded his thighs lightly and kicked her purr up a few notches. He gave in and started to pet her.

"She appears to be missing her tail," Larry said, sounding very concerned for someone whose people eat cats.

"She's a Manx," I told him. "She never had a tail to be missing."

"Ah," he said, relaxing and turning back to our conversation. "I think the half-bloods are Bonarata's."

"Last we heard, he was still in Italy," Adam said.

"That's what I've been told, too," agreed Larry. "But on Friday, the goblin watching the seethe reported that there was some kind of disturbance there." He paused, then explained, "Wulfe's presence necessitates that any observation of the seethe is done at a fair distance. Electronic devices are not useful."

He looked at us and appeared to make a decision. "For here, either, you should know. Our interior devices quit working shortly after the three-legged wolf came to your pack."

Our bond told me how unhappy Adam was that the goblins had been spying on us, unhappy but not surprised. Outwardly he gave no sign.

Larry continued, "Our outdoor devices quit after Underhill opened her gate." He paused. "We still get pictures from those cameras, but nothing that we can trust—and occasionally, I am informed, the Disney Channel."

"Huh," I said. I had not previously thought that Tilly had a sense of irony. Or knew what the Disney Channel was.

"I haven't noticed any problem with *our* cameras," said Adam.

"Underhill is a guest at your home," Larry said. "Of course she can't interfere with your cameras, which have the purpose of defense."

"So there was a disturbance Friday at the seethe?" I asked, redirecting the conversation. If Larry thought Bonarata was here—or that his minions were acting here—I needed to hear about it.

Larry nodded. "A number of black luxury vehicles with very dark windows entered the gate of the seethe. Nothing too out of the ordinary. There were more lights and more activity than normal—but again, nothing so unusual as to require my goblin calling in. No noises, but Wulfe ensures that the neighbors are not disturbed. At two in the morning, though, fifteen vehicles left, and she could not see into them to determine what they held. None of my people have seen any of Marsilia's vampires since that time, so we assume that they left in the cars."

"They haven't seen any of them?" I asked, startled. Larry's

goblins were scattered all over the Tri-Cities. They saw everything. "But Wulfe came here sometime on Saturday."

Larry tilted his head. "My goblin who watches here did not see him. Unfortunately, that isn't unusual with Wulfe. Are you sure?"

"Yes," said Adam dryly. "He slept in my bed."

Larry leaned back, his long, four-fingered hands finding the sensitive area beneath Medea's jaw. "Marsilia was right, then. You do have good reason to see Wulfe returned to the grave." His thoughtful eyes were on Adam. "Would you describe Marsilia's performance to me one more time? With as much detail as you can remember?"

This time Adam took point; he remembered it more clearly than I did, though I was able to add in a few details.

"Brimstone, not sulfur?" asked Larry when we were finished.

"Brimstone," Adam confirmed.

Brimstone was to sulfur what hydrogen peroxide was to water, except the charge was magic. A mundane human couldn't tell one from the other because they wouldn't sense the charge of power that made sulfur into the more magically useful brimstone.

"Interesting," Larry said. "Possibly the brimstone helped her with the smoke tricks. But brimstone would also conceal her scent. What does scent do for you, besides identification?"

"It helps in detecting lies," I said. "But she wasn't lying." I paused. "I don't think. After a while, when you can use your nose to be certain, you get a feel for what lies look like."

Adam agreed with a nod. "If she were going to lie, she wouldn't have been so careful with her words." He pursed his lips. "We can smell blood," Adam said slowly. "There was something . . ."

"On her neck," I said, tapping the side of mine just below my jaw. "A cut, I think. It had definite edges. But if it was damage from whatever happened in the seethe on Friday . . . I wouldn't expect a werewolf to still be showing the effects of battle. How quickly do vampires repair their wounds?" It was a rhetorical question. Vampires could heal very quickly as long as they could feed.

"Or a goblin, either," agreed Larry. "A vampire? If one is feeding regularly and the wounds are not severe, a vampire can heal very quickly. Hours rather than days."

"She could have come to us if she needed help," I told them. "Our pack—or even you, Larry. She can teleport." And so could Stefan. I didn't know if Larry knew about that.

"Yes," said Larry. If he hadn't known, he was concealing his surprise very well. "Though I don't think that she'd have come to me. If she and Stefan are not here, it's because they don't want to be here." He raised a palm at my indrawn breath. "There are many reasons that could be. Let's add that to the ongoing mystery."

"Hostage," said Adam grimly. "Marsilia spoke like a hostage in a terrorist propaganda video. Very careful with her words."

"Or maybe," I added, "as if someone who could tell if she were lying would interrogate her."

Vampires didn't have a supernatural ability to sense if someone was telling the truth the way werewolves could. But our local seethe did have a magical artifact that used blood, pain, and magic to detect lies. I rubbed the palms of my hands together in memory.

"*Hic sunt dracones*," I murmured involuntarily.

Larry looked up sharply.

"What?" Adam asked, his glance falling on me and then Larry.

"Here there be dragons," translated Larry. "Why do you say so?"

I started to brush it off, and then decided there was a possibility it might actually mean something.

"After I hit the spell web, I had a . . . I *think* it was a dream." I told them about it.

"Who is Daniel?" Larry asked when I was done. "There isn't a Daniel in your pack or in the seethe."

"You didn't see the ghost in Stefan's house?" Cats could see ghosts—for some reason I thought that meant that goblins might, too. "Daniel was one of Stefan's people." The rest seemed a little complicated, so I simplified it. "He was caught up in vampire politics—not his fault—and"—I stole Larry's phrase—"returned to the grave. Now he haunts Stefan's house, though so far I'm the only one who can see him."

"He was sitting on the couch while we were fighting the spider," Adam told me.

I didn't know what that meant. Had Daniel gotten stronger? Or was Adam picking up abilities from me the way I could sometimes borrow his voice of command?

"You saw him, too?" Larry asked me. "At Stefan's house just now?"

"Before, during, and after both fights," I said. "Though he didn't come upstairs with us when we left."

"He was fresh in your mind when you hit the spell web." Larry's voice said that the conclusion was obvious.

"Yes," I agreed, remembering opening my eyes to see Daniel's face close up. "Very fresh. I guess seeing him in the dream was more expected than not." Or maybe he'd been pulled into it with me.

"Was it just a dream," mused Larry aloud, "or was it something else?"

"Her fur had frost on it, and her breath was cold," Adam said. "As if she'd been running in an arctic forest for a while."

"Dragons, lions, and wolves," said Larry.

I cleared my throat. "Dragons, lions, and *Wulfe*, I think."

"Does that mean something to you, Larry?" Adam asked, because the goblin king had stiffened.

"Other than a fair warning," Larry said after a second. "It's just . . . You know how vampires, the old ones, are given Names?"

Larry's voice made the last word start with a capital letter, as if it meant something different to him.

"Like Bonarata is the Lord of Night and Stefan is the Soldier?" I said. "I was told it was because people hesitate to speak the true name of evil, just in case it hears you."

"An old superstition," Larry agreed. "Though some of those have more than a grain of truth. But a Name can also be a powerful thing, affecting how one is seen. People hear that Stefan is the Soldier—and they discount him. They only see that soldiers take orders."

Adam grunted. He sounded amused.

I hadn't thought of it like that. "The Lord of Night must be important and powerful," I said.

"And the Monster terrible," Larry agreed. "And he was."

The Monster was dead. Had returned to the grave with my help.

"We call Wulfe the Wizard now," Larry said. "But before he was broken, they called Wulfe the Dragon."

Dragons, I thought. I'd had my fill of dragons. We'd had a zombie dragon, a baby zombie dragon that still made me wake up in tears and shivering terror. Then there had come the smoke dragon, who got into the heads of its victims with a smokey bite. I realized I was rubbing my shoulder where it had bitten me.

"The Dragon," murmured Adam, giving Larry a sharp look. Me? I wouldn't be capable of sharp anything until after I got a few hours of sleep. My bones ached with weariness.

"Do you think that Wulfe himself might be responsible for the trouble the vampires find themselves in?" Adam asked. "Not Bonarata?" He considered it. "Wulfe could hold Marsilia and Stefan so they couldn't come to us. I could believe that. But to what end?"

Larry shrugged. "I don't know. But Wulfe's motivations are clear only to Wulfe. If you boil down what Marsilia said, it was a request for you to find Wulfe."

"And a warning that if we didn't, it would be disastrous for us—for our pack," I murmured. "But where would Wulfe have gotten a pair of spider half-fae? Bonarata is the one who collects useful half-blooded fae." I hadn't dealt with those much myself because I'd been a prisoner, but Adam had been to Bonarata's court.

"I'd rather it be Wulfe than Bonarata, too," I added, then realized that wasn't true.

"Would you?" Larry examined my face, then shrugged. "Where do you think Bonarata learned to court useful people and make them his own? That's why they called Wulfe the Dragon. He hoarded treasures of all kinds. Silver and gold were the least of them. His library would have made Charlemagne weep with envy. He gathered scholars, musicians, and artisans—" Larry paused. "I grant you that he mostly let them go out into the world again rather than turning them into acolytes or serfs like Bonarata does."

Conventional wisdom maintained that goblins' lives were as short as humans', or shorter. I'd questioned that before, and Larry's distant gaze—as if he was remembering something that he greatly desired—was confirmation of my suspicions if I needed it. Larry had seen the Dragon's treasures.

He shook himself from his brief reverie. "He found unusually beautiful women like Marsilia. Unusually dangerous men like Bonarata and Stefan. He did not usually change them into vampires, but there were exceptions."

"*Marsilia* turned Stefan," I told him. I was not arguing with him; I simply wanted more information.

"And could not control him because he should have belonged to Wulfe," said Larry. "We will help look for Wulfe. We are already doing that. I'll contact you if any of my people see any of Marsilia's. Or Stefan. They are somewhere in the Tri-Cities, if Marsilia came to you at Uncle Mike's. There is a limit to how far they can travel."

I didn't tell him that Stefan had taken a person with him and teleported from Spokane to the Tri-Cities. That felt like Stefan's secret. I'd need to get some sleep before I decided to share Stefan's secrets with Larry.

"We'll check out the seethe and Wulfe's house tomorrow," said Adam. "I'll make a few phone calls just to be sure Bonarata is still where he's supposed to be."

Larry nodded. "My people are always on the lookout for Bonarata. His aircraft have not landed in any of the local airfields. But he has a helicopter, and those may land where they will."

Larry stood up, setting Medea down in his spot with an absent pat. "My advice is that you don't go to the seethe without more people at your back. Someone created a nasty little trap at Stefan's—and it was probably aimed at you."

My mate grinned, showing his teeth. "Interesting times."

7

⚉⚉

AFTER LARRY LEFT ON HIS SHAGGY PONY WITH DAWN a whisper over the river, we headed up to bed. Daytime slumber in pack central was not going to be easy to accomplish.

While Adam fiddled with the drapes in an attempt to keep as much light out as possible, I scrubbed my tired face and brushed my teeth. By the time Adam had finished doing the same, I was buried under blankets and most of the way to sleep.

He climbed in, bringing a wave of cold air with him, and I growled a faint protest. But when he pulled me into his arms, his warmth more than made up for any disruption to my comfort that his entry into my nest of blankets had made. Of the many benefits of marriage to Adam, sleeping together was pretty high up on my list. He liked to cuddle and he radiated heat.

"Stefan is alive, right?" murmured Adam.

I nodded.

"I didn't want to ask with Larry around," he said. "But I was pretty sure that you wouldn't be sitting around chatting if he was gone."

"I don't know anything else," I told him. Unlike the mating bond I shared with Adam, the vampire's hold on me wasn't a bond between equals—if Stefan didn't want to contact me, there wasn't much I could do about it.

"Is that on purpose?" Adam asked softly.

"One of my least favorite things about marriage is this penchant you have for keeping me up when I want to sleep," I grumbled.

He gave me a comforting squeeze. "I know you don't like to think about your connection, let alone talk about it. But it might be important. Is Stefan keeping you in the dark on purpose?"

"Do you mean, why isn't Stefan jerking my lead and dragging my butt to wherever he is?" I wiggled to put some distance between us. Thinking about being tied to Stefan left me claustrophobic. "I have to assume it's for the same reason he hasn't shown up here."

Stefan had appeared in my living room before. He'd made me do things, too. Mostly things that had saved my life or his, but the idea that Stefan could force his will on me made my skin crawl. I finished with, "I have no idea."

Adam followed my wiggle but didn't touch me other than to kiss my temple. Even with the pumpkin-bruise, the brush of his lips was so tender it didn't hurt. I knew if I pulled away again, he'd let me be.

I sighed and snuggled back into his warmth. "Assuming we don't find him, I'd planned on trying to contact him through the blood bond after I'd gotten some sleep. I thought I'd wait until dusk."

Adam grunted his approval. Eventually I felt him relax, but now I couldn't follow him into sleep because thinking about Stefan's bond left me edgy. My thoughts kept chasing each other around until, finally, I saw a new angle on Marsilia and decided Adam needed to take a look at it, too. A kind person would have left it until morning, but since he'd made sure I wasn't going to fall asleep, I felt justified in waking him up.

"I am pretty sure she likes you," I said thoughtfully, and felt him wake up.

He waited, but he's not the only patient hunter in our family. Finally, he said, sounding a little wary, "Who likes me?"

"Marsilia," I told him. "She likes you, and so sending you after Wulfe probably means that he's not behind the weirdness at the seethe."

He huffed a laugh at my logic.

"She'd send me no matter what, of course," I continued. "You remember that she sent me after a vampire possessed by a demon."

"I do," agreed Adam with more heat in his voice than that deserved. It had been several years ago.

She was not happy that I'd survived and the demon-possessed vampire had not. She'd had plans for him.

"But she doesn't like me," I said. "She *does* like you."

"She likes you better now," Adam said. "She tells me that she enjoys watching you spread chaos over other people's plans."

I gave him an amused snort. "Not enough to care whether I live or die." I thought about that for a moment, because Marsilia had unarguably risked a lot to help Adam find me after Bonarata had kidnapped me. I added, "As long as it didn't affect her alliance with you."

There was a little silence.

"If she thought Wulfe was someone who needed to be stopped,"

Adam said carefully, "she would ask us to stop him. Instead, she's sent us to find him."

I lifted my head and glanced at his face to judge the seriousness of his expression. I put my head back down and said, in a voice that was smaller than I wanted it to be, "You think Larry is right."

I could not for the world have articulated why I didn't want Wulfe to be making trouble. Part of it was that I was more scared of him than of Bonarata. I'd escaped Bonarata. I was pretty sure I wouldn't have escaped Wulfe. Part of it, perversely, was that at some point I'd put Wulfe, terrifying as he was, on "our side." He was one of our people.

Larry had been right: I didn't think like a werewolf.

"I believe Marsilia sent us after him, and I doubt it's for the reasons she gave us," Adam said. Not quite arguing with me, just making sure I saw his point of view, too. "Other than that, I don't know why she thinks we need to find him, and neither does Larry."

"Larry is scared of Wulfe," I said after a minute. "That might be affecting his judgment."

"Yes, I think so, too," Adam said. "That doesn't make him wrong."

"Does he scare you?" I asked. "Wulfe?"

Adam thought about that for a moment, and I was drifting off to sleep when he said, "In some ways. Bonarata scares me more. Bonarata wants your hide to nail to his wall as a trophy. I don't think Wulfe would hurt you."

That woke me up. "Why don't you think he would hurt me?" I sat up and scooted around until I could see his face. I didn't think Wulfe would hurt me, either. My certainty was based on Wulfe's actions and manner. I hoped Adam had better reasons.

"Vampires are selfish creatures," Adam told me. "They have to be, in order to become what they are. Whatever it was that you did to him in Elizaveta's backyard when you were laying those zombies caught Wulfe's attention. Made him think you are important to him or his survival."

I'd been laying the spirits of the collected zombie dead that belonged to generations of a black witch family. Not being educated in the matter, I had been working with pure instinct. I'd managed to lay the zombies, but the spell effects had knocked Wulfe flat. I wasn't sure if he'd been in some kind of waking coma or if I'd done something worse. What I'd done had been a product of a long and terrifying night, with magic of all kinds thick in the air, and I wasn't sure I could ever do such a thing again.

Given that it was probably not repeatable, I didn't *want* Wulfe to think it was important to his survival. That sounded like an unhealthy thing for me in the long run.

"How is it important?" I asked.

Adam pulled me back down into the bed and pulled the covers around me. If I hadn't been there, he'd probably have slept on top of the covers. But I liked covers, and he liked to cuddle me, so he dealt with sleeping too warm.

"I don't know. Neither does he," Adam told me. "If he weren't as confused about it as you are, he'd do something more pointed than following you around and giving you inappropriate gifts. Until he figures it out, he won't hurt you. And that"—he hugged me tightly—"puts him far down the list of things I'm afraid of."

From the roughness of his voice, I understood that there were things he was afraid of, things that he didn't want to talk about. Like the fact that we were both worried about Elizaveta's lingering curse. That Sherwood could still be a problem, even if he was a Cornick. That our pack might not be up to the task of protecting our territory, and our failure to do so could end in a war, with the humans wiping out any supernatural they could find.

We both had nightmares, both from our pasts and from what might happen in the future.

"Larry thinks that Wulfe has taken over the seethe with plans of taking over the world," I said. "Do you think that's likely?"

Adam's husky laugh ruffled my hair. "Asking me the same question again won't get you a different answer. I know why Larry is worried. I don't know if that worry is justified. Something happened to the seethe. I think that there should be at least six hours of sleep between us and any further answers."

I growled at him, just to make him laugh again. All the worries in my stomach relaxed a bit when Adam did.

"I expect we'll find out eventually no matter what we do or don't do," he said. "We should sleep so we can deal with it when all hell breaks loose. Again."

"Sufficient unto the day is the evil thereof," I said direly.

He pulled me close and kissed me. "That's my optimist," he said, settling back in the bed to sleep.

"Love you," I told him, then yawned.

"Love you, too," he said.

I DREAMED.

I sat on the edge of the abyss from my earlier encounter with the spell web. It loomed below me, both a bottomless, empty hole and a presence of blackness that was the embodiment of solid darkness.

Instead of the snow I'd walked in previously, the ground be-

neath me was something like the forest floor in the Douglas fir–
dominated wilderness I'd grown up in. It was deeply packed with
dried fir and pine needles until it made a cushiony layer over the
hard ground. That was not the sort of ground one usually found
on the edge of a cliff, since needles were easily scattered by a good
hard wind. I dug my fingers into it.

Can't argue with what is, I thought, tossing my handful of dirt
and needles off into the abyss, feeling the tickle of the falling earth
against the bare skin of my dangling foot. My other foot was
tucked up and hooked under the knee of the leg that hung over
the edge.

It didn't feel like I was doing anything very dangerous. It felt
like I was dangling my foot off the branch of a very tall tree I'd
climbed. Just enough frightening to make my stomach tingle a
bit. I twisted around until the abyss was to one side of me instead
of in front of me, though I left one leg hanging off the edge.

Spread out on the ground in front of me was a white linen
tablecloth set with an elegant tea service, the kind with porcelain
so fine you can see your fingers through the sides. There was a
plate with those little creamy sandwich cookies I associated with
France but could now buy at Costco. There was also a plate of
brownies, but those looked a little unreal, as if whoever had made
up the plate couldn't quite remember what they looked like.

A warm breeze rose from the abyss and caressed my bare foot,
leaving sharp prickles behind. It wasn't really painful, more like
I'd gotten too close to a Fourth of July sparkler, the ones they give
little kids. I was connected to the abyss in some way that made
me uneasy. I started to pull my foot up, but Stefan spoke.

"Mercy."

I hadn't realized he was there, sitting cross-legged on the other side of the tablecloth. He wasn't looking at me; he was frowning at the brownies.

I looked up at the sky, which was that bright cerulean blue that artists are so fond of. But I couldn't locate the sun.

"Is this a dream?" I asked slowly. "Or are you doing this so you can talk to me?"

"I wouldn't do that," Stefan said absently. "That would be too dangerous. Someone would notice. But everyone dreams."

His words seemed important. I tried to make sure I'd remember them exactly. Marsilia's words had been important, too, but I had only remembered the gist of what she had said. Hopefully I would do better with these.

"Dangerous for you?" I asked.

He laughed. And it was wrong. Stefan had a warm laugh, and this was full of broken things like dreams and hope.

"No," he said, wiping his face as if there might have been tears on his cheeks. "Not for me. Marsilia and I, we are survivors. We are powerful enough to be useful, but not so powerful that we are threats. It's our friends and allies that we have to sell out so we can survive."

He looked up at me then and I sucked in a breath. Someone had gouged out his eyes.

I made as if to get up, to go to him, but he put up a hand. "*No.*"

There was such command in his voice that my body stopped moving without my volition. Suddenly my heart pounded, my hands and face felt numb, and I couldn't breathe as one of those stupid panic attacks gripped me. I hadn't had a panic attack in . . . maybe a whole week. The last one had been spurred by a dream, too. I'd dreamed of Tim and the drink from a fairy goblet that had stolen my will.

Just as Stefan had stolen my will.

If Stefan told me I was happy, I'd feel that way. It was the nature of the vampiric bond. If he told me to kill Adam . . .

"I don't think that would work," Stefan told me in a detached voice. "I don't think anyone could make you kill Adam." He paused. "Except maybe Adam himself, if he got you mad enough."

I stared at him. There was nothing wrong with his eyes. They were the same rich brown as always, a couple of shades lighter than Adam's. My panic attack had stopped. Just stopped. And I wondered if he'd told me not to be afraid. And not to remember that he'd told me so.

He turned his head to the abyss as if he were ashamed.

"I am sorry," he told me. "I can't— I'm not . . . Anyway. Marsilia and I have given you a game to play." His fingers worried at the edge of the tablecloth that dangled over the ledge. "If you lose, you die. If you don't play the game, you die. And even if you win . . ." He wiped his cheeks again. In a whisper he said, "I am so tired of the people I love dying while I go on and on." He bowed his head and, still very quietly, asked, "Do you know the prayer? 'If I should die before I wake . . .' But the Lord doesn't keep the souls of vampires safe, Mercy. Vampires don't have souls."

"Stefan," I said.

"Don't worry about me. Don't worry about Marsilia," he said forcefully.

"Are you all right?" I asked. "Are you safe?"

He laughed that terrible laugh again. "No. And no. But I'll survive. That's what I do. Tell me what happened when you went to my house."

I frowned at him. "How do you know I went to your house?"

"I was informed. Please?"

I told him what had happened in more detail than I would normally. I didn't know if that was an effect of this place or not-place, or something Stefan wanted from me.

"Is this a dream?" I asked again when I was finished.

"Have a brownie," he said, instead of answering my question. "You like brownies."

I gazed doubtfully at them. "I'll take a macaroon instead, please. I don't like the look of your brownies."

He laughed, and this time it sounded like his laugh—if a little tired. "Macaron," he told me. "Macaroons are the stodgy ones with all the coconut."

"I'm sorry about the piano," I offered without taking a cookie. "And, really, most of the living room furniture. The stairway. Some of the books got pretty wet, too, when the frost all melted."

"I don't care about the piano," he said. "Things can be replaced. Even books." He was frowning at me. He leaned sideways, getting a better look at my dangling foot. "What's wrong with your foot? Your feet? Why are you keeping that one way out there?"

I looked at my foot, too. "It's the one that got a bit of spider spine stuck in it." Hadn't both of them been hurt? "I'd forgotten. It doesn't hurt."

"Show me," said Stefan.

I raised my dangling foot and lost my balance, as if it were a lot heavier than I'd expected. Stefan swept forward like a striking snake and grabbed my ankle, sending the teapot spiraling off the edge and into the darkness.

He kept his grip until I regained my seat.

"Don't fall off the cliff, please," he said, sounding a little shaken. He gave the abyss a wary look. "Literally or figuratively. I don't know what it is or why it's here."

"Okay," I agreed.

I knew I hadn't been in any danger. I trusted Stefan to keep me safe.

I examined that last thought as Stefan looked at my foot. I knew that the only person I trusted to keep me safe with such bone-deep certainty was . . . no one. Not even me.

I frowned suspiciously at Stefan. What else *had* he said to stop my panic attack?

"Give me the other one."

I managed that without overbalancing myself.

"You should get them looked at," he said, releasing the foot he held. "Show them to Zee, I think. And soon."

He released me and began folding up the tablecloth with quick, almost angry movements.

"Are you afraid?" I asked abruptly.

He stopped moving, then his hands tightened on the tablecloth before he flung the whole thing—half-formed brownies and all—into the darkness, which swallowed them up.

"I'm always afraid, Mercy," he said, looking into the endless black. "Always."

I don't remember anything after that.

THE NEXT TIME I WOKE UP, IT WAS TO THE SOUND OF my bedroom door opening and the smell of the good hot chocolate. This was accompanied by the scents of bacon, cheese, and all sorts of breakfasty foods.

"Mmm," I said. "Marry me."

"Okay," agreed my husband. "This afternoon at two p.m. work for you? I might manage one thirty in a pinch."

"Sorry," I murmured, burrowing deeper under the pillow, "I think I have a date with this guy."

"Do you?" There was a clink as something, presumably my breakfast, was set down.

"Yep." I yawned. "Some hot guy. Used to be special forces. Don't know that he can compete with a man who cooks breakfast for—uhumf."

He inserted a muscular arm under my belly and heaved me out of the blankets and over his shoulder.

"Mine," he said smugly, a hand patting my butt.

I let myself go limp and muttered, "The things I put up with for breakfast."

He laughed and set me on my feet. That hurt for a second— and then it didn't. I returned his butt pat with interest on my way to my chest of drawers, where my breakfast awaited.

Adam had evidently rolled the walking stick aside to make room for the plate. I hadn't caught it moving—I seldom did—but I was pretty sure Adam wouldn't have put the plate half-on, half-off the chest.

The walking stick had been first made by Lugh who knows how long ago and had destroyed itself saving me. It had re-appeared a few weeks ago, looking as if it had never been reduced to splinters and bits of melted silver. I rolled it over so I could push the plate back on solid ground. I wondered if the walking stick still counted as an ancient artifact after remaking itself in my dreams.

Dreams. I paused, remembering that dream—or whatever it had been. I decided I'd eat breakfast and digest the dream a bit before I shared it.

"Any news?" I asked, wolfing . . . coyote-ing down crispy hash browns and bacon. Adam was a wonderful cook. I could bake good brownies.

Adam shook his head. "I thought we could both use fuel before we tackled mysteries."

He sounded a little preoccupied. I smiled to myself. I hadn't worn anything to bed, and I wasn't wearing anything now.

"Sex fiend," I told him. "The tabloids are right about you."

"Unusually so," he agreed. "Almost as if they had an inside source. Are you through eating yet?"

"SO WHAT DO YOU THINK IT WAS?" ADAM ASKED, NEARLY an hour later, as he put away the pans he'd used to make breakfast.

"Did I have a dream, or was it a message from Stefan?" I wiped down the sink and shook my head. "I don't know. It had the same feel as the one in Stefan's house—and neither of them felt quite like my normal dreams. But Stefan didn't say anything materially that I didn't know, and what was new was something I could have made up." I paused. "But I am going to have Zee look at my foot. It looks and feels okay—but it should be more painful, I think. It hurt when I stepped on those spiky things, and then I forgot about it." *Feet*, I thought. I needed to have Zee look at both of my feet.

"I'll go with you. Afterward we should gather some of the wolves and go pay—" He stopped talking as the sound of a car outside caught his attention. He glanced at me.

"George," I said with certainty. George drove a ten-year-old Mazda sedan. There was another Mazda in the pack, but it had a smaller engine. I knew cars.

A second car followed the Mazda. Brand-new cars could be trickier—less individual than older cars.

"And," I said, "someone driving a newer Chevy Malibu."

GEENA REED'S HAND SHOOK AS SHE BROUGHT THE cocoa up to her mouth. Sleeplessness ringed her eyes and tightened a mouth that looked as though it usually wore a smile. She was short, plump, and maybe fifty.

We made her very uncomfortable. Interestingly, it was just Adam and me who bothered her. She appeared to be quite at ease with George.

We had gathered in the living room because the kitchen seemed a little close quarters for someone who was as scared as she was. The living room had more choices of seating where she could get some distance without looking like she was trying to hide from us.

"Geena has been in the Tri-Cities for about two weeks," George said. "We met at my club."

George's club was where he joined other people who practiced BDSM. Geena didn't look like my idea of someone who belonged to a BDSM group. But I didn't look like most people's idea of a mechanic, either.

"I'm a witch," she told us—unnecessarily because witches carry a distinctive scent. Or rather there are three kinds of scents that belong to three kinds of witches.

White witches use only their own power to create magic. Being a white witch usually meant being a good person. Anyone witchborn who wasn't a good person—and who had a lick of self-preservation—became a gray witch. Gray witches pulled their power from the strong emotions of other people. I understood that negative feelings—pain, anger, grief—worked better. To stay a gray witch, the sources that they harvested from had to be willing—or at least *unwitting*. That gave them a lot more power than a white witch had.

Black witches didn't bother with finding volunteers. White witches, weaker and full of potential, were black witches' favorite victims, but they weren't fussy.

"I'm a white witch," Geena said, as if she were used to explaining herself. "Word has gone out that you don't tolerate black witches, and that's why I came here. I belong to a group of about thirty white witches. Most of us haven't been here long. A year ago, I am told, there were only six of us."

She looked at the cocoa in her hand and said, "We all thought . . . hoped, really, that this would be a safe place."

George helped her set her cocoa down on the side table. He looked a bit rough around the edges, like a man who could handle himself in a dark alley. He also appeared young enough to have been her son, though he'd been born sometime in the late nineteenth century.

There was an air of protectiveness in George's body language that was interesting—and none of my business. That last didn't lessen my interest. He took Geena's hand and kissed it. He didn't say out loud that he wouldn't let her be hurt—because Adam might take offense at that. But his kiss made it very clear that he considered her to be under his protection.

"I was asked by my coven to talk to George because we're friends," she said. George had not released her hand, and now her fingers closed tightly around his.

"And I brought her here because I thought you needed to hear what she knows," George said, when she didn't say anything more. "Witches have been disappearing and worse."

"Three witches have disappeared, we think," Geena said, sounding a little tentative. "No one from our coven. But Sandy is one of us."

Good for Sandy, whoever that was, I thought, when she quit talking. And did that mean that Sandy had disappeared, and we had four missing witches? Or had something else happened to her? Or was she the one who knew about the missing witches?

Geena's group wasn't really a coven, not a proper one. I'd been told that specific criteria were required to have a coven. For one thing, they had to have an exact number of members—I couldn't remember if it was nine or thirteen. But I knew it wasn't thirty. A coven had to have representatives from multiple families of witches—most of whom have died out. I was also pretty sure, because the implication was that all the witches had to be people of power, that a real coven wasn't formed by white witches. Still, Geena was welcome to call her group a coven if she wanted to. I didn't care.

"Sandy knows someone who disappeared?" inquired Adam before the silence grew any more desperate on her part. His voice was gentle. George wasn't the only one feeling protective.

Alphas and dominant wolves tended to be protective. It was both endearing and annoying, depending upon whether it was turned toward helpless, kindly women who looked like they baked bread for the homeless on a regular basis or directed at me.

"Sorry," she said, her voice tightening until it was nearly a whisper.

It wasn't that she was a naturally anxious person, I didn't think.

BDSM wouldn't attract the faint of heart. But a person could be taught fear—and white witches had plenty of reason to be afraid.

I ran through reasons she might be worried about us—and not George—and tried one.

"Geena," I said, "our job is to protect the people in the Tri-Cities. We can't do that unless we know what's going on. We appreciate very much that you've brought this to our attention. Whatever you tell us will help us keep your coven"—if she used the word, so could I—"safer."

She lifted her chin then and stared at me. She raised one hand toward me, palm first, and I felt a fine tickle of magic slide over me. Then she closed her eyes and nodded.

"Truth," she said. "Truly meant. Sorry, sorry." She sounded, this time, as if it were an apology rather than a fear response.

She straightened her back, let George's hand go, and said, in a much firmer voice, "Sandy is one of my coven. She shares a house with a woman called Katie, who is also a witch. Last Friday night, Katie went into her meditation room and locked herself in, as was her habit. Sandy went to bed, got up in the morning, and went to work. She's a nurse and has a regular Saturday shift. When Sandy got home, she noticed that the room was still locked. No one responded to her knocks or calls."

She frowned at us. "Meditation is a way to increase power, but you can get caught up in it, and that is dangerous." She waited until Adam nodded, and I wondered if she was a teacher of some kind. She seemed made for the role of elementary teacher—I really wouldn't have picked her for one of George's club members in a thousand years. Some people were hard to pigeonhole. Maybe Geena was a banker or an insurance salesperson.

"Sandy had to take the hinges off the door to get it open," she said. "When she did, Katie was gone. The room was empty."

George nudged her.

"It is a converted closet," she explained hastily. "There are no windows or other doors. The lock is a bar dropped into brackets on the inside of the door. That's why Sandy had to take off the hinges."

"Is that something a witch could do?" Adam asked. "Vanish from a locked room?"

"A black witch maybe?" Geena hazarded. It was obvious that she didn't really know. "Sandy says Katie was a gray witch, but not a powerful one, not even measured by white witch standards. And Sandy said that the room felt *wrong*. She's sensitive to things like that."

Stefan could have taken a witch from a locked room. Or Marsilia. I didn't like that thought one little bit. "When was this again?"

"Saturday," she said. "Or at least sometime between Friday night and Saturday late afternoon."

Friday night something odd had gone on at the seethe. On Saturday, Wulfe had brought me the girdle.

"You said that there were other witches missing?" Adam asked.

She nodded. "We think that the first was Ruben Gresham. He disappeared a few weeks ago. He was a white witch with a little more power than most men, from an old family that has a reputation for producing a few male witches every generation. I didn't know him—he vanished before I moved here. He wasn't a member of the coven, exactly, more of a loner. But he had a few contacts there. Maybe he got scared and just left." Her voice grew darker. "We white witches know how to run."

"Yes," I said.

That seemed to be what she needed. When she continued, her voice was steadier. "But if Ruben ran, he left everything behind, told no one, and knocked over his dining room table in the process. That was about four weeks ago. We called his family—one of my group is a cousin of sorts. They came and cleaned out his apartment, but none of them had heard from him. Not that they admitted to, anyway. Probably if it weren't for the other two, no one would have thought much about his disappearance."

"White witches don't file missing persons reports," George said. "If one of their people has reason to run, they don't want to have the police—or anyone else—searching for them."

"He's right," Geena said. "There might be more. These are the ones that no one thought would run. The third witch was Millie Sawyer."

Adam stiffened. "I know her. About eighty years old? Lives in West Richland near the pizza place? Elizaveta brought her in for some work once." He glanced at me. "Back when I was still married to Christy."

"Nearer to ninety according to what I was told," Geena said. "She didn't get out much, but some of my coven would go play bridge with her on Sundays. Two weeks ago, they found her door broken and no sign of Millie. Like Ruben, she didn't seem to have packed up and gone anywhere. Her car was still in the garage."

Adam looked at George. "Those are the three witches who disappeared. You sounded like something else is happening, too."

"Yes." It was Geena who answered. "I don't have a real name for this one. Sarina, she called herself. S-A-R-I-N-A but pronounced like the title. She pretended to be the reincarnation of a Russian Czarina—"

I couldn't help my snort.

Geena smiled briefly. "I'd have been more inclined to believe it if she'd said she was the reincarnation of a chambermaid or cook myself. Anyway, Sarina does—*did*—readings, virtual and in person, in a room she rented in the upstairs of an antiques store in downtown Kennewick owned by another witch."

She wrinkled her nose as if she didn't approve of the store owner.

"On Monday, one of Sarina's regular customers told the store owner, Helena, that the door to the reading room was locked. The owner sent the customer off and went upstairs to check for herself."

Geena pulled out her phone, opened the photo gallery, and handed it to Adam. "Helena—who is a gray witch—texted the leader of our coven, sent her the photos, told her to be careful, and said she was leaving for a while."

I leaned over his shoulder so I could see, too.

There were a series of photos. It took four of them to understand what we were looking at because the photos had been taken too close: a human body sliced up by something sharp. There was a pattern to the cuts, which were evenly spaced, but I couldn't quite see it.

"Why hasn't this been in the news?" asked Adam with a frown.

"No time," George said. "Geena took me by the store. There's a 'Closed until further notice' sign in the window, and the door is bolted. I thought about breaking in, but I called the police instead—about an hour ago."

I raised my eyebrows. George *was* "the police."

He gave me a faint smile. "I called the Kennewick police."

That was an interesting thing for him to do. The more usual thing was for us to cover up crimes we were sure only involved the preternatural community. Those were too dangerous for human law enforcement.

"Was the body still there?" asked Adam.

George nodded. "I was surprised about that."

"Helena must have been seriously spooked to leave the corpse," Geena said. "For a gray witch, a murder victim . . ." She hesitated.

"Christmas and birthday present all in one?" I suggested.

She nodded. "As long as Helena wasn't the killer—and I don't think she was—such a body would be the source of spell components, even if it wasn't fresh enough to supply magical energy."

"Do you mind if I send the photos to myself?" Adam asked, still thumbing the images back and forth.

"No," she said. "Of course. You should have them." She grimaced. "Ugly things."

"I'm putting my number in your contacts, too," Adam said as he tapped on her phone. "Feel free to call me if you need us."

"Us?" she asked.

"The pack," Adam said, handing her back her phone.

"Thank you," George said, putting a hand under Geena's elbow, urging her to her feet. "We'll get to the bottom of it."

"Just the three missing witches?" I asked.

George shrugged. "If you don't count Helena, who ran."

"Do you think they are all related?" Adam asked. "White witches . . ." He looked at Geena and stopped.

"Are prey," she finished for him. "I've heard whispers of others disappearing, not just witches. People with just a bit of magic or fae blood. Some of the weaker fae, even goblins. There are whispers that say that you and the Gray Lords don't really care what happens to us weaker beings. You just want to appease the humans. That the idea of the Tri-Cities as a refuge of safety is just a political sham—or worse, a trap."

Geena raised her chin. "I told George I didn't want to come here. That if you are killing your allies, or letting others kill them, what do you care about some missing witches?"

"Killing our allies?" I asked.

"Geena says Wulfe is missing." George sat back a little.

Encouraged, Geena nodded. "That's what people are saying. They say that when Marsilia confronted you about it, you threatened to kill all the vampires the way you killed the black witches. They say that you already killed Wulfe."

She looked suddenly terrified. I'd be terrified of someone who could kill Wulfe, too. She looked up at George, who sighed.

"*They* say," George said, with a little emphasis on the vague pronoun, "that maybe we killed the Hardesty witches not because they were evil but because they threatened our power. And now we're doing it to the vampires, too. Or at least that's the story Geena's coven has. Is Wulfe missing?"

I exchanged looks with Adam.

"We don't know," Adam said. "But Marsilia told us we needed to find him."

"When did you hear about a confrontation between Marsilia and us?" I asked.

"This morning," Geena said. "I heard she met you at Uncle Mike's."

"I was the first one to leave," said George, half-apologetically and half-irritated.

"The only people who were there when Marsilia showed up

were Uncle Mike, Sherwood, Zack, Adam, and me," I said. "Do you think any of them were on the phone this morning talking about it?"

"The pack knows," Adam said blandly. "I called them myself."

I threw up my hands. "I'm wrong again," I said. "I forgot *you* can't keep your mouth shut."

Adam laughed. "I get your point, though. I didn't talk to anyone this morning. I got in touch with Darryl about two hours ago and gave him the story and told him to make sure it traveled through the pack."

"Whoever is talking," I said, "it's not coming from us."

"*Did* you threaten to kill all the vampires?" asked George, sounding a little too eager.

"No," Adam said. "We're allies. Marsilia asked us to look for Wulfe, and Mercy and I spent the rest of the night doing just that."

"Huh," I said. "Marsilia said we'd be blamed . . . but I didn't quite believe it. It sounds like we really do need to find Wulfe." I glanced at Geena. "And the missing witches. And the missing anyone else."

George's eyes narrowed. "Huh."

"Interesting," Adam said. "I wish this wasn't so interesting."

"I don't believe you are killing witches, having met you," Geena said earnestly to Adam. Women tend to look at my husband with just that expression. George gave me a faint smile.

I was glad I hadn't responded by rolling my eyes, because Geena turned to me next. "You aren't a ruthless killer—you care about people." She made an odd brushing motion, one hand over the other. "My hands do not lie to me about the nature of a person."

"Good to know," I said. I had, in fact, killed people ruthlessly. Or at least without regrets.

"Come," George said. "Let me see you to your car."

"Thank you for your insights," Adam said. "I am sorry that we failed to keep your people safe. We will find out what's going on and stop it. Please, if you find out anything more, let us know. You can call me or George anytime."

She looked at all of us and then nodded her head. "Thank you."

George escorted her to the door. "I'll be right back."

As soon as the door shut, Adam picked up the phone and called Larry and briefly explained what we'd just learned from Geena.

"White witches always go missing," said Larry.

"Yes," Adam agreed. "But that is not usually accompanied by a wave of gossip accusing my pack of making them go missing. There's a dead witch, too." He told Larry about the fortune-teller.

"Our informative witch also said there are rumors about other people going missing, Larry," I said, knowing Larry could hear me. "Goblins, lesser fae. People who don't have anyone to watch their backs."

"Those also tend to use travel as a means to keep themselves safe," Larry grumbled. "Except for the goblins."

He didn't say anything more for a moment.

"She said goblins are going missing?" he asked. "Did she name names?"

"No," Adam replied. "She only had rumors. Are goblins going missing?"

"I hadn't thought so," Larry said. "But there are a couple of my people I haven't heard from in a while. Recluses. If there are missing people, that means we have an enemy who knows our home and our peoples very well."

"It could just be rumor," Adam said. "But I would appreciate it if you could find out."

"Information is my game," agreed Larry, and disconnected.

"I'll have Zack and Ben check into it, too," Adam told me.

Zack knew a lot of the more vulnerable supernatural folk around town. They used him to communicate with us because he wasn't as scary as the rest of the werewolves. Ben was a computer genius, and in his own words minus expletives, if there was a database he couldn't hack, it was because he didn't want to.

George returned in the middle of the call to Zack and waited with me while Adam made the call to Ben.

When Adam finished with Ben, George resumed his seat.

"White witches are perfect victims, aren't they?" He made a face. "Not a surprise to lose a few, not a surprise to have them run away. We don't even bother to look for them when they disappear."

"It's more surprising that Geena's people are talking about the missing witches," Adam agreed, sounding both tired and sad. "They don't usually want to call attention to themselves that way."

George nodded. "Do you remember me getting called away from the gathering last night?"

Adam lifted an eyebrow at the change in subject but nodded.

"It was the grocery store over on Road Sixty-Eight in Pasco," he said. "The smaller one."

"I haven't looked at the news this morning," Adam said. "What happened?"

"It's not on the news yet—though it will break soon," George said. "Some college kid was shopping with his roommates, separated to go to the baking aisle, and disappeared. One of the stocking clerks found the body about fifteen minutes after the last time his friends saw him. The thing is, his body looked an awful lot like the body in the photos Geena had."

"Was he a witch?" I asked.

George shook his head. "Smelled human to me. But I don't think his killer is. Geena's pictures don't show it—but I saw the body. The weapon is some sort of sharp blade, and he swings it like this." George moved his hand in a figure-eight motion. "He cut the body on the cross movements. Left it with crosshatch diagonals with a little roundness on the edges as he came around. I think at least the first four strokes were done as the body fell. Then the killer rolled the body over and finished up. The wounds are very deep, down to the spine."

That's why George had called the police on the dead witch. There was a human involved. He just hadn't wanted to say so in front of Geena.

"A witch Monday," I said. "And a human last night. Pretty quick."

"What else do you know?" asked Adam. "Is the victim connected to Monday's witch?" He rubbed his face. "And are they connected to the missing witches?"

"I don't know. I gave Tony a heads-up about our Pasco murder when I told him about the dead witch." Tony Montenegro was with the Kennewick PD and liaised with various supernatural groups—mostly because he was a friend of mine.

"This," George said, "is going to be a political nightmare for the pack. Especially if someone tells the police about the missing witches."

Adam nodded. "That's for sure. What can you tell us about last night's murder?"

"Not as much as I'd have thought in a place as public as a grocery store. We spent half the night out questioning anyone we could track down who had been at the store. We have some video of the victim, but nothing that shows the killer. The cameras that covered the area the body was found in were off."

"Off?" Adam's business was security. "As in someone switched them off? Who has access to do that?"

"It's a closed system, runs only out of the security office. That office was locked up before the cameras cut out and during the murder. The cameras turned back on while the office was still locked, just before the clerk found the body. It was off for about ten minutes."

"Any suspects?" I asked. "No one saw anything?"

"Sort of." George had a funny look on his face.

"What?" asked Adam.

"Thing is, it is probably a red herring," George said. "But one of the assistant managers went off shift about the same time our victim disappeared. He swears he saw the Harvester walking behind his car as he backed out of his parking place—which was not too far from where the body was found."

"The who?" asked Adam.

"The *Harvester*?" I asked. "You mean like in that movie? Dressed up like a scarecrow wearing a cloak and carrying a sickle?"

"The assistant manager said it was a scythe. Said he was watching his backup camera when somebody dressed like the Harvester walked behind his car. But when he turned to look himself, there was no one there."

"You believe him?" asked Adam.

George made a thoughtful humming sound. "The employee parking lot is big, well lit, and, at that time of night, mostly empty. We have the incident partially on camera. He definitely hits the brakes hard and stops for a bit before backing out. The security camera doesn't have a good view of the area behind his car, though—it's black-and-white and a bit grainy. The shadows around the back of the car were too dark. There might have been movement or maybe not."

"The grocery store on Road Sixty-Eight," I said. "Isn't there a movie theater right around there?"

George nodded. "And they were having a special showing of *The Harvester*. It had just let out. Theater manager said a number of people came dressed as the Harvester."

Adam exchanged a grim look with me. Jesse, Izzy, and Tad had gone to *The Harvester* last night. There were other theaters in town, but that one was their usual choice.

George said, "I have permission to take the two of you to the murder site and to the coroner's office to get a look at the body. Thing is, your nose is better than mine, Mercy. You might pick up something."

Magic, he meant.

We'd been getting ready to head to the seethe. I looked at Adam. "We should hit this before we go visiting the seethe," I said.

"After we stop by your shop," Adam said.

I frowned at him. "To do what?"

"You need Zee to look at your feet," he said.

I frowned at him. "There's nothing wrong with my feet."

"Spider?" he asked.

For a minute I couldn't think what he meant. Then a cold chill slid over my skin.

"Yes," I said. "I think we'd better."

8

"WELL NOW," SAID ZEE, CLEANING HIS HANDS WITH the gritty orange soap we used to get tough grease and other substances off. "You stepped on a spider-like half-fae creature and got punctured. And the vampire told you to have me check your feet." He paused. "In a dream."

"It sounds really stupid when you say it like that," I told him, in an irritated voice that was meant to cover up the butterflies in my stomach. I suddenly really, really didn't want him to look at my feet.

He dried his hands off and then looked at me. "I can't help how it sounds, *Liebchen*."

The phone rang, and he gave a hiss of irritation and his eyes flashed with real temper. "I am going to pull that thing out of the wall," he growled. He looked at Adam and lowered his lids in consideration—the expression made him look like a fiend contemplating the next child he was going to eat.

"You," he said, "and you." He looked at Adam and then

George. "Go out and answer the phone. Keep the people who come to bother me—"

"Customers?" said Adam dryly.

Zee brushed that away with a flick of his fingers. "Customers. Pests. *Nenn sie wie Du willst.*"

"Let's call them customers, please," I said. "They pay me so I can pay you."

Zee snorted dismissively and waved his hands at my mate and George. "Go and tell them we are closed for an hour at least."

I waited . . . hoped . . . for Adam to take offense at Zee's tone. Then maybe I could delay Zee examining my feet.

Adam gave me a shrewd look, jerked his head at George—who was the one who looked stung by Zee's attitude. When Adam closed the door behind him, it did have a bit of a snap, but he left me alone with Zee anyway.

And that was good, right? Because I needed Zee to look at my feet. I couldn't figure out why I didn't want him to do it.

"I cannot do this," Zee told me with a frown, "without a payment."

Which was the beginning of negotiations. There were good reasons for the fae to bargain when you asked them for favors. Balance was very important for fae magic, and it ran in their blood and bones the way that the need for success ran in human culture. Despite the shard of hope I felt at his first words, it soon became apparent that Zee was feeling mellow. Or maybe he was worried about my feet, because he didn't bargain very hard.

As payment for his doctoring, he demanded I tell him everything that had happened, starting with my bruised face and ending with me sitting on the cold concrete floor of the shop with my feet in Zee's lap while he sat on the short mechanic's stool.

I'd negotiated so I could leave out the bit about Sherwood because that was pack business and had nothing to do with the mess the vampires were in. I could probably have left out the part about the missing and dead witches—and the dead young man at the grocery store. But Zee was a useful source of information. The more I told him, the better the chances were that if he knew something, he could tell me about it.

"Spiders," said Zee thoughtfully as he ran a grease-darkened finger over the bottom of my foot.

I had been getting more and more uncomfortable, almost jittery. My hands and butt were too cold from the chill concrete. The garage stank of burnt oil, diesel fuel, and rubber—which it always did, but now it made me feel as though I couldn't breathe. The overhead lights were too bright. Mostly, I very much didn't want the old iron-kissed fae to put his hands on my feet. Not at all.

Overcome by a desperate urgency, I pulled one of my feet away, but managed to keep from trying to free the one Zee was holding. Zee's eyebrow went up—and he tightened his hand around the ankle of the foot he still held.

Adam opened the door and stuck his head in the garage bay. "What's wrong?" he said sharply. He must have felt my sudden panic.

"Mercy has been infected by a particularly malicious bit of magic," said Zee clinically. "Next time some fae spider shoves a bit of themselves into her, could you bring her to me right away? It would have been a lot easier to fix right after it happened."

When I jerked my leg, he kept his hold on my ankle without visible effort.

"I think," Zee said thoughtfully, "that you and your comrade should clear out the office, lock the door, and put up the 'Closed' sign. When you are done, both of you come in here. This will take a bit longer than I had assumed."

He glanced toward the front of the garage, and the motors that powered the bay doors switched on. The big doors clanged and shivered and closed me in.

I DIDN'T ACTUALLY SEE MUCH WHILE ZEE WAS WORK-ing on my feet because I spent most of the time facedown on the concrete. George held me down with a knee between my shoulders and both hands wrapped around my wrists, which he held in the small of my back.

It wasn't comfortable at all, the kind of hold that would usu-ally be used on someone Adam felt was really dangerous. But I'd broken free of the first two holds they'd tried. Adam had a leg over the back of my knees and held my feet so I couldn't kick anyone while Zee worked.

"Certain kinds of fae can reproduce this way; several of those share some characteristics with spiders. Though they like to claim that spiders share characteristics with them," Zee said as he worked. "Some of them have bodies covered with fine quills designed to break off inside their victim's flesh."

The foot he worked on burned, and flashes of electric pain shot up my leg and through my spine and wrapped around my forehead like one of those awful contraptions that black-and-white science fiction and horror movies so love. I screamed.

Unfazed, Zee continued talking. "The bits become the equivalent of fertilized eggs. Once that happens, they release a magical contaminate to turn their host into a guardian who will defend them in whatever way possible."

There was a metallic clink. It sounded just like when Zee dropped a nut into a tin pan. I couldn't see what he was doing because George didn't allow me enough freedom to turn my head far enough. I grew convinced that he was breaking off pieces of my feet and what I'd heard was the sound of my discarded bones—now turned to gems by the dangerous old smith.

"If you had waited much longer," Zee said, "we'd have had to find one of the healers to deal with it, and the cost for that would be a lot higher than a story."

"Story?" Adam's voice was rough with the wolf's rage.

"Mercy paid me with the story of what happened last night—except for some pack business, which we both agreed could be private. She told me about the vampires and Stefan, the missing witches and the dead people. I might have a little to add to that." There were several more clinks.

It took him about twenty-five minutes to do my feet. By the time he'd started on my second foot—which apparently had absorbed fewer bits of spider—my determination to stop him at all costs was mostly gone. That allowed me to quit screaming, though by then my throat was raw.

"Better?" Zee asked.

I nodded. "George can get off of me."

"No." Zee's voice was firm. "I'm not done. Stay where you are, George."

On my back George stiffened at Zee's tone, but he didn't say anything. I wondered what had put the old fae in such a foul mood. Now that I was thinking more clearly, it had been odd for Zee to be so abrasive earlier. I had hoped that Adam would take offense—but Zee usually didn't go out of his way to push like that. He liked Adam and understood the role of an Alpha wolf.

The earlier rudeness I could attribute to worry over me. Maybe. But to act that way now was odd. I thought of Izzy's story of Zee rescuing her and the way it had worried me. Most of the time Zee acted like—no. He *was* a grumpy old mechanic who showed his soft heart to very few people. But there was another truth, a Zee who was *more*. An ancient being who was brutal and dangerous, and *that* old fae was capable of serving a father wine in the bejeweled skull of his child.

When Zee finished with me, I was covered in sweat and dirt. My throat hurt and my shoulders were sore. I sported more bruises—though none that would be visible if I wore long sleeves. My wrists weren't even sore, though George had had to hold me hard—the fine balance must be some skill he'd learned as a police officer. Or as a BDSM participant.

Both of my feet were sore—the right one was a lot worse than the left.

"I am glad my corpse isn't going to be giving birth to six-legged spider-thingies," I told Zee, my voice hoarse, which was as close to thanking him as I could get.

We'd agreed on a payment, but thanking him would place me in obligation to him. He wouldn't do anything about it, but he'd worry and lecture.

"You fought the fae in your coyote form," Zee said thoughtfully.

"Yes."

"Let me see your hands," he said.

If Adam hadn't been standing between me and my best exit, if his reactions hadn't been what they were, I might have escaped.

Adam held me wrapped in his arms, trapping my legs between his, while George held the hand Zee wasn't working on.

My hands took longer than my feet had.

When Zee was done, Adam sat on another stool with my sweat-stained, dirt-covered self in his arms. I buried my face in his shoulder and breathed. Letting his scent—he'd broken a sweat, too—remind me that I was myself again. If I had needed a reminder that there were worse things than being linked to a vampire, one that I mostly trusted, this had been it.

"So," said Zee, "I told you that I have an addition to the story Mercy told me. She said the grocer saw the Harvester, the villain in the horror movie, in his rearview mirror?"

That distracted me from my fit of post-terror shakes. Not that Zee had picked out that aspect of the story I'd told him, but that Zee knew the name of a character in a movie. Zee didn't go to movies, and seldom—if ever—watched TV.

"Yes," George said. From his tone of voice, he was still ruffled by Zee's rudeness.

"In the movie, the main character acquired a sickle that turned him into the Harvester."

"Zee?" I asked slowly. "Did you *see* the movie?"

He narrowed his eyes. "What of it?"

"It hasn't actually opened yet," I told him. "Did you see it last night?"

"Yes." His face dared me to make something of it.

"Did you follow Tad?" I asked. Then I held up a hand. "Wait. Izzy said you fixed her car for her." I stared at him. "Did you ensure that her tire would go flat at a time when she would naturally call here?" She hadn't called, though, had she? "Or that Jesse, hearing how close Izzy's car was, would call you to help her?"

He flattened his lips and didn't reply.

I sat up straight on Adam's lap, put my feet on the floor, and then pulled them up again because that had hurt. "Is Izzy in danger from you?"

"Everyone is in danger from me," the old fae snarled.

"Is she in danger from you because she and Tad are dating?" Getting information out of the fae depended upon asking the right questions.

"If she is no threat to my son's well-being," Zee said carefully, "then she has nothing to worry about from me."

We stared at each other.

"There are some things our friendship would not recover from," I told him. "Harming Izzy is one of them."

He angled his head, as if in thought. "I will agree," he said slowly, "to accept your arbitration if she hurts my son."

"You won't do anything to her without talking to me about it," I interpreted. "And if I tell you to leave her alone, you will do so."

He nodded his head abruptly, and I relaxed.

"Unless he dated while he was back East in college, Tad hasn't had a serious girlfriend before," said Adam thoughtfully. "I get where you are coming from."

There was so much sympathy in his voice that I craned my neck around so I could see him.

"You didn't follow Jesse around," I said.

Adam didn't reply.

"I am disappointed in both of you," said George solemnly. Then he ruined it by saying, "Zee, you have great magics at your beck and call and you followed Tad around like a mere mortal. Adam, you have all the spy-tech anyone could ask for, and a whole pack of werewolves to call upon."

"Tech would have been a betrayal," Adam said. "If Jesse'd caught me skulking around, she'd have had my hide. But if she found out I was watching her with cameras . . . she would never trust me again."

I'd been watching Zee's face.

"He caught you," I said, amazed. Thoughtlessly, I put my feet on the ground so I could lean forward, but then pulled them back up again. "Tad caught you when you followed them to the theater."

Zee's face and his whole body stiffened for an instant, then he relaxed and a huge grin lit his face. "That boy is smart like his mama," he said. "I am proud."

And that's why he'd given in when I confronted him about Izzy. Tad knew about the car thing, too. I relaxed further. Zee couldn't do anything to Izzy without Tad finding out. And that made Izzy a whole lot safer.

"You were going to tell us about the Harvester?" I suggested.

"Of course," said Zee, his smile fading. "This is a film about a man possessed by a sickle—which, for some reason I do not understand, they called a scythe."

"We heard about that," Adam commented.

"*Ja, gut*," Zee said. "In the movie, this sickle drives the man to kill—and then to stalk and kill in more and more elaborate ways, *ja*?"

"Okay," I said.

"There was such a sickle," Zee said heavily. "I do not know how it came here, to this place. But about forty years ago, some damned fool boy found it—or was given it. This sickle is sentient—like your walking stick, Mercy. But it is more than that. It conscripts people to its purpose. This boy, he started killing people."

"People?" George asked with a frown.

Zee nodded. "But the victims were carefully chosen. Magic in their blood, but not too much. No one tied with a larger group—no vampires, no black witches, no greater fae. A few lesser fae, goblins, white witches, a weak gray witch, half-bloods of any of the preternatural folk."

"Are you saying that this sickle is sentient enough to make those kinds of calculations?" Adam asked.

"I am telling what happened," said Zee curtly.

"We don't have enough bodies to have a pattern," George said. "A witch, yes. But the second victim is human."

Zee didn't address that directly. "There was a policeman. In those days we hid ourselves, but there are mortals whose eyes are open. They do not try to find mundane explanations for inexplicable things. This policeman was one of those. When he saw bodies slashed to pieces as if someone were harvesting wheat . . . he did not look at them and think a normal human had killed them. His involvement concerned someone who decided to do something about the situation. She had an inkling about what was happening, and so did I come to the Tri-Cities. The sickle was not of my making, but she didn't know that."

Zee shrugged and straightened a few tools on one of the rolling carts, his face casually turned away from the rest of us. I wondered if it was indignation at answering a summons, but I didn't think that he'd have hidden that.

My phone rang.

I dug it out of my pocket, but I was watching Zee and caught a glimpse of his expression.

Avarice was one of the deadly sins, wasn't it?

I glanced at my phone's screen. The caller's number was unavailable. Thinking about what I'd seen on Zee's face, I hit the green button.

"Hello?" I'd called Samuel this morning, looking for information on Sherwood. He hadn't picked up, so I'd left a message. Sometimes his calls registered as unavailable.

"Hello?" I said.

Silence. Telemarketing companies sometimes auto-dialed and ended up with more calls than their people could handle at once. They usually hung up after a few seconds. This one didn't.

I couldn't hear anyone breathing, but I could hear something. Faint whispers of the wind and traffic. Something set the hair on the back of my neck crawling. I knew it wasn't Samuel on the other end. I don't know how or why, but it didn't feel like Samuel.

"Stefan?" I asked.

With a click the call disconnected.

"Mercy?" Adam asked.

I shook my head. Now that I'd disconnected, I couldn't put my finger on why I'd gotten so freaked-out. I flexed my hands and they hurt. I shivered.

"Mercy? Was it Stefan?" Adam's voice centered me.

"It's nothing. Paranoia." I waved my hand, taking in the daylight streaming through the skylights. "It's daytime. Stefan would be asleep—and he's not likely to call me and then not talk." Some vampires could function during the day. Wulfe could. "It was a telemarketer." By then I was able to make the last sentence a truthful one. "Anyone spiked by spider-fae-from-hell gets to be paranoid for a few hours."

"I can find out who it was." Adam took out his own phone and texted.

George grinned. "Are your people illegally hacking into the phone system?" he asked. "Again?"

"You are a cop," Adam said. "How stupid do I look?"

"If you can't find anything, you can give it to me," George offered. "I have friends."

I looked at Zee. "Do you see what I have to put up with? A telemarketer calls and all hell breaks loose."

"I told you what would happen when you started dating an Alpha werewolf," Zee said without sympathy.

The call over–dealt with, George's face grew serious. "How many people died, Zee?" he asked. "When was this? I've served my time on cold cases and attended some serial killer seminars, a couple focusing specifically on the ones who operate or have operated in Washington, and I haven't heard about people being killed with a sickle."

"You would not have heard of this," Zee said. "Most of the victims were never reported—like your disappearing witches. I think there were official reports on three—though those were destroyed. The situation was managed so that nothing was publicized, and the investigating officer was shut down." Zee frowned. "I did not like that part. He was a good man doing a hard job, and the way he was quieted was crude. He quit his job soon after."

"You caught the killer," I said.

"It stopped," Zee told me heavily. "It was not me. The sickle and the boy it had used were left for me. They were left where Uncle Mike could find them, but it was understood by both of us that they were left for me."

"What happened to the sickle?" Adam asked.

"I destroyed it." Zee's lip curled. "It was crude old black craft. Witchcraft." He paused as if reconsidering his opinion. "Effective," he allowed. "But still crude."

"Bodies slashed as if they were harvested wheat," George said. "That's how I'd describe the boy last night. But you destroyed the sickle."

"I destroyed *a* sickle," Zee said. "One that was presented to me as the murder weapon. It was not the sickle I'd come here to find."

A thoughtful silence followed his words.

"I should have heard about them," George said with certainty. "Paperwork or no paperwork, people saw the bodies. Whoever hushed it up did a good job."

"And yet"—Adam's voice was careful—"we have a movie."

"Yes," Zee said. "We have a movie. Based on whatever stories an old policeman told his grandson. Outside of the broad strokes—a killer controlled by a cursed sickle—the movie is completely fictional."

"Huh," I said. "I guess I'm going to have to go to the movies." I looked at Adam. "Date night."

He nodded but didn't look happy about it. Slasher-type horror movies were not healthy fare for a werewolf. Sudden noises, too much tension, and a theater packed with fear-laden people was a recipe for disaster.

"You could take Tad instead," suggested Zee. "When I told him this morning that the story of the Harvester was based on an actual occurrence, he sounded as though he planned on watching it a second time."

"The kid at the grocery store could certainly have been killed with a sickle," George said, not to be distracted by a movie. His phone chimed and he looked at it. "Tony says he's ready to leave the Kennewick crime scene to the forensic people. If we go now, Tony will meet us at the grocery store in Pasco."

I eyed Zee. "How would you like to come with us to look at a crime scene?"

Zee shook his head. "No."

"You are staying here," Adam told me firmly. "Your feet hurt."

WE ALL WENT, OF COURSE.

"Alpha werewolf meets coyote," murmured George gleefully from the back of Adam's SUV as I hopped in. "Fae—"

"Stop," said Zee, climbing in beside him.

George didn't lose his grin, but he quit talking. George was not stupid.

The grocery store was closed.

"We don't want to hinder any investigation," the manager said as he locked the front doors behind us.

He was a solidly built man in his late forties or early fifties, his hair the silvery-wheat color of a platinum blond going gray. He had a rounded, Santa Claus–type face, an impression that was enhanced by a short white beard. He'd given me a sharp look but hadn't said anything.

"You need to find out what happened to that poor boy." He sounded a little fierce.

"Was it you who saw something in your rearview mirror?" Adam asked.

He shook his head. "Nope. That was Andy. Andy Vargas." He paused, keys halfway to his pocket. "Andy isn't someone you'd think would make things up," he said soberly. "He's an honest man, and he was terrified last night." He shrugged. "Today he's mortified and regrets saying anything to anyone. He is convinced it was someone in a costume."

I put my nose to the floor and did a quick sniff around the entrance. There were a lot of scents, nothing that stood out as unusual to me.

"Excuse me," the manager said, a little diffidently, "is that a coyote?"

Adam nodded. "It is. She'll give us a little more insight into what happened."

"You didn't bring one of your—" The manager fumbled to a stop as Adam looked at him. It's uncomfortable for a man used to being in charge to meet someone like Adam.

My mate smiled, and the manager relaxed. "I didn't think you needed any more monsters here," he said.

"You aren't monsters," said the manager unexpectedly. "I live out in West Pasco. Your wolves took down that zombie cow not a hundred yards from my house, and my grandchildren were home visiting."

Adam's head tilted. "Thank you for that. Let's say, I didn't want to scare anyone any more than we had to, then. And she's better for something like this anyway."

"A coyote?" asked the manager.

"Mostly." Adam considered me. "Let's go directly to where

the boy was murdered first. Then see if she can track the killer either backward or forward."

The manager led us directly to the back area and stopped in front of a wide swinging door. "It's just beyond here," he said with a nervous smile. "I'll leave you to it. If you need anything, I'll be up in the offices doing paperwork. Otherwise, when you're done, you can leave via any of the exit doors—they lock automatically."

"Thank you," George said. "We'll be fine."

The manager's sigh of relief as he walked away would probably not have been audible to a normal human. We followed George through the door to the murder scene.

It was, I supposed, exactly what anyone would expect the loading bay of a grocery store to look like. A forklift was parked in one corner next to a stack of orange traffic cones and a bunch of tent-type signs leaning against the wall. The one I could see read *Caution: Wet Floor.*

A bay roll-up door large enough for a semi was flanked by two more doors. On the far side, between the big door and the wall, was a second roll-up door, this one sized for a forklift. The nearer door was a push-bar type with an *Exit* sign overhead. Next to that door, covered with warning signs, was a machine used to flatten cardboard boxes for recycling. I knew that because it was full of flattened cardboard boxes, now drenched in blood.

Fenced off by crime scene tape hung over plastic delineator posts, the forklift, the push-bar door, the nearest walls, and about a ten-foot square of concrete floor were also covered with dried blood. Some of it pooled on the floor, but a lot of it was scattered around in sprays of various heights on walls.

Looking at the blood-spattered area, I recalled Lady Macbeth's line: *Yet who would have thought the old man to have had so much blood in him?* I was a predator and I killed—mostly mice and rabbits. Blood usually didn't bother me. But there was something about the blood spray here that made me feel less like a predator and more like prey.

I'd been with packs of werewolves when they took down elk and once a moose. Both of those had a lot more blood volume than a human-sized body did. And yet . . .

"It's as though whoever did this wanted to spread the mess as far as they possibly could," said Adam. "A lot of this is blood cast from the weapon the killer used. I've seen something like this before, when I went into the jungle with Christiansen a few years ago—"

David Christiansen had been Changed at the same time as Adam. David ran a small group of mercenaries who specialized in rescuing ransom victims.

"We were after a drug lord over there who killed people in particularly gory ways in order to terrify people—his followers as much as his enemies." Adam's eyes drifted high up on the wall. "It worked."

"We've been asked to stay outside of the taped area," George said.

Zee dropped down to squat on his heels in a way that no one who looked as old as Zee did should be able to and examined the room. He tipped his head so he could see the high spatter on the walls.

"Four cuts, you said"—Zee stood up again—"as the body fell." His arm made a different motion than George's had when he'd been describing the killing blows. George had been graceful and quick. Zee's were also quick, but they were jerks back toward himself rather than a fluid figure eight.

"That's not how the body looked." George frowned, watching him. "The cuts are in the front."

"Then the victim was facing away from the killer," said Zee. He frowned at the blood pattern, then nodded. "A sickle is sharp on the inside curve. You used it in a circular sweep, hooking back toward yourself. Assuming the murder weapon is a sickle. But this is not dissimilar from the single kill site I saw before our sickle wielder died." He frowned at the patterns of blood spray. "If we are not looking at a repeat of history, this"—he waved a hand—"could be done with a long knife, I suppose. I could tell you if I saw the body."

"I was planning on taking Adam to see the body," George said.

"I will go also." Zee dusted his hands off, though I had not seen him touch anything. "Mercy, have you found our killer's scent?"

Ah yes, I had a job here, too. Part of the compromise I'd made with Adam was to wear my coyote shape. Thirty-five pounds divided over four feet was easier on my wounds than my human weight on two feet. It hurt for sure, but I wasn't going to let anyone see it. The nice thing about four sore feet is that limping isn't much of an issue.

I put my nose on the ground and tried to find individual trails. The victim's scent was easy—his bodily fluids saturated the loading bay in iron-bound spatters. I didn't know the dead boy's name, but I knew his scent, a thing far more intimate than a spoken name could ever be. I knew what shampoo he used, and I could have picked his antiperspirant out of a lineup.

There was magic here, too.

When I shifted into my coyote form, largely I was still me. But the coyote me had senses that the human me did not. And the coyote processed that information just a little differently. Every once in a while, that caught me by surprise, especially if I was in a kind of place where I didn't usually wear my coyote form.

That's why I thought at first that the weirdness I was sensing was just the coyote in a grocery store for the first time. I'd caught something while we'd been walking back here, but with my nose to the ground—I could taste darkness.

Magic shimmered through the fur on my coat, and something altered about the dead boy's scent. I *knew* who he was. Not his name. His name wasn't important. I knew he'd been impulsive and cheerful. He cared deeply for those around him, but not so much about school or work. I got a fair sense of his fae half—the singed scent told me he was associated with some fire fae. The magical boost I was getting from it told me his mother had been able to fly—and that she was dead.

I was drowning in his scent, in the magic that bloomed in the wake of his death. Magic that sought to become . . .

I was dismally aware that I would remember who this boy was until the day I died. It was so overwhelming that it took me a while to be able to look beyond the victim.

I thought it was something about the way the young man had been killed that had created the magical soup that swamped me. I tried to shake it off and get something about the killer.

Intent on that, I heard a new voice speak quietly. Tony had made it here from the Kennewick crime scene.

I ignored him for the moment, worried that if I took my attention off my job, I'd drown in the swamp of *knowing* and not be able to pull myself out. It took some effort, but I forced the tide of magic back so I could detect something other than the dead boy and his murder.

I found people who worked at the store. I knew that was who they were because their scents were layered over days and weeks. I found the police officers who carried with them the metallic smell of weapons—gunpowder, gun oil. I found forensic people who smelled of chemicals and their nitrile gloves. Despite the darkness that filled my mouth, those scents came to me as scents usually did.

There were bloody footprints that led to the push-bar door, and I tried to scent the killer around them. Police tape meant I couldn't get right on top of them, but that shouldn't have mattered.

The footprints smelled of the blood of the victim. I was going to smell him in my dreams. I almost gave up. Had lifted my head to look at Adam—when I figured it out.

"Mercy?" Adam said.

I ignored him. I closed my eyes because this was ephemeral, this was something that I shouldn't be able to detect. Along the edge of the bloody footprints and the understanding of who the victim was—right on that edge, I felt the abyss.

I had felt it in that vision I'd shared with Stefan and in the one in Stefan's house when I broke through the spiderwebbed spell. I'd forgotten the endless, unfathomable depth of it. It didn't smell of anything and it smelled of everything at the same time. Magic. Madness. As I became aware of it, I could feel it feeding upon the death here, feeding but not consuming.

And I had been able to taste it since I fell through the spiderweb

PATRICIA BRIGGS

of magic and attracted its attention. I should have panicked, but in my coyote form, I was focused on following the not-scent the killer had left.

Adam caught me with a hand over my chest before I blundered past the yellow tape. I floundered a moment with the scent of the abyss in my head—how could I follow it if I couldn't go past the tape? I was aware that my mouth was open and I was panting as if I was in pain as I struggled with Adam.

"Open it," Adam said.

George opened the smaller of the roll-up doors, on the far side of the big bay door, well away from the police tape. Adam set me down and I ran out, hopped down the concrete steps, and bolted to the outside of the door the killer had left by. It, too, was sealed with crime scene tape, but I didn't need to go in through the door.

I caught the scent that wasn't a scent; I caught the *feeling* of the abyss and followed it to the small lot marked *Employee parking*, where it disappeared.

I tried again. Ended up back in the parking lot, where the scent stopped. Not like the killer got into a car or something. But like he vanished.

Like Stefan could vanish.

It didn't smell like Stefan. I put my nose on the ground again to make sure.

I had been raised by werewolves, by monsters. I'd seen monstrous things. I knew what vampires were capable of. Stefan was capable of this. He could kill a young man who'd gone to the store to buy groceries. He was very old, and the ties between us meant he could order me not to recognize his scent—that could be why I couldn't smell the killer except for the taste of the abyss it carried with it.

I thought of the self-loathing in Stefan's voice.

"I'll survive. That's what I do," he'd said. And, "Marsilia and I have given you a game to play."

Stefan could have done this.

I trotted back into the store and followed the victim's scent, because it was easier to track than the abyss. I tracked the young man to the place he'd been taken—in the middle of the flour and spice aisle. I wondered if that had been on purpose, because the overwhelming scent of spice made it very difficult to smell anything else.

Sneezing, I tried to catch the slippery feeling that the abyss had left behind. It was like those optical illusion pictures that became three dimensional when you unfocused your eyes. That wasn't an exact analogy, but it was close.

I followed it. I was so focused that only when I reached the wide door to the back area did I realize I'd caught the trace of the killer taking the victim to where he'd been killed. I broke off, went back to where the victim's scent encountered the abyss, and cast around a bit. Nothing. It was as if the darkness coalesced right there, right where his victim had been taken.

I might believe that whatever had killed here was able to teleport like Stefan and Marsilia. Maybe just like, though the thought made my stomach hurt. But common sense told me that the killer had to have located his prey somehow. Found the right victim and waited until he was alone.

I looked up.

This store wasn't like Costco or some of the other warehouse stores that put in overhead shelving to store merchandise. But the top of the shelf was still pretty high, a couple of feet over head height. Not really out of sight, but there were a lot of magical creatures who could remain unseen if they were still enough. Werewolves could. I was pretty sure vampires could as well.

I hopped onto the top shelf, landing on bags of flour. I trotted along the ridge where the two opposite-facing shelving units met. Nothing.

I leaped to the other side of the aisle—and found the abyss. The killer had waited on the shelving for a while. I could tell because of the depth of the darkness. I backtracked it from that perch and along the top of the shelving—it was dexterous enough to run along a path no more than an inch and a half wide. I had no trouble with it, but I was pretty sure that I couldn't have run it wearing my human form. At the end of the aisle, I dropped to the ground, but the darkness disappeared.

After a moment's consideration, I jumped on top of the next aisle and found it again. It wandered from one unit to the next and finally dropped to the ground near the front entrance. I trailed it almost to the doors before it disappeared again. I looked out the window and thought that something that could teleport might be able to look through the window and show up inside the store.

I didn't know why they hadn't just come through the open door.

. . . *a game* . . .

Or maybe I did.

9

~~~

ADAM

ADAM LED ZEE, GEORGE, AND TONY TO THE BENTON County Coroner's Office, a small building set in the corner of the massive criminal justice center. Technically the grocery store murder victim's body should have gone to the Franklin County Coroner's Office, but Benton County had a specialist for supernatural crimes, so both the boy's body and the witch's body had been taken there.

"You okay?" George asked.

Adam nodded. It was as close to lying as he allowed himself. His wolf was very unhappy leaving Mercy behind in the SUV.

After she'd returned to her human shape, his mate had been unusually quiet and wracked with shivers. Normally he'd have said she was in shock—but normal went out the window when dealing with Mercy. She'd refused his offer to get food for her, and with the others in the car, he hadn't pressed. When she'd proposed that she stay in the car because her feet hurt, he'd trusted her to know best how to take care of herself.

That had been a hard-fought battle. It was his nature, man and beast, to take care of the people around him. When he was courting Mercy, he'd come to the reluctant understanding that taking control of her life—even and maybe especially for her own good—was the opposite of care. Experimentally, he'd applied that understanding to his pack, and he'd seen it become healthier, stronger. Larry the goblin king had not been wrong when he said that Mercy was changing Adam and the pack.

Still, knowing that leaving Mercy when she asked him to was the right thing to do didn't make it any easier.

Before abandoning her in the car, he'd wrapped Mercy in his coat because she was still shivering as if the SUV heater wasn't blowing hot enough to boil water. He'd given her a look to let her know that he expected her to tell him what was going on as soon as she could. She'd nodded. And that unspoken promise had allowed him to shut her door and leave her behind.

Shivering.

There were a lot of reasons that she could be shivering like that. All the easy ones would have been something she could talk about in front of everyone. He frowned darkly.

Neither he nor his wolf was happy with her alone in the SUV. Something more bestial than his wolf stirred to life and brought a growl rising to his lips. He stopped that before it became audible.

Mercy still believed that Elizaveta the witch had called the malformed beast into being. Mercy had thought that when she broke the witch's curse, the evil creature—who only resembled his

wolf as a tank resembled Mercy's beloved and deceased Rabbit—
should have gone away. When it lingered, she had decided it would
just need time to fade.

Adam knew better.

Elizaveta might have given it form, but that beast had been his
for longer than Mercy had been alive, born when a God-fearing
boy, who'd thought the world was mostly a good place peopled
with mostly good folk, met a war in Southeast Asia. Adam had
grown that beast to protect himself and used it to wade through
scenes of such horror that, even though he'd lived as a werewolf
for half a century, the memories still appeared in his worst nightmares. Adam had used the beast to follow orders that no moral
being would have been able to carry out, because he knew that
those orders were the right ones, no matter how horrific.

He had learned to control that monster, when other soldiers
had given in to theirs. He'd killed some of those people—the man
who hunted Vietnamese children after his platoon had been blown
to bits by a shoeshine boy. The colonel who collected fingers.
Adam didn't even remember most of them, because their deaths
had not bothered him and the graveyard in his soul was full to
overflowing with the dead he did regret.

When Adam had first been bitten, controlling his wolf spirit had
not been very difficult for him. He'd been staying on top of a far
worse monster for a few years by then. His time in Vietnam had
ended. He hadn't needed the older, more primal beast, so he stuffed
it in a cage and forgot about it until Elizaveta had freed it once more.

Adam was pretty sure it was here to stay this time. For a moment he flashed back to a night in Mercy's garage when the beast
had taken him by surprise and broken free.

Belief, he reminded himself fiercely, was important. He *could* control his monsters, both of them. And he'd use them to protect his pack, his territory. His mate.

"It is a bad sign when you growl, *ja?*" asked Zee.

"He's good," George said. "Hard to leave that little coyote when she's having a bad time of it. Not like Mercy to stay behind when we go look at bodies. Maybe there's a ghoul just waiting for us to leave her alone." George was behind him, but Adam could hear the baiting grin in his voice. "He's got to think like that. Tough to be the Alpha." George thought Adam could control his monsters, too.

"Not helpful," Adam told him, knowing George would hear the grateful lie in his voice. Having George voice his confidence *was* helpful.

"Not accurate," said Tony firmly. "She's armed. She's dangerous. And she is sitting in the parking lot of the criminal justice center, not in an ancient graveyard in the middle of Transylvania."

Which had been, more or less, the thought that had allowed Adam to leave her when she'd requested it of him.

Adam held the office's door open and waited for the others to go in. George gave him a sympathetic glance as he passed by. George was a reliable wolf; he did as he was asked, made good decisions on his own, and took care of the people around him as best he could. He generally thought a lot more than he talked—which was a good thing for a policeman and a werewolf.

Tony Montenegro . . . Mercy had acquired Tony before Adam had met her. He was quick-witted, adaptable, and—although Adam had never seen him in action—moved like someone who had been in a lot of fights.

Tony'd been an undercover agent. According to Adam's contacts, Tony had been in deep cover a few times, though not in the Tri-Cities. He'd helped to bring down drug traders and a couple of rings of human traffickers. Adam rather thought that Tony probably had his own version of Adam's beast. If so, he carried it well.

Tony was the ideal person to be their liaison with the KPD because Tony knew when to lie and he did it well enough that not even his fellow police officers knew when he was doing it. It was hard to find a liar with personal integrity.

Last to enter was Zee.

That story about the skull cups with jeweled eyes had not surprised Adam. Some of the Gray Lords in the local reservation had been considered gods—and they still walked softly around Zee. The only one who didn't, Uncle Mike, was, in Adam's judgment, the kind of person who ran toward danger rather than away.

Mercy treated Zee like a grumpy old mechanic, and that's who he had become. Belief like that was important when dealing with magic. The longer Zee wore his glamour, his disguise, and the more people believed in that version of the Smith, the more the disguise became real.

Belief was important.

Adam's wolf approved of Zee because he made their mate safer. Adam took great care to treat Zee the same way Mercy did, tried very hard to look at the stringy muscles and thinning hair and see only a tough old man. But he never forgot how dangerous the old iron-kissed fae was.

The interior of the coroner's office was decorated in government cheap and long-wearing. It smelled like death. While a feral part of Adam came to alertness, the coroner, an Indian man in his early fifties, greeted George and Tony like old friends.

"Rahul, Tony and I've brought a couple of extra people," George explained. "This is Zee Adelbertsmiter. Zee, Rahul Amin. We're here to look at Aubrey Worth and Sarina, last name unknown."

Amin gave the old man in the greasy mechanic's overalls a professional smile. He did a pretty good job of professionalism when Adam was introduced, too, making an effort to treat Adam as he would any other visitor. He almost succeeded.

Adam had grown used to being a local celebrity, and he enjoyed the more recent addition of hero status because it meant fewer people were outright afraid of him. Like Mercy's sword— her late sword—the locals viewed him as protection for them and not a dangerous weapon that could backfire. That attitude made everyone a little more safe.

"Dimitri, our specialist, won't be here until tomorrow," the coroner said as he led them through the door into the morgue proper. "So I have to ask you not to touch the bodies."

"Of course," Adam said.

The morgue was dominated by the large refrigeration unit on the wall opposite the door they entered by. The floors and walls were covered with materials chosen for easy cleaning. It could have been the kitchen of a high-end restaurant except for the smells. The whole room had a meat locker scent—fresh meat, old meat, old blood and new. Food.

Once upon a time he would have fought to put that thought to the back of his mind, but he'd accepted that he was a monster, that the wolf did not care what kind of meat he ate. He also was not much bothered by the smell of rotting flesh.

"Who do you want to see first?" Amin asked. "Fair warning, Sarina spent a couple of days at room temperature." He glanced at Zee and Adam. Evidently the police officers were presumed to have stronger stomachs than the civilians.

"It is of no concern," Zee said. "The woman first."

Amin, not having expected the decision from that quarter, glanced around at the others. George nodded at him. With a small shrug, the coroner pulled open a metal drawer.

The room was small for the five of them. Adam fell back, and caught Tony's and George's eyes so they did the same, leaving Zee and the coroner the space around the dead woman.

Her face was unharmed, and from it, Adam judged Sarina the witch to have been a well-preserved sixty. Her sleek black hair was short and sharply defined even after the indignities her body had suffered in dying and afterward. She'd worn her makeup heavy, nearly stage level. A spray of blood droplets scattered across the pallor of the cheek nearest Adam. Her blood-red lipstick was smeared.

The photos George had shown them had been accurate, as far as they went, but had missed the point. Viewing the actual body, it was obvious that though the wounds impacted the front of the woman, the worst of the damage was to the sides. The cuts were deep—the body nearly severed in two places that Adam could see clearly from where he stood.

He'd seen a lot of dead-by-violent-means bodies over the years, enough to form opinions of his own. The weapon had been wielded by someone who was stronger than a human, but it was in need of sharpening because the cuts were ragged. He also thought that the damage done reflected pretty accurately the scenario Zee had demonstrated at the kill site rather than George's original version.

Zee ran his left hand over the body about an inch from her skin, and Adam was pretty sure that if he'd had Mercy's senses, the room would have been filled with magic. As it was, the hair on the back of his neck was standing up. The old fae had a sour look on his face—which was his standard thoughtful expression. Adam was pretty sure Zee had not found anything that surprised him.

Adam wondered if he should warn the coroner that this corpse would be a target of any gray witch who knew about her—though Amin's specialist should be able to tell him that. What could have spooked Helena, the witch who owned the antiques store, so she had not taken the corpse herself? What had scared her?

Like any predator, most gray witches had no problem with squeamishness. She had stopped to take photos. Why hadn't she taken the body? Or parts of the body—the organs were the most useful, and there was no sign that anyone had tried to take the dead witch's heart or liver.

"Zee?" Adam was starting to think he should have insisted on bringing Mercy in, and not because he was worried about leaving her alone. "Could you learn more if you touched the corpse?" As Helena presumably had—before leaving not only the crime scene but the whole city. What had she discovered?

"*Ja*," he said, straightening up. He glanced at the coroner and said, "But we are guests here. I am ready to look at the boy."

The second corpse hit Adam unexpectedly hard. He'd seen a lot of bodies, a lot of death, and nowadays, unless the dead person was someone he knew, he was generally unaffected. But Aubrey Worth was—*had been*—Jesse's age.

While his daughter had been half a block away watching a movie, someone had ripped Aubrey's flesh open, spilling his life onto a polished cement floor. He'd had plans, people he loved who loved him back. Now there would be a hole in the world where his life had previously fit.

They would find his killer and make sure that no more people died before their time. Adam made himself think about something else before his wolf decided to show itself.

The coroner must have figured out that Zee was scary while Adam was distracted. Or maybe he'd added two and two and gotten five when Adam asked Zee about touching the body. Whatever the reason, Amin had quit trying to make conversation and moved a few steps closer to Tony and George, without abandoning his post near the drawer. He looked a little protective of his dead charges, as if he was fighting not to put himself between Zee and Aubrey Worth's corpse.

Zee began by treating the young man's body the same as he had the first. But when he was done using his hands, he put his face quite close to the body. Amin looked as though he was going to protest—but Tony put a hand on his arm. Not restraint, exactly, but requesting cooperation.

Ignoring the silent argument, Zee closed his eyes and inhaled. Adam knew about scenting things. Sometimes holding the air in your lungs for a couple of seconds and then letting the air back out through your nose gave you a different take on subtle scents. He didn't think that the old fae's nose was as good as a werewolf's, but he could have been wrong.

He was watching quite closely, so he saw the moment Zee froze. The old fae's eyes opened, but Adam had the impression he wasn't looking at anything. Zee's eyes were usually some intermittent shade between blue and gray, but now they were the color of a shimmering silver blade, with neither pupil nor white in evidence, and the air in the morgue acquired the sharp scent of ozone and potential danger.

Zee closed his eyes again and took in another breath. When he straightened at last and opened his eyes, they looked stormy but human. Then he frowned slightly and turned to Adam.

"I think that we could use Mercy's nose here," he said, sounding utterly like himself.

In front of the others, the old fae would never say, "Mercy can smell some kinds of magic better than I can." But Adam was sure that was what he meant.

Adam nodded. "I'll ask her."

Zee looked like a battered old mechanic again, hands in pockets, and thoughtful. But the air still smelled of ozone, and Adam's skin twitched as he turned his back on the iron-kissed fae.

ADAM FOUND MERCY STILL HUDDLED IN HIS COAT. Her face was tucked down into the fabric until only the top of her head stuck out.

He said her name before he tapped on her window to get her attention, so he wouldn't startle her. She jumped a little anyway— a sign of how tense she still was. When he opened the door, the heat boiled out of the car, though he could hear her chattering teeth.

Since no one was watching, he unclipped her seat belt and pulled her against him, holding her the way he'd wanted to for the past hour. She snuggled against him. After a bit, her shivers died down.

He spared a thought for George and the humans trapped in

the morgue with an unhappy fae. But this was more important—and he trusted Zee not to take out his temper on innocents with any more deadly weapon than a few sharp words. Probably that king's children whose skulls had been turned into cups had not been innocents.

"I needed that," Mercy said, her voice muffled in the folds of his coat. "Thank you."

"Do you want to tell me what's wrong?" he asked.

A car turned into the parking lot, but the driver didn't turn her head to look at them. This mostly empty corner of the lot was a fair distance from the justice center; doubtless she was looking for a closer parking place.

Against his neck, Mercy whispered, "The killer didn't have a scent."

She sounded thoroughly spooked.

"He's using some sort of magic that shields his scent?" Adam speculated. "But you followed him anyway." He wasn't doubting her assertion—he hadn't been able to pick up the killer's scent himself. But he knew what a hunt looked like, and she'd been on a trail.

She nodded her head and said with obvious reluctance, "This is going to sound stupid."

He waited.

She sighed. "So when I broke through the spider's spell web, I told you I saw a great dark abyss, right? And it was there again in my dream with Stefan. He didn't know where it came from."

He kissed the top of her head.

In a small voice she said, "I think I brought it with me. I think it sunk its jaws into me when I broke through the spider-thing's web, and it's been with me ever since."

"Do you think it's connected to the spines that Zee took out of your hands and feet?" he asked.

She considered it but shook her head. "No. It was somehow connected to the second spider-thing, the one in the basement, I think."

"Okay," he said. "How does that tie into the fact that the killer had no scent? Just so you know, I couldn't scent him, either. My nose isn't as good when I'm not the wolf, but I should have been able to pick up the killer's scent when I was standing right next to his bloody footprints."

She hesitated. "I worked out a theory while you were in the morgue. It's pretty far-fetched."

"Hit me," he said.

"I tracked that killer by feeling the abyss," she said. "It wasn't really a scent, but it was a trace of something sort of like magic." She paused and said, "I really need to talk to Zee about that, because there was something weird going on with magic at that scene."

"He wants to talk to you, too," Adam said. "But go back to the abyss that you think has its claws sunk into you—and is also tied to the murder of that boy."

She shrugged. "I told you it was weird. *Is* weird. I don't know how to describe it. It's something with will and power and—" Her voice tightened. She didn't finish that thought. "What I was following, the killer's trail, was a trace it left behind."

"Zee told us that the sickle—the one he came here looking for—was sentient," Adam commented. "What if what you are feeling is that sickle?"

She nodded. "Someone is using it to kill people. Someone

without a scent—but because I have this tie to the abyss, the sickle, I could follow it."

"Your instincts are pretty good," he said.

He did not doubt for a minute she was correct. Her magic, a gift of Coyote, was exactly like any gift a trickster god might bequeath—irrational, chaotic, and only sometimes useful. But Mercy was adept at sussing out how to deal with it using instincts and intellect.

She was also good at throwing herself into danger, following where her magic led her. An image of the dead woman's ruined body flashed in his mind. That would not happen to Mercy. He wouldn't let it.

"You believe me?"

"I do," he told her.

"Okay," she said. Then her body stiffened a little as though she was forcing herself to talk. "I think that the murderer might be Stefan."

"Why?"

Like Adam, Stefan was a killer. But there was a reason his name in the vampire world was the Soldier. Like Adam, by preference, Stefan's kills were neat and quick. The kind of theatrics at play here didn't feel like Stefan, even if he were wielding an artifact.

An artifact that Zee had told them could control its wielder. Stefan was old and powerful. Adam had a hard time believing an artifact could control him.

"Because I trailed the killer," Mercy said. "He appeared, just appeared, in the store. Then disappeared in the back lot. He didn't get in a car—there's a feel to the trace when a door closes."

Adam knew what she meant. Since he hadn't been able to

sense the killer, he didn't know how what happened to scent when someone got into a car translated to whatever Mercy had sensed. But he trusted her judgment that whatever and whoever the murderer was, he had disappeared in the same way that he had come. And that sounded like something Stefan could do—Stefan and Marsilia, Stefan's maker.

"Could it have been Marsilia?"

"There wasn't a scent," Mercy said. "Stefan could tell me not to recognize his scent."

"He couldn't have told me," Adam reminded her. "I couldn't scent the killer, either. Marsilia can teleport, too."

"After he'd killed—" She hesitated. "After he or she killed the boy—" She paused again.

"Aubrey Worth."

She sighed and bounced her head against the side of his jaw gently. "I didn't want to know that. I didn't want his name."

"After he or she killed the boy . . . ?" Adam asked, since she didn't seem inclined to finish her thought. When she still didn't say anything, he said, "Maybe the sickle makes it so we can't scent its wielder."

She made a frustrated noise.

"Once you add magic in, it's hard to know how to limit it," Adam observed sympathetically.

"It was magic—or rather there was a lot of magic all over." She let out an irritated huff of breath, sounding, for the first time, almost normal.

She got like that when she was trying to explain magic with words when all she had were feelings. Especially since, as a female mechanic, she was leery about explaining things that might be called into question without empirical evidence—even to

Adam. The more "woo-woo" (her words) something was, the more defensive she got.

"I'd like to talk a bit to Zee about what I think I felt there. What he thinks it all means. When that boy—" Her voice broke off. "Okay, okay."

She sucked in a breath, gave an irritated growl, and wiggled to put some space between them. When she was done, she was sitting sideways in her seat as if ready to get out of the SUV. He stepped back against the open door so she could get out if she wanted to— and to give her space, which is what he thought she really needed.

He wasn't hurt. He'd been expecting her physical withdrawal as soon as her shivering lessened. Mercy wasn't much given to public displays of affection—still less if they were driven by a need for comfort. She didn't lightly reveal weakness—he understood that entirely.

She waved her hands as if in surrender. "Okay. Okay," she said again. "It helps if I talk through this. I'm sorry if it's too woo-woo."

"No problem," he said.

She gave him a suspicious look, but evidently he was successful in hiding his amusement at her discomfort, because she started talking. "When *Aubrey* died, there was some sort of explosion of magic, too. I could feel the remnants of it. It felt as if the blood on the floor was still connected to the killer in some way. I could trace that feeling both ways."

"To Aubrey and to the killer," Adam said, not liking the way that sounded.

She nodded, and her body gave a convulsive shiver. Her eyebrows rose a bit, and she took another deep breath. She met his eyes.

"I think I could track that magic because it's attached to me, too. A sort of awful three-way tie." She glanced in the backseat, and her face tightened.

"Company?" Adam asked. He'd gotten used to that aspect of her power. "I can't tell."

He could sometimes sense the ghosts—even see them, as he'd seen the boy in Stefan's house. But if he could, it was a bad thing. Whenever he walked into Mercy's old house, he felt like a long-tailed cat in a room full of rocking chairs.

She nodded, a flicker of relief crossing her face. He couldn't tell if she was relieved that the ghost was weak enough he couldn't perceive it, or if she was relieved that she didn't have to talk about it and risk making it stronger. He could make an educated guess about who the ghost was.

"That magical connection gave me insights into the boy"—she grimaced and twitched her shoulder as if someone had prodded her—"into *Aubrey* that I don't normally get. Sort of a spiritual equivalent of the scent of a person. You know how a good sniff can tell you what shampoo they use, if their car has leather upholstery, how many cats claim them?"

Adam nodded.

"Well, I can tell you that our victim was not too bright but sweet as they come. He was half in love with one of his roommates and half in love with a cute girl in one of his study groups that so far he had been too shy to speak to. He loved bubble tea and sushi. Someday he wanted to visit Japan. He was good at math but had no business being enrolled in computer science."

That evidently got some sort of reaction from the ghost because Mercy scowled over her shoulder before catching herself. She rubbed her hands over her face and slid out of the car. She stiffened just a little but otherwise covered up the fact that her feet were still sore. She moved into Adam and let her forehead fall forward until it rested on his chest.

"Makes it feel like you lost a friend instead of a stranger," Adam said gently, rubbing her arms. He made a point of not looking in the backseat, where he was pretty sure Aubrey's ghost was sitting.

She nodded. Silence fell between them, and he was content with that.

After too short of a time, Mercy said, "Why are you out here without the rest of them?"

"Zee sent me out to see if you would come in. He wants you to look at the bodies. Something he figured out in there made him pretty upset." Adam considered his memory of Zee's face. "Angry, I think."

Both of her eyebrows shot up. "He wants me to do what? Since when am *I* an expert on dead bodies?" She pursed her lips to disguise her smile as she continued in an appalled tone. "And you kept them waiting in the morgue while I chatter on about stupid woo-woo stuff? When Zee is angry?"

"They'll wait," he said.

She snorted and clambered back into the SUV to turn it off. She locked it, handed his keys to him, and set off for the coroner's office, limping.

"Do you want to go coyote?" he asked, following her closely. He didn't ask if he could carry her in; he wasn't stupid.

She shook her head. "I can't talk that way. If Zee needs the coyote's help, I'm sure there's a bathroom I can change in so I don't shock anyone."

She stopped abruptly. Tensed. Adam looked around, but he couldn't see anything to cause her reaction.

"Okay," she muttered to herself. Then she turned and looked at someone standing on his right—Aubrey's ghost, he presumed.

"Look," she said. "You need to go. Go into the light or whatever." Pause. "I don't know what light. There's supposed to be a light. Or a path." Pause. "Look, I don't have a freaking manual. I don't know what to do—but I think that you should." Pause. "Because most people die and go somewhere. Their souls don't linger around even if their ghosts do. I don't think it's good for you." Much longer pause.

Adam put his hand on her shoulder and his lips to her ear. "Pull on the pack," he said. "On me. Tell him to go."

"What if that just leaves him wandering around somewhere away from me?" she said, her shoulders hunching under his hand.

"You can't help everyone," he told her.

She gave him a look. "The day you take that advice is the day I listen to it from you."

That was fair.

"Can you call someone to help?" he asked. "Your brother, Gary? One of the other walkers?"

She shook her head. "Tad always says that the real cool thing about being half one thing and half another is that no one can figure you out. He was being sarcastic about the 'real cool' part."

"I gathered."

"Even Gary's powers work differently than mine do," she said. She frowned a moment, and Adam felt her draw on the pack bonds—he pushed a little to speed things up.

"Aubrey Alan Worth," she said with the punch of Alpha that let Adam force his pack members to obedience.

Adam hadn't known Aubrey's middle name. He didn't think that anyone had said it aloud in Mercy's hearing, either.

"Your time here is done." Her voice, for all the power she was putting in it, was gentle. "Be at peace."

Adam seldom felt magic—other than the magic inherent in being a werewolf and Alpha of his pack. But Mercy was his mate, he was touching her, and she was using his power to amplify her voice. He felt the weight of her magic—and he felt the backlash as something cold and old and empty pushed back.

She staggered, and for a moment Adam was sure that the only thing keeping her on her feet was his hold. She reached up and grabbed one of his hands with her cold one and held on tight.

"No," she said quickly, her voice soothing. "I see. I see. I understand. You can't go yet. No. Don't panic. We'll fix it. *Calm down.*" That last she put another push of pack magic into.

"Okay," she said. "I understand. But I won't take you into that building because it's not a good place for you. Could you wait by the SUV?"

She waited, then released Adam's hand to stride off toward the coroner's office, muttering, "If I'm going to be haunted for the rest of my life, at least it will be by a sweet boy who takes orders."

"Do you think that's likely?" he asked, keeping his voice down. Whatever had happened had scared her, and she needed to distract herself. It scared him, too, because it hadn't felt like anything a big bad wolf could protect Mercy from.

Mercy started to shrug and then said, "I think that if we can find the killer, we might be able to break whatever is keeping Aubrey here. It's not what Frost did to Peter, but it's the same effect."

Frost had been a vampire who fed off the souls of the dead, keeping his victims tied to their bodies, including one of Adam's wolves. Frost had been a nasty piece of work.

"Okay," he said, putting confidence in his voice. They'd handled every other damned thing that had come their way, including Frost. They'd handle this one, too. Hopefully.

"I don't know what I'm talking about," she reminded him. "I wish there were a Haynes or Chilton repair manual on how I work."

"You'll figure it out," he assured her earnestly.

She turned to him, eyes alight with ire—and then frowned. "Quit baiting me."

He grinned. Unable to help himself. What a gift she was.

MERCY SNIFFED AGAIN. LIKE ZEE HAD BEEN, SHE WAS careful not to touch the boy's body. Her brows were drawn in puzzlement, and she tilted her head as if trying to catch some faint sound. Abruptly, she stiffened and closed her eyes, and Adam felt her draw upon the pack—not for power but as an anchor. Instinctively, he stepped forward and reached out to touch her.

Zee got in his way. Had it been anyone else in the room, Adam would have knocked them aside. But Zee was protective of Mercy, and he knew magic. If he didn't think Adam should touch her, Adam had to trust his judgment. He didn't have to like it, though.

"You know something of their deaths," said Amin, watching Mercy. "Is there anything that I should tell Dimitri to be careful of during the autopsy?"

Mercy straightened, shivered, and looked at the coroner. "I think that you should put off the autopsies as long as possible. You aren't going to learn anything helpful that points to this killer," she said. "And . . ." She glanced at Zee.

The fae's anger had not eased at all while Adam was gone. It gathered around Zee like the moment before lightning struck and felt a lot bigger than it had when Adam went to get Mercy. The awareness of the danger slid down Adam's spine, and the smell of iron-rich battle fury brushed his nose like a future memory.

Adam was pretty sure Mercy could feel it—she just wasn't moved by it. Growing up in the Marrok's pack of crazies had left Mercy pretty unimpressed by temper.

George had put himself between the fae and the other two, which told Adam that George knew what was going on. But Tony and the coroner weren't plastered against the wall and shaking with fear, so he figured they had no clue. That was probably just as well.

"Probably it would be safe enough," Zee said, sounding cool as a cucumber. "But only probably."

"It's our job," Amin said. He waved a hand at the refrigeration unit. "They are our charges. Dimitri's and mine."

"Could you give us a week?" Mercy asked. "We don't really know what's going on yet. If you could give us some time, we will know more."

"Do you know who the killer is?" he asked.

"We know what killed them," answered Zee. "The other question may be less interesting than you think."

Amin shook his head. "We take care of them," he told them. "'Probably safe' is good enough. Let me know if you find out 'definitely not safe'; otherwise, we will follow procedure."

AT ZEE'S REQUEST THEY STOPPED AT THE CEMETERY off the Bypass Highway that separated the Yakima River from Richland. He hadn't said why, and no one in the SUV was stupid enough to ask. Tony was pretty sharp. He had caught on that there was something wrong. Probably from the way everyone but Mercy was treating Zee.

Zee directed them through the maze of well-tended gravel drives before he had them stop. Then he took Mercy and made the rest of them wait at the SUV.

"I hate this," Tony muttered, watching the old man and Mercy traipse between the stone markers inset to make maintaining the grounds easier.

"I don't much like graveyards myself," admitted George, leaning against the SUV in a way that boded ill for the paint job.

Adam thought about objecting, but scratches were not what brought the resale value of his vehicles down. It had been a few years since he'd actually had one survive long enough to be traded in or sold.

"Graveyards are fine." Tony tossed George an irritated look. He glanced over at the manicured grounds, green even in the late autumn chill. "Well, not fine. And this is a cemetery. Graveyards are next to churches. What I hate is knowing fuck all about what is going on while bodies are falling around me." He frowned at Adam, as if Adam knew what was going on and was keeping it from him.

"You didn't spend any time in the military, did you?" asked George wryly.

Adam felt his own lips twist. George's time in the military had been during World War I, but some things did not change.

Zee and Mercy had stopped by a grave. Mercy sat down cross-legged on the grass and put her hand on a gravestone. Huh. Zee had said that Mercy had a better nose for magic than he did. And

Mercy's magic, nose driven or not, worked better with the dead. Not that she was happy about that.

Adam pulled out his phone and checked. This cemetery had been in existence since 1956.

"YOU WILL TELL ME WHAT'S GOING ON WHEN YOU know?" asked Tony in a voice that clearly said he didn't expect them to do that.

George shrugged. "You know how it is."

They'd stopped at Mercy's garage, where George and Zee had left their cars. Adam didn't think that Mercy was planning on opening the garage until tomorrow, but she and Zee were fighting with the office door lock, so evidently she and Zee had something planned. Maybe she'd left something inside, but more likely they were going to talk through what they'd found.

Tony's complaint at the cemetery had hit a chord with Adam. How often would knowing just a bit more above his pay grade have resulted in fewer people dying? That was a set greater than none, he thought.

"Tony," Adam said thoughtfully, "just how far do you want to go down this rabbit hole?"

Tony stiffened, giving him a look. "Is that an offer?"

"You have had our backs for a while now," Adam said. "I think it's fair that you know where the bodies are coming from. I think they're"—he nodded toward the door, where Mercy had stepped back and was watching Zee manage the lock—"not sure what's going on. But I will tell you when we have a working theory."

"Catch?"

"You'll have to lie about it to your fellow officers, knowing that ignorance might get them killed—though maybe slower than actually knowing what's going on."

Tony's eyes narrowed. "You think that's new to me? I might not have fought in an organized war, but I've been in the trenches, where it's hard to decide who is friend and who is foe."

"Organized," said George carefully, "war. I haven't been in one of those."

Adam gave a huff of laughter. "Isn't that the truth." He returned to the subject at hand. "There is still a hard limit to what I can let you know. Secrets that aren't mine. I'll share what I can without regard to your safety—but I will impose silence on you about things that outsiders cannot know. That will mean that sometimes when those bodies fall, you will know that it was your silence that let them die. Your silence, and not just mine."

Tony met his gaze and held it long enough that Adam had to put a hold on his wolf.

"Fair offer," Tony said. "Can I think on it?"

"Open offer," Adam agreed. He waited outside until George's car pulled out of the lot.

10

I FOLLOWED ZEE INTO THE GARAGE, WHERE PRESUM-
ably he'd tell me all about what was going on. I felt like I had too
much information and none of it went together. I had a box of
jigsaw pieces, but I felt like I couldn't tell if they all went to one
puzzle or three different ones.

I clutched Adam's coat around me, probably looking like an
idiot. I was tired, sore, and scared—and well beyond caring what
I looked like, or at least caring enough to do anything about it.

Aubrey followed me.

I'd quit talking to him, though it was probably already too
late. I didn't know if my paying attention to him affected Aubrey
anyway because he wasn't a typical ghost; I hadn't really figured
that out before I tried to help him "go into the light" or whatever.
Ghosts are spirit, what's left behind sometimes when people die.
Aubrey was the whole kit and caboodle minus his body—soul
bound to this earth as if he were still alive. And not really without

body, either, though that was dead, all right. But when I'd tried to send him on, I'd felt that the ties that bound him to his body weren't cut the way they should be.

Zee took a seat on one of the short mechanic's stools, the kind on wheels, arms crossed and mouth set. The unhappiness that had begun earlier today and built into anger through the visit to the grocery store, morgue, and cemetery was still with him. Zee could hold on to rage longer than anyone I knew.

"Mercy," he began, but I stopped him.

"Could you wait for Adam?" I asked.

He raised an eyebrow.

Adam couldn't perceive the kind of magic that Zee and I had been wading through all day. I wasn't sure I was getting all of it. What I did get, I hoped I didn't understand what it meant— because what I thought it meant was bad. I had the distinct feeling that Zee's explanation wasn't going to make me feel any better, any less afraid.

I'd had a spider-fae lay thorns or something that had turned into eggs infesting my hands and feet, and those embryonic creatures had taken control of my mind. The spider eggs were going to give me the willies for days once I allowed myself to think about them. I'd waded through the magical and physical leavings of a killer and viewed the bodies he'd left in his wake. If I was going to get more horrible news—and I was pretty sure I was—I wanted Adam to get the horrible news with me.

I raised my chin in response to Zee's eyebrow lift to indicate that I didn't care if Adam added to the discussion or not, I wanted to wait for him. That seemed to amuse Zee—without cooling the rage I could feel radiating off him. He shrugged to indicate that he was fine waiting for Adam even if he thought I was being stupid.

My hands and feet hurt, a dull irritating ache that didn't keep me from pacing. Pacing meant that Aubrey had a harder time trying to invade my personal bubble. As a bonus, as I walked, the minor pain of my feet distracted me from the worst part of my day so far.

The awareness that I was somehow tied to that dark entity hadn't faded like it had after I'd dreamt about it. Maybe if I hadn't tried to send Aubrey to wherever souls go when their bodies die, or maybe if I hadn't examined Aubrey's body, if I hadn't tracked the killer using my ties to that endless darkness—hey, maybe if I hadn't gotten up this morning—I wouldn't be noticing that the taste of darkness in my mouth was strong enough to choke on.

Probably, as Larry the goblin king had not-so-usefully warned me after the fact, it really hadn't been a good idea to use my body to break the spider-fae's web. Something about that surge of aimless magic had made me vulnerable enough for the abyss or whatever it was to connect with me.

I heard Adam open the office door and lock it behind him. That was smart; no need for a customer to come in and overhear us talking about a serial killer.

Adam walked in and I immediately felt better. His air of competence and confidence was contagious. It worked on the pack and it worked on me. With Adam in the room, I knew he would find a path forward that was, at the very least, less stupid than all the other paths forward—no matter how bad the situation was.

Adam glanced at Zee, who might have looked a little ridiculous squatting on the short stool if he hadn't felt so dangerous.

That Adam took note of Zee first told me that he considered Zee a threat. My mate is not stupid.

Adam looked at me—and I caught the moment he saw I was still wearing his coat, indoors where the temperature was fine for shirtsleeves. He met my eyes and smiled. It wasn't amused, that smile. He liked it when I wore his clothes. I went from feeling ridiculous to feeling sexy in one smile.

"Let me start," Adam said, holding up a finger. "Mercy's been tied to some kind of intelligence since she broke the spell web at Stefan's, and it is getting stronger."

"This is true?" Zee turned to me.

I shrugged, glad of the warmth of Adam's coat. "Yes."

"That is not good."

"Agreed," Adam said with a growl. He held up a second finger and said, "At the grocery store, Mercy could tell that that intelligence was tied to the killing of the young man—which means presumably also the witch earlier this week. She thinks this intelligence is feeding off the deaths—and using them."

Zee nodded.

Adam held up a third finger. "The ghost of the boy from last night is following Mercy around, unable to move on because he is being held by that intelligence. I think from your reactions to the bodies in the morgue and because we visited the cemetery afterward that the magic the intelligence is working is also tied to the bodies of its victims."

He held up another finger without waiting for a reaction from either Zee or me. "Fourth." Adam stopped speaking and shook his head. "You have no idea how much this disturbs me. And if I weren't living with Mercy's walking stick, I wouldn't be able to conceive it was possible. *Fourth*, the intelligence Mercy found is the artifact that you, Zee, told us about, the one that killed people forty years ago. The cemetery we stopped at dates back to well before the time when those people were killed. I presume that some of the victims were buried there and you both were checking out their graves. I'd guess you found that those bodies were still bound to souls that should have gone on decades ago. Prisoners, in fact."

He tilted his head and examined Zee's face. "Some damned *thing* controls people, picks out victims, works magic to bind them, and defends that binding. And now it's attached itself to Mercy." Adam's voice roughened with anger on the last bit, but his focus stayed on Zee.

"*Ja*," said Zee. "To be fair, it is a very old thing." He shrugged, the motion making his stool squeak. "And magic applied over time is a strange and powerful force."

"Finally," Adam said, "you're mad as a wet hen because someone pulled the wool over your eyes all those decades ago by slipping you a sloppy ringer when you were hunting a powerful artifact."

"Perceptive for someone who has no feel for magic," said Zee sourly. He considered Adam a moment, then said, "I believe that the intelligence that Mercy is sensing is an artifact known as the *Seelennehmer*."

"The Soul Taker?" I asked, dusting off my rusty German. "Like in the children's prayer?"

Zee looked blank, so Adam recited it for him. I joined him on the last line, remembering that Stefan had quoted that, too. "If I should die before I wake, I pray the Lord my soul to take."

Zee stared at us. "And that is a prayer for children to recite?"

I nodded.

He grimaced. "Charming. Yes. The Soul Taker. Or possibly

the Soul Stealer. *Ja.* I have been hunting this artifact for a long time. Four decades ago I was told that it might be here, and that possibility was the reason I came." He gave Adam a savage smile. "That I *followed orders.*"

"I get you," Adam said.

Zee nodded. "When I came to look, the killer was found dead and I was given a weapon that *could* have been the murder weapon. It is my shame that I did not look beyond my disappointment." He frowned, and for a moment the whole garage smelled of his rage before he quenched it into something colder. "Someone played a game with me."

"They had a second sickle that could have killed people the way Aubrey was killed?" I asked, because that part of the story didn't make sense. "Something just sitting around for them to use when you appeared on the scene?"

"That is why I did not look further," Zee said in an aggrieved tone. "Who would have such a thing? It was inferior to the Soul Taker, but still an artifact that had taken a great deal of time and effort to craft, for all that it was mortal made. A few centuries old, it was valuable in its own way. And, too, a sickle is not a usual weapon to be so crafted. It is far more useful as a farming imple-ment."

Adam grunted, then said, "Convenient that someone produced both a sickle that could have done the job and a dead body who could not be questioned. I presume you are sure that the body was the one who had been doing the killing?"

Zee nodded. "Yes. And I never found out who left them for Uncle Mike to find. I made assumptions, but I didn't push it fur-ther because I wasn't interested in how or why, just in acquiring the Soul Taker."

"You came here to find it," I said. "You thought that the sickle was the wrong one and destroyed it. And you stayed here. Why?"

He paused and his chair squeaked again as he rocked back. "I had been looking for the Soul Taker for a very long time, and creatures as old as I am eventually run out of things that make life interesting. I decided to settle here and wait."

"You've been waiting for forty years to see if an artifact turned up?" I asked.

"It started that way," he said. "Forty years is not a long time, *Liebchen*. I am patient."

Adam pulled over one of our shop stools and bumped my leg with it. "Sit," he said. "You make my feet hurt."

I sat down with a thump.

Adam stepped behind me and put his hands on my shoulders. "We have some unknowns to address," he told us. "It is possible that forty-odd years ago an artifact was found by chance and some clueless kid—" He paused, and Zee nodded.

"He was no one special. An average human teenager before he was taken," Zee said.

"But someone killed him and slipped you a ringer," Adam continued.

I hadn't realized that Zee had calmed down during our discussion until he got angry again.

"Yes," Zee said.

"We don't know who that is," Adam said. "But I am going to assume, based on the evidence that the Soul Taker is active again, that the person who killed that teenager and gave you a replacement sickle is the one who saw to it that the Soul Taker is out killing people again."

Zee nodded. "I agree. And possibly that person is responsible for the last time, too. Before that incident, the Soul Taker was last active three centuries ago in Eastern Europe. Someone brought it from there to here."

"Second unknown person is our current killer," Adam said. "This killer, we think, is not a mundane person." He glanced at me.

"Teleported," I told Zee, making a bouncing gesture with my hand and making pop-pop sounds. "I think it might be Stefan, but something is interfering with my ability to pick up a real scent." I got that out as if it didn't matter to me, but Zee gave me a sharp look and Adam's hands tightened on my shoulders.

"It could be Marsilia," Zee said. I shouldn't have been surprised that he knew she could teleport, but I was. "Or any of their bloodline who got that gift."

"That's what I said," Adam agreed. "But I just can't see either of them giving their minds over to an artifact, no matter how powerful. Vampires have mind magic naturally, and Marsilia and Stefan are old and powerful."

"Agreed," Zee said thoughtfully. "There is the possibility that the Soul Taker is being used without taking over its wielder—but then it is even less likely, because the vampires, more than any of us, do not want bad publicity. They do not want *any* publicity."

I thought about my dreams. "What about torture?" I asked.

Adam caught what I meant immediately. "You mean the way Stefan showed up with gouged-out eyes."

"Torture weakens the will," said Zee, with more confidence than I wanted to see in someone I considered a friend. He nodded slowly. "That might do it, but it would take weeks, if not longer, to break the shields that master vampires can call to protect their minds."

"Could the artifact give someone the ability to teleport?" I asked. "I mean could we be looking at a normal human given magical powers by the artifact?"

Zee shrugged. "If I had ever held the Soul Taker in my own hands, I could tell you. My own weapons can make an unskilled warrior more skilled. Give them strength, endurance, and other things." He frowned. "Other fae artificers have done more, cloaks that make one invisible, or change the wearer into a stag or a horse." He held up a finger, asking us to wait while he thought. Eventually he shook his head. "Giving its wielder more power is not something the stories credit the Soul Taker with. It is possible, but unlikely." Seeing my face, he said, "It is an uncommon gift, but there are fae who can teleport, as well as a few other beings. Uncle Mike will know."

"Okay. Please let me know if he comes up with some possibilities," I said. Then I altered the subject. "Whether it has anything to do with the Soul Taker or not, something is going on with the seethe. Stefan is missing. We are looking for Wulfe, too. And Larry says that all of the vampires in the seethe got into fancy cars and drove away, leaving the seethe empty."

"Larry thinks that Wulfe is shaking things up," Adam said. "I don't disagree with him. If Bonarata weren't in Italy, I'd look to him—though he has used Wulfe to work his mischief before." He shook his head. "But I'm not sure that it is connected with the Soul Taker."

"Except," Zee said softly, looking at me, "that Mercy tells us that the Soul Taker noticed her and attached itself when she broke through the spell woven by the spider-fae at Stefan's house."

I nodded, flexing my hands reflexively.

"There is something about spiders and the Soul Taker," Zee

said. He tapped his forehead. "It is in here somewhere, but I am very old and I think it is an old story. I will think on it some more. There are people who might remember."

"It sounds like we have one problem and not two," said Adam. "I don't think that makes our situation better."

"No," I agreed.

"I am not going to be able to come in here tomorrow, *Liebchen*," Zee said in a total non sequitur. "Either you'll have to work the shop or close it for a day—which is bad for business."

It became obvious that he wasn't going to elaborate until I responded.

I rubbed my face and glanced at Adam.

"We're going to break into the seethe tomorrow," he said. "I've arranged to bring some of our pack with us. 'With us' can be 'with me' if you need to open the shop. If we run into something where we need you, we can always call."

I should go with him. But I was exhausted mentally and physically. The idea of coming to work and doing something I knew how to do was very appealing. At the very least, I was unlikely to have spider-fae lay eggs in my feet if I was taking apart carburetors.

"Mary Jo was going to come with us to the seethe," Adam said. "If you stay here, I'd ask that you keep her with you here for the day."

He met my eyes and waited. This was not an "I want to keep you safe, little woman" request. This was the Alpha of our pack not wanting to let one of his pack members who may or may not have put herself in the sights of a supernatural serial killer work alone in a place where she would predictably be found.

"She can do paperwork." Adam offered up Mary Jo to my least favorite job without evidence of a qualm.

After a few terrible incidents, Mary Jo and I were coming to an odd sort of acceptance of each other. It wasn't quite friendship, though the possibility was there—more a matter of mutual respect.

"You mean I get to torture her?" I asked.

Adam threw back his head and laughed.

"Of course I'm coming with you," I told him. "I'll close the shop for the day." I glanced at Zee. "If we don't take a random day off every once in a while, our customers will think they are in charge."

"*Passt*," said Zee, the satisfaction in his tone conveying the meaning of the German word, which meant I probably wouldn't bother looking it up in the *Langenscheidt's German-English, English-German Dictionary* I kept tucked in a drawer in the office.

"Zee," I said. "We need to talk about the Soul Taker. What it is. What it's doing. And how to render it harmless."

He stared down at his boots. Then he laced his fingers together and stretched them, as if preparing for an arduous task.

"Most artifacts are made with intent," he said. "On purpose rather than by accident. And if so made, most are crafted by the fae."

He reached out a hand and pulled the walking stick, my walking stick, from the air. I had been looking at his hands and couldn't quite pinpoint the moment in which the walking stick had appeared. It felt as if, somehow, the artifact had always been there, in Zee's hands. He turned it as if examining it, letting the artificial lights overhead illuminate the old wood and silver.

He eventually continued, "Humans can also create magical items, but being mortal, most are not concerned with making something that outlives them. The more conscientious mortals are very concerned, in fact, that nothing they make outlasts them so that they do no unintentional harm." His face composed itself into something subtly more gentle, as if thinking about someone specific. "A witch's magic dies when they die, usually. And if not, it fades over time. Humans are rarely able to make true artifacts. There are, outside of the fae and human magic users, few other beings whose magical crafting lends itself into making artifacts."

Everyone in the garage bay knew all of this. My feet hurt. I was very tired. And, I realized, hungry. I should have let Adam get food earlier. Zee was seldom long-winded, I reminded myself. If he was taking time with this, it was because he thought it was important.

"Among the fae, there have never been many who could make even such a minor artifact as this once was."

He tapped the walking stick lightly, then spun it. I would never have suspected that the old fae had the skills of a drum major, but he twirled it so fast it blurred.

Still spinning it, he said, "Ariana"—Samuel's mate—"was one of the best of the makers before she deliberately crippled herself."

He tossed the walking stick up and caught it.

"Lugh."

As he spoke that name, a spark of light twinkled in the worked silver that bound the gray wood of the artifact Lugh had crafted who knew how long ago. Possibly Zee had an idea, but I doubted it. The few very old beings I knew tended not to dwell on the past or count the years.

"An artifact is made—and then *finished*, sealed in its wholeness so it neither gains nor loses magic. Nor can its purpose be changed. Lugh was careless in his later years, though mostly that just meant that his artifacts lost power, became less, and then broke."

He tossed the walking stick at me without warning. I caught it. Or possibly it came to my hand.

"It is not the case that your walking stick was improperly made," Zee said. "Extraordinary things happened to it while it was in your hands to change it. To allow it to change." He looked at me.

"I didn't mean to," I said.

I had done something to the walking stick, a lot of *somethings* that had resulted in the object I held in my hands. I'd used it to kill an immortal monster. I considered that and amended it to multiple immortal monsters—at least one of which might have been considered a god. I'd gifted it to Coyote—which, in retrospect, might not have been the smartest thing I could have done. The walking stick had gained in power, in versatility, and . . . sentience. I didn't know what it could do, or would do, and neither did anyone else.

"Because there is another way for an artifact to be made." Zee's voice was soft. "Worship. Blood. Desperate need—the way that you remade Lugh's walking stick. Other catalysts include time and belief."

He reached into one of the pockets in his overalls and pulled out a small metal object. He threw it at Adam, who caught it easily.

Adam opened his palm and I saw a dull gray metal ring. "Heavier than it should be unless it's made out of lead."

"Iron," Zee told him.

I touched it and pulled my finger back with a hiss. It hadn't hurt exactly, but it left me with a feeling of *wrongness* and *seeking*.

I told Adam, "Give that back to him."

He tossed it back to Zee.

I took Adam's hands in mine and examined them, turning them. I had no idea what I was looking for and didn't find anything, but the palms of my own hands itched. Possibly that was still because I'd had spider eggs dug out of them.

"Go wash," I said. Running water was effective at dispelling magic. It should wash away any taint that foul thing had left behind. "You don't want any of that sticking to you."

He didn't argue or ask what "that" was. As soon as I heard the sound of the faucet in the bathroom being turned on, some of my urgency dissipated—leaving room for anger.

"What were you *thinking*?" I growled. "That isn't something you just toss around as if you'd picked it up at Walmart. And you don't, by God and all his angels, you don't ever throw something like that at my mate."

Behind me Adam laughed. I turned to give him an indignant look to see him drying his hands off with a shop rag. But he was looking at Zee.

"Bran looks like that when she lays into him," he told Zee. "Affronted, but also sort of incredulous and delighted. When was the last time someone yelled at you for a"—and his voice lost its amusement—"dumb stunt?" He let the words ring a moment and said, "Are you going to tell me what that was?"

"Haunted," I said.

"An artifact," Zee answered at the same time.

Zee shrugged. "Haunted might be right. Your mate was in no danger. It takes time to feel its effects, and once it is no longer in skin contact, its magic dissipates."

"I stand by my objection," I said. "I don't care how harmless you think it is. Don't throw cursed objects at my husband."

Zee threw up his hands. "Fine. Fine."

Adam got us back on track. "What would it do if I wore it for longer than five minutes?"

Zee looked at me. "People who wear that ring on a regular basis kill themselves. Eventually."

"Is that like most of the people who have worked with you?" I snapped, and Adam stifled a laugh.

Zee contemplated me sourly.

"If you don't throw dangerous objects at people I love, I won't snap at you again tonight," I offered after a moment.

"Done and done," he said, satisfied. "The ring is a minor artifact."

"Minor or not, that thing is foul." I rubbed my fingers together to rid myself of the feel of corruption. "You just carry something like that around in your pocket?"

Zee raised an eyebrow. "I carry a lot of things around in my pockets," he said in a superior tone. "It is what pockets are for."

Adam's grin flashed, and I said, "Don't encourage him." I turned to Zee. "No one made that ring magic?"

"Correct," Zee said. "It's old—maybe fifteen hundred years. A lot of bad things can happen to people in fifteen hundred years, and enough of those bad things happened to people around that ring that eventually it started carrying those things with it. You called it haunted, Mercy. Maybe that is true. But the ring has a predictable magical effect on anyone wearing it, and after not being on a human hand for nearly two centuries, it has not lost any of its power. Those two things make it an artifact. A naturally occurring artifact, one might say. And because it was *made* without intent, it has changed a lot over the years. The last four people who died wearing it all starved themselves to death. A thousand years from now it might not have any magic at all—or its mere presence might cause everyone in the city to quit eating."

"The sickle that killed Aubrey is something like that ring," I said.

Zee nodded. "It is."

He paused and pursed his lips, pushing his stool back and then forward like a teenager might. I was waiting for him to spin it in circles when he stopped.

"For a very, very long time, whispers of the Soul Taker came to my ears," he said. "The first story I remember hearing was of a blade that turned a child of eight into a warrior who killed the bandits who attacked him. The boy died, and the sickle disappeared for a few hundred years."

I looked at the walking stick in my lap, remembering a battle with a group of fae warriors when the walking stick had used me to fight them. A blue spark danced down the length of the wood, brushing over my fingers with a faint bite on its way to the end that sometimes turned into a blade. It was the same color of spark that Zee had called out of it with Lugh's name.

"You chased after it?" Adam asked.

"It is my habit to find wild-made artifacts, particularly weapons. It is not wise to leave such a thing in ignorant hands because— as you see with the ring—artifacts that have not been properly finished can grow more powerful with age. Being prudent, I find them before they fall into the hands of my enemies."

He smiled, and it was a fierce, chill smile that didn't belong on my friend's face. "But the Soul Taker is different." He closed his hands as if he could feel it in his grasp.

"I think it might be the single most powerful naturally occurring artifact that has ever existed," he said, and the creature in the room with us was the Dark Smith of Drontheim. He was the Smith who turned the skulls of his enemies into drinking cups and turned their eyes to gems.

"You have felt it yourself, haven't you?" He was not addressing Adam, and his voice sent shivers through my bones. "It has a purpose. You can feel the ties that bind the bodies and souls together."

"Yes," I said. Then, unable to help myself, I reached out and grabbed Adam's hand in a hard grip. "And me, too," I told them. "It's got me."

Zee's head gave a funny jerk, he blinked twice, and it was my old friend who sat across from me once more with an expression of grave concern on his face. "*Ja.*"

I took a breath. "I was kind of hoping that you could help me with that one."

Zee shook his head. "My magic is cold and rooted in stone and metal. I do not do bonding of mind and body. I could only just barely sense the connections between the Soul Taker and the dead." He paused, considering. "I don't know any of the fae who might be able to help that I would trust with this. Not as power starved as my people have been."

Adam looked from Zee to me. "What aren't you saying?"

"I am pretty sure," I said apologetically, "that the Soul Taker is preparing a sacrifice."

"I have come to believe that the Soul Taker was forged as an instrument to bring death to honor a god," Zee said. "In the old religions, sacrifice was more usual than not. The sickle, a symbol of harvest, was a common instrument to use."

"You were supposed to disagree with me," I told Zee.

"What god?" Adam asked. He'd moved to stand behind me and put his hands on my shoulders.

Zee shrugged. "*Keine Ahnung.* Perhaps, given that the sickle is a tool of the harvest and the harvest gods were commonly blood-soaked, it was one of those—though I still think there was a connection to spiders." He frowned but shook his head. Evidently the memory was still not coming. "I can say that its magic does not have the feel of any god I have encountered—though I could tell you more if I held it in my hands. When I say that the sickle is very old, I mean just that. It was old on the day I first heard of it. The name of its god is long lost."

"But not the god itself," said Adam.

"Sadly, gods seldom die unless someone kills them," said Zee, who had done so at least once that I knew of.

MY PHONE RANG ON THE WAY HOME.

"Are you going to answer that?" Adam asked.

I looked at the caller ID.

"Unavailable," I told him. "I don't need a warranty to take care of repairs on the van. And no warranty is going to help your SUVs."

He grinned appreciatively. "True. But you might have a twenty-year-old tax bill that you can take care of now—or else the feds will come calling."

"You get more interesting spam calls than I do," I told him.

More seriously he said, "My people couldn't trace the last crank call you got. If it's the same people calling now, I'd like to give them another shot. Why don't you pick it up and see how long you can keep them on the line? If you make it three minutes—"

While he considered rewards, I said, "I get to pick the color of your next SUV."

He snorted. "Do I look stupid? Pick up the call, please."

"Fine," I said and accepted the call.

"Mercy?"

Samuel's voice took me by surprise. I'd almost forgotten I'd asked him to call. Sherwood wasn't precisely the least of our problems, but he was no longer the most immediate one. The SUV slowed momentarily and then resumed its former speed. It was getting dark out, so Adam turned on the lights.

"Hey," I said. "How's Africa?"

"Still a continent," Samuel answered, but his voice was wrong.

I stiffened, moving to the edge of the seat as if I could leap up and help him from half a world away. "Is there something wrong?"

There was a pause.

"Samuel," I said insistently.

"Can't fool you," he said, sounding almost relieved.

"Ariana?"

"She's fine. I'm fine." Those words hung in the air for a moment.

"Liar." I called him out on it. "Do you need something? Is there anything I can do?"

"Or I?" Adam asked. My phone wasn't hooked up through the SUV's sound system, but that didn't matter. "Or the pack? Whatever you need, you know that."

"Thank you, my friends," Samuel said, sounding weary, but

also better somehow. "I think we have it covered for now. You were my second-string but my first-string has the ball."

"Football metaphors aren't like you," I tried.

"You would not believe how competitive a bunch of doctors can get," Samuel said, sounding more like himself. "I've played a lot of football—proper football and not American—this past year."

"Where are you now?" Adam asked.

Africa was a whole giant continent. I never had been able to pin down exactly where Samuel and Ariana were on it. Sometimes he talked about where they'd been last week or last month, but not where they were.

"Middle of a snowstorm," Samuel said. "In more ways than one. I have about three minutes of battery left on my phone, Mercy. What did you need?"

"Snowstorm in Africa?" I asked. Granted it was a whole continent, but when I thought of Africa, I thought of jungles and deserts.

"What did you call me for?" Samuel said.

From the sound of his voice, he was done talking about himself.

"Sherwood's memory came back," I said.

"Hah!" Samuel said, and I could hear his smile. "I told Da he wasn't faking it."

"Did Bran think he was?" I asked.

"You know? I'm not sure. It seemed to irk Da a whole lot, though."

He was sounding more like himself, but there was still an undercurrent of something, a little edge that told me he was in the middle of something desperate. If talking about our mysterious Sherwood gave him some amusement, some respite, then we could talk about Sherwood—for the next three minutes, anyway.

"Just who is he?" I asked.

"I'm not sure I am at liberty to tell you," Samuel said.

"I can tell he's one of you—a Cornick. And he's old."

"Did you ask him?"

"Who was it who told me never to ask old wolves about their pasts?" I asked in return. If Sherwood had intended to tell us who he was, he would have done it.

"Did I do that?" He laughed. The honest amusement made him sound tired.

I exchanged a look with Adam, who was frowning.

"Yes," I said. "If your phone gives up before you tell me, I'm going to sell your Christmas present on eBay and donate the proceeds to—" I tried to think of somewhere he'd hate. "The John Lauren Society." The John Lauren Society was an anti-fae, anti-werewolf, anti-supernatural hate group for the Upper Ten Thousand.

Samuel laughed. "What the hell. He's Da's oldest brother."

I'd finally gotten Samuel to tell me how he and Ariana met. That had taken in a lot of history I hadn't expected to hear about.

"All of Bran's brothers died saving Ariana from her father," I said. "You told me that story."

"He left Grandmother's pack long before that," Samuel said. "His escape was one of the reasons Grandmother came hunting Da. She couldn't find"—he started to say another name and changed his mind—"Sherwood."

I exchanged a look with Adam. What had Bran been thinking to stow his *brother* with us? Had he been protecting us? Protecting Sherwood?

"Look," Samuel said. "Be careful with him. Of him. You know what Charles does for Da?"

"Goes out and kills rogue wolves?" I said.

"And scares the rest into behaving," agreed Samuel. "It's a horrible job, but necessary. Sherwood was my da's bogeyman before Charles was. It's not a job that leaves someone stable and well-adjusted."

"Bran wasn't the Marrok before Charles was his bogeyman," I said.

"Wasn't he?" Samuel sounded amused.

"Sherwood is dangerous," said Adam.

"We are all dangerous," Samuel told him. "He's worse than that." I heard a faint beep. "Love you," said Samuel. "Got to go. Bye."

He hung up before I could say anything more.

"I don't like that," I said.

"If you didn't know Sherwood was dangerous, you haven't been paying attention," Adam said.

"Not that." I waved the issue of Sherwood away for later consideration. "I meant Samuel."

"I know," said Adam gently. "But he's an old wolf, and not stupid. He has backup if he needs it. Sounds like he has Bran involved already."

My phone rang again.

"Samuel?"

The person on the other end of the line didn't say anything. I couldn't hear breathing, but I could hear the faint sound of the wind in some trees. I disconnected.

"Wrong number or something," I told Adam. I had more interesting things to think about than a crank caller. "First-string wouldn't be Bran. Bran's not part of the team. Bran would be . . . I don't know. Coach, maybe. Or the franchise owner. First-string—that's Charles all the way."

"Agreed," Adam said.

I nodded. "Okay, that's good. He'll be okay if Charles has his back."

"And he knows he can come to us," he said.

"And I can check with Charles to make sure that there really isn't anything we can do."

"Yes."

It started to rain. Out of habit I checked the temperature, but we were a few degrees too warm to have to worry about freezing rain. This rain would only get us wet.

"What do you think is so bad that it has Samuel on the run?" I asked, my voice sounding small in my own ears.

"I have no idea," said Adam.

He put his hand on my knee and gave it a squeeze. For absolutely no rational reason at all, that helped.

JESSE AND TAD WERE DOING HOMEWORK ON THE kitchen table when we got home.

"Glad you're alive," Jesse said. "There's pizza in the fridge— we saved you some. Kind of nice just having the three of us plus one in the house. When you put something in the fridge, it doesn't magically disappear."

"Glad you're alive, too," I said with maybe a bit too much emphasis.

Both Tad and Jesse looked up.

"I thought that your death had been indefinitely postponed, Dad." Jesse sounded worried.

"It was," Adam said. "But since we never want boredom to be a thing in this household, today it's Mercy's turn to have a killer on her tail."

Tad and Jesse both looked at me.

"The Harvester is out to get me," I said with perfect truthfulness. Almost perfect truthfulness. "We think."

There was no way to be sure that the Soul Taker was after me just because I was connected to it. But Zee and Adam had both decided that probably I was in its sights, metaphorically speaking.

Jesse rolled her eyes, but Tad, who could hear the truth in my answer—or at least knew a little bit more about the story of the Harvester than he had last night—stiffened. He looked at Adam, who nodded once.

Jesse missed that exchange. She had other things on her mind.

"Dad, you've been to Southeast Asia. Have you been to South Korea?"

"Yes?" he said cautiously.

She narrowed her eyes at him. "How long ago?"

"Ten years?"

She pointed at the seat next to her. "Sit down, right here. I need you. You will be my primary source."

She looked at me and waved her hands. "You. Stepmother. Eat your pizza somewhere else while I quiz your man about the way women were treated ten years ago in South Korea."

With a grin, I loaded a plate with a couple of pieces of kitchen-sink pizza, a third piece with pineapple and what looked like poblano peppers, and started for the back door.

Tad hopped up and opened the door for me. "If you have a killer out hunting you, maybe I should come out with you."

"Don't you have a paper to write?" I asked.

But he was right, I needed to be more careful. When he followed me out the door, I didn't object.

Normally I'd have said our house was the safest place for me to be. But normally there were three or four werewolves here as well as a demon dog. We'd sent them all away.

It was chilly outside, but I'd recovered from my earlier shivers. I'd given Adam back his coat, but I'd kept my own on. Tad only had a sweater on, but he didn't look cold.

Tad and I had worked together for years. I felt no need to make conversation as I walked out to one of the picnic tables and put my plate on top of it.

Rather than use the bench, I climbed onto the table and sat cross-legged, facing the house. Tad sat on the other half of the table, facing the opposite direction—toward the gate to Underhill and also toward my old house, the one he was moving into in a couple of days.

Before I started eating, I took out my phone and looked up "snow in Africa." Apparently the Atlas Mountains in Morocco regularly got dusted in snow. I switched to my weather app. It wouldn't have Aspen Creek on it—or at least it hadn't last time I checked. But Troy, Montana, was close. They had a winter storm warning until Saturday noon. The area expected high winds and snow accumulation up to eighteen inches in the next twenty-four hours, as much as three feet of snow in the mountains.

"You okay?" Tad asked.

"No," I said. "Worried about a friend."

"Anything I can do?"

"Nope," I told him. "Me, neither."

"That sucks," he said.

"For sure."

The pepper on the pizza wasn't poblano but something a lot hotter, though it went with the acid-sweetness of the pineapple in a way I wouldn't have predicted.

I looked up at the moon, which made a C shape, and smiled. A long time ago I'd sat on top of a picnic table while Samuel told me about the science of the moon's phases. I'd told him that the way I could tell a waning moon was that it looked like a cookie monster had bitten into it and left a "C" in its place. I'd sung him the "C Is for Cookie" song. It was the first time he kissed me.

That had been a long time ago. And it had probably been for the best that Bran had put an end to our romance, though I hadn't been grateful at the time. When you're sixteen, sometimes you need the adults in the room to step in.

"You and Izzy okay?" I asked. Tad wasn't sixteen. But he was still pretty young.

"Can't help your other friend so maybe you can help me?" suggested Tad gently.

"Keep my nose out of it?" I asked.

He sighed. "For now. I warned her about Dad, about me, too. But I guess she hadn't listened."

I took another bite of pizza and crunched through a pepper that had been lurking beneath the cheese, spicier than the first. I looked around and realized I hadn't brought out anything to drink.

"I'll get you a water," Tad said, jumping off the table and escaping from our discussion of his love life.

I looked back up at the moon as the door closed behind him.

Then I oh-so-casually let my gaze drift back down to the house again. There was something wrong with the roofline.

As if he had only been waiting for me to notice him, a shape pulled away from the shadows to stand silhouetted against the sky. He walked a few deliberate steps until the faint light of the moon fell on him, so I could see him clearly.

He was dressed in ragged clothing—like a scarecrow, like the Harvester from the movie. There was no question that the resemblance was on purpose. A small part of my brain noted that it might be a good idea if Adam and I actually watched the blasted movie. The rest of me sat with a piece of half-eaten pizza in one hand and didn't move.

Though he was backlit by the moon, I had good night vision. I should have been able to see his face. But, as in the movie poster, all I could see was blackness. It didn't matter. I didn't need to see his face to know who it was.

"Oh no," I said, my throat dry. "No."

He held the Soul Taker in one hand. In my head, I'd seen a shining blade, something worthy of the power it carried. But it wasn't like that at all. The blade was pitted and rough-finished. The handle was wrapped in something that could have been leather—or electrical tape, something dark.

I stood up, as if the extra height would help me pick out details more clearly. I peered into the blankness that was his face and tried to decide if it was a mask. He angled his head, following my motion, obviously returning my attention in a way that felt almost mocking.

He walked toward me, the steep angle of the roof not affecting the grace of his movements.

Tad opened the back door, a glass of water in his hand. His

body stiffened and his eyes looked behind me. He was facing the wrong way to see the Harvester drop down and disappear into the shadows on his way to the ground. I stared at where he'd been for a second, trying to process exactly how he'd disappeared.

"What is that?" said Tilly breathlessly. "Oh, what is that?"

I jumped off the picnic table and turned to face Underhill. Red curling hair hung in a tangled mess nearly to her feet, which were filthy. Usually she appeared in the guise of a child, but tonight she chose to be a teenager, and she was bundled up in a jacket that looked very much like Adam's—exactly like Adam's.

She smiled brilliantly at me, her face alight with greed—an expression I'd seen on Zee's face earlier today. Because of that, when she said, "Usually they are disappointing, don't you think? But that was even better than in the stories. It was so dark and vast. Empty and full at the same time, an abyss that stretches across the universe. Can you get that for me, Coyote's daughter? If you get that for me, I will—" Tad stepped between us, and she broke off, pouting.

"Iron-kissed son," she spat like an annoyed cat. "Have a care."

"Mercy," said Tad, "I think it might be a good idea to finish eating inside."

"Me, too," I said.

"Get *it* for me," Tilly said, "and I'll keep your people safe."

I gathered my food and thought hard. I had to say something, because rudeness was likely to be more dangerous than silence.

"I fear, Tilly, that acquiring such a thing is beyond my abilities," I managed.

Watching her with narrow eyes, Tad walked backward as he escorted me to the house. When I took a quick glance over my shoulder before I went through the door, she was staring up at the roof, her face moonlit and rapt.

Adam was on his feet by the time I got inside.

"Marsilia was right," I told him. "We need to find Wulfe. He's the one who has the Soul Taker."

11

~~~

I DREAMED.

"Why don't you ask our lady how to find him, Stefan?" I muttered to myself, imitating Andre's somewhat prissy tones. "She knows where he is."

I hadn't expected to be wandering around the countryside when a prudent man would be fast asleep, but my lady sometimes had a peculiar sense of humor. It was night, but the full moon and the brilliant stars left plenty of light to see by, even though the path was little more than a game trail at the edge of a field. The air smelled of the memory of the sun, and even the shadows had a friendly feel.

Just when I had started to think I'd gotten the directions wrong, I saw it. A huge old tree, like something out of my *nonno*'s stories, rose above the nearby trees, dominating the woods around it.

Just above eye level, the trunk split into two. In the bench formed between the halves, a youth lounged, eyes closed, with a vielle in one hand and a bow in the other, as if he'd fallen asleep in the middle of playing.

He was clothed all in white. His loose tunic, belted at the waist, hung over hose that were tied at midcalf. Peasant clothing, except that no peasant could have kept white clothing that pristine, and his belt, doubled and redoubled around his narrow waist, was heavily embroidered silk.

The boy's feet, one braced against the trunk half he was not leaning against and the other dangling carelessly, were bare but clean—as if the mud of the fields did not dare cling to his skin.

A glowing waterfall of pale gold hair, backlit by the moon, spilled over his shoulders. It was caught back from his face in dozens of thin braids laced together. His skin was a shade lighter, even, than his hair, unblemished as if he'd never seen the sun nor aged a day past childhood.

Before I could speak and without opening his eyes, he pulled the vielle into position and drew the bow across a pair of strings, producing a strong, dual note. It was a harsh thing, that first note, breaking into the muted sounds of the night. But as he played, the music softened.

I closed my mouth, unwilling to interfere.

Though his face was still, his body rocked with the movement of the bow. The fingers of his left hand danced over the fingerboard of the boxy, ornate instrument, drawing out of it such music as I had never heard, not even in the courts of the princes.

I had come here to thank the healer who had saved me after I put my body between a knife and she whom I served. I had no memory of it, but my friend Andre had described my festering wounds with more detail than I needed. They believed I was dying.

Then my lady brought a healer who had stayed alone with me in my room for two days and nights. When he left, my friends had discovered me sleeping and my wounds clean of infection.

My lady had laughed when I told her I needed to thank my benefactor. But she'd told me where to find him anyway—a strange place to find a strange man, she'd said. She seldom used his name, calling him "*my traveling scholar*" or "my poetic friend." He was a mysterious man who brought her books, told her stories, and taught her mathematics and geography and foreign languages—a man who appeared to no one but her. I had had no idea he was a healer as well.

My friends had seen nothing but a heavily cloaked figure when he'd come. But learned men, in my experience, were old and hoary, possessed of beards and creaky bodies. They were not youthful beauties who played music to the stars with eyes closed and the expression of a man who beheld, behind his closed eyes, the face of God.

"Are you an angel?" I whispered.

A wicked, carnal smile lit his face. He opened his eyes, which were as blue and dark as the ocean deep, and beheld me. His music did not falter as he sat up. Only then did I recognize the belt as a girdle my lady had favored, a gift from one of her wealthy lovers, now wrapped three times around the youth's narrow waist.

"Nor anything like, darling Stefan," my lady's scholar answered in lightly accented but serviceable Italian. "How kind of Marsilia to send me a present."

I WOKE UP, MY MERCY SELF ONCE MORE. THE SCENTS of my home centered me, as did Adam's leg entwined with mine. I told myself that I should have expected to dream of Wulfe under the circumstances.

But I'd dreamed of him through Stefan's eyes, and that wasn't how my dreams usually worked. It hadn't had the sharpness, the feeling that I was present, that a real vision had. But even though tonight's adventure hadn't felt *real*, it felt *true*.

Beside me, Adam rolled over. He was a light sleeper.

"Okay?" he murmured. If I'd been asleep, I could have ignored him.

"Dreaming of Wulfe," I told him, still uneasy in my own skin.

"Oh?" His voice was a low growl that seeped into my bones. "Think I should do something about that?"

I didn't get back to sleep for a while. When I did, sated and limp with pleasure, I dreamed—

—of Wulfe.

"STEFAN, STEFAN!"

The locks on my door rattled with her urgency.

"Marsilia?" I had feared her dead, hoped that she had fled. I stood up, ready to do whatever she needed of me.

She got the door open, and I saw she stood with a guard to either side of her. I wobbled a little as if weakened by my long confinement—which was true enough, so far as it went. I saw them relax as if that weakness meant I was not a threat, which

257

was not true. I was always a threat. I had been a threat when I had been merely human. I had been a threat in the centuries I had served as my lady's daytime servant, caught in the twilight world of fledgling so long as I had been useful there. It would take more than a little starvation to make me less dangerous.

"Get to your rooms," she ordered me urgently. "Get a bag and pack. Do not take time. He has said I may go. I may take you and Andre. We are to be exiled."

It was almost enough to make me thank the God I had long ago abandoned. Then the torchlight fell upon her and I understood the price our lord and master had extracted, and I took my thankfulness back. If we made it out of here, I would be thankful, properly, to *my lady*, who had made it possible. If we did not, I would spend the rest of my life—likely not that long—exacting what vengeance I could.

In the weeks since I had seen her, my lady had gone from rounded health to cadaver thinness. Her hair was limp and dirty, and a red mark ran along the edge of her hairline as if he'd threatened to scalp her. Her face—I did not flinch. I would not flinch.

He liked to damage his playthings, did our lord and master. Her nose was destroyed. In the uncertain light, and beneath the dried gore, I could not tell if he'd just beaten her or actually cut it off. He had written sonnets about her loveliness, this woman he loved. The nose was recent damage, perhaps even a few hours ago. Her eye looked as though the damage was weeks old.

"It is no matter," Marsilia said impatiently, glaring at me through her one good eye. "Stefan, go. Meet me—" She stopped, glancing at her escorts. "You know where he keeps my treasure. Meet me there as quickly as you can. I think I can take that treasure with us."

She didn't say, because there were witnesses, *as long as we leave before he changes his mind*, but I knew our master as well as she did.

My instincts were to abandon my things and accompany her. Where she was going, where her treasure was, was not safe. But she was as dangerous as I, even wounded, and better—those escorting her would never think her so. And I had money and jewels in my rooms, useful for life in exile.

I HEARD THE SCREAMS BEFORE I GOT TO THE LEVEL where the secret dungeons were. There was only one prisoner here, in the secret depths of the palazzo, and he did not scream anymore. Something was wrong.

I dropped my bags and drew the sword that had still been hanging in its proper place in my rooms, as had all my belongings. I hadn't been able to decide if the Lord of Night thought I would just resume my place at his side, or if I was too negligible to draw his attention. Knowing him, it could be both.

I was weakened, but not so weak as a mortal would be, and more skilled than any of the vampires who would have worked down here. As long as the fight was short, I did not doubt that I could prevail once I got there.

The door at the top of the stairs had been ripped off its hinges, but there was a turn at the bottom so I could not see what was going on. It had grown, suddenly, very, very quiet.

"Stefan," said Marsilia, her voice quite calm.

"Yes?"

"Move with care," she said.

I took the stairs in two leaps, but obedient to her wishes, I slowed as I turned the corner. The area was dimly lit by a single flickering torch. Even with my ability to see in the dark, it was hard at first to understand what had happened. There was blood everywhere—both fresh and rotting—but that was to be expected in a torture chamber.

The bodies were less expected—my lord liked to keep his workspaces clear of corpses. Marsilia stood very still next to one of the cages, whose crude wooden door was open.

Like the room, she was covered in blood.

"I opened his door," Marsilia said. "And then he killed everyone but me."

I didn't understand what she meant, and then saw the figure crouched at her feet, dirty hands wound around the bottom of her dress. He did not look like anything so much as an animated skeleton.

Seeing me, he came to alertness with a hiss and flash of blue eyes—the only part of Wulfe that was recognizable at all. I stopped and waited for him to decide what to do about me.

The bloody remains were Marsilia's escorts. I recognized the shape of one man's shoe. They had been vampires and alert—and it had done them no good at all.

"Are you sure it's—" I asked, not because I doubted, but because I didn't want to believe.

"Yes," my lady said.

Wulfe, our clever and flighty friend, had been down here for centuries in Bonarata's loving care, and we had not known it. A chance remark in the bitter fight Marsilia had with Bonarata over the werewolf bitch he'd taken to his bed had sent me hunting. After a dozen false starts, I'd followed some drudge from the kitchens to this secret space.

When this place had belonged to Wulfe, he'd kept his treasures in these rooms—musical instruments, tapestries, a poorly woven basket a child had given to him in exchange for his healing of her mother. Wulfe had been as likely to hoard dried flowers as exquisite jewelry.

I'd gotten only close enough to these rooms to sense him. It had been Marsilia who brought me over, after Wulfe disappeared, but my ties to him were still strong enough for me to feel him when I got close enough.

I was not such a fool as to think I could break him out and escape with him on my own. I'd gone to my lady.

For Wulfe's sake, she'd confronted our dangerous lord, because we both knew that it had to be him banishing us. If it was our idea to leave, he would hunt us to the ends of the earth.

At the sound of my voice, the thing that used to be Wulfe scuttled across the floor on all fours, but no less agile for that. As he approached, the smell of him was indescribably bad. I tried not to look at the most awful parts of his mutilated body. Bodies could be healed with enough time and food. It was his mind, quick and unconventional, that would be harder to restore.

He fastened his fangs in my calf, but only took a taste. He sat at my feet, considering—then scuttled back to Marsilia.

"I expected to find you here," said a familiar voice behind me.

Wulfe disappeared behind Marsilia's skirts with a sound of panic.

Cursing silently because I'd let myself be distracted, I turned and raised my sword in the same movement.

Iacopo Bonarata gave my blade an amused look. "You'll want these," he said with a charming smile and feral eyes. In a careless movement, he tossed my abandoned bags at my feet.

He looked at Marsilia and, for an instant, all expression fell away from his face, and he did not look charming at all. "So it was never the wolf. Or rather it was a different Wulfe." His mask reappeared. "My beautiful, deadly flower, my Bright Dagger, you dare more than I can allow. I will die of sorrow and boredom without you, but it must be done. There are servants above with a carriage that will take you to an estate in France where you will stay." He glanced at Wulfe and then me before turning his face back to Marsilia. "Do not make yourself a threat to me."

"It *was* the wolf," she said, and unlike Bonarata's, her sorrow was real. "Both of the wolves. All of the self-indulgences and the petty cruelties. But it was when I found out about this, about what you had done to *him*, then I knew that the man I loved was no longer inside your skin. Iacopo Bonarata, prince of my heart, would never be capable of this."

I thought she was wrong. Bonarata had been a charming, ruthless, self-involved bastard from the first time I'd met him, and becoming a vampire had not improved matters.

Bonarata's face did not change.

"You can take that," he said with a nod toward Wulfe. "And"— he produced a wadded-up mass of embroidered cloth of gold—"you can keep this, too." He looked down at what was left of the angelic, gifted scholar Wulfe had been. "*It* seemed to be particularly attached. I left it in the cell for the first year or two." He smiled. "A kindness."

Here, I thought, *look at him, Marsilia. Here is the real Bonarata.*

He dropped what he held on top of my bags, and I saw it was the girdle he'd given Marsilia, his mistress, when we all had been human. I think he'd been a monster even then.

Marsilia said, "You tell me this was vengeance? For something he never did, centuries ago? *I* gave him the girdle."

"I did this for you, my Bright Blade," Bonarata said. "A gift of memory. When you betray me, remember it will never be you who suffers." He turned to leave.

"You didn't do this for vengeance," I told him. "Not just for vengeance."

He froze and turned to me, an incredulous look on his face, as if one of his horses had decided to speak. It was my habit to let him think the less of me, to treat me as her servant—which I was. And if he forgot I was dangerous, that was a good thing. But I wasn't going to let her live believing what had been done to Wulfe was her fault.

"You were afraid of him," I said, meeting his eyes.

We stared at each other in that filthy dungeon. But it was Bonarata who turned and walked away.

THIS TIME WHEN I WOKE UP, THE SKY WAS STARTING to lighten, and Adam was showering. I got out of bed, went to the closet, and opened the safe where I'd put the belt—the girdle— Wulfe had left on the bed.

I hadn't really needed to check, because I'd known even while I was dreaming Stefan's memories that the belt Wulfe had worn when Stefan met him for the first time, the belt Bonarata had tossed on top of Stefan's bags, and the belt hanging in my safe were all the same one.

"Morning," Adam called. "I'll make breakfast."

"Thanks," I said. "I'll be down in a minute."

I showered, thinking about Wulfe, about gifts that were not gifts at all. About vengeance and sacrifices.

I dressed in my usual work clothes—jeans and a T-shirt.

Braided my hair and stared at the thin white scar on my cheek that
I'd gotten the last time I'd gone up against a god. I came down the
stairs in time to spot Tad and Jesse headed out the door.

"This is early for you," I said. On Thursdays their classes
didn't usually start until eleven.

"Study group meeting at seven thirty," Jesse said, rolling her
eyes.

I couldn't tell if she was rolling her eyes at the hour, the study
group, or Tad opening the door for her. It could have been any or
all of them.

"Good luck," I said.

Jesse stopped and looked at me. "Don't die," she told me.
"Don't let him die." She poked a finger toward the kitchen.

"Don't die," I returned. "Don't let him die." I poked a finger
toward Tad, who laughed.

Jesse contemplated him, sighed, and said, "Sometimes sacrifices need to be made." Then she stomped out the door.

"Is the sacrifice that you keep me from dying?" I could hear
Tad ask her on the other side of the door in a cheerful voice. "Or
am I the sacrifice to be made for others' safety?"

"Get in the car, Tad," she said. "I hope you and Izzy make up
soon. I don't know if I can stand being around just you for long."

The car doors shut and Jesse's car drove off.

Sometimes sacrifices need to be made.

"HEY, YOU," I SAID TO ADAM AS I ENTERED THE KITCHEN.

"Morning, Sunshine," he answered, handing me a cup of cocoa. "Ready to storm the seethe today?"

I blew on the steaming liquid. "About that—" I faltered to a stop.

Adam waited for me to finish. He would listen to me. He wouldn't tell me that my evidence was ridiculous, even though it was. I tried to think of a way to talk about it that didn't begin with "I had this dream . . ."

When I didn't complete my sentence, Adam let it be. I knew that it was only a temporary stay, though. If I didn't address it, he'd press me on what I'd been going to say.

Turning his attention to the giant omelette he was cooking, he said, "Sherwood did a drive-by on Wulfe's house last night. It's empty with a Realtor's sign in the front. He called the real estate agent this morning, who told Sherwood that it's undergoing renovations and just went on the market on Tuesday. He's going to meet the Realtor there at nine and check it out. Sherwood has a good nose. He'll be able to tell if Wulfe has been there between last Saturday and today."

"Sherwood called the Realtor this morning?" I checked the clock; it was barely seven.

Adam saw my look and nodded. "He told me that the early bird gets the worm."

"He's right," I conceded. "But it was still rude. If I were the Realtor, I'd have told Sherwood to meet me at two in the morning."

Adam smiled, but asked, "What were you going to say about the seethe?"

I'd known he wasn't going to let that pass.

Before I could decide how to answer, the doorbell rang.

Adam pulled the pan off the burner, checked his concealed carry, and waved at me to tell me to stay in the kitchen while he got the door. I wasn't wearing a weapon this morning—and as soon as I had that thought, I noticed the walking stick lying on the kitchen table.

Before Adam got to the door, whoever it was had switched to knocking. I picked up the walking stick as Adam opened the door. I set the artifact down on the counter, where it would be a little less noticeable than on the table, as soon as I heard Larry's voice.

"Adam," he said, sounding pretty intense. "We need to talk."

I don't know if Adam gave a soundless invitation, but he certainly didn't say anything before the firm quick steps of someone wearing hard-soled boots heralded Larry striding into the kitchen. I blinked at him.

Gone was the nearly naked, barbarian goblin. Or the good-old-boy goblin. Today Larry was dressed like an upscale Texas businessman who wanted to be a cowboy, in gray boots made of some exotic skin. His western-cut shirt and jeans had to be bespoke to fit him that well. The only thing missing was a hat.

When I was growing up in Montana, we sniggered at people who wore clothes like that. Most of the time. But sometimes you could tell that the person wearing the expensive want-to-be-a-cowboy garb had really spent a lot of hours on a horse. Larry wore them in a way that made me confident that, unlike a certain Montana politician, if he were wearing a cowboy hat, he'd have known which way to put it on.

Ignoring my surprise at his appearance, Larry thumped a copy of the local newspaper down on the table without bothering to greet me. "Have you seen this?"

"Not yet," Adam told him, picking it up to look.

A couple of months back, our last paper-delivery person met

Joel in his tibicena form and refused to come back, which was fair. I didn't know what the newspaper paid its delivery staff, but it wasn't enough to brave a volcano god's demon dog.

I stepped in close to Adam so I could see the newspaper, too. The headline read *15 People Gone Missing. Where Is the Pack?* They'd used a picture of Adam in one of his dark suits with Warren in wolf form. The photo, I knew, had been taken at a recent training exercise Adam had conducted with the emergency response people in the hope that humans who had repeatedly been exposed to werewolves would be less likely to shoot them when the wolves were trying to help out. But the shot, with the river in the background, made Adam look like a playboy. Or maybe a wealthy but dangerous criminal. It was a hazard of his looks.

To save time, I read the first line and the last line of the article, just like one of my old college professors had taught me. Our local reporter sounded shaken, I thought, and honestly concerned that we had too much on our plate—that we couldn't keep the city safe.

I checked the byline, but I was pretty sure who'd written it because I recognized her style. Tamra Chin was young but sharp. She was a good journalist, and she'd done a few pieces on the pack.

"Bingo," I muttered, and both Adam and Larry looked at me. I said, "Marsilia warned us this was coming." I thought, *motivation, motivation, motivation.* "Public distrust to undermine our pack's position as protectors."

Larry nodded at the paper. "This is my fault. After you called me, I sent my people out to search and ask questions. As you see, we found a few more missing people than George did. All of these fit your criteria—connected to the supernatural, but not powerful themselves or associated with powerful groups. For comparison, we had three people who disappeared between January and July. About what I would expect, given the mobile nature of our more vulnerable people." He wasn't just speaking of the goblins. He was talking about the people who lived in our territory. He wouldn't have done that last week. He was taking his offer of friendship seriously.

"No one went missing in August," he continued. "Ten people disappeared the last two weeks of September and five more this month."

Adam hissed through his teeth. "That's a lot of bodies to dispose of," he said. "Or people to stash."

Larry jerked his head in agreement. "Bodies, I'd think. They weren't interesting enough for anyone to go to the bother of keeping them prisoners."

He pulled a piece of paper out of his pocket and put it on the table. On it was a neat list of names, designations (things like "witch" or "half-blood fae"), dates (presumably the dates they disappeared), and how they vanished. "This is in time order," he said.

"It's your fault the newspaper got the story so fast?" I asked as Adam began reading through the list.

Larry nodded. "One of the goblins I set out searching is no friend of the fae. When she found out the numbers of people missing, she decided you were sacrificing those people to the fae or the witches or the vampires to maintain the safety of the Tri-Cities."

"Sacrificing?" I murmured.

He glanced at me. "That's the word she used. She took the names with her to a friend at the newspaper." He grimaced. "At least her friend is more restrained. The article doesn't accuse you of being the reason the people are missing—just not doing the job you claimed to be able to do."

We had been, I thought, lucky that it had been Ms. Chin doing the piece.

"If fifteen people were snatched under our noses before we figured out something is going on, we aren't doing our jobs," said Adam.

"You don't seem upset about the article." Larry looked inscrutable. "Just the missing people."

"Publicity is pretty far down the list," I said.

"Publicity sparks mobs," Larry said.

"We need to deal with whoever is taking our people first," Adam said. "Then we can manage publicity."

Larry nodded. "All right. All right. I agree." He looked at me. "You said Marsilia warned you. But I thought she told you that you needed to find Wulfe before people started to mistrust you. Not that you needed to find out who is making the vulnerable members of our community disappear."

"I told you about the witch who was killed on Monday," Adam said. "The boy at the grocery store Tuesday night—Wednesday morning—was a half-blood fae."

Aubrey hadn't made the news yet, but Larry would know about his murder. Larry's people traded in information. I think Adam was going to tell Larry that we knew Wulfe was the killer—and that was why Marsilia sent us after him—but Larry's shocked reaction distracted him.

He pulled out a chair and sat down, clearly processing information.

"It's Bonarata," he said. "My people told me last night that he was still in Italy, but it's Bonarata."

I nodded. "That's what I was going to say," I told Adam. "Earlier when we were talking about the seethe."

Adam nodded. "My people say he's in Italy, too. But he's a vampire, and people believe what Bonarata tells them to believe. Once we knew Wulfe's role, it had to be Bonarata." He was watching Larry. "But you didn't know about Wulfe. What is it about the last two deaths that tells you it's Bonarata?"

"I'd assumed that the gray witch had killed the fortune-teller," Larry said. "I have photos. I have photos of the boy, too. But I didn't connect them because I thought he was human." He paused. "And that stupid movie—*The Harvester.*"

"You know about the Soul Taker," I said.

"How is it connected to Bonarata?" Adam asked.

"Well, he's had it for a long time, hasn't he?" said Larry. "Centuries. He likes to collect things, does Bonarata."

He leaned back in the chair and stretched out, crossing his feet at the ankles. Those boots were definitely custom-made, too. Larry's feet were too oddly shaped to fit in shoes built for human feet.

"I had a call last night from Uncle Mike. Did I know how a dead body and an artifact that resembled but was not the Soul Taker ended up on his front door forty years ago? Zee wanted to know." He looked a little indignant. "I was in Iceland forty years ago, didn't come to the US until 2000."

"So you don't know?" I asked.

"Of course I know," he said, sounding even more indignant. "I didn't connect Uncle Mike's inquiry with our current problems. Zee has been looking for that damned artifact off and on for nigh on a thousand years. Possibly two thousand years. It has been one of the driving forces of my people to keep it out of his hands."

I opened my mouth to ask why, but Adam asked his question first.

"How did the dead boy and a ringer for the Soul Taker get left for Uncle Mike to find forty years ago?"

Larry's eyebrows shot up. "One of my goblins put them there." He tapped a finger on the table and gave Adam a look. "Not something we'd do now, but the goblins here were without protection. They worked for the seethe, perforce, and hid from the fae. But they watched. And they knew things." Larry flashed his sharp teeth. "Just as we watch and know things now."

"What did they know?" asked Adam.

"Bonarata exiled Marsilia to the New World as soon as travel was practical. And once he found out there was a desert, a sunny place with few people—he made her move her people here. You know this much."

We nodded as he'd invited us to.

"Once international travel became quicker and easier," he continued, "it became Bonarata's habit to visit every couple of decades. He stopped doing it"—a faint smile crossed Larry's lips—"about forty years ago."

He quit sounding like the voice-over in a documentary for a moment to add, "I did some research on Bonarata after our visit to Prague. Called a few friends in Italy. I have quite a file on him. I think a psychiatrist would have a field day."

He cleared his throat and resumed his storytelling. "Most often, Bonarata would announce his visits and require them to stage celebrations as he culled vampires he thought looked to be too powerful. A few of those he kept alive and took for his own use, but mostly he just staked them out in the sun. He also killed promising fledglings. He made sure that none of Marsilia's people were too loyal to her."

Larry pursed his lips. "Marsilia put herself in a sort of hibernation—a thing old vampires can do." He smiled darkly. "We have an eye on one or two who've been sleeping for centuries."

"So does Bran," Adam said.

"Maybe I will compare notes with him." Larry returned to his story. "Marsilia's people roused her for his visits—but such wakings are only half-effective. It can take an old vampire decades to truly awaken from a hibernation. I have not been able to find out if she did this because she thought she would save her people that way, or if she was just trying to escape the misery of her situation."

"Interesting that she decided to reawaken now," said Adam thoughtfully.

Larry smiled at Adam. "Isn't it just. Starting a decade ago, really. When you came to the Tri-Cities with your pack, making the supernatural community here much, much stronger than it had ever been before." He looked at me. "You came here about the same time, didn't you?"

"When did you come to the Tri-Cities?" I asked before he could put those two events together.

Larry just gave me an amused look. When he spoke, he resumed his prior subject. "At other times, Bonarata would conceal his presence, but the goblins always knew. At those times, he would just watch Marsilia's people—who were primarily under the leadership of Stefan and Andre." He tapped the table. "You remember Andre, don't you, Mercy?"

"Of course," I said.

I'd *killed* Andre after he set a demon-possessed vampire out to hurt the people I loved. Stefan and Wulfe had conspired to keep my involvement in Andre's death from Marsilia. Stefan, I think, because he cared about me. Who knew why Wulfe did anything. It was not something that I talked about even now, but it didn't surprise me that Larry was suspicious.

Larry gave me a thoughtful look. I don't know what he read on my face, but he returned to his story with a shake of his head. "One or the other of them might have been able to handle the seethe—though neither was someone I'd consider a leader. Together, they were a near disaster. Maybe Marsilia thought it was better that way." He appeared to consider it.

"But, even so, about forty-five years ago, the vampires organized themselves and seized control of the Tri-Cities' supernatural community—a control that only waned when Mercy stood on a bridge and claimed us for her own." He smiled at me with sharp teeth. "We goblins appreciate that more than I've told you, I think."

"You're welcome?" I said, and his smile widened.

"I always found it odd that the two of them managed that," said Adam. In answer to my raised eyebrows, he clarified his reasoning. "Stefan's name in the vampire community is the Soldier, Mercy. Soldiers take orders, they don't give them. And Andre . . ."

"I've always thought it was Wulfe," said Larry slowly. Then he spoke more briskly. "But I wasn't here then. Bonarata came on one of his stealth visits around forty years ago and found that Marsilia's seethe was thriving, with money and power enough to survive without his support. He disliked that. As you know, the vampires' hold on our fair cities used to be based on a Mafia-style protection racket."

"Like ours," I murmured. "Except we don't get paid."

Adam laughed, turned, and kissed me on the mouth. "I knew we forgot something."

Larry cleared his throat. "Bonarata, in a plan that now sounds strangely familiar, decided to strike terror into the hearts of the nonvampires who were supporting and giving their money to Marsilia's seethe. He brought in an artifact that he had stored away for a rainy day—the Soul Taker. Obviously time had made him complacent about it, though he wasn't fool enough to take it up himself. It was the right tool for the job, because it does hunt down folk with a little, just a little, magic in their blood. No one knows why."

"Zee thinks that it is collecting sacrifices for some ancient god," I said. Though I didn't go into the gathering souls part of it because I didn't want to get Larry off track.

Larry grimaced. "That sounds even worse than I thought. At any rate, he sent it off to kill folks, and it did. And some bright person thought to ask one of the more powerful fae, a Gray Lord, for protection. Once she'd had her attention drawn to it, that one of the Gray Lords summoned Siebold Adelbertsmiter."

He shook his head. "I don't know if it was a smart move or a stupid one. Neither does she, because she's dead. At any rate, that news came to Bonarata in some fashion."

Larry stopped and gave me a hard look. "Mercy, it is important that you know this. I know you think he's your friend. But no one wants the Dark Smith to get his hands on the Soul Taker."

"I've got that," I said.

Larry nodded. "Bonarata does not, either. He killed the mortal child the Soul Taker had taken possession of and had one of the goblins drop the body and a replacement artifact on Uncle

Mike's doorstep. Uncle Mike being the only one my goblin could be sure would call Zee to deal with them, instead of stealing the sickle for their own use and leaving Zee still on the hunt."

Larry gave a little cough. "Uncle Mike called me this morning and let me know that Zee is perturbed none of the goblins told him that he'd been given the wrong sickle. But since I was not here then, he will let matters lie." He paused.

"If Bonarata pulled the Soul Taker out of play forty-odd years ago," Adam said, "why did he bring it back now?"

"Higher stakes," I said. "Getting rid of us is worth the risk of losing control of the artifact." I looked at Larry. "Even to Zee."

"Maybe he doesn't know the Dark Smith stayed," Larry suggested.

I shook my head. "No. I told him myself just a couple of months ago."

"Maybe he thinks he can get Zee to work to his ends," Adam said. "Given a big enough bribe."

"That's a twisty thought," Larry said. "Could be, could be." He gave Adam an interested look. "You have a reputation for being straightforward."

Adam smiled but didn't say anything.

"I know what the movie has to do with it," I said in sudden astonishment. "Holy wow. It's pretty clear from this viewpoint, isn't it? The Tri-Cities is bigger than it was forty years ago—and we have a much larger population of lesser magical people because of the treaty. Lots and lots of new people who aren't a part of any community yet. And we know they are transient, so when they disappear, we don't worry."

Adam nodded. "I think you're on the right track. Bonarata was taking out the people who counted on us to save them." His voice was a little rough. "But no one noticed. Maybe that was intentional. When he'd done enough damage, maybe he planned on making a call to the newspapers." Adam tapped a finger on the one Larry had brought with him. "But then posters for that movie went up all over town—a movie based on the time when he set the Soul Taker loose here."

Larry rubbed his face as if he was very, very tired. "He realized he had a more dramatic way to rock the illusion of safety that we've been maintaining. He set the Soul Taker out to kill here again."

"Yes," I said.

12

~~~~~

"YOU DECIDED IT WAS BONARATA, TOO," I SAID. "WHEN?
Why didn't you say anything?" That was a little disingenuous
because I'd only come to the conclusion our enemy was Bonarata
after I'd dreamt about him.

We'd spent the morning working. Adam mostly stayed on the
phone with his people to take care of the issues that had developed while he'd been out of the office. I slogged through some of
the endless paperwork that owning the shop entailed.

We'd eaten lunch and now were headed to my garage to meet
the other werewolves, prepared for battle. My cutlass was toast,
so I wore a similar-sized katana from Adam's store of weaponry.
I had my concealed carry in my waistband, covered with a light
jacket over my usual T-shirt. The lamb that served as my holy
symbol was safe around my neck on the new chain that also held
one of Adam's dog tags and my wedding ring.

It was daytime, but I wouldn't have gone into the seethe without my lamb unless someone dragged me kicking and screaming.

Adam said, "I wasn't certain. I'm not certain now. It could turn out that there's a cult of fae spiders who practice some sort of mind control."

When I winced, he glanced at me. "Sorry. A little close to the bone."

"Next time, you get to be the spider incubator," I told him.

"Fair enough," he agreed meekly. "Anyway, the whole focus on scaring the public and reducing confidence in our pack's ability to do our job is right in line with the reason Bonarata kidnapped you."

He stopped speaking, and when I glanced at him to see why, his eyes were glittering bright gold.

"Truthfully, I am surprised that he moved again this soon," I said, as much to give Adam something to distract himself with as to communicate anything important. "It sounded to me as though you convinced him that the real power in the Tri-Cities rests with the Gray Lords, who are using us as a public shield."

Adam had managed that because it was absolutely true.

He nodded. "Honestly, I expected him to move against us—if only because we make Marsilia's position more powerful in a way that does not depend upon him. But Bonarata has the reputation of being a long-game thinker. So I expected him to spend the next forty years building his game before he engaged with us again."

I thought about the silk belt in our weapons safe. Adam was right, Bonarata was a patient hunter.

"For a straightforward man, you think awfully twisty."

"Thank you," he said. "It's all those years of dealing with Bran. He gets in your head."

I winced theatrically. "People have been disappearing since September. That means this all started just a couple of months after we got back from dealing with Bonarata in Europe."

"Maybe this isn't something new," Adam said slowly. "Maybe it's a continuation of the vendetta he's had against Marsilia since he banished her however many years ago."

"That sounds about right," I said. "So maybe my kidnapping this summer was a part of a much longer plot."

Adam smiled grimly. "God help us. It's like trying to unweave something Bran put together—or claimed credit for. I imagine we'll figure out everything eventually. As long as we survive."

Our wolves were waiting for us in the parking lot. I was a little surprised to see one of the bay doors open and Zee standing outside talking with Adam's second. Zee looked frail and small next to Darryl's muscular sleekness. No one would suspect that he was the more dangerous of the two.

I got out of the car and waved at the assembled werewolves but headed straight for Zee.

"I thought that you weren't going to be here today," I said after greeting Darryl.

"Do you have a minute that we can talk?" Zee asked.

I glanced at Adam and said, "Give me five?"

"We're still waiting for Warren and Zack," he said. "Take your time."

Zee led the way to the bathroom and shut the door, turning on the fan for good measure. He listened to the gentle hum and made a sound of disgust.

"The fan in the old building would have kept our voices from carrying to a werewolf sitting with his ear against the door," he complained.

He turned off the fan and waved a hand. I felt his magic fill the room.

"Bonarata is here," he said.

"We think so," I agreed. "Both Adam and Larry have word that he's still in Italy, but all signs point to that being wrong."

"Talked to a friend in Seattle," Zee said. "Bonarata is building a home there. My friend says that there's been a black copter flying in and out of the property three, four days of the week. The only person who uses that helicopter is Bonarata. He's been in Washington State for five, maybe six weeks."

"Okay," I said. I'd felt better when we weren't certain.

"Bonarata's at the heart of this," Zee said. "Found out that he's had the Soul Taker for centuries. I didn't look in that direction because, given a few centuries, I would have thought that the Soul Taker would have found a way out of his hold, one way or another."

"You said that you didn't think it could take Bonarata," I said.

"Bonarata doesn't fill his castle with old, powerful vampires," Zee said. "It should have found someone." He frowned. "I think he found a way to contain it. After you helped me understand exactly what it's doing with its dead, a web of death magic that spans an abyss we have no way to measure, I don't think anyone is safe. Not you. Not Bonarata. Not me."

I thought of the vast blackness of the abyss I could sense at the edge of my awareness and shivered.

"Okay," I said.

There was a bead of sweat on Zee's forehead. I knew the temperature of the bathroom was sixty-five degrees because I'd lost the battle with him to raise it to seventy. Talking about the Soul Taker scared me—it did something else to Zee.

Zee had settled in the Tri-Cities more than forty years ago because he thought there was a possibility that the Soul Taker would show up here again. The Soul Taker had the same effect on him as the full moon did on a werewolf. I could smell his eagerness.

"How did Bonarata protect himself?" I asked. "Is it something we could do?"

"Not anymore," Zee said. "That's where the spider-fae come in. Uncle Mike remembered the story. About eight hundred years ago, a colony of spider-fae discovered the Soul Taker. When it was done with them, they were all dead except for two half-breed younglings who had learned how to contain its power so that it could be handled without danger."

"The ones we killed at Stefan's?" I asked.

"They match the description I was given," Zee agreed.

"Okay," I said.

"You should tell all of that to Adam and your people," he said. "But this is what I wanted to tell you alone."

"Okay?"

"When you find the Soul Taker, do not touch it. Do not let those you care about touch it. Kill its wielder and call me."

WHEN I CAME OUT OF THE GARAGE, ADAM WAS IN THE middle of explaining everything we knew about the enemy so far. He glanced at me.

"Bonarata's here," I said. "He's got a place in Seattle and a helicopter. He's been here for over a month."

Adam glanced at Zee, who nodded.

Normal people like me would be scared to find out the Lord of Night had come to visit. I could see the pack come to alert, their bodies stiffening. That the feeling I got from them through the pack bonds was eagerness for the hunt was a testimony that all werewolves are crazy.

Adam looked around at them, lips quirked in a smile that told me he'd caught the same thing I had.

"Are we going up against him at the seethe?" asked George. "Because if we are, we need more people."

"Probably not facing Bonarata today," Adam said. "Larry says the seethe is empty. Bonarata might be patient, but he has better things to do than sit around in an empty building like a spider waiting for flies to hit his web."

"Can we stop with the spider metaphors?" I asked politely. I could tell by the grimaces that George had passed around the story of the spiders.

"Are Marsilia's people still friendly?" asked Mary Jo. "If Bonarata's involved, isn't that like Bran getting involved? Don't they owe allegiance to him?"

"I don't think we've gotten to the point that we need to worry about Marsilia's people attacking us," Adam said.

"Except for Wulfe," I reminded him. "You all should know about Wulfe."

Adam explained about my encounter with the Harvester.

"We are going into the seethe in the middle of the day, people," said Darryl when Adam was finished. "Any vampires up and about are going to be weaker and slower."

"Don't count on that if it's Bonarata," Adam told them. "If you see him, don't engage."

"Don't know what he looks like, boss," said Warren flatly. He was, uncharacteristically, dressed in an all-black T-shirt and black jeans. His body posture was . . . wrong, his usual relaxed casualness nowhere in sight.

"If you run into a vampire you don't know," Adam told him dryly, "assume it's Bonarata until someone who knows what he looks like says it's not."

"He looks like a Mafia thug," I told them.

"Not always," murmured Zee. He looked at Adam and spoke more loudly. "I know him. Do you want me to come with you?"

Adam tilted his head. It was a motion I saw the werewolves do all the time—but humans seldom used it.

"I appreciate the offer," Adam said carefully. Zee was old enough to find "thank you" problematic and rudeness objectionable. "But if I'm wrong, I can justify bringing the pack through Marsilia's door. I don't want to explain to her that I let the Dark Smith into her home without more cause than we have. This is just a quick sweep to confirm that our allies are not there, and possibly find some clues into where they've been taken."

"Fair enough," said Zee, settling back into the body language of his old-mechanic guise. I hadn't realized until that moment that he'd dropped it.

I wouldn't be surprised if he gave us time to do our search and then went out and did his own.

"If Larry says the seethe is empty," Darryl said, his voice a little sharp, "why are we going at all?"

Adam looked at him and said in an unfriendly voice, "Do you have anything better to do?"

Darryl's nostrils flared. He didn't like the vampires, and I didn't blame him. I felt the same way about most of them. He didn't like being put in his place, either.

"Marsilia's our ally," I told Darryl before the situation had a chance to get worse. "Someone spirited her and our vampires off. There may be clues. Emails, letters—something that tells us where they went and why."

"Fair enough," said Darryl. He had an easier time standing down with me than with Adam. I wasn't an Omega like Anna, but I wasn't a threat in any way, shape, or form, either. So his wolf didn't bristle—and as the Alpha's mate, I had enough authority that he didn't feel the need to put me in my place.

Adam wasted no time loading two vehicles with the ten wolves. It might have been eagerness to get on with the task. But I wondered if it didn't have something to do with Zee. Warren and Darryl ended up in Honey's Suburban together. Usually this wouldn't have been a problem. They liked each other. But Darryl was on edge because of the vampires, and whatever had been bothering Warren was still bothering him.

Adam saw it, caught Zack's attention, and our pack submissive found a seat next to Warren in Honey's car. Disaster hopefully averted, we loaded Adam's car with the rest.

"Assuming I don't die," I told Zee as I stepped up to the shotgun seat of Adam's SUV, "I'll come back and relieve you this afternoon."

Zee shook his head. "No, Mercy. It is all right. I have the shop today."

"Okay," I said. "Don't drive off customers."

"I wouldn't dream of it," he said innocently.

I pretended I hadn't noticed him baiting me, waved my hand at him, and closed the door.

We got about half a block down the road when Ben, speaking from the far backseat, said, "Any of you sodding wankers know what's done Warren's nut for him?"

"Any of us sodding wankers know what Ben just asked?" George's voice was very dry.

"On it," Adam said, answering Ben, not George. "I've told him he has two days to tell me what his problem is. Just don't push him before then."

"Did you tell that to Darryl?" asked Mary Jo.

"I told Auriele," Adam told her.

"Maybe he should take shotgun in your rig on the way home," I suggested.

"No," said Adam. "In my ride, that's your spot."

"Okay, then," I said, a little surprised—and, unexpectedly, a little happy—at the growl in his voice.

IT HAD BEEN A WHILE SINCE I'D VISITED THE SEETHE. A couple of years, maybe. It was in an area of town where I didn't have much reason to go—and maybe I'd been avoiding it. Stefan was my friend, but I was with Darryl when it came to the rest of the vampires.

I'd been aware, peripherally, that there was a lot of building going on along 395, the highway that was the demarcation line between east Kennewick and the rest of town. But I hadn't thought about what that meant to Marsilia's home.

The last time I'd visited, it had still been surrounded by the shrub-steppe that was the Tri-Cities' version of virgin wilderness. Now the seethe was surrounded by new houses.

"Didn't there used to be these weird two-story brick pillar-thingies around here?" I asked as we turned down the paved road that had replaced the single-lane gravel drive. I could see the gates of the seethe, so we should have already passed between the brick edifices.

"Taken down as a hazard," George said. "About the same time as this housing development was built."

Upscale houses surrounded the still-expansive grounds of the seethe. The eight-foot cement walls that marked out the vampires' home ground were far more substantial than the walls that surrounded the seethe the last time I was here. The huge wrought-iron gates were the same, though.

"Some people have no sodding sense of self-preservation," Ben marveled. "Look at how close the fucking houses are."

I saw why Adam had insisted on packing all of us into as few vehicles as possible despite the possible danger of cramming dominant wolves together. This was a neighborhood that would notice a bunch of cars driving into the seethe in the daytime.

"I wonder if all these people are trying to figure out why they're having nightmares every night," Mary Jo said.

Adam glanced up and down the road. We were too late for lunch and not early enough for kids to be getting home from school. There was no one in sight. That didn't mean there weren't people looking out from all those blank windows.

"Mercy, slide over and drive," he said as he got out.

Adam was up and over the eight-foot-high gates in a quick movement that would have been easy to miss, even if someone was watching. He did something at the control box on the other side and the gates swung open. I drove through with Honey close on my tailpipe.

I negotiated the whole of the wide circular drive until the front of Adam's SUV was nearly touching the gates, which were sliding shut. If we had to go fast, I didn't want to waste time. *I* would have left the gates open to facilitate that, but Adam was probably thinking about not letting anyone else in.

As I turned off the engine, Adam walked up to Honey's window and spoke to her. In response, she maneuvered her Suburban around until she was parked beside me, effectively blocking the vehicular entrance.

The main building was a two-and-a-half-story Spanish-style house that we could have fit two of our house inside—and our house was not small. Graceful arches and architectural details mostly served to hide the lack of windows. Behind the main house were extensive gardens, a swimming pool, and a guesthouse—or at least I assumed they were still there. The front drive where we were parked had been walled off from the rest of the grounds except for a single-lane paved road that followed the outer wall, presumably leading to the guesthouse, which had its own garages.

The aboveground edifices were mostly a façade, a place to show guests and greet local dignitaries and politicians. Most of the seethe's grounds were riddled with tunnels and layers of basements that truly housed the inhabitants of the seethe.

The occupants of Honey's car burst out as if there were a swarm of bees inside. Warren's face was flushed, his eyes yellow. Darryl looked none too happy, either. Zack caught Adam's gaze with a wide-eyed look of alarm.

"Warren," Adam said sharply.

Warren jerked around and met Adam's gaze for nearly three

seconds before he took a deep breath, closed his eyes, and nodded once.

"Sorry, boss," he said.

He pivoted back toward Darryl without raising his eyes—and we all saw the effort that took.

It was a pretty well-kept secret that if he wanted the post, he probably could have beaten Darryl for second, both by combat and by dominance. Adam and I knew it. Warren knew it. I was pretty sure that Darryl knew it, too (which wouldn't have helped matters while they were trapped together in Honey's SUV). But although Warren was more accepted by the pack than he had been a few years ago, that he was gay would still be an issue. Our pack, like most packs, was composed mostly of men born in the last century. The opinion of the pack held sway in pack magic, and his rise to second would disrupt it.

This was not the time to disrupt the pack. And Warren didn't *want* to be second. Darryl was good at his job, Warren had told me a few months ago: "Why fix sumthin' that ain't broke?"

"I'm sorry, Darryl," Warren said sincerely. "I've got some things riding my hide. But I don't have to take it out on my friends."

Darryl considered him a moment—which was enough unlike his usual response to make me wonder how bad the altercation in Honey's Suburban had been. Or maybe whatever had Warren acting weird was spreading through the pack. When Darryl nodded, it was pretty obvious that he was still riled.

"It's the seethe," Adam told me quietly.

I nodded. Darryl's dislike of vampires had solidified when he'd spent a few days as the unwilling guest of Marsilia's vampires not long after he'd first moved here, a long time before I'd been a member of the pack. It had been some sort of misunderstanding. Darryl had stayed behind in New Mexico when the pack moved up here to finish up some work projects. Adam hadn't been expecting him for another week. Marsilia hadn't known he was coming at all. She had still been pretty immersed in her hibernation-lethargy at the time, so she did not police her people as well as she did now. Maybe, considering the timing, the incident with Darryl could have been *why* she'd started to wake up again.

At any rate, a group of vampires found a strange werewolf running around and decided to bring him home to play. Though blindsided because he'd been told that the vampires and werewolves here were not actively hostile, Darryl had still torn two of them apart. The other three had succeeded in capturing him and had treated him just as if he'd killed two of their buddies.

Someone apprised Marsilia of the situation, and she'd stirred enough to contact Adam. Darryl had been released, but he nursed a mean grudge. Unhappily for him, the incident meant he knew the layout of the seethe better than any of the other wolves, or else Adam could have left him out of the expedition.

Adam surveyed his troops. "Mercy and"—he hesitated long enough that I knew he'd originally planned on sending me with someone else—"Warren, you search the main house. Start from the ground floor and work up. Darryl, Auriele, Honey, and Zack— go out to the guesthouse, hit the tunnels, and work back toward the main house. Ben, George, and Mary Jo are with me. We'll enter the tunnels from the main house and plan on meeting in the middle. If you run into trouble, call out. Cell phones won't work in the tunnels, but wolf calls will travel. Don't split up from the groups I've assigned you."

"What about damage?" said Darryl. His voice was usually

deep, but unhappy as he was, it had dropped until it was almost difficult to distinguish words. "Can we break down locked doors?"

Adam nodded. "We need to clear the seethe, and we aren't going to dawdle about. No unopened doors, no unsearched rooms. Be thorough."

The designated four jumped the wall, taking the shortest way to the guesthouse. I found I could sort of catch a glimpse of its roof if I hopped a bit for more height.

"Mercy," said Adam.

"Just making sure it's still there," I told him. I caught up to him as he got to the front door.

It was unlocked.

I couldn't decide if that meant anything. Marsilia wouldn't be worried about thieves, but I'd have expected her to lock the whole place down during the day.

"Like a flytrap," Ben said, hesitating before he entered the foyer. "You know—open maw to sucker the flies inside."

"Thanks for that," I said, and he grinned, though he didn't look any less spooked.

The interior of the house hadn't changed since the last time I'd seen it. Like the exterior, it showed the influences of the Spanish explorers in the tiles, textures, and color choices of the decor. Our summer heat meant that Spanish-influenced architecture was pretty common in the Tri-Cities.

"The entrance into the basement is in the kitchen," Adam said as he led the way.

"I know," I said. "The first time I came here I escaped that way."

He nodded. "This house is mostly for show, but Marsilia is unpredictable, so don't get complacent." That was directed at

Warren and me, I thought. No one could get complacent in the tunnels, which reeked of blood, death, and vampire. "Look for anything that might tell us where they went."

"That's more likely to be in the guesthouse," I said. Marsilia spent her daylight hours in the smaller building, where her enemies would not expect her to be. "But we'll stay on our toes and look everywhere."

I met his gaze and he held it for a minute, then nodded.

The kitchen was the same as it had been the first time I'd seen it. Bird's-eye maple cabinets and cream-colored Spanish stone countertops added to the effect of the backlit stained-glass panels on the walls, making the kitchen appear bright and airy despite the lack of windows. The stainless-steel elevator doors were in line with the fridge and a walk-in freezer, making for a wall of metallic gray without so much as a fingerprint smudge.

Adam and his team got into the elevator—and Adam looked at Warren. "Don't get complacent."

"You got it, boss," drawled Warren. He looked more like himself than he had when he'd gotten out of Honey's SUV, but I didn't miss the tension in his shoulders.

After the elevator closed and hauled my mate down to the bowels of the earth, I said, "Sorry you got stuck with babysitting duty."

As the least able fighter, I was always destined to be stuck with exploring the main house because it would be the safest place. All the scary stuff would be down in the tunnels. Warren, however, was one of the pack's big guns.

"Best use for me," Warren said. "I'm unlikely to pick a fatal quarrel with you." Almost to himself, he growled, "I could really have refrained from poking at Darryl before he had to face vampires."

"What's wrong?" I asked.

He looked at me thoughtfully. "Bonarata is challenging our ability to protect our territory. Our vampire allies have disappeared—except for Wulfe, who is killing people with a cursed weapon. People we are responsible for protecting are disappearing and dying. Fuel costs more than it did this time last year, and I'm still stuck with the conviction that it should be twenty-five cents a gallon. Financial disparity is at an all-time high."

I frowned at him. He knew what I meant.

"It's nothing," he said with a growl in his voice. "It's fucking nothing, Mercy." Warren didn't swear much. He saw my look and said, "Leave it."

"Are you sure I can't help?" I asked.

He looked at me, then away. "I am very tired of being pushed," he said. "Let me tell you how this is gonna be. We are gonna look through this house and find damn all. And you are going to leave me the fuck alone while we do it. I am tired of you sticking your Little Miss I-Can-Fix-It nosey self in my fucking business."

I blinked back sudden hurt tears.

I was tired. I was scared. I was worried about Adam and the rest down in the tunnels. I was worried about Zee. About poor Aubrey, who would never get to kiss his secret crush.

I had two choices. I could stand here and cry—or I could get mad. Guess which one I chose.

Warren started methodically searching the kitchen. I did the same beginning from the opposite side.

The fridge and walk-in freezer had never been used—nor had the dishwasher. Both still had that fresh-out-of-the-box smell, even though I was pretty sure it was still the same fridge that had been here three years ago. The cupboards were empty of food, though there were dishes and cookware in appropriate locations.

"Staged," Warren said, surveying the empty pantry. "Shall we move on?"

I didn't respond. Didn't look at him. I just stalked out of the kitchen to the next room I came to. We worked in silence while I nursed my righteous anger until I could pretend that I wasn't hurt.

Mostly.

Despite knowing that the whole huge house was mostly a decoy, I had expected that exploring the home of our local seethe would have been more interesting. But Warren had found the right word—it was staged. The whole house aped a place where people lived. Closets and drawers were empty. Rooms were beautifully decorated, walls filled with good but not expensive art. There was not a trace of personality anywhere.

Adam was risking his life in the tunnels, and I was wandering through a house that could have been a showroom for a Southwestern-themed furniture catalog. And I was doing it with someone who was tired of me.

He was so obviously in a hurry that I'd started slowing down just to irritate him. We were going through the last room on the main floor, the second room we'd run into that was pretending to be an office, when Warren finally snapped.

He had gone through the desk, both closets, and a small bookcase and had to wait for me. He tapped his foot once as I shut the bottom drawer of the totally empty three-drawer filing cabinet I'd just spent five minutes looking through.

I looked at his foot. Then I tipped the filing cabinet on its side so I could examine the bottom, just in case there was a concealed hiding place. But it was solid.

"What *are* you looking for?" Warren growled. They were the first words that either of us had said to the other since we'd left the kitchen.

I blinked at him. Set the filing cabinet back on its solid metal bottom and contemplated the room. He'd looked through the closets and the desk. I looked at the bookcase. It was not a big bookcase. Four shelves, each with a matched set of books. I squinted at the titles—they appeared to be books on banking and the stock exchange.

"I used to make secret compartments in books," I said thoughtfully. I went back to the bookcase and pulled out the first book on the top shelf, *Bank Audits and Examinations.*

"My foster mother showed me how to make them." I didn't look at him while I spoke. Looking at him might make him think I thought he cared about anything I had to say. "I still have one of them. You glue the edges of the pages together and cut out the center to make a hollow."

"You have got to be joking," he said.

I almost smiled at his tone. There was still irritation, but it was edged with wariness. As if he'd finally started to figure out he was not going to (*hurt me*) snap my nose off and swear at me without paying for it.

"Adam said to be thorough," I told him, putting that book back on the shelf and picking up another one. I wasn't moving particularly quickly.

To my delight, the next floor up had bookshelves in all the rooms. It was as if someone had told Marsilia, "Human habitations have bookshelves on the second floor." The books were all in sets, but otherwise seemed completely random, the complete set of Charles Dickens's work placed next to a specially bound set of Thoroughbred studbooks from the turn of the last century. Just exactly the sort of collection guaranteed to irritate a man who really loved books the way that Warren did.

He knew why I was going through each book—and he knew that all he had to do (probably) to put himself out of his misery was to apologize. He didn't, so I opened every book on every shelf.

Two rooms and four bookshelves later, I opened a book and found it hollow. Sadly, there was nothing in it, but someone had made a hiding space in—I checked the title—Gibbon's *The History of the Decline and Fall of the Roman Empire*, Volume 4, printed in 1974.

"I always thought I should read Gibbon," I said. Not to Warren. I wasn't talking to Warren yet. More as if I were talking to an invisible friend who might be interested in what I had to say. "But I made it through *War and Peace* and decided I'd paid my toll to the gods of history." I closed the book but set it aside.

"It was probably hollow when she bought it," Warren said, looking with unhappy resignation at the book that was going to justify my search.

I'd actually had the same thought, which is why I'd set it aside so I could tell Marsilia about it. I didn't say so to Warren, though.

Giving up—but not enough to apologize—Warren joined me in going through every book we found. He was a lot faster about it than I was.

"I am sorry I swore at you," Warren said. "But quit poking."

I considered how to respond. An apology that starts with an "I'm sorry" and ends with a "but" isn't an apology at all.

"You know," I said, putting *A Child's Garden of Verses* back on the shelf between *Strange Case of Dr. Jekyll and Mr. Hyde* and *The Black Arrow*, "while we are thumbing through books that no one has ever so much as opened, our compatriots are wallowing through eldritch abominations."

Unsaid but plain to be heard was *And if you'd let someone help you before now, you'd get to go play in the scary dungeons instead of facing near-fatal boredom babysitting the useless coyote.*

Maybe I was upset about more than Warren getting mad at me for trying to help. The rest of them hadn't run into anything bad, though. I wasn't Adam, who could pick up quite a lot from the pack bonds when he wanted to, but a fight in the tunnels would have been close enough for both Warren and me to sense.

"Teach me to pick a fight with Darryl," Warren muttered, picking up the last of the white leather-bound collection of H. P. Lovecraft's work.

We moved to the next room. Five more bookcases, half-full of books. The next room also had five bookcases.

Somewhere along the line, the growl went out of Warren. Warren loved books. Despite the obviously ridiculous amount of I-don't-care that had amassed the titles on Marsilia's shelves, there were some good ones plunked between a complete collection of World Almanacs 1900 to 1965 inclusive and Time-Life collections. The Time-Life books were really too thin-spined to make good hiding places, but I looked in them anyway.

"Warren," I said, staring at the book in my hand. There was a close-up of a knight whose raised helm showed a spectral mist, and the gold-embossed lettering informed me I held *The Enchanted World: Ghosts.*

Maybe I should have been paying better attention to what we were here for instead of trying to get under Warren's skin and worrying about Adam.

"What?"

"There should be ghosts here," I told him, putting the book back on the shelf.

There were always ghosts where vampires sleep; traumatic death was one of the things that created ghosts. I'd used ghosts to track down vampires' lairs before—that's how I had located Wulfe's house the first time.

Warren came to alert and looked around. "Here in this room?"

"No," I said. "Here in this house."

"I thought you told me ghosts avoid vampires," Warren said, his manner all business, since we were actually talking about something that might be useful. "Like cats—except for yours."

"When the vampires are out and about, you won't find a ghost anywhere near them," I told him. For truth's sake I said, "Not usually. But when they're sleeping, their dwelling places tend to fill up with the shades of their victims."

Stefan's house didn't. But as long as I had known him, he'd been very careful that the people he and his fledglings fed upon lived to see another day. Daniel was the only ghost at Stefan's house.

"Is there a vampire running around here?" Warren asked.

I tapped my nose. "The last time a vampire was in this room was maybe six months ago." My nose, we had found as we dealt with more and more vampires and zombies, was better when it came to dead-but-still-moving creatures than the werewolves'. Especially if we were still running around on two feet instead of four.

"Were there ghosts here the last time you were here?" asked Warren.

I had to think about it. "Not in this house," I conceded. Though I'd felt them on the edges of my nerves in the tunnels.

"Maybe Marsilia has the house warded some way," Warren said, going back to his book with studied casualness. Not like he was interested in the ghost angle—more like he was interested in the book and didn't want me to know it.

"I'll ask her about it," I said.

My mother once told me to be careful of punishments that ended up going two ways. My hands were filthy—and the skin on my face itched where I'd touched it. Handling books wasn't quite as bad as handling money, but those books had been sitting around for years with nothing but a light dusting.

We trudged up the stairs from the second floor to the third floor, which was only half the size of the house. With no windows and no light filtering in from below—because we'd turned the lights off as we finished with each room—it was pitch-dark. I could see in the dark, but not in the absolute dark, and we were near that now. I fumbled along the wall on my side of the staircase and heard Warren doing the same on his.

My hands hit a switch and I flipped on the lights. We stood at one end of a long hallway with three doors on either side and one at the far end of the hall. This floor was so seldom used that it didn't even smell like vampires.

"Left or right?" I asked, since Warren and I were talking to each other again.

Warren gave a shrug because we both knew it wouldn't matter. With sudden decision he stalked to the first door on the right.

He turned on the light and froze in the doorway. Curious as to what had made him stop so suddenly, I followed him and peered into the room. It was a bedroom with a bed, a nightstand, and a dresser. Oh, and all the walls were covered with floor-to-ceiling bookshelves that were packed with sets of books. There were hundreds, possibly thousands of books, most of which were so boring that the publisher had to make them look good in order to sell them.

"No one puts hollowed-out books on the third floor," I said decisively.

Warren laughed—and not just a little bit; he leaned against the door frame and whooped like a hyena.

"Well," I told him sourly, "if there was anyone lurking up here, they know we're here now."

After he'd quit laughing, he said, "I'm sorry I snapped at you. I know you were only trying to help—"

"If you say 'but' again and blame me for it, we are going to go through each and every book in that room," I warned him.

It made him laugh again. Which made the whole we-must-search-each-book punishment a success.

"I'm sorry I tried to help you," I told him. "I should know by now that there is no help for you."

He hugged me. "You did help," he assured me.

It took us about three minutes to search that room, including under the bed—and Warren was back to his pre-whatever-was-putting-him-in-a-temper self. That reassured me that whatever had gotten his tail in a tangle, it wasn't life-threatening, so maybe I should trust him to deal with it.

I was in the closet when a heavy thump made me jump and

pull my gun. I came out of the closet, ready for enemies—and saw Warren on the floor in push-up position, looking under the bed. He thrust himself to his feet, using only the power of his arms, and smiled innocently.

"Did I startle you?"

I put the safety back on my gun and returned it to my waistband holster. Then I shook my head sadly. "Those who do not learn from history are destined to repeat it."

He laughed again. "I'm sure," he said.

The other five rooms were identical to the first except that the sets of books were slightly different. One room, the last of the identical bedrooms, had bookshelves filled only with sets of encyclopedias—several of them were incomplete, judging by the book-sized spaces left where the missing volumes had been, or should have been. If we all survived this, maybe I'd ask Marsilia about them.

We searched each of the rooms thoroughly—which was easy. There wasn't anything in any of them besides a bed, an empty chest of drawers, an empty nightstand, and the bookshelves. Warren did his thump-producing pratfall to search under all of the beds. We'd stopped checking individual books, but we'd looked behind the books for papers. Each room had a safe behind the painting above the bed. Like the three larger safes we'd found in the lower levels, they were all unlocked and empty and had the combination taped on the outside.

The door at the end of the hall led into a master bedroom suite.

There was a bathroom, a bedroom, and a small office off to the side. The ceiling was taller than the other bedrooms had been—maybe around twelve feet. A huge chandelier hung from a fancy medallion in the middle of the room. About half of its light-bulbs were out, maybe because it would take a ladder to change the bulbs. Maybe because no one cared.

The bed was the only piece of furniture in the room, and I probably could have described it pretty accurately before we opened the door. It was a huge thing, built of mahogany, and framed with velvet curtains. It might have walked off the set of a 1950s Zorro movie and was exactly the bland sort of choice that a decorator would have picked for this house.

"I'll check the office," Warren said, surveying the room. "You do the bathroom. Then we can go downstairs and lounge in the kitchen and wait for the others to get back."

"And you can grab that Lovecraft book and keep reading," I said.

He gave me a shamefaced grin but didn't deny it.

The bathroom, like the bed, was exactly the kind of bathroom that I expected to find in a house that looked like this one. There must be a decorator somewhere who specialized in creating rooms that looked exactly like they should.

"Maybe this is a room from the world of forms that Socrates talked about," I murmured, knowing Warren would get the ref-erence.

He'd told me once that he'd carried Plato's *Republic* in a saddle-bag for two years and read it every day. I'd had to read it for a college class and pass a test on it. He had passages memorized, and all I could remember was the bit about the world of forms. And that Socrates liked to teach people by asking them questions.

"The form that all other Spanish-style mansions are modeled

on," intoned Warren from the office on the opposite side of the bedroom.

There was a huge antique claw-footed bathtub in the corner of the room, surrounded by small tables holding trays of empty hand-blown glass bottles that should have been filled with soaps and bath oils. White fluffy towels were piled on a wire rack, close enough that a person bathing could just reach out for them.

I turned and caught a glimpse of myself in the mirror. My face was filthy from where I'd touched it. I looked at my hands.

"Marsilia sure has a vast collection of dirty books," I said.

There was a pause. "You *are* in a bathroom," Warren told me, a hint of laughter in his voice. "I'd guess you could wash your hands."

"Do you suppose she'd mind?" I asked. I tried to make it funny, but the bathroom had an untouched quality that made me uneasy—as if it didn't want to be used.

"If she does, you can buy her a new towel to go with the doors Darryl is taking pleasure in destroying." Warren's voice was dry, as if he understood my hesitancy and thought it ridiculous.

Which it was.

"Thanks," I said.

"Anytime, darlin'," he said, sounding as though he'd come back into the bedroom. I could hear him drop down to look under the bed.

The soap on the dish wasn't wrapped, but it didn't look as though it had ever been used. I turned on the water and watched it suspiciously. Sometimes if a faucet wasn't used often enough, the water was gunky. It looked and smelled okay—and it even warmed up fast. The soap smelled of lemons, but not too strongly.

I used a washcloth to scrub my face and spent some time on

my hands. When the water ran clear, I turned it off and dried on a nearby towel. The white towel was smudged when I finished, so apparently I hadn't gotten all the dirt with the washcloth. I bundled the mucky things together and set them beside the sink, where the cleaning crew couldn't miss them.

"Bathroom is clear," I said, starting for the door—and caught a glimpse of something in the huge old bathtub. There hadn't been anything in it when I'd checked it a few minutes ago.

Now it held an assortment of encyclopedia volumes. Five of them were leaned up against the back edge of the tub, braced by the three on the bottom. They were mismatched and from different places in the alphabet. The first one was *The World Book Encyclopedia* in gold-embossed leather, Volume 19, W-X-Y-Z. The second one was from a set of *Encyclopedia Britannica*, Volume 1, A-ak, Bayes. My eyes had moved to the third one, registered it as the T volume from a different set of *World Book*—and that's when I realized that, taken as a whole, they spelled WATCH OUT.

Schooled by Hollywood horror movies, I dropped to the floor. Nothing happened. I felt like a fool as I got to my feet. I hoped Adam hadn't felt the way my heart had pounded.

"Warren?" I said. "I think I found the missing encyclopedias. And possibly the ghosts that should be here."

He didn't say anything.

I thought of that thump I'd heard. The one I thought meant that he was looking under the bed. An unconscious body falling to the floor would sound like that, too. I drew my gun but stayed where I was.

"Warren?"

I couldn't feel any distress from him through the pack bonds.

He wasn't dead. He wasn't feeling pain or stress—I was pretty sure I'd know it if he were. If this was another joke, I'd shoot him. My gun wasn't loaded with silver bullets so it probably wouldn't kill him.

All of the lights went out.

13

ADAM'S WORDS RANG IN MY HEAD. "DON'T SPLIT UP. Don't get complacent."

We had done both, Warren and I. My fault more than his. But I didn't have time for "should haves" and "what-ifs" right now. I concentrated on here and now.

"Guns don't work in the dark without specialized equipment," Adam had told us on some training session or other. "If you can't see your target clearly, you're too likely to shoot your friends."

The werewolves and I could see just fine at night, outside where there was always some sort of light. In this house with no windows, I was blind.

I holstered my gun and drew the sword. I didn't bother to be quiet about it. Whoever had taken down Warren already knew where I was. It was as dark as a cave, and my enemy thought that these conditions would benefit them. It was my job to make them wrong.

I wasn't helpless without sight. Movement would make floor-boards shift, fabric rub, and my ears were very sharp. I concentrated on what my senses could tell me. I heard one person breathing and hoped it was Warren.

We were in a vampire's house. It might be midafternoon, but I had seen Wulfe awake and moving during the daytime before. Vampires only have to breathe when they want to pretend to be more human or when they want to talk—which requires air. I had a very good nose, even among the werewolves. I opened up my other sense, too, the one that let me feel magic in the air.

I heard and smelled nothing. Moreover, when I tried to reach Adam using our mating bond, I could not get through. It was still there, but I couldn't touch it. The same was true of the pack bonds and my bond with Stefan—which I tried in a fit of desperation. Someone was interfering. Some*thing*. I knew what it was.

"Soul Taker," I said.

A brush of air current had me raising the katana across my body. After I held it there, something hit it. A touch, not a blow, metal on metal that rang softly rather than a proper clang.

Wulfe was mocking me.

I had to assume that my opponent knew exactly where I was. Maybe Wulfe had some of that specialized equipment Adam had talked about. Maybe vampires didn't need any light at all in order to see. Either way, standing around waiting to be attacked when he could see me and I couldn't see him seemed stupid.

I bolted out of the bathroom, finding the doorway by memory. My shoulder caught something that yielded like flesh, but not hard enough to do more than send me sideways for a step until I caught my balance. I didn't let the brief misstep slow me down much.

I had assumed that the lights had gone out all over the house, but the light edging the bottom of the bedroom door said differently. My attacker had shut the door, trapping us inside, and turned off the lights just in this suite. The light under the door was not enough to penetrate the darkness, even for someone like me who could see in the night. But it gave me a goal.

The bedroom was very sparsely furnished, and everything was pushed up against the walls—there was nothing to trip me up as I sprinted to the door. But it was a huge room, maybe twenty feet by thirty feet that I was crossing on a diagonal.

Wulfe chased me. I couldn't hear him, couldn't smell him, but I could feel the floorboards move under my feet. And I knew that he was just behind me.

I slapped my hand on the switch, illuminating the room once more, and bounced off the wall like a swimmer on a turn. When speed is your only superpower, you learn to keep moving. This time I ran toward where I'd heard the sounds of breathing. Toward Warren.

Behind me something hit the door hard—as if to slam it shut when I'd never tried to open it. That sound told me I'd done the right thing by going for the switch instead of the door. I hadn't considered escape with Warren apparently incapacitated, but it was nice to know that the morally reprehensible choice would not have worked anyway.

Warren was collapsed on the floor not far from the bed; his body was totally lax, a little too much like a corpse. I reminded myself fiercely that I could hear him breathing. I couldn't stop and didn't want to lead Wulfe to him, so I kept going.

Abruptly the whole room was filled with magic so dense that I coughed as my throat buzzed with it and I tripped. I rolled when

I hit the floor and came back to my feet. Something had been shielding itself but had decided to come out of hiding, and it tasted like darkness.

"Olly olly oxen free," I said.

I'd stopped in the middle of the circular rug that had been centered in the empty space between the bed and the door. It was as good a place to begin as any. And it put me between Warren and Wulfe. Warren and the Harvester.

He stood next to the door, the rough-bladed sickle in his left hand. He made no move to turn the lights off again. As if that had been a joke that had run its course and didn't need to be revisited.

He was, as he had been on the roof of my house and in the movie, clothed in ragged dark brown robes that resembled monk's robes and a sort of hooded cloak. But this time there was no darkness obscuring Wulfe's face.

Even so, the Harvester didn't look quite as much like Wulfe as he had last night on the roof of my house. His body language was hunched in a way that reminded me of the broken creature I'd seen in Stefan's memories. Wulfe's face was drawn, hollowed, as if he had neither fed nor rested in days, and it was missing a couple of important parts.

No wonder the darkness hadn't bothered him.

"Bonarata have something against eyes?" I asked, holding the katana defensively in front of my body and wishing for the cutlass that I'd trained with until it was nearly a part of my body. The katana was similar, but its weight and balance were off enough that I had to think about what I wanted it to do.

I wondered what Wulfe was waiting for.

His robes moved, as if touched by a ripple of wind, but the air in the room was stagnant. When the Harvester spoke, no words passed through Wulfe's lips.

My servant does not need eyes, the Soul Taker said in my head.

It was the same way Adam and I could talk to each other. Having this thing do it felt like a violation. A corruption.

But I set aside my revulsion to be dealt with at some later date and considered its words. I thought of Marsilia's thick veil, of the way that she hadn't really met anyone's gaze. The glint of something I'd seen behind her veil could have been open wounds. I thought of Stefan. In one of the communications we'd had, he'd been missing his eyes, too, hadn't he?

Eyes let your enemies see into you.

The second time I felt the Soul Taker speak in my head, I realized I'd gotten it a little wrong. Adam spoke to me through our mating bond. The Soul Taker spoke through a different bond, one that was stronger than I'd realized.

I wondered why it had stopped to talk. But no matter how horrible having that thing talk to me, inside of me, was, the longer I kept it engaged, the better the chance that Adam would come looking for me.

It wasn't just words filling my head, either. I received concepts, dozens of them, one on top of the other. I understood that the sickle's realm was one of souls. I understood the truth in the belief that eyes were the gateway to the soul. At some fundamental level I also gained an understanding of why vampires could freeze their prey with their gaze. I knew if Wulfe still had his eyes, someone like Marsilia could have saved him from serving as the sickle's vessel.

All of that in less than the tick of a clock.

I understood that Bonarata had tortured Stefan, Marsilia, and

Wulfe. He had given Wulfe to the Soul Taker—but prepared the other two vampires to be wielders should they be needed. Bonarata thought he'd taken their eyes because he'd wanted to. He did not understand the necessity.

"Does Bonarata know that you make some of his decisions for him?" I asked out loud.

The Soul Taker laughed inside my head.

I wanted to shake my head to rid myself of its laughter, but I couldn't take my gaze off Wulfe. I'd seen him fight. I needed to see when he decided to come at me before he moved. The clothing he wore obscured my usual cues—I couldn't tell when his shoulders tightened, and it was going to be hard to see his weight shift. And, of course, I couldn't watch his eyes.

I still didn't know why the Soul Taker had stopped to talk to me. But I knew it couldn't last. This encounter would turn to blood soon enough. That was the purpose of the Soul Taker—to take souls.

I had better than a decade of martial arts training under my sensei and three years of daily sparring with Adam. I was pretty handy in a fight with someone vaguely in my weight and ability class. Wulfe was a vampire who had been fighting with a blade since sometime before the Renaissance.

I was, I thought, a little faster than he was in the same way I was a little faster than most of the werewolves—not enough to be a significant advantage. I was also smaller and not nearly as strong.

If I had to depend upon my katana to save me, I was doomed.

"Why me?" I asked, to see if I could keep it talking. If the Soul Taker was feeling chatty, maybe I could figure out a way to survive. I'd already learned that if Wulfe could see, then someone might be able to wrench him free of the Soul Taker. Not likely to be useful until he'd fed enough to regenerate his eyes—which wasn't going to happen in the next few minutes.

"I don't seem to be in your usual category of victim," I said, when it did not reply.

Sacrifice, it corrected me. The echoes of its voice made me understand that my death would serve a greater purpose. That I should feel joy as the blood of my body pooled on the ground and the magic of my death and my soul linked with those who had gone before. I even gained an understanding of the depth of that phrase "those who had gone before."

Souls caught together and stretching through time, still as connected to the Soul Taker as they had been on the day of their death. And the Soul Taker perceived them all individually in the same thorough and extensive way that I had tasted Aubrey Worth's soul. Not quite the same way. I was sad that Aubrey had died; the Soul Taker felt nothing. No. Not nothing. Satisfaction.

"So many people," I said involuntarily, their numbers pressing upon me like a great weight.

To release my lord into the world requires the sacrifice of many, it said.

I understood that as the years had passed, the definition of the kind of sacrifice who could be brought into the magical web this thing was creating had narrowed. The web had taken on the characteristics of the sacrifices before and become less elastic in what it could accept. Many had died uselessly before the Soul Taker had understood that it needed to refine its hunt.

Magic ability, but not too much, nor with too much training. Magic ability still malleable, able to be shaped.

I understood that as it touched me when I'd destroyed the

spider-creature's web, it had been able to see further through me than it usually could before it made a sacrifice of someone. I'd exposed my soul (yes, that had really been a stupid thing to do, I decided; next time I'd throw a chair or something), allowing the Soul Taker to perceive that I was connected to a spark of divine that might be the single power needed to make the spell work.

Coyote's daughter, it had called me the first time I'd seen it.

But it wasn't just Coyote. It was the wolves of our pack—and I had a moment to think that it was a very good thing that we'd broken from Bran, or it could have taken every werewolf Bran was connected to, assuming Bran wouldn't be able to stop it. It was the seethe through my blood tie with Stefan, who was tied to all the vampires in the seethe, to his maker and her maker before her. To Bonarata and everyone he was tied to.

Bonarata was in control of all the vampires in Europe and, Marsilia had told Adam, most of the vampires in the US. He and his vampires in turn controlled thousands of humans by blood bonds.

The Soul Taker understood souls, and apparently all of the blood ties that connected wolf to wolf and vampire to vampire were soul bonds.

I really, *really* should have just thrown a chair.

"But you have Wulfe already," I protested out loud.

Vampires are dead. They cannot be sacrifices.

For an instant I understood, really understood, what that meant—that they were missing the magic that defines life—but there were too many things getting shoved into my head, and I didn't try to keep that one. The Soul Taker needed a living conduit into the vampires' web of blood bonds, and for some reason—

Coyote, among other things, was a guide for the dead. I tried very hard not to let the Soul Taker see that thought.

—for *reasons*, my bond with Stefan would work, when other bonds with other living things did not.

I understood that my death, by means other than the Soul Taker's blade, was the only way to prevent the Soul Taker from doing as it wished. Right now, there was no feasible way for me to do that in such a way that the Soul Taker could not take a final blow before I died by other means.

By sacrificing you, I finish my task, the Soul Taker said.

"I see," I said, my mouth dry.

So why was Wulfe just standing there? Why didn't the Soul Taker have him kill me this minute? Why was it talking to me?

How would it be, I thought, to have existed all those years—and I knew that it was old in the same way that I understood Aubrey Worth's life. How would it be to have had a single task for all those years, and then come to an end of it? What would happen to it? Would it cease to exist?

Was it afraid?

I opened my mouth to ask, but the Harvester moved, and then I was too busy for conversation. I felt the Soul Taker withdraw its awareness from me as Wulfe occupied it fully.

Drill is the secret sauce to creating a fighter. If you have to think about what you're doing, you're doing it too slow. I had drilled and drilled and drilled with my cutlass. Not with the katana. The automatic reflexes still helped, but the differences between the blades threw me off.

As I struck and whirled in the deadly dance I was engaged in, I wondered why Bonarata had given Wulfe to the Soul Taker rather than Stefan. Marsilia he had bigger plans for. She would either become his devoted slavish follower or he would kill her in some spectacular fashion that would be spoken of for centuries. Bonarata was jealous of Stefan. And between Stefan and Wulfe, I would think that the Soul Taker would have an easier time using Stefan.

"Stefan," I said out loud, "is old and tough and strong, but he's not a freaking witch wizard crazy person. So why did Bonarata pick you, Wulfe?"

The sickle made a wicked quick slash at me, but I moved a quarter of an inch and it missed my throat. I dropped and thrust the katana like it was a foil or a spear and forced the Harvester back, a wet stain over one of his hips.

"Why you?" I asked.

In my mind's eye I remembered *the skeletal thing crouching against Marsilia's skirts, surrounded by the blood-drenched dungeon and the dead.*

I blinked and was back in the unused master bedroom just in time to get out of the way of Wulfe's elbow. That jump back into Stefan's dream-sending thing had been dangerous. I couldn't do that again.

Bonarata had tortured Wulfe for centuries. He'd turned him into that creature—and still Wulfe was his own person, broken as that was. Bonarata had tried to use Wulfe to undermine Marsilia, to spy upon her, and Wulfe followed Bonarata's orders exactly as they were given—and somehow defied Bonarata by twisting those directives on their heads.

I thought of Stefan's long-ago words. Bonarata was still afraid of Wulfe. Something kept him from killing Wulfe outright. I did not know what those reasons were. Maybe it was as simple as the fact that by killing Wulfe, Bonarata admitted that he was afraid. But he did not expect Wulfe to survive the Soul Taker.

I understood now, in a way I hadn't an hour ago, exactly what the Soul Taker did to those who wielded it. I understood why Bonarata would assume that Wulfe would die a servant to the blade.

But I'd seen the damaged thing Marsilia and Stefan had released from Bonarata's prison. And he'd survived. If I were a betting woman, I'd put my money on Wulfe. Long shots have always appealed to me.

Adam said it was the Coyote in me. Of course, I'd never know how it turned out because I would be dead.

That's when it hit me how odd it was that I wasn't already dead. I had calculated that my life span after we started to fight would be in seconds. It should have been over in seconds.

I hadn't kept track of the time we'd been at this, but I'd broken a sweat and my breathing was starting to be more labored. I knew this state from practice bouts with Adam. From that I estimated that we must have been fighting for three or four minutes.

A minute is a very long time in a fight, especially a fight with sharp things. I wasn't good enough to last this long in a fight with Wulfe.

Did the Soul Taker not want to kill me and finish the purpose of its existence?

We exchanged more moves and countermoves, and I could feel myself slowing down. He knocked me back and it took me too long to get my guard up. He should have hit me—and he didn't.

Some king had enslaved Zee, and Zee had made cups from the king's son's skulls and got the king and his wife to drink from them. Some people made very bad slaves.

I bet, I thought with a surge of hope, that it would be really difficult to make Wulfe do something he didn't want to do. I wouldn't want to try it.

The tip of the Soul Taker slid along the top of my scapula, cutting the shirt and my bra strap away and ripping a slice in my skin. I felt my awareness of it grow, felt its magic sliding into me, even as I spun away and lashed out with a low swing that forced the Harvester back.

Wulfe was serving the Soul Taker, exactly as well as he had served Bonarata. And that was why I was still alive after roughly five minutes of fighting.

That was a bad idea, Bonarata, I thought. *It's going to bite you in the butt.*

Teach him to play with the daughter of a chaos deity. Send the Soul Taker out to kill me and see what that gets you.

I turned aside the Soul Taker again—and Wulfe's head jerked down and he bit me. Surprised, I rolled away and—

I WALKED BESIDE SOMEONE IN THE FORMAL GARDENS at the seethe with rosebushes taller than my head on either side. Some part of me was very concerned about this. It felt like a very dangerous thing to do. I shouldn't be walking in a garden. I should be—

"Pay attention," said Wulfe sharply.

I started to turn my head to look at him.

"Do not," said Wulfe, and I froze before my eyes found him. "We don't have much time."

I knew that what I should be doing was fighting off the Harvester—who was Wulfe, or at least partly Wulfe. My body was defending itself on pure reflex while Wulfe pulled me into his dream.

"Do you remember Frost—" he said.

Frost? What did our situation have to do with Frost? Forgetting his injunction, I looked at Wulfe incredulously. But my perceptions were altered by my ties to the Soul Taker, which had tasted my blood and which operated in the world of souls.

I *saw* Wulfe.

THE SICKLE HOOKED MY KATANA AND RIPPED IT OUT of my hand at the same time that Wulfe . . . that the *Harvester's* elbow cracked against my jaw, knocking me to the ground.

I rolled with the blow and came to my feet, meeting the backhand swing of the sickle with a blow of my own with the walking stick almost before I realized that the walking stick was in my hand. I didn't try to hit the sickle with the walking stick; I took aim at Wulfe.

"Steel loves flesh," Adam liked to say, though he said it as if he were quoting someone else. "Wood loves bone."

I hit the back of Wulfe's wrist with the wooden stick and heard the bone crack. The Harvester dropped the sickle—and there was a moment when I could have grabbed it before he did, but I would sooner have stuck my hand into a nuclear reactor than touch that blade.

I knew what Wulfe was. I had *seen* him, seen the power he still held, and twisted and broken as it was, his capacity to wield magic to protect his mind was infinitely larger than my own small measure of ability. The Soul Taker had control of *Wulfe*. If I touched that thing, I wouldn't have a chance.

The Harvester picked up the sickle in his right hand, almost before it had touched the floor. He continued the fight as if I had not hurt him.

If the katana had thrown me off balance, the walking stick was . . . odd. Better, I decided, in some ways, even than my own cutlass, because it felt as if I'd always fought with the walking stick in my hand. But if I'd been careful to turn aside blows rather than risk a full-strength sickle-to-blade strike with the katana, I was even more careful with the walking stick.

I had the feeling that if that sickle dug its corrupted blade into the walking stick, something very, very bad was going to happen. But something bad was going to happen really soon anyway. We had been fighting for a relative age for this kind of aerobic full-on, full-contact fight. We were both bleeding.

If I didn't change the nature of this fight pretty soon, my death was going to be the bad that was going to happen, even if Wulfe was managing to play a reluctant attacker. If I died, according to the Soul Taker's own calculations, it would have repercussions I was not willing to be a part of.

But I had *seen* Wulfe.

I used the movement of my body to center myself and gathered my magic, the magic that allowed me to speak to the dead, a magic that I understood better after the Soul Taker had shown me its world of souls and ties between life and death. I tried to form it the way I had when I'd laid to rest an army of zombies. When I'd done that and accidentally included Wulfe in my workings, I'd knocked Wulfe for a loop. I was hoping it would work again.

All this time I'd wondered if I had simply knocked him out that night. Given him the vampiric equivalent of a concussion. There was no question it had affected him more than just physically. He'd behaved more like someone who'd had too much to drink. So it was possible he'd gotten the edge of what I'd thrown at the zombies and been sort of hotboxed.

But, however it had happened, I had just *seen* Wulfe. If I weren't fighting for my life, I might have struggled to explain how I'd seen into him. But I'd just had the Soul Taker in my head, and I didn't have time to lie to myself.

I'd seen his soul. I knew why he stalked me and what he wanted from me.

Having *seen* him in his dream time in the garden of the seethe, I understood exactly what I'd done in Elizaveta's backyard. For a very brief time, I'd given Wulfe back himself, the person he'd been before Bonarata had tortured him all those centuries ago. Once again, he'd been the traveling scholar, Marsilia's poetic friend, the man who had played a vielle while sitting in a tree in the moon-light.

Wulfe hoped that I could make him whole once more, perma-nently this time. That I could save him. I was pretty sure—having seen the scars of his past and the person he was—that I could not. Though I might give him brief respite, fixing what had been done to him was beyond any magic I could lay claim to.

I could not undo the damage done to him, but I thought I might, just might, be able to shake the Soul Taker's hold on him. After all, the Soul Taker itself had told me that it did not think it could have held Wulfe had Bonarata not blinded him first.

I pulled on whatever magic lingered in the room, no matter that it was the Soul Taker's magic. Although my mating bond and my pack bonds were intact, the Soul Taker—or possibly some magical protections that Marsilia had on her seethe—was block-ing me from pulling on that power. Instead, I called upon the ghosts tied to the seethe with unbreakable bonds of trauma, and they came, despite their fear of the vampire in the room with me. And, when the walking stick fed it to me, I took power from the dance of blade and staff that the Harvester and I engaged in.

When I could hold no more magic, I dropped the walking stick, slipped my head under Wulfe's arm, shoved my neck into his armpit, and reached up with my hand so I could touch his face, the only place his skin was exposed.

His flesh was chill under my battle-and-magic-heated fingers as I whispered, with all the Coyote-born magic within me, *"Be at peace."*

He stiffened, smooth movement suddenly clumsy. But he didn't stop.

Wulfe twisted and got a hold on my shoulder. He was a lot taller than me, stronger, and I was pouring everything I had into the magic. I had no defense. He threw me across the room. He caught me with some magic, too, but its effect and the shock of hitting the wall with the back of my head mixed together into a miserable, pain-filled instant.

Get up, get up, Aubrey whispered in my ear. I felt icy cold hands on my face.

My vision came swimming back. Aubrey, if it had really been him, was nowhere in sight. But the Harvester was.

He walked toward me, casually swinging the sickle like a tennis player warming up. There was no need for hurry on his part. I was still stunned by the impact, either of the wall or his magic. My eyes worked, so I could stare into the crusted wounds where Wulfe's blue eyes should have been. He stood in front of me for a second. I managed to move my shoulder. If I'd had a couple of minutes, I thought I could shake it off.

The sickle came at me, cutting the air so fast that it made a noise.

The blade missed, sweeping by me and up in a strike I would never have been able to get much force behind. But Wulfe was a lot stronger than me. The pitted old blade dug into Wulfe's own belly, spilling entrails and splashing me with blood. It was so unreal that it felt almost like I was watching a scene in a Quentin Tarantino martial arts movie.

The Soul Taker's enraged howl rang in my aching head without making an audible sound as Wulfe laughed. My magic, it seemed, had worked after all. Though I hadn't dreamed that this was what Wulfe would do with the moment of freedom—vampires were not built for self-sacrifice or suicide. They were vampires, in fact, because they refused to die.

Blood pooling at his feet, Wulfe tried to open his hand, fingers relaxing. But before the sickle fell to the ground, his hand moved like a striking hawk, closing around the leather-wrapped handle. He stood still, armed with the sickle, as blood continued to drip.

I tried to gather myself and managed a sort of full-body twitch. The Harvester staggered away from me, toward Warren, his footfalls heavy. Warren, who was unconscious. I was helpless to do anything to interfere as the vampire dropped to the ground and bent over the werewolf. From where I was, I couldn't see exactly what he did, but I could hear it when he started to feed.

Feeding was how vampires were able to heal their wounds because—although I now knew, somewhat to my surprise, that vampires had souls—they were not truly alive. They did not reproduce sexually, and they could not heal using their own biological abilities. They needed to borrow healing from the living blood they fed upon.

The Soul Taker had decided to fix Wulfe's body before sacrificing me. I looked at the blood on the floor in front of me. There was a lot of it. I wondered why it chose to feed on Warren instead of me.

"That one is dangerous," said Coyote conversationally. If I could have turned my head, I imagined I would have seen him squatting on his heels beside me.

"Which?" I whispered.

Wulfe took no notice of my words—which meant that Coyote was keeping our conversation private.

"Both," Coyote said. "All. But you need to destroy that weapon, Daughter. The opening it is building does not call a well-meaning god into this realm." He considered his words. "It could be summoning a world eater."

My brain was still not quite tracking. I could tell because I was having a conversation with Coyote while the Soul Taker used Wulfe's body to feed upon my friend. And because the next thing I said was sort of stupid.

"We killed the river devil," I said. I sounded offended—which I was. We'd killed that being, the world eater, at great cost. I was pretty sure that it should stay dead.

"The river devil was a conduit for great destruction," Coyote said. "That body was a means by which our world could be devoured. A metaphor."

"Pretty concrete for a metaphor," I said. "It laid me up for months and put me in a wheelchair that I couldn't move because my hands were hurt, too."

"There is nothing in the world that says a metaphor cannot be concrete," Coyote chided. "But if that thing—"

"The Soul Taker," I said, and then my heart froze in my chest because Wulfe's body stiffened and he quit drinking.

After a moment, he began feeding again.

"Don't name it," said Coyote kindly. "Not unless you want its attention."

"It wants you," I told him. "Through me."

Coyote nodded. I couldn't see him do it, but I knew he was nodding. "Dangerous." He paused. "It *is* more likely that it is summoning something that has long since dissipated or reintegrated with the Great Spirit. Still, a summoning of that size is likely to end in disaster. You are my hands and heart in this world, Mercedes Athena Thompson."

"Hauptman," I said.

"Ah," he agreed. "That is a very important part of your name. Don't forget it."

Warm fingers pressed against my head in farewell or blessing. Or possibly "Good-bye. You are going to die today." With Coyote, it could be difficult to tell.

A few seconds that felt like hours later, my head cleared and I could work my arms and legs again. I didn't think this was anything Coyote had helped me with, but I was too frantic to worry about it one way or the other.

Vampires were not supposed to kill their meals. In return, no one would tell the mortals that vampires were real. It was a pact that had stood for a very long time. It was better for all of us. The vampires followed the agreement, more or less, and were careful to hide the bodies when they "forgot," which was often enough to leave vampires' homes haunted by their victims. I couldn't trust Wulfe, in his altered state, or the Soul Taker to leave Warren alive.

I reached out and grabbed the walking stick without looking for it—the best way I'd found to make sure it showed up. As soon as my fingers closed on the carved surface, I surged to my feet.

The door exploded.

Well, not really "exploded." But it burst open with a noise that indicated bending metal and splintering wood. It *felt* even louder than it actually was because as soon as the door opened, the bond I shared with Adam lit up with information.

And if I had ever, once, doubted that I was loved, if I had ever doubted that my husband was a scary monster who would kill anything that threatened me, that moment disabused me of it. Which was only fair because I felt the same way.

Adam went for the vampire feeding on Warren. But without even looking up, the Harvester vanished. I hadn't known Wulfe could teleport—though Marsilia and Stefan could, which implied an inherited gift. No reason that it could not have come from Wulfe.

Deprived of his target, Adam hit the bed rather than tripping over Warren. The two-by-eight of mahogany that served as the long side of the bed frame cracked and broke, and the legs dug deep gouges into the hardwood floor. It hit the wall with the speed of a locomotive, and other parts of the bed and the drywall and the wainscoting took an impressive amount of damage. Adam kept on his feet but howled his rage at missing his rightful kill, as the pack, all of them still in human form, poured into the room.

"So," I said into the silence that followed, "I'm afraid we got complacent, even after two warnings. Maybe next time you should give us three?"

Without a word, Adam stalked over and wrapped me in his arms, picking me up off the ground. It hurt all of my various bruises. Most especially it hurt the long cut across my back. There had been several moments during which I'd been pretty sure I wouldn't get to do this again. I hugged him back.

"Warren's breathing okay," Darryl said. "But there's something weird about the way he feels in the pack bonds. Feels like corruption."

Adam let me go. "You're sure you're okay?" he asked.

"A few cuts and a cursed weapon to hunt down," I told him briskly, ignoring the aching bones and muscles that I knew would get much worse once the adrenaline wore off. "I'll find time to gibber in a corner with fear as soon as we're all safe. But I'm good."

Adam went to Warren, who hadn't stirred. Mary Jo, a trained EMT, was going over the back of his head and neck with careful hands. There was a fireman's axe on the ground beside her, her favorite weapon.

"I don't know why he's unconscious," she said. "How long has he been this way, Mercy?"

"I'm not sure," I said. As much as I wanted to check on Warren with my own eyes, I stayed back. Mary Jo and Adam were better with first aid. "I was busy, and that makes time feel odd. And I got hit with a magical whammy that laid me out. The Harvester took Warren by surprise. Maybe he hit Warren with a magical whammy."

Yes, said Aubrey from right beside me. *I can see it. But it's fading.*

I didn't respond.

"The vampire's trying to bind him," said Darryl flatly. "I can feel it."

His eyes were gold, the pupils small. I wondered how long he'd been dealing with his wolf trying to get out. From Auriele's surreptitious glances, I figured it might have been a bit too long for comfort.

Adam nodded. "I can feel it, too."

"We can keep him in the cage until we can get Marsilia to free him," Darryl said.

"Assuming she can," said George.

"She freed me," Darryl growled.

"Those bastards who got you weren't Wulfe," Auriele said, sounding worried.

Adam moved Mary Jo aside and sat on the floor beside Warren. "I learned a little trick while we were in Italy," he said. "Let me see what I can do."

He pulled Warren around, then leaned forward and kissed him on the forehead.

Lips still touching skin, Adam said, "*Wake up.*" The words carried the push of the power of the pack Alpha, and I could feel him draw upon us. This was nothing unusual. Adam could call upon any of his wolves.

Warren's eyes opened and Adam caught his gaze.

The gateway to the soul, I thought.

Adam forced power down the pack bonds and thrust it into Warren. The magic rose in every werewolf in the room until they all wore their wolf's eyes. I heard a few growls.

Warren's body jerked in reaction, but he didn't fight to break eye contact.

"*Change,*" Adam told him. Outwardly that wasn't anything special, either. Forcing a wolf's change could help them heal. I'd also seen it used as a disciplinary move a time or two, in order to reinforce the knowledge that the Alpha was the wolf in charge without resorting to outright violence.

But what Adam did with his power as Warren began to change was different. It felt like he was burning through Warren with what I could only describe as spiritual fire as Warren's body altered.

Warren was dominant and old. His change didn't take as long as some of the others. But it wasn't my instantaneous change, either. It took maybe ten minutes for him to complete it, but the vampire taint was gone after the first few moments of his shift. Adam stayed where he was and held Warren's eyes until a wolf stood where the man had been.

Mary Jo cleaned my various cuts. There were a number that I didn't even remember. Fights were like that. The worst of them was the long cut across my back. Honey produced a safety pin and rerouted my bra strap so it still worked without pressing across the cut.

I gave them an abbreviated version of what had happened.

"This was the last room we were checking," I said. "I took the bathroom, Warren got the office. The Harvester knocked out Warren and cut the lights."

"The Harvester?" interrupted Auriele. "Isn't that Wulfe?"

"Yes," I said. "Sorry that I'm being confusing. We fought."

"And you're still alive?" Her surprise was not flattering, but I shared it, so I didn't take offense.

"The Soul Taker wanted to kill me," I told her, "but Wulfe didn't." I decided I was too tired to run through the whole fight, and I'd only get lost babbling about the woo-woo part of it. So I said only, "Wulfe managed to break free of the Soul Taker's hold for a moment and stabbed himself instead of me." I waved at the blood on the floor. "Which is where you all came in. Thank you. How did your search go?"

"Marsilia is going to have to replace a lot of doors," Auriele said with an admiring look at Darryl.

He snorted. "We didn't find a thing. Not so much as a body. Empty room after empty room." He looked at me. "But we did not get complacent."

"We should get Warren home," Adam said, rising to his feet. "We're done here."

14

~~~

DECIDING WE NEEDED TO GET WARREN HOME QUICKLY, Adam loaded Warren, Zack, and me in his SUV and sent the rest of the wolves to ride with Honey back to the garage. Darryl took Warren's key fob, rescued from the shreds of Warren's jeans, and promised to deliver the Subaru.

Zack hopped back out of the SUV and went over to have a word with Darryl. I turned to Adam.

"Not now," he suggested.

Warren, curled up on the flattened half of the back passenger seat, looked as though he were asleep. But I took Adam's point. There were a lot of things we needed to talk about, but adding Warren and Zack into the mix just now was probably not useful.

Zack slid into the side of the backseat that hadn't been turned into cargo space and belted himself in. "*Auriele* will drive the Subaru to our house," he said, possibly to Warren. "Darryl will pick her up there."

No one talked much on the way to the house Warren and Kyle shared with Zack. Zack must have texted, because Kyle came out as soon as we drove up.

He accepted Warren's shredded clothing with a muttered, "Maybe he wasn't wrong about expensive clothing and werewolves." But his eyes were on Warren, who'd hopped out of the SUV, stretched, and then trotted up to Kyle, tail waving gently.

Kyle gave Adam an anxious look. "I couldn't tell what happened from Zack's text. 'Warren got a magical whammy but he's fine' doesn't really mean a lot to me."

"Keep an eye on him," Adam said. "The whammy was nothing to worry about, but he was bitten by a vampire. You should make sure he eats and drinks."

"Vampire?" Kyle said, his hands closing on Warren's fur. "It's the middle of the day."

"Some of them are active during the day," I said.

"If you get worried, get Zack to take a look at him," Adam told him. "If you get really worried, call me or"—he hesitated—"Sherwood."

"Sherwood?" asked Zack, looking startled. "Are you sure?"

Kyle looked from one to the other and said, "Definitely not calling Sherwood. What's wrong with Sherwood?"

"What's not wrong with Sherwood," I said. Weariness from the fight had started setting in. My feet and hands ached for some reason—it took me a minute to remember that Zee had dug spider bits out of them yesterday. That seemed like a long time ago. My arms hurt, my left hip hurt, and the place on my jaw where I'd caught an elbow hurt every time I moved my mouth. "But call him anyway if you think Warren isn't right. He's got more experience with magic than any of us."

"I thought he didn't remember anything?" Kyle narrowed his eyes.

I gave Kyle a look, met his gaze, and then jerked my head away. "Sometimes I wish Warren had fallen in love with one of his fluff pieces instead of a lawyer. I will answer your questions when we all have better answers. Warren needs to lie down in front of a fire and sleep. Zack can tell you about our adventures today. I need to get home and wash and change and not keep standing on your driveway answering questions I don't know the answer to."

There was a little silence. The air echoed and I realized I'd yelled the last few words.

"You look like you killed someone," Kyle said. "Too late to hide it from me, I'm sad to say. But if you wash up quickly and burn those clothes, I'm sure no one will ask." It sounded as if he were snapping back, but I knew Kyle. He was worried. But he knew better than to ask me what was wrong when I'd just asked him to stop asking questions.

"Don't you have to report it when you think someone might be a murderer anyway?" Zack asked Kyle, his tone one of casual inquiry.

I threw my hands up—which made the cut on my back burn—and stomped back to the SUV. They talked for a little bit more, but with the door shut I could pretend not to hear them.

"I thought she just dyed your hair blue when you weren't looking, or put stuff in your coffee that made you pee green," Zack said. "I didn't think she yelled at people."

"She yells at me," Adam told them.

"Probably because you wouldn't care if she dyed your hair blue," Kyle answered. "She gets mad when she's scared. What's scaring her?"

Adam got into the SUV eventually without answering that question because he didn't know the answer to it yet. He gave me an opportunity to say something, but when I didn't, he started the engine and we headed home.

"Bran taught me how to use the pack bonds to break the ties that vampires use on their prey," he said into the silence. "That's how I knew what to do for Warren. I asked about you and Stefan, but Bran said a consensual bond was a different matter."

I nodded. My newfound and unwelcome understanding of the way the bonds worked with souls allowed me to visualize the problem. Consensual bonds were like two-ply rope instead of string. Just like I understood how blood made those ties possible and stronger.

I knew all of that because the connection between the Soul Taker and me was stronger now that it had tasted my blood. The cut along my shoulder blades burned. I was pretty sure it was just a normal cut, but the significance of feeding my blood to the Soul Taker made it feel as if it was the worst damage I'd taken in that fight. Maybe it was.

I wanted to run, but I was trapped in the SUV, bouncing the heel of one foot. The problem was that right now there was nowhere to run from or run to, but my adrenaline-infused body didn't know that.

"Bran says if it becomes a problem, killing Stefan is the easiest way to break it," Adam said. "I could do that."

I wasn't as sure of that as Adam sounded, but I nodded again. I knew Adam wouldn't kill Stefan without a good reason—I wasn't going to get upset with Adam for suggesting it, because I was pretty sure he wanted me to react. It was kind of him to try to distract me, but manipulation was a bit much. Maybe I should dye his hair blue. I rubbed my eyes because I didn't want to cry. That would send the wrong message.

"Mercy?" Adam asked, his voice low.

"I'm thinking," I told him. "Let me get it straight in my head first."

He nodded, "Can do, darlin'."

After a while I asked, "Did you take Warren home and send the rest with Honey to keep me away from Zee?"

"Yes," he said. "If I had taken you straight to the garage and he asked you about the Soul Taker, what would you have done?"

I didn't answer. I wasn't sure of the answer. "What could I have told him that he doesn't already know?"

"That you'd call him in when you found out where it is," Adam said. "I thought you should have some time before you deliver a powerful, ancient, and cursed artifact into a powerful, ancient, iron-kissed fae's hands. I'm not saying we shouldn't do just that—but we should only do it after due consideration."

I didn't say anything to that, either. He wasn't wrong.

"Did you blow up at Kyle because you are scared of the Soul Taker?" Adam asked.

"Yes," I said. "And Wulfe."

Adam didn't respond because he knew I wasn't telling him all of it.

"I'm scared of what will happen if Zee has the Soul Taker," I said, though I wasn't sure I'd been all that worried until Adam had made sure I didn't see him until I had time to think it over.

I'd known Zee for ten years. I loved him as if he were my family. He'd saved my life more than once. But I agreed with Tad when he worried about Zee's interactions with Izzy. Adam was not wrong that we should be wary of Zee's interest in the Soul

Taker. I thought about that bead of sweat on my old friend's face as he spoke of the artifact. I couldn't think of anything I lusted after enough to make me sweat—except for Adam. I understood the way the Soul Taker worked on the people around it—not just its wielder. Zee and the Soul Taker sounded, now that I really thought about it, like a very bad idea. I just wasn't sure we were going to have a choice in the matter.

"And?" Adam asked. "You're scared of something else, because none of that is anything that would make you yell at Kyle."

Me. I thought. *I'm scared of me.*

"Vampires have souls," I said abruptly. It was not the change of subject that Adam probably thought it was.

I could feel him looking at me, but I kept my face turned away. "Old souls are—not bigger, exactly, than newer, younger souls. They just have more twists and turns."

"Did you have a philosophical discussion with the Soul Taker while you were fighting?" Adam asked dryly.

"Wulfe was always screwed up," I said, picking at the fabric of my jeans. "Some sort of experiment, maybe." I had a fleeting impression of vague faces that told me not much. Had they been his parents? They didn't feel parental. "He was a pet, maybe," I heard myself say. This wasn't the important part. I sorted through what was important and got back on track.

"Witch and wizard and mage and vampire and something fae that's mostly gone now." It had been a wisp I could sense but not put my finger on. "Riding all of those magics was a balancing act, but he managed, mostly." He'd killed his progenitors and wandered the world haphazardly for longer than I'd realized. He might be as old as or older than Bran. "He found Marsilia first, then Stefan, and finally Bonarata. They took care of him. He knew so much, understood so much, and was so lost. Bonarata persuaded Wulfe to turn him. Wulfe was old even then, but Bonarata was his first—the first vampire he made."

"Who have you been talking to?" Adam asked.

I shook my head. "Bonarata didn't understand what Wulfe was. Didn't understand what maker meant—that Bonarata would have to obey Wulfe. He dealt with it until one day Wulfe scared him. Bonarata doesn't deal well with fear, so he set out to destroy Wulfe." I paused. "And I think he was jealous, too—of Marsilia's feelings for Wulfe. That's why Wulfe let Bonarata be the one to turn Marsilia. But Wulfe doesn't understand jealousy very well."

"Mercy?" asked Adam, sounding wary. "Do I need to take you to Sherwood? Or Bran?"

I reached out and he caught my hand. His was very warm or mine was very cold.

"I think we just need to get rid of that damned artifact," I said in a normal voice that made me realize how singsongy and dreamy I'd been. I cleared my throat. "Coyote is affiliated with the soul and with death—and I think that is playing with the effect the Soul Taker is having on me."

"Okay," Adam said, his hand still holding mine.

"Let me tell you about Wulfe, because it's important and I don't know if I'll remember the important bits later." *Or I might be dead and you need to know about Wulfe. If you, my love, are the one left to face him and that artifact.*

"Okay," he said.

"And I don't know things until I say them out loud," I said. "So some of the out-loud parts aren't going to be important." I had looked into Wulfe's eyes for a very short period of time, and that had been in a dream. And I had seen everything. My head ached worse than the cut along my shoulder blade where it pressed against the SUV seat.

"Okay." Adam's voice was very soft.

"Bonarata set out to break him, but he didn't really understand what he was dealing with—because Wulfe never told him. Bonarata knew Wulfe could wield magic and that he was a little wrong, but he didn't connect the two. I don't know why Bonarata doesn't kill Wulfe. Or rather, *Wulfe* doesn't know why. I think it's because Bonarata is scared of Wulfe, and killing him would be an admission of that."

Adam nodded. "That's how Marsilia reads it, too," he said. "She thinks that if Wulfe dies before Bonarata conquers that fear—then Bonarata will be afraid of Wulfe forever."

"I don't know why Wulfe hasn't killed Bonarata," I said.

There was something, some reason, but I could not find it in my mental image of what I'd seen when I *looked* at Wulfe.

I just knew there was a reason, something Wulfe had kept hidden from me as soon as he knew that I was seeing into him.

"Is it important?" Adam asked.

"I don't know," I told him. "But other things are. Bonarata tried to break Wulfe—but Wulfe was already broken. Wulfe isn't stubborn, he is like . . ." A kite in the wind, and Bonarata was the wind. But what I said was "Like the lizard with the two dark spots on its rump that look like eyes, to fool predators. Wherever your enemy thinks you are, be somewhere else." That was all I could tell him. There were other things he should know, but I couldn't put them into words.

"You think that the Soul Taker doesn't have as strong a hold on Wulfe as it assumes," Adam said, because he was good at reading between the lines.

That was it. I nodded, then shook my head. "None of them do. Not the Soul Taker, not Bonarata, and not Marsilia."

The SUV was very quiet; I realized we'd stopped at a red light. We were near the turn that led to my garage.

"Now why don't you tell me why you aren't looking at me?" Adam asked. "I thought maybe you had a headache, but you're deliberately not looking at me."

"Remember how I told you that I was tied to the Soul Taker somehow?" My voice was tight.

"Yes," he said.

"Today, while we fought, it cut me. Tasted my blood. And now when I look into someone's eyes, I *see* them. I *saw* Mary Jo when she was cleaning me up at Marsilia's. I *saw* Kyle."

"You saw them," Adam said cautiously, turning onto Chemical Drive. "You don't mean with your eyes?"

"Yes, with my eyes," I snapped at him. "Sorry, sorry. It's with my eyes the same way I smell magic. Only I can smell magic without my nose. With this I have to meet their eyes."

That wasn't quite true. I'd seen Wulfe and he didn't have physical eyes to look into. He'd had to use a dream for that.

"Mercy?"

"Wait, I'm having a revelation." Had Wulfe meant me to see him? Was that why he'd bitten me—blood magic—and pulled me into a dreamscape?

Even after looking into him, I wasn't sure. I pulled my mind back to the explanation I owed Adam.

"I see"—I clutched his hand with my suddenly clammy one—"into their souls. When I remember it—it comes like a visual. But I can tell you things about them that the visual shouldn't tell me. It feels like my senses are confused. Like I can taste music or

337

hear colors. I looked at Wulfe and I know things about his past that looking at him shouldn't be able to tell me."

"As a person who tried LSD a few times," Adam said, "I probably understand better than you might think."

"You?" I asked, genuinely shocked. Not that people did LSD, but that *Adam* had.

"Vietnam," he said shortly, as if that was an answer—and maybe it was. "But I understand how perception can get miscategorized."

"It's like what happened with Aubrey," I said. "Except they aren't dead. Mary Jo—" I hesitated. What I saw when I looked at her, at Kyle, was something I had no right to know, let alone repeat.

"Do you think it's permanent?" Adam asked.

I slumped in the seat. "No idea."

We drove in silence for a while, past the fairgrounds.

"Can we stop by my shop?" I asked.

We'd have to backtrack to do it now.

"Do you want to see Zee?" There was no emphasis on the "see," but we both knew what he meant.

"No," I told him honestly. "If I use this to look at him, I don't think he'd ever forgive me. But I think I have to. Because if we get the Soul Taker, the only thing I can think of to do with it is give it to Zee. And I just don't know if that's a good idea or not."

Adam didn't say anything.

"The Soul Taker is really bad news," I said in a small voice. "It scared Coyote."

"When did—" Adam began, but broke off. "Never mind. That doesn't matter right now. Zee is the only person you think can deal with this artifact." He grunted. "All things considered, he's still the only person I'd ask to deal with it, too."

"Larry left the Soul Taker with Bonarata rather than tell Zee where it was," I said. "And Bonarata was so ignorant that he gave Wulfe to it. I have to tell you right now that the Soul Taker riding Wulfe scares the pants off me."

Adam still hadn't turned around, and we were now closer to home than to the garage.

"Did you change your mind about Wulfe after you saw him?" asked Adam.

"No," I said.

"How about Mary Jo or Kyle?"

I saw where he was going. "No."

"You know enough about Zee to decide what to do," Adam said, and I could breathe again because he was right.

He didn't take me to the garage. We drove home instead. There were no other cars parked at the house, so Jesse was still out.

Adam got out first because he wasn't stiff from sitting after a fight. I heard him laugh as I slid gingerly out of the vehicle—but I didn't see why he was laughing until I shut the SUV's door.

Some joker had left a pumpkin pie on the porch step. It was store-bought, one of those in a clear plastic keeper. In orange Sharpie they'd scrawled *For Mercy, with apologies, from Her Little Pumpkin.*

I picked it up and took it inside. There were three small pumpkins sitting on the stairway. One of them had a three-by-five index card with *Score is 1–0. Want to try again?* A second had a big spider drawn on it with marker. The third was covered with itty-bitty spiders.

I could have sniffed them to figure out who it was—even if they'd used gloves, they had transported the loot in a car. But that would have been cheating.

I walked past the stairway and into the kitchen. I set the pie on the table next to Medea, who was not supposed to be on the table. She rolled over on her back without any sign of guilt, and I rubbed her belly.

"You are a weird cat," I told her, as her stump tail swatted back and forth with pleasure as if she were a dog.

Adam came up behind me and put the stairway pumpkins on the table next to the cat and the pie. He wrapped his arms around me and said, "What can I do to help?"

I turned around and stood on tiptoe to kiss him, finding his lips by feel because I kept my eyes closed. As his mouth caressed mine—and then changed into something fiercer—I felt the tension that had invaded my body ever since I saw the encyclopedias in the bathroom ease into a different kind of tension.

Passion didn't make my stomach hurt, didn't make me want to curl up under the blankets like a child afraid of the dark. Passion—at least passion with Adam—made me feel brave.

"That," I said. "Yes. That's good. Nudge."

"Upstairs." His voice was gravelly and sent a zing up my spine because my body knew what happened to it when Adam sounded like that.

I nodded and he picked me up—I wasn't so far gone that I didn't wince at the feel of his arm across the cut on my back and the flexing of stiff muscles. I was pretty sure that I'd pulled something in my lower back, because it spasmed when I twisted.

Adam was observant by nature and training, so it didn't surprise me when he took me to our bathroom instead of our bed. He undressed me carefully. When my shirt tried to stick to the cut, he held a wet washcloth over it until it pulled free.

"Mary Jo looked at it," I told him. "She said it was my choice for stitches, but her opinion was the stitches would bother me more than the wound."

"She's a werewolf," Adam said, looking closely at my back. "Stitches are always unnecessary for her, and she'd already be healed from something like this. She cleaned it?"

"Yes," I said. "Did she bring her little first-aid kit just for me?" I don't know why that hadn't occurred to me. But anything the werewolves couldn't heal from in minutes would be too much for that little kit.

"Yes," Adam said, and I snorted at his "of course" tone.

He stripped me down to my skin. He paused here and there to check other cuts and bruises. But I knew there wasn't much. His fingertips touched the muscle in my side that had given me fits when he picked me up in the kitchen.

"Bruised," he said.

"The wall." The impact had been on my back. Good. Bruises healed faster than pulled muscles—or at least they quit bothering me sooner.

He wet another clean washcloth and delicately cleaned my face, my hands and arms, making me remember that I was splattered with blood.

"Most of the blood is Wulfe's," I said. And told him about how I'd tried to free Wulfe from the hold of the Soul Taker—and how he had used that freedom—in more detail than I'd given the pack.

"He cut himself open to save me," I said. Possibly that wasn't the only reason, but I didn't want Adam to know quite how much the Soul Taker wanted me or what it thought that would mean. Not because I wanted to keep anything from Adam but because

I needed to make love with him. And if I got started on the whole woo-woo mess of my visit to the seethe, I wasn't going to want to make love for a while.

"He could have killed me anytime he chose," I told Adam's shoulder—because he was holding me again by that time and because if my face was buried in his shoulder, there was no possibility of my catching his eyes.

"There are people I would less like to make an unwilling slave of than Wulfe," Adam commented. "But they are fewer in number than the fingers of my right hand."

"How come you have all your clothes on and I'm naked?" I complained, because I was done talking about Wulfe and the Soul Taker right now.

He laughed, a small private sound. "Because you plastered yourself against me before I could get them off."

I backed up and sat on the cold marble of the vanity countertop because my feet hurt and because it put some distance between us. I could watch him strip without being tempted to touch—which might slow us up.

Watching Adam undress was one of my favorite things.

"What?" he asked, stepping out of his jeans.

I remembered to shut my eyes before I accidentally looked into his. "What do you mean, what?" I asked.

"You were grinning."

I felt it happen again. "I am just surprised that some enterprising women haven't put a hit out on me in sheer envy," I told him. "And they don't even know that the outside package isn't a tithe on the man underneath."

There was a pause, and I felt my smile soften, but it wouldn't go away. I hurt all over. I was an exhausted mess. As soon as I let myself think again, I was going to be a scared, exhausted mess. And it didn't matter. Adam made me happy.

"You can look at me, you know," he said, nearer than I'd expected. "You don't need the Soul Taker to show you my soul—you've already been there, done that."

My mate had a generous and open heart. Beside him I was a hopeless coward. It would not matter to me if he'd seen my soul bared once, I still would not want him to do it again. I would be too afraid of what he'd see.

I swallowed. "I have my heart set on jumping your bones," I told him. "That other is distracting."

He gave an Adam grunt, and I heard the soft footfalls that told me he had gone into the bedroom. I opened my eyes and gingerly got off the vanity. My skin wanted to stick so I had to peel myself off. Standing on my feet had been getting more uncomfortable, but sitting on the vanity had been the wrong choice. Hopping down wasn't pleasant.

Adam missed all of this—as I intended him to. When he came into the bathroom, I was standing on the tile and he was holding one of his silk ties—deep blue with chocolate highlights that were the same color as his eyes.

"Not that one," I said. "It's my favorite."

He lifted it and wrapped it around my eyes anyway. "Mine, too," he said. Then he put his lips against my ear and whispered, "I like it when you wear my clothes."

I didn't object again. There were always dry cleaners.

He picked me up again—this time avoiding both the cut on my back and the sore muscle. He took his time getting from the bathroom to the bed. By the time he set me down on the cool sheets, I had forgotten all about my aches and pains.

It took him a while, but eventually I forgot my own name. I remembered his, though.

Sweaty, panting, and happy, I lay contentedly facedown on the bed while Adam cleaned the mess we'd made. He put ointment on my back and only then untied the tie covering my eyes.

"I think it will survive," he said, sounding a little surprised.

"Quality pays off," I murmured.

"You should eat something," he said.

If I moved, it was going to hurt. Right now nothing hurt at all.

"Go away or come to bed," I told him.

"I thought it's supposed to be men who have to sleep after sex," he complained, but there was a thread of laughter in his voice. I made Adam happy, too.

"I fought a possessed vampire. I get to sleep."

"Fair enough," he said, patting my butt. He pulled the sheet and then the blankets over me.

I probably should have worried about the ointment on my back getting on the sheets. But I couldn't work up the energy.

Adam pulled down the shades to darken the room, then took a shower. I was asleep before he came out of the bathroom. Someone tried to wake me up for dinner but left me alone after I yelled at them. If I dreamed, I didn't notice.

I WOKE UP TO A DARK ROOM AND ADAM SLEEPING beside me. I'd stolen all of the covers and he lay naked, facedown on the bed. I couldn't help but smile—and it had nothing to do with his hard-muscled body. He could have unrolled me from the covers, but that would have woken me up.

"*Frost*—"

The memory of Wulfe's voice made me frown. Why had he wanted to talk about Frost? Frost was dust, Adam and I had killed him between us, but when Frost was walking the earth, he'd had a talent for souls. He'd fed off them.

Adam stirred. I rolled out of the blankets and covered him.

"I'm up," I whispered. "Go back to sleep. I'm going down to grab some food."

He grunted and reached out. I touched his hand and leaned over to kiss him. Then I grabbed a set of sweats I kept in the top drawer of my dresser and put them on before leaving the bedroom.

The house was quiet. I could hear even breathing from Jesse's room. Medea joined me at the top of the stairs, twining around my ankles all the way down to the kitchen. There was a Tupperware container of food obviously portioned for my dinner— spaghetti and salad. The pumpkin pie was on the same shelf with two pieces missing. I gave Medea a meatball in her food dish, then sat down and ate like I hadn't had food in a week. When I'd finished the dinner I'd been left and a big piece of pie, I went back to the fridge and gathered sandwich makings.

And on my second bite of sandwich, I realized what Wulfe had meant. It was a lot of meaning to get from one word, but I was pretty sure I was right.

My absent gaze fell on the window, and I realized that Tilly, in her favorite guise of a ten-year-old girl complete with long, tangled hair and a dirty shift, was sitting on the picnic table I'd been sitting on when the Harvester had come calling.

Blood chilled, I wondered how long she'd been there.

I was going to start using the curtains in this room at night, I decided. After a second, I changed my mind. Curtains would mean that I couldn't see what was on the other side of the window.

She beckoned me outside.

I looked at the cat. "I don't think this is going to be good," I said, but I went out, sandwich in hand. If the Harvester came back, he would be occupied with Tilly and not me.

"To what do I owe the pleasure?" I asked as I closed the kitchen door behind me.

She had a lumpy mass of rough fabric sewn with thick thread that might have been gut sitting on the table beside her. Something roundish about the size of a small cantaloupe was inside the makeshift bag.

"You are going to get the Soul Taker," she said with more confidence than I felt. "And I have a gift for you to give the old Smith, with my compliments. I'd give him the other, but I can't remember where it was left." She held a finger up to her cheek and dimpled at me. Someone had been watching too many Shirley Temple movies.

I finished my sandwich, taking my time, then wiped my hands on my pants. When I started toward her, she pushed the bag in my direction.

"You bring the Soul Taker to me," she said, her voice no longer sounding like a child's voice, "and I will see that it troubles you no more. You bring me the Soul Taker, and I will see that no harm comes to you and yours for a mortal generation. You bring me the Soul Taker, and I will owe you a favor commensurate with the gift of the sickle."

She opened the bag, pulling the fabric back so that it worked as a presentation cloth for the object it had held. Then she lit a lantern—or created one, because I hadn't noticed a lantern before this. Maybe she thought that I hadn't figured out what it was and I needed the light.

I looked her in the eyes—then flinched away when I remembered I shouldn't do it. But it had been only Tilly's dirty face I saw. She smiled slyly at me when I met her eyes a second time. "Is it that I don't have a soul, do you think?"

"I think that it would take more than the magic of an old artifact to let me see into you," I said.

She laughed delightedly. "I do like you," she said.

I stared at the thing on the table. "If I take it to him, you will extend the agreement—the one that allows you to have a door in our backyard and pledges that you harm no one who lives in our home—to my house over there." I waved at the single-wide. "So I can rent it to someone without worrying about the tenant."

If one of the fae asked me to do something, it was expected that I ask something in return. I didn't let on that it was important to me—just a balance for the delivery service.

"Agreed," she said easily, unwittingly making Tad's life safer and easier. She probably wasn't going to be happy about it, but it was a valid bargain. "And the other?" she didn't bother to hide her eagerness.

I picked up the cup—it was neither as large nor as heavy as it looked, though it appeared to be molded out of pure silver. There was no question it was a work of art—exquisitely beautiful, even if it was in the shape of a skull. I'd instinctively lifted it with my hand cupped beneath the round part, and it felt comfortable there.

I'd pictured it with lower jaw attached, but it was only the single complete piece of skull, though the socket where the bottom jaw fit was clearly visible. The teeth from the upper jaw were a little irregular and one eyetooth was missing. I couldn't tell what color the gems set in the eye sockets were at first. But when I tipped the cup, the lantern made the gems flash blue.

"You think of him as a mentor. As one who fixes machines.

You think he is your friend," Tilly said. Interesting that she didn't name him. She wasn't usually worried about drawing his attention.

"I do," I agreed.

"He searches for artifacts to bring back the magic that was once his," she told me.

That was also true, though a little misleading. I expected deceptive truths with Tilly. Collecting his own weaponry had been a casual hobby of his for as long as I'd known him. I had the impression that it was more in the nature of gathering his children around him. I hadn't been aware that he was collecting wild artifacts as well until he'd told me. He wasn't mining them for lost power.

I was pretty sure.

"You don't know him." Tilly watched my face closely. "A decade to one of his kind is a mere breath to one of yours. You look at this." She bobbed her forefinger toward the cup I held. "You look at this, Mercedes Thompson Hauptman, and you remember what he is—the Dark Smith of Drontheim, who killed his own daughter."

She paused, but I didn't react. That story I knew.

She frowned at me in obvious disappointment before continuing. "Wayland Smith, who forced a king to drink from the skull of his child. You *remember* what he is, the truth I have given you. Then you bring the Soul Taker to me. It is not the only powerful artifact I have kept safe—and kept others safe from."

She scooted off the table and grabbed the empty bag, taking it with her as she skipped back to the door in the wall. Only then did it occur to me that she hadn't touched the cup herself. It didn't feel dangerous in my hand.

Even though I'd heard the kitchen door open, I didn't turn my back to Tilly until she was gone, her door shut behind her.

Adam didn't speak as I brought the skull cup into the kitchen and set it among the pumpkins with a clink. He put an arm across the top of my shoulders as we contemplated the delicate detail that made the gruesome object beautiful. The gems were deep blue, cabochon, and the size of a robin's egg—sapphires, I assumed. But I wasn't an expert; they could have been something else—gemified eyeballs, at any rate. They were a little smaller than the eyes that originally fit in the sockets. I supposed they had shrunk when Zee had changed them.

"I know where Bonarata has our vampires," I told Adam. Wulfe had given me the clue when he'd asked me if I remembered Frost. "We need to go there tonight. Just you and me, I think. I don't want to give Bonarata reason to declare a war—and I don't want any of our wolves to accidentally pick up the Soul Taker."

He pulled out a chair and I did the same. We spent the next ten minutes making plans. I was glad I hadn't explained how anxious the Soul Taker was to kill me and gather every person tied to me. If I had, he might not have agreed to go alone with me tonight, and I had a strong feeling—a Coyote-urging-me kind of feeling—that we needed to do this *now*.

Adam had dressed before coming downstairs, so I left him penning a note to Jesse while I went up to put more appropriate clothes on. I didn't know where the katana had ended up. Presumably one of the others had grabbed it—or it was still in Marsilia's unused master bedroom.

I called Tad while I opened the safe.

"On my way," Tad said. "Adam texted that you needed me." He yawned.

I talked to him while I took down my chosen weapon. I considered bringing other weapons, too. In the end, I only added my usual concealed carry gun. If I needed more firepower, the walking stick would serve me as well as anything.

"I see," Tad said. "I'll be there in ten."

Adam had come up while I'd been on the phone. He reached over my shoulder and took a *rokushakubō* from the safe. There are many varieties of *bō*, and Adam had two or three favorites—all of which he kept in the safe. This one was a little longer than he was tall (as the name suggested) and made of unvarnished hickory. About a foot from each end were three one-inch bands of steel.

He glanced at my weapon.

"It's not polite to return a gift," he said.

I looked down at the silk belt I held in my hands. "I don't think it was a gift," I told him. "I think he brought it here for safekeeping. Bonarata took it from him once, and he didn't want to give him the opportunity to take it again."

Any museum curator would have cringed at the way I wrapped it around my waist and tied it. But I didn't think Wulfe would mind. It was a belt, after all.

"Are you going to tell me where we're going?" he asked.

"Benton City," I said. "The vineyard where we killed Frost."

15

~~~

BENTON CITY WAS A SMALL TOWN TEN MILES ON THE other side of the Tri-Cities from where we lived. Most of the people who lived there worked in the Tri-Cities or out in the nuclear-cleanup complex of the Hanford Site. The rest of them grew fruit or made wine.

It was about three in the morning when Adam drove to the abandoned vineyard in the maze of hilly agricultural land surrounding the little town. The property was still covered with gray skeletons of grape vines that had been left to die. It was unusual that good grape-growing land had been left to lie fallow like this for so long.

But on the site of the burned-out winery, someone had recently built a very large house. The land around the house was ripped up and scored—obviously where someone was still working on proper landscaping—but the house itself looked finished.

Anyone could have been building a house, of course. But

Adam had checked the county records and found that the land was owned by an Italian company. If I had any doubts that our vampires were there, the big black helicopter sitting on a pad beside the house eliminated them. The helicopter also meant Bonarata was there, but we'd known that was probable.

Adam drove on about a quarter of a mile and pulled into the property via a side road demarcating the line between the dead vines and live ones. The road was graveled and wide enough for a car and a half to drive on it, but there was cleared ground on either side of it.

The ground sloped—as good vineyards do—and we drove over a hump of land before we stopped. Adam parked out of sight of the house, next to one of the rows of dead grape vines, and we got out.

I heard a nighthawk cry and the distant sound of the interstate traffic. Coyotes exchanged a few barking yips—and when I replied, they showed up to check us out. An adult and three half-grown pups. One of the latter looked as though it wanted to investigate further, but the adult headed out for better hunting grounds, and the pups followed her.

"You're still sure that the Soul Taker will come out and find us?" Adam asked.

I nodded and thumped my temple—not the side the pumpkin had hit—and said, "It knows we are here. It wants me. It will come."

The only question was if the Harvester—the Soul Taker and Wulfe—would come alone.

We had been there for about twenty minutes when the helicopter engines roared to life. I looked at Adam, who shrugged. He didn't know what the helicopter meant, either—except that the game was probably ready to begin.

"I love you," I told him.

He smiled and set his steel-shod *bō* against his shoulder to get it out of the way so he could kiss me.

"Very touching," said Bonarata, his accent both faintly British and Italian.

We'd hoped for Wulfe and the Soul Taker alone, but Adam had thought it unlikely.

Neither Adam nor I reacted to Bonarata's presence, letting the kiss come to a natural conclusion a few seconds after Bonarata spoke. Then I stepped back and let Adam do the talking.

"You are trespassing on our territory without permission," Adam said.

It wasn't that Bonarata didn't look dangerous; he just didn't look like a monster. He was maybe four inches taller than Adam and had a boxer's square build, a big man who looked like a brawler. His nose had been broken and badly set—probably when he'd still been human. The skin around his left eye had been split and scarred. Even in the hand-tailored suit that he wore, he looked like hired muscle.

He smiled at Adam, and the smile changed his face, giving it the kind of dangerous charm that had sent women after bad men for as long as there had been women and bad men.

"Ah, please forgive me. I was visiting my people. I had forgotten that I should have let you know that I was here."

He knew that Adam could hear the lies he spoke. He didn't care.

"Oh, you let us know," I said. But I said it quietly enough that he could ignore me if he wanted to, and he didn't pull his attention off Adam, who was smiling with white teeth.

"I wasn't speaking of your visit," Adam said gently. "Though I accept your apologies as meant; Marsilia can have whatever visitors she chooses. She is my ally and I accept her judgment. I was speaking of this—" Adam swept out a hand to indicate the vineyard and the house we couldn't see but all knew was there. His other hand held the *bō*. "You should have put the property in someone else's name if you didn't want us to find it."

"This?" Bonarata said, brows raising in mock surprise. "This is a gift for Marsilia. She complained to me that so many houses have been built around her seethe that they pose a risk to her people. When it is finished, I shall present her with the deed."

That, oddly enough, was truth.

"A surprise gift," Adam said. "She didn't know about it."

Bonarata's smile widened. "That is true. But how else should you present such a gift to the woman you love?"

I snorted and drew an unfriendly look. He wouldn't think it odd that I avoided his eyes. Smart people didn't look vampires in the eyes.

He returned his attention to Adam. "Next time I come, I will be sure to give you warning," he said. "When I next buy property, I shall speak to you as well. As you can hear, I am getting ready to leave." His smile widened again, giving us a glimpse of fang. "My work here is done."

I tapped my hand twice on my thigh, giving Adam warning. When the Harvester appeared at Bonarata's side, teleporting in, Adam had already let the *bō* slide into both of his hands, ready for action.

Wulfe had fed again since Warren, I thought. The iris of his left eye was white, still in the process of regeneration, but his right eye was clear. He could see. That would change things a little, hopefully in our favor. I wondered that Bonarata had allowed it, then realized it was the Soul Taker that understood Wulfe's ability to see made him more difficult to keep in thrall.

"This one," Bonarata said, indicating the Harvester, "belongs to Marsilia." His words rang with a power that seemed to take him by surprise.

I had done that a few times. Said things in the heat of the moment, and it was like the universe listened. That was how our pack ended up in charge of a supernatural neutral zone.

I could see from Bonarata's face that he hadn't meant his statement to be real. But there had been truth in his voice, and something—fate or the universe or magic itself—had decided to take the man at his word.

A binding between Bonarata and Wulfe broke. I saw the Harvester's robes sway.

Wulfe had always been a spy in Marsilia's camp, Bonarata's unwilling servant. If Wulfe and Adam and I survived this night, I'd be pretty interested to see what this changed.

Adam stepped forward, disrupting the moment. "This is my territory," he said—and there was a bit of unintentional magic in his voice, too.

Maybe he should have waited another minute, because our territory had just expanded again.

There was something in the air tonight, I thought. Then my eyes found the battered sickle in Wulfe's hand. I knew how dense the collection of souls the Soul Taker had amassed was. Something like that could leave a magical charge just by being in the vicinity.

I put my hand on the girdle—not on purpose, just reflex, to make sure it was still there—and it was warm, a few degrees warmer than my body. It took me by surprise. I had not thought the belt to be anything but an antique. Not only was it warm, but I could feel a few bits of sparking magic caressing my skin.

The Harvester—Wulfe—turned his face toward me, and I saw the exact moment he noticed what I was wearing.

The girdle's magic had distracted me. Adam and Bonarata had exchanged a few words, but Adam's growl brought my attention back to them.

"The Harvester may not hunt in my territory," Adam said.

Bonarata stepped back and waved a gracious hand. "By all means, Alpha. I have told you he is not mine." His voice had a snap to it I didn't think he intended because the last two words were nearly a purr. "Stop him."

Adam didn't run precisely, though he moved with speed. Wulfe looked at the girdle I wore for half a breath longer before turning to engage with Adam.

I moved to the side so I could watch the fight and keep an eye on Bonarata at the same time. Adam and I had a backup plan if Bonarata threw in—but Adam didn't think he would. If he attacked Adam in our territory when he was a guest, he would lose face—and provide an opportunity for Bran to claim the attack was an act of war. Our pack might be officially separated from the Marrok, but Bran claimed all of North America. He could legitimately recognize any unprovoked aggression on Bonarata's part. More to the point, Bonarata knew that Bran would do so.

Adam didn't think Bonarata would risk a full-scale war with the North American werewolves. Of course, for Bran to act, there had to be witnesses.

I touched the belt again, just to make sure that I hadn't been imagining things. But it felt entirely normal now. Maybe I *had* just imagined it.

Like the sickle, the *bō* had started out as an agricultural tool. It was, essentially, a good, stout stick. Adam used the metal bands on the ends of his stick to protect the wood from edged weapons.

Even though Wulfe was taller by several inches, the *bō* gave Adam the advantage of reach, letting him stay well out of range of the Soul Taker. Wulfe wasn't giving Adam any opportunities to break bones. The only reason I'd been able to do that was because Wulfe hadn't expected me to snatch the walking stick out of the air.

The fight was a near stalemate, an exhibition in martial arts done at supernatural speed. Adam had told me that, having seen Wulfe fight a time or two, this part of the dance might last as much as five minutes.

As long as neither of them made a mistake.

A gun might have been the best choice of weapon—and we had discussed that, too. I had my concealed carry tucked in my waistband, though Adam had left his in the SUV. Adam wasn't sure that he could kill a vampire as old as Wulfe with a gun, and we didn't want to do that anyway. Our goal was to separate Wulfe from the Soul Taker. Marsilia needed him in the same way that we needed Sherwood.

I'd thought Wulfe had been holding back when we fought, and I'd been right. Someone who didn't understand what was going on might think that they were deliberately not hitting each other. But that wasn't true. They were predicting each other's moves and getting out of the way. I could do that, a little. I could do it better when fighting with people I'd trained with for months or years. Adam and I could put on a pretty good show. But nothing like this.

There weren't any giant leaps—once a fighter's feet left the ground, his trajectory couldn't change until he hit something. That made him an easy target. Those kinds of flashy moves were for demonstrations, or for fighting someone you held a considerable advantage over.

I wasn't the only one fascinated. I caught the moment when Bonarata leaned forward and watched the fight, moving subtly as if in participation. When he'd been human, he'd been one of the condottiere, a captain of mercenaries who'd gained power and wealth by waging war.

I might have enjoyed watching it, too, if I didn't know what the Soul Taker was. If so much didn't ride on Adam being just that little bit better than Wulfe.

Just that little bit. Or maybe if Wulfe managed to figure out why I brought his silk girdle with me. I wanted to touch it again, to see if it was still sparking magic. But Bonarata hadn't noticed it yet, so I kept my hands still.

Gradually, Adam forced Wulfe to fight defensively. And the fighting had slowed down a little. Not because anyone was tired, but because they'd taken each other's measure and quit wasting effort.

At that slower pace it was easier to understand what they were doing. The sickle was knife-sized, and so was best used just outside of grappling range. The *bō* allowed Adam to stay farther away than that, in the outer circle of the fight. He could hit Wulfe—as long as he was fast enough that Wulfe couldn't grab the *bō*. But Wulfe was forced to stay too far away for the Soul Taker to touch Adam, who used the ends of the *bō* to keep Wulfe away from him.

I judged the duration of the fight more on the way they were fighting than a clock. Adam's shirt was wet with sweat and Wulfe was making irritable movements when his Hollywood-inspired costume got in his way. He pulled off one of the flowy sleeves and flung it on the ground with a snarl that would have done credit to Adam.

I unwrapped the girdle from around my waist—and it was once again warmer than it should have been. I coiled it up so I could hold it in one hand, but when I got to the end, I wrapped it around my wrist. I didn't want to lose it too easily.

"What do you have?" Bonarata asked.

I looked up, almost caught his gaze, and managed to focus on his mouth instead.

"Bait," I told him. "And anchor." Then I let out a single yip and bolted for the fight.

Adam hit Wulfe hard in the chest, making the vampire take a step back and a little to the side. Then Adam took two quick steps out of the pattern of the fight—away from Wulfe. Leaving Wulfe facing me while focused on Adam.

I stopped about ten feet from him, and using the power that flowed from Adam, I said, *"Wulfe."* It was more than his name, it was a reminder of who he was. I held up the girdle stretched between my two arms as I caught his gaze.

I heard the crack of a gunshot, but it didn't hit me or Wulfe, so I ignored it. I was aware, peripherally, that another fight had broken out between Adam and Bonarata, but I could not afford to look. Adam had told me that he'd keep Bonarata from interfering with what I was going to try to do.

Using the knowledge the Soul Taker had given me, I found the soul bond it had initiated between me and it and hit that with a blaze of the pack's cleansing power—just as I'd watched Adam do to keep Warren from being enthralled by Wulfe's bite. I didn't try to break the bond between the Soul Taker and me. Instead, I sent the spiritual fire through the artifact and into the slave bond between the Soul Taker and Wulfe. Then I twisted the cleansing power and let it burn.

I couldn't quite burn through the bond, no matter how much power I threw at it. Wulfe wasn't ours in the same way that Warren was, so the pack magic couldn't completely destroy the Soul Taker's hold.

Wulfe's eyes, one clear and one cloudy, met mine as he walked up to me and held out his hand. Despite the war I knew was raging inside him, there was no tension on his face. I gave him the girdle and he closed his fingers upon it. The serene expression on his face reminded me forcibly of the memory Stefan had shared with me of his first meeting with Wulfe.

As soon as he touched it, the Latin words and the phoenixes embroidered along the belt began to glow. It wasn't flamboyant, more like the embers of a fire. He closed his eyes, brought the fabric to his face—and dropped the sickle.

I quit pouring power into him and collapsed on the ground in the same instant. I don't think I could have managed even a second longer—but it had been enough to give Wulfe a chance, and he'd taken it.

I had called him to himself, then given him the belt—a reminder of a time before Bonarata had broken him, something for him to cling to. And with that anchor, he'd been able to destroy the hold the Soul Taker had on him all by himself.

"Because a kite needs to be tethered in order to fly," Wulfe said, as if pulling the thoughts from my head, which he very well could have been. He opened his eyes and met mine. "And Marsilia"—his hand tightened on the old silk—"is my anchor."

They had been lovers once. More than that. Marsilia, Stefan, Andre, and Bonarata had been his family. The reason for his existence. But when Bonarata had broken him, Marsilia had given him a touchstone of safety. I didn't have to close my eyes to remember the skeletal creature that had clung to Marsilia's skirts in that long-ago dungeon.

I could see that Wulfe was thinking the same thing. And I knew why he'd never killed Bonarata. The simplest reason of all. Wulfe loved him.

Wulfe looked away, breaking that intense communication— and I realized for the first time that the reason I hadn't looked away first was because I couldn't have. He leaned down and kissed the top of my head, and then vanished.

A wailing roar reminded me that there was still a fight going on—and I knew that sound. I knew what I was going to face before I turned to look.

Adam . . . the beast that fought Bonarata wasn't anything like a werewolf. Though his hind legs were articulated like a wolf's, he stood mostly upright by choice—aided by overly long arms that could balance him when necessary. Adam's face was a monstrous distortion of a wolf's head, with an undershot jaw and teeth that would have done credit to a predator twice his size—and he was huge.

Bonarata must have gotten closer to me than we'd planned for Adam to have given himself up to the cursed monster. Then I noticed there were pieces of a gun scattered about. Somehow, though we went armed with guns ourselves, neither of us had considered what might happen if Bonarata had a gun.

I thought of the shot I'd heard. Unlike his change to the wolf, Adam's change to this beast could be instantaneous, quick enough for him to stop Bonarata from shooting me. To save me, Adam had given himself over to the beast.

Adam's monster was built for fighting. It was faster than his wolf form and armed with outsized claws and fangs. Even though Adam wasn't in charge of this form, his instincts were still honed by half a century of fighting and training.

Bonarata looked fragile next to Adam. He'd armed himself with Adam's *bō* but he still should have been outmatched.

I had never seen anything like the beauty of that fight.

I'd known Bonarata had been a fighter. But I'd just watched Wulfe fight—no-holds-barred—and if he had not lost to Adam, he had not won, either.

Maybe if Adam had been fully in control of that beast, he might have stood a chance, but it was obvious to me after watching for a few seconds that Bonarata was going to kill Adam.

I drew my own gun—but the speed at which they were moving meant that I'd have a better chance of hitting Adam than Bonarata because Adam was bigger. My hand was shaking so badly—from the after-effects of the magic I'd poured into Wulfe—that I didn't dare try.

My foot touched the sickle and I felt it tug at me.

I could help you kill the vampire, the Soul Taker whispered. The sound of its truth wound around my heart.

I jerked my foot away . . . and hesitated.

The fight between Adam and Wulfe had been almost musical,

the percussive sounds of weapon on weapon and light feet on the ground. The fight between Bonarata and Adam was not. I had the feeling that if I understood Italian, Bonarata's vocabulary would have rivaled Ben at his best as he screamed insults in a stream of rage. Adam's monster's inchoate howls and roars made Bonarata's battle cries insignificant.

I saw Bonarata swing, and this time Adam didn't move away in time. There was a crack that sounded like a baseball bat hitting a home run, and Adam reeled back, one arm at a funny angle. He grabbed that wrist with the opposite hand, overlarge even on such a huge body, and jerked it. The arm snapped again, though not as loudly. It was hard to tell, because none of his limbs looked as though they were natural, but I thought he must have either reset a joint—or pulled a broken bone straight so it could heal.

The whole thing took only a second. Adam reengaged with Bonarata, though he visibly favored the arm that had been injured. While Adam was dealing with his arm, Bonarata had glanced at me and seen the Soul Taker.

I didn't see him do it. I felt the Soul Taker take notice.

Take me up, it told me. *Take me up or face me in the hands of the Lord of Night.*

Bonarata caught Adam in the ribs and broke the *bō* on him. The monster fell but rolled back to his feet immediately. Now Adam's breath was harsh and labored, and he whined with each intake. The arm Bonarata had hit seemed to be okay now, but there was a dent in Adam's rib cage.

He will be better than the last one, the Soul Taker told me. *The Lord of Night is strong. I can break strong.*

Bonarata was moving the fight so that it neared the place

where I stood, indecisive and scared to the bone. I bent down to take up the sickle—and Bonarata lunged for it at the same time.

I could have beaten him to it, but I could not force myself to touch it. Bonarata's hand closed on the blade, and it cut his flesh. I felt a cold chill sweep through me—the Soul Taker's joy at the power of the blood of the Lord of Night. There was still a moment left for me to grab the handle. I could not do it.

Through the blood tie that stretched between the Soul Taker and me, I understood as soon as it did that the artifact could never bind to the soul of the Lord of Night. Not in a week. Not in a century. Influence, yes, but the vampire's mind was impenetrable in a way that the Soul Taker understood better than I did.

Bonarata smiled at me as he let Adam rip the Soul Taker from his careless hold while I screamed a hopeless protest.

Adam's oversized hand made the sickle look absurdly small. He jerked it back and Bonarata hissed, his blood splattering the ground and me.

Adam roared at him, and for a moment I thought everything would be okay—but only because in that moment the only thing I could feel was my mate. Then Adam dropped to the ground as if he'd been shot. He curled around the hand that held the Soul Taker as if to protect it, hiding both hand and artifact from view. Every muscle of his body was rigid, the corded veins growing more defined. He made an indescribable noise that hurt my ears as the Soul Taker began to turn Adam into its wielder.

Bonarata put his hand to his mouth and licked delicately at the wound the Soul Taker had left.

I brought my gun up—and Bonarata slapped me in the face with the back of his free hand. It didn't knock me unconscious, quite, but I couldn't protest when he kicked the gun out of my hand and walked a few steps away.

I heard a soft noise, and something bumped against the tip of my nose. Cold and old and fathomless.

I rolled away from the blade of the Soul Taker, but sick and dizzy, I could only manage to come up to my knees before I sat down again. My nose bled from Bonarata's slap, but it was the feel of the Soul Taker I tried to wipe away with the back of my wrist. Adam hadn't meant to touch me with the sickle. I doubt Adam knew I was here at all.

The beast that held the soul of my mate was curled around himself, one arm outstretched as if to keep the sickle as far from the rest of him as he could manage. He was writhing slowly with the effort of his fight.

Bonarata was sitting on his heels about ten feet from me—which was way too close—a three-foot section of Adam's *bō* tucked into the crook of his elbow. He was smiling, but his eyes were as empty as the grave.

I quickly looked at his chin. I did not want to see into Bonarata.

"I'm glad you woke up before I had to go," he said. "I wanted to take this moment to tell you why I am here."

"Evil overlord's classic mistake." My voice was tight. My face hurt where he'd hit me, and Adam's pain was sliding through our mating bond.

He laughed. I imagined that people who didn't know what he was would have found the sound warm and reassuring.

"Not at all, Mercedes Thompson Hauptman," he said. "It is necessary that you understand why so many people died. Why I destroyed the Tri-Cities seethe and your pack."

"Pack's not destroyed," I said grimly.

His smile widened as he nodded at Adam. "You do understand what the Soul Taker is, don't you?" He looked a little thoughtful. "I wonder if it ever will collect enough souls to bring its god back." He shrugged. "It doesn't matter, though. Because in an hour or two, it will have your mate, the Alpha of the Columbia Basin Pack. Through the pack ties it will own your whole pack."

I didn't say anything.

"It will leave you alone, though," he said. "Coyote is a little too much like its own god for the Soul Taker to risk drawing his attention."

That's not what the Soul Taker believed, but I wasn't going to take up that argument with Bonarata.

"And there are some things even the Soul Taker cannot force its wielder to do," Bonarata continued. He shrugged. "If I'm wrong, I'm wrong, but in my judgment, Hauptman could not be forced to hurt you."

He tapped Adam's *bō* into the ground a couple of times, watching Adam's shuddering body. "I expect that the Dark Smith will eventually wrest it away from him. A pity, but once you killed my Uttu and Ninhursag, my sweet spiders, I knew it was time to let the Dark Smith have his plaything. Siebold Adelbertsmiter might even free your mate rather than killing him. What do you think Adam Hauptman will do after a day, or a week, or a month of killing innocents?"

I didn't say anything. There wasn't anything to say.

"That's what I think, too," he said. "Do you suppose that he'll drown himself like Bryan did?"

I didn't know how he knew about my foster father, but I tried very hard not to give him a reaction. We'd been wrong, Adam and I, when we'd determined Bonarata's motivations. This hadn't been about Marsilia or sabotaging our neutral territory. This had been about me, a coyote shapeshifter who'd made a fool out of the Lord of Night.

"I will follow you for the rest of your life," he said pleasantly. "It doesn't matter if you live to be a hundred or five hundred. I understand it's a toss-up with Coyote's children." He pulled out his phone and hit a button. We both listened to my phone ring for a few seconds. I thought about the crank calls I'd been getting, the ones Adam's people couldn't trace. The calls that had happened during the day.

"After a few months," he said, brushing a thumb over the screen of his phone to cut the call, "I suspect that you'll think of me every time you hear a phone ring."

"Whenever the whim strikes me, I will kill everyone you care about and anyone who cares about you." His voice was conversational. I don't know what he was reading in my face. "They will die, and you'll know it is your fault." He stood up and dropped the broken section of *bō* on the ground.

"I will not have it said that the Lord of Night was bested by you," he told me. "I hear the whispers. But no more. For centuries they will talk about what happens to people who dare to thwart my will. Your fate will be a lesson for them all."

He walked away. After a couple of minutes, I heard the helicopter lift off.

"Mercy."

I think I was still half-dazed by the blow Bonarata had dealt me, because I'd been staring after Bonarata instead of trying to help Adam. I was sitting on the ground, and I didn't try to get up for fear I'd just fall back down again.

I crawled to Adam.

His mouth wasn't made for speech, and the words came out garbled, if urgent. I understood them anyway. "Get Sherwood." "Bran." "Run." And then my name, over and over again. I don't think he even realized he was doing it. His eyes were closed.

I put both hands on his face. The reddened hide felt strange—almost rubbery under my hands. At my touch he opened his eyes. In this form, his eyes were always human.

I *saw* him.

I was too tired, too hurt to try to free Adam the way I'd helped Wulfe break free. In any case, the power that I'd used for that had been Adam's and the pack's. He was already using it to fight the Soul Taker. The pack was feeding power to Adam as fast as he could take it.

I could *see* that as I looked into him. I could feel the pack bonds the way he did, as connections to each of us. Through those bonds I felt their frantic effort to help Adam—and I felt when Sherwood stepped in, his power sweeping through every wolf. I only barely managed to shield myself from being pulled in.

The power that pulsed into Adam was more focused, more useful, with Sherwood directing it from his end. But I could feel the Soul Taker's triumph as Adam began to lose the battle anyway.

So I opened myself up to Adam, let him see me the way the Soul Taker had forced me to see others. Let him see how the Soul Taker worked so that he could take the power that Sherwood fed him and—burn the bond the Soul Taker was building.

Ours, roared the pack magic, *our Alpha, our mate, ours*.

Adam opened his hand and released the Soul Taker.

16

ADAM PUT HIS HANDS OVER MINE, WHERE THEY STILL rested on either side of his face. He closed his eyes, breaking the searing, jumbled *knowing* that flowed between us.

It was through the pack bonds that I felt him gently stem the flow of power, feeling his gratitude and reassurance slide back down those channels. And I knew, because the pack knew, that everyone would be heading toward us as soon as they could.

My phone rang and I flinched. Adam's rang, too, as his body spasmed with his change. Normally I would have let him go—changing was painful, and his change from the beast to human was much worse than the change from wolf to man. But I needed to touch him, and he made no effort to back away. Maybe he needed me to touch him, too. In due course, the sounds of his bones reshaping themselves died away.

The flesh between my hands smoothed and softened until it

was Adam's human face I held. I bowed my head until my forehead rested against his collarbone. After a moment I felt the first sobs rise up.

Eventually I ran out of steam and just lay there. At some point he'd sat up and pulled me into his lap.

"Stupid," I said into his shoulder. I pulled back so that I could swipe at my snot-and-tear-wet face with the corner of my T-shirt. I got half of it done, but the other half of my face was too sore to touch.

"What's stupid?" he asked, his voice a little hoarse.

"I should have known that you were too pigheaded for a mere ancient artifact to swallow down."

He put his head on the top of mine and said, "Swear to God, Mercy. Best two out of three. Best two out of three."

After a while, we helped each other to our feet and staggered back to the SUV.

His clothes were trashed, but that was a common hazard of being a werewolf, so we always kept spares in his SUV. While he dressed, I called Zee.

"Hello, Mercy," he said.

"Hey." My throat closed. I looked over at the Soul Taker and thought about how much power it represented.

"*Liebchen?*"

I thought of the night that Zee had come out to fight zombies with me. I thought of the collection of blades and other weapons he had once made that now resided in a secret room inside his home, where they would do no more killing. If Zee wanted to go out and slaughter people, he didn't need the Soul Taker to do it.

"I have a bargain for you," I said.

MARY JO BROUGHT HER FIRST-AID KIT AND SUPPLIED me with painkillers and an ice pack. She didn't comment about tear tracks or snot while she gently cleaned the sore side of my face. When I insisted on sitting on the ground next to the Soul Taker to make sure that no one touched it, she and Honey stayed to guard me.

Adam had taken a lot more damage than I had, but he was already mostly healed by the time the first of the wolves had found us. Once assured that I wasn't going to die anytime soon, he took the rest of the wolves to see what Bonarata had done to our vampires.

Zee came about fifteen minutes later, walking through the pack vehicles to get to us. I expected him to go straight to the Soul Taker, but he stopped and squatted across from me first.

He scowled at me. "I have decided," he said, "that the bargain you offered me still left me in your debt."

I might have said something smart-mouthed, but it hurt to talk. I only managed an "Oh?"

He nodded almost angrily. "To regain the balance between us, I give you this."

He touched his index finger to my forehead and coolness washed over me, taking with it the pain of the last week. I shivered with sudden exhaustion and only just remembered not to look him in the eye.

I opened my mouth and he put his finger on my lips. "Do not," he said sourly, "even think about thanking me."

I nodded. Then he stood up, dusted off his hands, and grabbed the Soul Taker. As soon as he touched it, I felt the blood bond I shared with it become muted.

He walked off without another word. As soon as she judged him to be out of earshot, Mary Jo said, "I didn't know he could heal people."

"Me, neither," I said.

I WENT TO WORK THE NEXT DAY BECAUSE I WAS A small-business owner and Friday was a business day.

I took my Vanagon, begrudging every mile I put on her. Part of me knew that was stupid—cars needed to be driven. But I wanted to choose when I drove her. It had taken me a long time to find the Jetta I'd totaled in August. Old VWs were scarce. I'd have to get serious about running down a replacement. Maybe I'd see if Adam wanted to take a weekend and head to Seattle.

About nine in the morning, I was underneath the greasiest engine compartment I'd seen for a couple of weeks, trying to find an electrical wire hidden in a half inch of mud-grease. I knew—from my own investigations on the upper part of the engine compartment—that terrible mechanics (or ham-handed amateurs) had worked on the wiring in this lovely cabriolet a number of times in its four decades of life. That meant the wire I was looking for could be anywhere.

Aubrey crawled under the car and scared the bejeebers out of me, and I shoved most of my face into the greasy mass above me before I realized what had happened.

He laughed, then apologized for it because he'd been a sweet young man. "Hey, Mercy," he said. "I just wanted to tell you thank you—and tell you good-bye."

"Good-bye?" I asked.

He smiled again—and it looked like the one Wulfe had given me yesterday: sweet with a hint of wickedness. "I get to go," he said, sounding excited.

"Yeah?" I asked, smiling back at him.

He nodded. When he hit his head on the car, there was no noise and the grease fairy didn't cover his face. "But they said I could tell you thank you."

"Time to go, boy," said a familiar voice, sounding kinder than he usually did when talking to me. That's fathers for you.

I skittered out from under the car, but quick as I was, Aubrey and his guide-to-wherever-dead-souls-go were gone.

About a half hour later I'd managed to get the grease off my face and most of my hair—and also found the wire about two inches from where it should have been. I was trying to decide how to bill a job that cost four dollars in parts and took me fifteen minutes to fix after I'd spent two and a half hours looking for a short. Two and a half hours was pretty good for chasing down an electrical fault, actually.

Once, Zee and I together had spent *three days* on a Vanagon, trying to find an intermittent short. We'd come out disagreeing on which wire was the problem, replaced them both—and had it come back in the next day. Tad, who was manning the shop while I went for lunch, had fixed it in ten minutes.

I'd just worked out the taxes on the invoice when I felt an odd tug inside my head. I grabbed the top of the counter, because I was sitting on a very tall stool, and held on while someone pulled a spiritual octopus out of me complete with a million arms loaded with suction cups. When it was finished, I was sitting on the floor, curled up in a ball with a bloody nose.

My phone rang.

I read the caller ID and answered it only because it was Zee.

"The Soul Taker is no more," he said, sounding satisfied.

Bargains, I thought, *are how you deal with the fae.* If I gave Zee the Soul Taker, he agreed to destroy it. And heal me, too. It had been a good bargain.

"Got that," I told him. "It had a few more holds on me than I thought it did."

"*Ja*, it happens like that sometimes. Good that you did not pick it up. Eat something, you'll feel better." He paused. "I am hungry, too. I'll bring lunch."

"Paper or plastic cups if you bring drinks," I told him. "No skull cups."

"Underhill wanted the Soul Taker," Zee said. "Tad told me what she said when she gave you the cup for me. She would have kept her bargain to keep your family safe. And a favor from Underhill is no small thing."

"Yeah, well," I said. "You had first dibs."

He laughed and hung up.

When he came in twenty minutes later, he brought street tacos from our favorite food truck. He handed me a soda in a can with a little emphasis. But what we talked about was fixing cars.

When lunch was over, he stayed to help, and we were both working on a twenty-year-old Mercedes convertible when the phone rang and the bell jingled at the front desk.

"Desk or phone?" I asked.

"*Pest oder Cholera—es ist ein und dasselbe*," he grumbled.

"If I go to Germany and everyone thinks I'm a grump, it will be your fault," I said. "And since when do we compare our customers to diseases?"

"Since I sold you the garage and they became your customers," he said. "I will get the phone."

I was still smiling when I walked into the office—to see Warren.

"Hey," I said. "How are you feeling?"

"Like I have a deadline," he said. "And it occurred to me that I have a friend I can ask for help."

Adam had given him two days to deal with whatever was making him so crabby.

"Always happy to poke my nose into your business," I said.

Loud and muffled German leaked through the closed door to the bays. "Hey, maybe if I can fix what's making you grumpy, we can try it out on Zee."

Warren gave me the faint smile that deserved. "I doubt it. Leopard don't change its spots. Come take a drive with me." He turned and walked out the door, tension obvious in the set of his shoulders and the snap in his voice.

Eyebrows climbing at the order—I'd have thought yesterday would have cured him of talking to me like that—I stuck my head back into the bays and called out, "Test driving. Back whenever it happens." I started for the door, then considered the new Subaru and stripped out of my greasy overalls.

I don't know what I expected, but it wasn't for Warren to gesture me into the driver's seat of his new car. I sat down on the leather and couldn't help but smile as I adjusted the seat to fit me.

I started the car with a push of the car-starter button. A message popped up on the space-age screen in front of me that said: Driver Not Registered. Do You Wish to Register?

Warren touched the tablet-like secondary screen that lay between the driver's and the passenger's seats, and the message went away. I gave him a quick glance because that touch had been overly quick and the tap had been a little harder than I'd have used on a touch screen I wanted to last a few years.

"Where are we going?" I asked.

"Howard Amon Park," he said, and he gripped the car door and gritted his teeth.

"Okay," I said.

I might work on old cars most days, but we could do new cars, too. Adam's SUV was brand-new and had all the whistles and bells. But it seemed to me that Adam's SUV had quite a lot fewer bells than this car—in a literal sense. I hadn't gone a block and it had beeped at me five times. Twice it was because I went over a white line, but the other three were so quick I couldn't figure out what it thought I'd done. There were little green and red lights that were on a heads-up screen that I was unsure of, too. By the time I pulled onto the highway, I was a little tense. I also was a lot more careful to keep the car between the lines.

"Use the cruise control," he said.

I did. Adam's SUV didn't try to steer for me, but I knew what automatic steering was supposed to do. As I was glancing at the cruise control buttons, the car dinged rudely, and a red banner flashed in on my dashboard and on the tablet between Warren and me: Stay Alert!!! I guessed that the second banner that the passengers could see was a courtesy to warn them that they were about to die.

I turned off the automatic steering because it was irritating having the steering wheel fight me, but after a mile I noticed it was doing it again. I turned it off a second time.

By the time I drove into Howard Amon Park, I was pretty tired of hearing all the beeps and dings. The car told me to keep my hands on the wheel when my hands were on the wheel. It told me to watch the road when I was watching the road, and also when I *wasn't* watching the road—which was even more annoying.

I parked the car and asked Warren to find the owner's manual. I took about ten minutes to skim through it and then got to work turning off all the helpful modern things designed to drive were-wolves (who were control freaks one and all) batty.

"There," I said, backing out of the parking space. "That should help."

I hadn't driven a mile before it was at it again.

The engine stopped while we were at a red light. I'd never driven a car that did that. It was supposed to save gas, but the mechanic in me worried about the starter. The Subaru restarted itself without warning, and both Warren and I flinched.

"I'm pretty sure that was one of the things I turned off," I said as the car informed me I'd crossed the lane marker and my hands weren't on the steering wheel. The tires might have touched the white paint between my lane and the shoulder, but both of my hands were on the wheel.

"Yes," he said. "Did you think I couldn't read an owner's manual?"

I cleared my throat. "It has not been my experience that owners of new cars read their manuals unless their names are Kyle." Kyle had highlighted his favorite parts—mostly having to do with safety.

A warning light flashed on.

"You are low on washer fluid," I told him.

A message came on the car's tablet-sized screen that said we were low on washer fluid. A moment later a red alert light came on the dash, and when I toggled it, it told me we were low on washer fluid. Warren's phone chimed and he didn't even look at it.

"It goes through a lot of washer fluid," he said. "Gets the windshield real clean."

I bit my lip and tried not to laugh.

"I'll have an email about the washer fluid, with an explanation on how to fill it up. And a number for the dealership if I'm too stupid to follow their step-by-step instructions and want a mechanic to fill my washer fluid." He paused. "Kyle will get the text and email, too."

I rubbed my face and the car dinged and told me to keep my hands on the steering wheel.

"He don't say anythin'," Warren said. "He just buys washer fluid and sets the bottles on my side of the garage."

"It's not supposed to turn all of its helpful technology back on," I offered. "I could try to troubleshoot it, but most of these kinds of programs are proprietary. Probably easier to take it in."

"It doesn't do it if I'm not in the car," he said.

I looked at him. I forgot for a moment that I was supposed to be careful not to look people in the eyes—but nothing happened when I met his gaze. I stared some more, just to be sure. That ability had evidently disappeared when the Soul Taker was destroyed.

The car told both of us to Stay Alert!!!

"Can you trade it in for something a little older?" I asked.

"Kyle gave me this car," he said carefully.

"I know that."

"Kyle grew up in a shitty home that taught him a lot of stupid things. Most of them he's shed like a snake sheds its skin. But the one thing that he's held on to is that he tells me he loves me with gifts."

I could see that.

"He don't want gifts in return," Warren said. "It ain't transactional."

"Okay," I said.

"But if he can't give me somethin', it hurts him. Took me a long time to figure that out. He's been trying to get me a car for two years and finally talked me into letting him do it. I told him to pick out anything—but it had to be something that wouldn't stand out, because that was the pretext he was using to buy me a car."

"And you think he won't understand about the dinging," I said.

"It don't do it if he's in the car."

"What?" I said.

"It don't do it if he's in the car."

"I heard you the first time," I told him. He grunted.

"I won't hurt that man," he said in a soft voice. "He only just survived his family. He don't let no one in as far as I am in. I won't hurt him by trading this car in."

"I see," I said. The only sounds in the car the rest of the way back to the garage were the sounds the car made at me.

Zee came out and scowled at me as we got out of the car. It wasn't his I'm-angry scowl, just his usual you-made-me-dealwith-customers scowl. I tapped the hood of the car a couple of times and said, "Zee, this car has a problem."

I explained what was going on, in detail. Zee pursed his lips, opened the car door, and looked inside. Then he held out his hand.

"Keys," he said.

I saw a flash when Warren almost reacted to the sharp note in Zee's voice, then he controlled it and tossed Zee the key fob. Zee was gone about ten minutes, and when he got out of the car, there was something softer than usual in his face.

"Kyle bought you that car," he said.

Warren nodded.

"He picked it out and drove it home—you didn't go with him."

"It was a gift from Kyle," Warren said. "I wanted it to be the gift he wanted to give me."

Zee smiled, a real smile, one of the ones he only shared with people he likes. "He wanted you to be safe," Zee said. "So he bought you a car that would keep you safe. And he thought about it all the way to your house—like a wish. And sometimes, if you happen to be around a lot of magic—like maybe your mate is a werewolf—a little magic happens."

I thought about the girdle—that hadn't felt especially magic to me until Wulfe had been nearby.

He gave Warren back the key fob. "It should behave itself now. If it starts up again, bring it to me." He paused. "I think you got a keeper," he said, and went back into the office.

I was pretty sure he wasn't talking about the car.

ADAM AND I WENT TO THE SPECIAL SHOWING OF *THE Harvester* at the pumpkin patch on Saturday night. I had tried to stay home. I liked horror films, especially bad horror films—but I had no desire to revisit the Soul Taker. However, Adam had a plan, and it was a good plan. I dressed up a little more than I usually would for a movie showing held in a barn.

Waiting for the show to start, Adam put his lips against my ear to murmur, "Marsilia called with thanks. She also told me that Zee has been spreading the story about how we took down Bonarata and gave the Soul Taker to him instead of Underhill because he would destroy it and free the people, our people, that it had killed. She said that our credit with the supernatural residents of the Tri-Cities is getting a pretty good boost from that."

"Zee is spreading that?" I asked. Zee didn't gossip.

"Uncle Mike," Adam said. "But he wouldn't be doing it if Zee hadn't asked him to."

"Damage control," I said. "And we're in better with the vampires than we have ever been."

Wulfe, Marsilia, and Stefan had taken most of the torture Bonarata had meted out on his visit. But it had been a lot of damage. The rest of their people were mostly newly made or weak, and Bonarata had scared them badly.

They'd been in pretty bad shape by the time the pack found them. Our pack had gotten them fed and transported back to the seethe before daylight. Physically, Marsilia had assured Adam, they'd be okay in a few weeks.

"Marsilia intends to move the seethe," Adam murmured.

I blinked. "To the house in Benton City?"

"No," Adam said. "She's going to build a new house. She asked me for the name of our contractor." He paused. "I don't know what to think about it—but she's bought Elizaveta's property in Finley."

I didn't know what to think about that, either. "I wouldn't live there."

"She says it has power."

"Yikes," I said.

His shoulders shook with silent laughter. We *were* in a movie-theater barn. Good manners said we had to be quiet.

I don't know if anyone else thought the movie was scary, but I spent a great deal of it with my face pressed against Adam's shoulder. Adam seemed to spend a lot of the movie trying not to laugh and saying things like "That's not what arterial spurting looks like" and "Heads don't roll like that. They aren't round, they're rounded." But he said them quietly, so we only got a few odd looks.

People knew who he was, of course, so we got some of *those* looks, too. But mostly Tri-Citians were respectful of our privacy. As long as there weren't scary monsters mucking about (werewolves were respectable monsters), people mostly left us alone.

After the movie was done, the writer came out. He looked nervous, proud, and nervous again by turns—but was a pretty interesting speaker. I had not expected that, considering the lines in the movie. He talked for about fifteen minutes and then took questions. The fourth question was about the two bodies found earlier this week in what looked like a copycat crime.

Adam had anticipated that question.

He stood up and introduced himself for the benefit of anyone who didn't know who he was. Then, with permission from the writer, he told the story of the Soul Taker. He didn't tell them everything—all the people in this room thought they knew what the Soul Taker was from the movie they had just watched—and if it had been scarier than that, they didn't need to know it. He touched on the killings of four decades ago and then credited an unknown evildoer with releasing the sickle into the wild because of the movie.

By the time he was finished, there was a hush in the room, and several local reporters Adam had called earlier today asked a few good questions.

We left eventually.

"Well," I said, "between your storytelling and Zee's storytelling, our wolves are once again the heroes of the Tri-Cities and Bonarata is going to be rolling in the grave he should be in."

Adam snorted. Then he said, "I feel bad for that writer. I took away his moment of glory."

"Don't feel too bad," I said. "You just made his movie into a cult classic."

THE FOLLOWING FRIDAY FOUND ME BAKING BROWN-ies for the gamers in the basement. Because there were no extra wolves living with us, I had all the ingredients I needed.

The pack's ongoing pirate LAN game was open to anyone in the pack who wanted to play. But a couple of weeks ago a spin-off adventure in the Dread Pirate franchise had been released, this one designed to be played Dungeons & Dragons style. Which meant that players had to go in as a team and survive till the end. It was intended for four to eight pirates, and tonight the diehards had gathered for a game-until-we-drop that was expected to run at least until dawn.

Adam, Mary Jo, Ben, Warren, and Darryl had volunteered to test the waters. I wasn't playing because the part of the game I really liked was killing my fellow pirates, not amassing imaginary treasure.

This afternoon, Sherwood had called me to say he was joining in. I didn't get to ask him any questions, because he said what he had to say and hung up.

Sherwood had showed up tonight, his one-eyed, half-grown kitten riding on his shoulder like a prince of India riding on an elephant. He hadn't said anything to me, just waved and headed rapidly downstairs, where the rest of the pirate crew were already gathered.

I put the brownies in the oven and licked the spoon. They'd been at it for about three hours. Jesse had watched for a while, but Tad and Izzy had come over. They'd set up in the big meeting room to use the projector system to play YouTube math videos. Calculus 101, I was informed, was a flunk-out course, and they were all planning on acing it.

The stairs creaked, and I looked over to see Sherwood carrying dishes.

"I've been knocked overboard and retrieved unconscious," he reported. "We'll find out in ten minutes of gameplay whether or not I survive."

Sherwood's eyes looked happy, I thought, as he reached up to scratch Pirate—the cat—under his chin. He flexed his white mittened feet into Sherwood's shirt and purred.

"Experiment a success?" I asked as Sherwood moved away to put the dishes in the sink.

He looked at me.

"No urges to kill Adam and become Alpha in his place?" I clarified.

He smiled. "None," he said, then sobered. "I still don't remember how to tone down how dominant I am when I want to. Which means that Darryl and Warren and I might have to dust up a bit to put everything in order. But not now—because my wolf understands that a dustup might hurt the pack's ability to defend our territory, and we are at war." He shook his head.

"Wolf logic for you. But yes, Adam and I are all right. And Warren and Darryl and I can engage in mock battle without anyone getting riled."

"Because?" I asked.

"Because the pair of you together make a better Alpha than I would," said Sherwood.

I frowned. "That's not how being Alpha works."

"Not usually, I grant you," said Sherwood. "But the way the magic of this pack works, you two are one." He smiled, a sharp expression. "Coyote's daughter brings something to the mix. I felt it that night—when Adam was fighting off the Soul Taker."

I narrowed my eyes at him. "We know that you were the Great Beast of Northumberland. Were any of the other guesses right in the betting pool?"

He grinned at me, a sudden happy expression, but before he could say anything, we were interrupted.

"*Pegleg!*" Ben's shout rose from the basement. "Get your arse down here. You're waking up and there's a bleeding kraken after us!"

"All hands!" bellowed Captain Wolf Larsen (Adam).

"Coming, Captain!" Sherwood's cat clung easily as Sherwood ran down the stairs.

I pulled the brownies out of the oven and set them to cool before I frosted them. As I got out the ingredients for the frosting, I heard the soft sound of a violin being played in my backyard.

I looked out the window over the sink. Night had fallen and it was darker outside than in my kitchen, so I couldn't see very well, but I thought there were people sitting on the picnic tables in the backyard.

I went outside, shutting the door quietly behind me. As I

stepped out, there was a flurry of movement and small shadows scattered away. My eyes couldn't quite catch them, though I could hear the sound of wings and the rustling of dry grasses.

"Your people?" I asked Tilly, who, in her guise of a ten-year-old girl, was sitting on the ground, her face intent.

She nodded but kept her rapt gaze on Wulfe as if she'd never heard music before. I listened for a few more bars, searching for the title of the familiar piece, and finally found it—*The Lark Ascending.*

Wulfe sat on top of one of the picnic tables. He wore a white dress shirt unbuttoned too far and black dress pants rolled halfway up his calves. His legs were crossed at the ankles and he was barefoot, though there was a chill wind that made me wish that I'd stopped and grabbed a coat. Wrapped around and around his waist was the embroidered silk belt.

Sitting on the bench of the picnic table nearest to Wulfe's concert platform was a figure shrouded in a black robe. A hood was pulled over his head and he wore what appeared to be a porcelain mask over his face. There was a small hole in the pursed lips of the mask, but the eyes were just painted on. I tried not to wonder about what his face looked like beneath the mask.

I sat next to Stefan and listened to Wulfe play. After a few minutes, Stefan stirred and tried to talk. But his voice was hoarse and slurry, as if there were something wrong with his tongue, so I only caught "owe."

I shook my head. "We're friends, Stefan. There's no account keeping between friends."

He made a sound that might have been a laugh, then he started coughing, a dry, dusty sound that made his shoulders heave as he bent down until his forehead pressed into his knees. I reached out a hand but didn't touch because I couldn't see how he was hurt.

Adam had told me that Marsilia had been in a bad way, but Stefan had been worse. I understood that Marsilia had already recovered thanks to heavy feeding, but Stefan would take more time. His damage had been more than physical, Marsilia had told Adam. But she hadn't chosen to elaborate.

Wulfe came to the end of his piece and brought his violin down to rest on his lap.

"If he doesn't try to talk, then he doesn't have to breathe," he said, watching Stefan.

Stefan nodded and the coughing diminished. He sat up with an effort as Wulfe slid off the table and put his violin in its case.

"You're done?" asked Tilly, clearly disappointed.

"Yes, lady," he said gravely.

She pouted at him, and he raised an eyebrow. "I come and go," he told her. "You'll hear me again."

She watched him a moment, her mouth twisted unhappily, but finally nodded. Then she was up on her feet and running into the darkness without another word. I heard her door squeak open— it didn't usually squeak—and the sounds of small creatures scurrying before the door clicked shut.

She hadn't once looked at me.

"Thank you for the concert," I said. "And for bringing Stefan here."

Wulfe smiled at me, and it was a real smile. He walked to me and dropped to one knee, then he took my hand and kissed it.

"*Bravissima*," he said. "Excellently well done, Mercedes Athena Thompson Hauptman. Well done."

I frowned at him. "Does this mean you'll quit stalking me?"

He laughed but did not answer, just went back to get his violin.

Stefan leaned down until his mouth was next to my ear. "Be afraid," he whispered clearly, and almost soundlessly.

I stared into his porcelain mask and knew that he wasn't talking about Bonarata.

Violin in one hand, Wulfe came back and picked Stefan up with careless ease.

"He should still be resting," he told me, "but he wanted to come with me tonight."

"I'm glad he did," I said sincerely.

The kitchen door opened. I didn't have to look to know that Adam was watching.

Wulfe gave me an angelic smile, then vanished.

ACKNOWLEDGMENTS

The following people either read this book in its various stages and helped me pound it into shape or they supplied information I needed: Sergeant Dave Allen (retired from the Pasco Police Department), Collin Briggs, Linda Campbell, Dave Carson, Katharine Carson, Michelle Kasper, Christine Masters, Ann Peters, Kaye Roberson, and Anne Sowards. I am grateful for their efforts, and anyone who reads this book should be as well.

Additionally, Zee is very appreciative of his friends Michael and Susann Bock, who keep his German correct and who understand exactly how he feels about customers.

Finally, I very much wish to thank Gertrude, my Subaru, for making me a better driver, whether I wanted to be or not.